### Also by Violet Marsh

*Lady Charlotte Always Gets Her Man*
*Our Dear Miss H. Is on the Case*

# Miss Wick and the Duke Dilemma

## VIOLET MARSH

FOREVER
**LARGE PRINT**

This book is a work of fiction. Names, characters, places, and incidents are the product of the author's imagination or are used fictitiously. Any resemblance to actual events, locales, or persons, living or dead, is coincidental.

Copyright © 2026 by Erin O'Brien

Cover design and illustration by Dawn Cooper
Cover copyright © 2026 by Hachette Book Group, Inc.

Hachette Book Group supports the right to free expression and the value of copyright. The purpose of copyright is to encourage writers and artists to produce the creative works that enrich our culture.

The scanning, uploading, and distribution of this book without permission is a theft of the author's intellectual property. If you would like permission to use material from the book (other than for review purposes), please contact permissions@hbgusa.com. Thank you for your support of the author's rights.

Forever
Hachette Book Group
1290 Avenue of the Americas, New York, NY 10104
read-forever.com
@readforeverpub

First edition: March 2026

Forever is an imprint of Grand Central Publishing. The Forever name and logo are registered trademarks of Hachette Book Group, Inc.

The publisher is not responsible for websites (or their content) that are not owned by the publisher.

The Hachette Speakers Bureau provides a wide range of authors for speaking events. To find out more, go to hachettespeakersbureau.com or email HachetteSpeakers@hbgusa.com.

Forever books may be purchased in bulk for business, educational, or promotional use. For information, please contact your local bookseller or the Hachette Book Group Special Markets Department at special.markets@hbgusa.com.

Print book interior design by Taylor Navis

Library of Congress Cataloging-in-Publication Data has been applied for.

ISBNs: 9781538739662 (trade paperback), 9781538739686 (ebook), 9781538782606 (large print)

*To Emma, Heidi, and Dottie*

# Chapter One

*London, late 1750s*

Inside was nothing but ashes.

Eoin Aucourte, the newly minted Duke of Foxglen at the age of only twenty-two, stared unblinkingly at the contents of the ornate box, the very container that had tempted him for more than a decade. It had always rested on the desk of Eoin's paternal grandfather, the late duke. When the old man had called Eoin into his office to upbraid him, Eoin had stared at the relief of silver serpents twisting and turning on the metal exterior.

Slowly, Eoin pivoted in the direction of his Uncle Hugh. Guffaws racked the forty-six-year-old man's body with such intensity that he barely managed to nudge Eoin's Uncle Francis, who was sitting next to Hugh for the solicitor's reading of the late duke's last missive. Although the peer had only died in the wee hours of the morning, his surviving children—Eoin's two aunts and two uncles—had insisted that they gather in the dining room with Eoin and the solicitor to learn what they would inherit.

"Do you see that, Francis?" Uncle Hugh asked as he clumsily batted at his younger sibling's arm.

Uncle Francis was laughing too. "I did. Nothing but char."

"All the times our nephew danced to our father's tune—just to get soot in the end." Uncle Hugh snickered.

Under the dining room table, Eoin's fists were clenched, but otherwise he displayed no emotion. Just as he'd been taught. Because his grandfather had promised that if Eoin transformed himself into the perfect heir, then he'd give him the mementoes of Eoin's mother locked away in the silver case.

"I don't even know why John wants to find *that woman* anyway. After all, she did abandon him at the tender age of six." Aunt Joan used the English version of Eoin's name rather than pronouncing it as "Owen." The late duke had insisted that no one use the Irish one that Eoin's working-class mother had chosen at his birth.

Although Eoin didn't bother to correct how Aunt Joan addressed him, he wouldn't allow her other falsehood to stand. Not anymore. Not with the former Foxglen dead and the precious clues to his family's whereabouts destroyed. "Mama and my older sister didn't leave me of their own free will. You know that the law dictated that your father—my grandfather—had the right to be my guardian."

"Why wouldn't the statutes favor my papa?" Aunt Joan tilted her delicately shaped chin in the direction of the solicitor. At forty-two, she was a strikingly handsome woman with golden hair and cornflower-blue eyes that matched her brothers'. "Should John's mother, a poor widow of a dead traitor, have been entrusted with raising a future duke? The laws of primogeniture prevented my father from disinheriting John despite John's regrettable maternal line, but at least Father had the right to raise John as he saw fit after my eldest brother died."

Frustrated rage burned in Eoin's gut, but he did not allow it to show on his face. He'd heard these accusations for the past sixteen years.

Before the solicitor could opine upon Aunt Joan's rather rhetorical question, a moan came from her sister Eliza. The forty-year-old was the youngest of the Aucourte siblings and, as far as Eoin knew, had always possessed the weakest disposition. Her hair and skin were both a shade paler than her more robust sister's, and she looked like an ethereal fairy queen.

"I cannot tolerate hearing about our late brother's death." Aunt Eliza's voice was so soft that Eoin wouldn't have understood her if he wasn't adept at reading lips—a skill his grandfather had thought would make Eoin an excellent choice for a courtier to the king.

"Eh? What did you say?" Uncle Hugh asked in his booming voice. He and his brother looked like graying princelings with their blond waves threaded with silver. Their behavior, though, had always been boorish.

"Eliza said she didn't want to listen to tales about our dead brother," Aunt Joan snapped. "And neither do I. I am here to learn what

Father left me. We already know that the entailed portions of the estate are unfortunately John's. But what am I to receive?"

Eoin noticed that the left side of the otherwise sober solicitor's mouth twitched. Upward. A glint of amusement?

Eoin stared closely at the staid man, whom he knew well. As part of his training to become the next duke, Eoin had accompanied his grandfather since the age of nine on most of the peer's business dealings. His task had been to silently observe without showing any inattention. Eoin understood the character of Foxglen's cronies better than his own personality. And the attorney, Mr. Lewis, was not prone to amusement. Ever.

At first glance, Mr. Lewis looked like a jolly sort with neatly trimmed white whiskers and perennially pink cheeks. Yet closer inspection revealed his true character. Even though his hazel eyes were bright, it was more with shrewdness than kindness. And he never smiled but always remained calm and self-possessed.

Except for today.

Now, instead of sitting perfectly straight,

Mr. Lewis leaned forward as if in anticipation. Normally when the lawyer reviewed documents, he kept them flat on the table. Currently, though, he gripped the pieces of parchment tightly enough that they crinkled at the edges. And...was that sound of a tapping foot emanating from Mr. Lewis rather than one of Eoin's aunts or uncles?

"Shall we resume?" Mr. Lewis asked as he glanced around the room, and Eoin wondered what he saw—probably a hulking young man with dark hair surrounded by his golden bevy of relatives. With his giant frame, Eoin had never fit in with his paternal family and their finely hewn features, a fact he was never allowed to forget.

"Yes. Get on with reading the letter." Uncle Hugh waggled his fingers in the solicitor's direction.

The man's mouth quirked northward once more, but his voice betrayed no emotion as he intoned the words penned by the late duke. "'I am sure that my surviving offspring are eagerly awaiting news of my bequest to them. They are, unfortunately, spoiled beyond redemption. I am afraid I should have not left their raising to their nursemaids, governesses, and tutors. Children, I have learned, require a firm hand, so I did not repeat my mistake with Viscount Malbarry.'"

Of course, his grandfather would refer to Eoin by his courtesy title. Because that's all Eoin ever was, an heir for molding into a perfect duke.

"Must we listen to the chidings?" Uncle Francis asked. "We had enough of that when Father was alive."

"Most definitely." Aunt Joan heaved out a sigh. "I much preferred his benign neglect in our formative years. He became much too invested in our lives after our eldest brother died in an otherwise forgettable uprising to overthrow King George. Father even forced us all to live with him if we wanted any luxuries in life instead of giving us an income, as was our due."

"Well, we are finally going to receive what we deserve," Uncle Hugh said impatiently. "That is, if you would all stop interjecting and allow the solicitor to continue reading."

Without ceremony, Mr. Lewis began anew. "'As both my sons drink like fish, I have arranged these flasks for them…'"

Mr. Lewis paused and rang a small bell. Immediately, the pocket door to the dining room pulled back, and two of Mr. Lewis's clerks scurried in. Both were holding flasks shaped like small, angry sturgeons.

"'As neither of my sons has developed any ability to handle their liquor with dignity, these containers are filled with naught but water. Drink up, my sons. This toast is on me,'" Mr. Lewis continued reciting.

The words were unnecessarily cruel but not entirely fiction. Both men had been ejected from polite society shortly before the death of Eoin's father. Perhaps Hugh and Francis could have emerged from their twin scandals of nearly vomiting on the queen at a ball (Hugh) and drunkenly crashing a carriage into the prized glasshouse of a royal duke while attending a house party (Francis). But their elder brother's treason had sealed their fates.

"This is unacceptable!" Uncle Hugh smashed

his fist against the table, causing Aunt Eliza to jump before she slumped back into her chair.

"That can't be all!" Uncle Francis shouted. "There must be more. The solicitor hasn't finished speaking yet!"

"Yes. Read on. Read on!" Hugh demanded.

As Mr. Lewis picked up the will once more, the clerks hurried from the room. Eoin followed their movements suspiciously. Were they running to retrieve an equally insulting gift for the women? Yet no one else noticed their exit as everyone's attention was upon the lawyer.

"'To my daughters—'" Mr. Lewis read.

"No!" Uncle Hugh's denial was angry and loud. "He cannot be moving on to my sisters already. Where is my inheritance?"

"And mine!" Uncle Francis echoed.

"You!" Uncle Hugh roared as he turned and hurled his fish flask at Eoin's head. "You knew of this, you damned sycophant."

Eoin didn't dodge the silver missile. Instead, he simply snatched it from the air. He'd always possessed an uncanny deftness that his grandfather had dismissively attributed to his common blood.

"No," Eoin said. "I did not."

"Like everyone says, you were his bloody shadow—following him everywhere, doing his bidding. Of course you knew about this bloody letter!"

"C-e-e-ease!" Aunt Eliza's voice was wavery and faint. "My nerves are already strained, and my head is beginning to ache. Please stop your shouting."

"Eliza's right. Yelling won't solve anything," Aunt Joan interjected grumpily as she crossed her arms.

"Venting your spleen will at least rebalance your humors," Uncle Francis announced in his most sagacious tone. He rather sounded like a pompous nincompoop.

"You just want to hear what Father left you, Joan, but I doubt it will be any better than our fish flasks," Uncle Hugh ground out.

"Ahhhhhhh," Aunt Eliza breathed out as if she were in physical pain, and perhaps she was. She did seem to suffer from megrims, but Eoin couldn't assist. She wouldn't welcome his help, and anything he said would only make her siblings shout more.

"Proceed," Uncle Hugh snapped at Mr. Lewis, the annoyance in his voice almost palpable. "We might as well get this intolerable exercise over with."

Mr. Lewis immediately began reading again as if he'd never stopped. "'As for my girls, I leave them these laying fowls...'"

Again, Mr. Lewis halted to ring the bell. Before the door even opened, Aunt Joan had leaped to her feet, and Aunt Eliza had slumped fully onto the table.

"A laying fowl? What does that even mean?"

As if in answer to her question, the two clerks emerged once more. They each carried a large basket containing a hissing goose.

Uncle Hugh and Uncle Francis laughed almost as uproariously as they had after witnessing Eoin's ash-filled box. Aunt Joan gasped in horror while Aunt Eliza seemed intent on ignoring the situation.

Mr. Lewis, however, chose to continue his recitation. "'As Eliza and Joan are nothing but silly geese who lounge about my home, I am providing them with companions who perfectly suit their temperaments.'"

If Eoin had allowed any emotion to show on his face, he would have frowned. Unlike his uncles, his aunts were not deserving of such condemnation. Their misfortunes had been brought upon them by the misconduct of their late husbands—husbands who their father had selected for them. It was not their fault that their spouses had died scandalously and in debt.

"Get that filthy thing away from me!" Joan backed away as one of the clerks approached her.

As Mr. Lewis's other subordinate placed the second fowl in front of Aunt Eliza, she lifted her head a scant inch. Unfortunately, the bird chose that moment to extend its ghastly-looking tongue, which was shockingly lined with what looked to be serrated teeth. Eliza's high-pitched scream echoed through the large room and bounced off the ceiling.

Her caterwauling caused the unwanted goose to rise. Below its flapping wings lay a cache of eggs. Abandoning its nest, the bird leaped onto the table. Its webbed feet struggled to find purchase on the lace-covered surface. Slipping and sliding, it waddled frantically, pulling the fabric every which direction.

Uncle Hugh and Uncle Francis clambered to their feet and scurried toward the protection of the wall. Aunt Eliza slumped in her chair while Mr. Lewis simply sat, holding the will, the left corner of his mouth still pointed up. His two clerks wisely decided to retreat from the room, their role fulfilled.

"Do something!" Uncle Hugh roared at Eoin because, even if they didn't like him, they still expected him to solve everything that plagued them.

Eoin stood up and stalked toward the goose, who promptly half ran and half glided in the opposite direction. Eoin made one swipe, but he only touched two tail feathers.

"It's moving!" Aunt Eliza suddenly screeched.

Eoin turned to see her staring in horror at one of the eggs, which had indeed begun to shake back and forth. The gosling inside was clearly in the process of hatching, but the sight was unsettling, especially to someone as prone to nerves as Aunt Eliza. However, instead of simply backing away from the basket as Eoin would have expected, Aunt Eliza chose to reach inside, grab the egg, and then hurl it.

Eoin acted on instinct and dove for the delicate projectile. After all, the creature inside was striving with all its might to be born into this world. How terrible would it be for that hope of life to be literally dashed against the floor?

Eoin landed painfully on his stomach, but the force of his plunge shot his body forward. Reaching out one long arm, he was just able to softly catch the egg before it hit the ground.

"You are to secure the filthy goose, not the egg, John!" Hugh demanded.

Eoin, however, ignored his uncle as he strode to the bellpull in the corner of the room. Unlike Mr. Lewis's hand-held one, this chime would call the house servants. Sure enough, a footman popped into the room a few seconds later. To the young man's credit, he remained stone-faced at the spectacle before him.

"Peter, can you bring Ann to catch the geese? My understanding is she recently came from the country, and she grew up on a tenant farm. Also, bring two more footmen with you to carry off the birds and their baskets," Eoin said, ignoring the utter chaos too.

Peter nodded and hastily exited. He returned

promptly with Ann, a wide-eyed lass of seventeen. It was clear that the maid was overwhelmed by being called into a meeting of the noble family, but she very expertly wrangled each fowl. Within moments, not even a single feather remained in the room, and a semblance of peace descended—or rather it would have if Aunt Eliza hadn't commenced sobbing and Uncle Hugh hadn't taken to muttering curse words.

Eoin, however, felt more at ease than he had since he'd open his box of ashes. If his aunts and uncles had received nothing, they were dependent on him and desperate for funds. He could easily pay them to tell him what they knew of his mother. Eoin doubted that they were aware of her location, but they must at least remember her maiden name. Perhaps they could even describe her. Eoin had only hazy memories of eyes as blue-green as his own and a voice singing to him in a lilting Irish accent.

"Let us all sit," Eoin said. As his relatives complied, he turned to the solicitor. "Mr. Lewis, if you would be so kind as to finish the rest of the letter."

"Certainly," Mr. Lewis said. This time when he read, he left the paper lying on the lace cloth. " 'If my four children wish to receive any more from my estate, they must earn it. It should not be difficult as it only requires that they do nothing. I have set up a trust with my unentailed wealth. For every five years that Viscount Malbarry does not locate either his mother or his sister, you'll receive one hundred pounds each. After twenty years, you shall jointly inherit Windy Hill.' "

Bloody hell. The old sot had been uncannily devious, even until the end. Although the estates produced enough income that Eoin could technically pay his relatives more than the trust, the price was simply too stiff. Too many souls depended on the duchy for their livelihoods, and Eoin wouldn't siphon away large amounts from the coffers. And he had no idea how he could compensate his aunts and uncles for the Windy Hill property, even if the house and the lands were relatively small compared to the rest of Eoin's holdings.

His relatives would be loath to help him even without the incentive that his grandfather had just offered from the grave. Now Eoin truly had no leads, and he doubted his mother would reach out to him. Even though his memories of his parents were fuzzy at best, he did recall his grandfather threatening to use his power to send Eoin's sister to a far-flung girls' school and to have his mother hanged for treason if she ever tried to interfere in Eoin's life.

Dimly, Eoin heard his aunts and uncles protest about the unfairness of waiting for their inheritance, but Eoin couldn't listen anymore. He'd spent years building fortification after fortification around his emotions, but for the first time in a long while, he felt a crack. A small crack but a crack nonetheless. And he did not want to break in front of Mr. Lewis and his paternal relations.

Without offering an explanation, Eoin stood and strolled from the room. He heard Uncle Hugh yelling "Stop," but Eoin didn't listen. He was duke now—even if he otherwise felt as powerless as he always had in this household.

As a boy, when he felt he could no longer endure his grandfather's endless restrictions, he'd slink away to the gardens behind the London townhouse. Now, however, he merely walked through the French doors leading from one of the sitting rooms onto the veranda. He couldn't leave the grounds, couldn't run from his responsibilities as duke, but he could afford himself this single, momentary retreat.

He weaved through the overgrown pathways, as flowers and plants had never been his grandfather's priority. He stopped in front of a folly built in the shape of a circular keep. The whimsical structure had been ordered by the late duchess, the grandmother who had died long before Eoin's birth. He wished that he felt some connection to her, some solace. But there was none.

With a sigh, he entered the structure. Nothing was inside. Not even an old, forgotten bench. Ignoring his silk finery, Eoin plopped on the ground and rested his back against the cool interior stonework.

Just then he felt a curious warmth on his palm. Glancing down, he found a little gosling lying partially in its cracked shell with its head nestled against Eoin's skin. He'd forgotten all about the egg that he'd rescued from his aunt's panicked fit.

Pink dimpled skin peeked out from between yellowy-brown feathers as the baby animal wiggled back and forth. With its down still wet, the gosling looked unbearably small and breakable. Yet despite its fragility, it still valiantly struggled to free itself from the confines that it had known its entire existence.

Could Eoin be so determinedly resourceful?

"You are a fierce little one," Eoin said, and then immediately felt sheepish. It wasn't in his nature to talk to animals as if they could understand his words. Yet now he found himself doing so in less than a space of a fortnight. Last time, he'd even awkwardly bowed to a sharp-tongued parrot named Pan.

Eoin couldn't stop his lips from twitching upward as he thought about that particular evening. But it wasn't the bird or even his own actions that brought a glint of amusement to his otherwise miserable day. No—it was the memory of Pan's mistress: Miss Hannah Wick.

The redhead was precisely the type of female that Eoin had been taught to avoid.

Her father was an English-born pirate who'd seduced and married the daughter of a viscount. Then, instead of having the grace to simply run back to the Caribbean and fade into distant memory, the society-defying couple had set up a coffeehouse in London that catered to all sundry of misfits, reformers, and downright dissidents.

They were exactly the kind of people that Eoin's grandfather abhorred, but Eoin secretly admired.

Although Miss Wick's family history had intrigued Eoin, it was her boldness that had utterly captivated him. At their first meeting, he'd been dressed in the clothes of a farm laborer, and she hadn't known his position as an heir to a dukedom. Yet when she'd laid eyes on him, Eoin had watched interest flare to life in her grass-green eyes. And Miss Wick, with her hoydenish expression and the wild Titian curls escaping her coiffure, had caused a rebellious want to riot through all of Eoin's staidness.

Perhaps it was because no woman had ever looked at him so brazenly. His height, title, and reputation for aloofness made debutantes and even their matchmaking mamas uneasy. Oh, they still flirted—he'd been an heir to a dukedom after all—but the coyness was always forced and definitely calculated. And Eoin had never known how to respond to their machinations. Yet there had been no artifice in Miss Hannah Wick's undisguised appreciation of his physique, and his own response had flowed naturally from him.

She'd even called him "storm-worthy," a clear innuendo that she'd like to breach all his walls. And, swounds, at that moment, he'd been ready to let his every defense crumble for her. But she and her companions had been in the middle of solving a mystery, and there had been no time for more than her few flirtatious words.

Solving a mystery.

Energy shot through Eoin, and his heart squeezed at the onslaught. The Black Sheep Coffeehouse was fast gaining a reputation as the place to go to receive help in unraveling enigmas.

And Eoin had the very devil of one. Even better, he would see Miss Wick again.

## Chapter Two

"I cannot believe that you allowed me to flirt with a bloody viscount!" Hannah Wick skewered her maternal cousin, Lady Charlotte, with her best glare.

And Hannah was an absolute champion at glowering. After all, her ability to convey authority and outrage with her eyes was an extremely valuable asset when it came to dealing with unruly customers at the Black Sheep Coffeehouse, which Hannah ran with Charlotte and her paternal cousin, Sophia.

Unlike most, Charlotte didn't squirm under Hannah's gaze as the three proprietresses washed dishes together in the back room of their establishment. However, the noblewoman may have permitted a single, demure swallow. Hannah couldn't be entirely sure.

Charlotte was always the picture of polite poise, the inverse of Hannah's own rough-and-tumble presence.

"Well, given the particular circumstances at the time, it seemed most prudent—" Charlotte began to say in that gracious, kind way of hers. When Hannah had first reunited with her estranged relative, Charlotte's demeanor had grated, but now Hannah had grown rather fond of her.

Sophia broke in to the conversation. "What Charlotte is trying to delicately say is that it wasn't the time to be dramatic."

"Dramatic! DRA-MA-TIC!" Hannah hung on to the last word, fully aware and not caring that she was proving Sophia's point. "Why shouldn't I be dramatic over this? He's not just any ordinary viscount, is he? And it's not even that he's next in line for a dukedom. He will be Foxglen—the FOX-GLEN— someday."

Sophia reached out and patted Hannah's arm. "But even then, he won't be the duke who stole farmland from our grandparents and then sent our starving fathers to the Colonies when they were caught poaching. That is the current Foxglen's sin, not Malbarry's."

"Pfft." Hannah barely stopped herself from slamming down the ceramic coffee cup that she'd been cleaning. "Any member of the Aucourte family is a nemesis of ours by default."

Sophia rolled her eyes as she gently disentangled the breakable piece from Hannah's grip and began to dry it. "We are the daughters of pirates. If we engaged in blood feuds, we'd have nothing but enemies. There is a reason that our investigations have always centered primarily on Foxglen."

"What do you mean, your investigations?" Charlotte asked as she stacked the earthenware neatly on the shelves behind the serving counter.

"Something is fishy about the Aucourtes," Hannah said. "For over a decade, there's been rumors of illicit dealings. Papa wanted to pursue the whispers, but my mother and Aunt Mary talked him out of his revenge. They didn't want to bring scrutiny upon the coffeehouse." The establishment was originally a meeting place for London outcasts, including reformers, ex-prisoners, and folks rescued from slavery and indentured servitude by Sophia's mother, who was known on the high seas as Brave Mary.

"And now I've gone and drawn attention to the Black Sheep by opening the back room," Charlotte sighed. The hidden space for men and women from all social strata to mingle had conversely become one of the most gossiped about locales in London.

Sophia waved her dishtowel dismissively. "The coffeehouse isn't in the same precarious financial position that it was when Hannah's parents first established it. Besides, your strategy increased business by twofold."

"Your plan has truly been a boon, Charlotte," Hannah agreed. Originally, she hadn't been keen on her noble cousin's suggestion, but the back room had become a lively enterprise that brought in a great deal of coin—money that Hannah was more than willing to spend on loosening lips when it came to the Aucourtes.

"But do you really suspect that Foxglen is committing crimes?" Charlotte asked. "He's notoriously obsessed with obeying every letter of the law."

Hannah squeezed the cup she was washing with enough force to send the earthenware shooting through the suds as it slipped from her soapy grasp. "His funds are nothing but ill-gotten gains from enclosing the land that my father's ancestors tilled for generations. Bloody sheep feasting on grass where wheat and turnips should be growing. Foxglen might act all high and mighty, but he's just a well-dressed thief."

"B-u-u-u-t," Sophia said, hanging on to the word, "despite his greediness, we have doubts over whether he's the architect behind whatever is causing the whispers. That's another reason why my mother didn't think it would be fruitful to chase down the rumors. It's always been more likely that Foxglen's sons are involved."

"Hmmmm," Charlotte said thoughtfully as she turned from arranging the earthenware. "That does make sense. It's widely known in Society that Foxglen maintains a tight rein over his sons' allowances. Too many drunken scandals. They're forced to reside wherever the duke does. Neither is known for their morals, so it wouldn't surprise me if they'd gotten involved in some vile business."

"Do you know any other rumors about the family?" Hannah asked eagerly. She'd been meaning to question Charlotte, but they'd been too enmeshed in other mysteries.

"Not really—at least not the sort that you're interested in," Charlotte admitted. "His daughters are widowed and don't attend many events since their husbands both died in disgraced financial ruin. The duke, himself, is in poor health and rarely attends social gatherings. His sole grandchild is Malbarry, who's known as the duke's shadow. You rarely see one without the other, and people say talking to the viscount is exactly like speaking with the duke. They hold the same views."

"Ugh." Hannah resisted the urge to smash the saucer that she was currently cleaning. "How could I even flirt with such a creature? What happened to my good sense?"

"If it is any consolation, you most assuredly disrupted *his*." A slightly impish expression had fallen over Charlotte's normally serene countenance. Hannah had been spying more and more such looks from her cousin. Normally, she liked the sight but not today.

"His what?" Hannah asked rather waspishly, even though she knew exactly what her cousin meant.

"His good sense," Charlotte clarified. "He has the reputation for being utterly and thoroughly staid, but you made him blush."

A spurt of warmth shot through Hannah, and her heart started squeezing like a laundry mangle. Ruthlessly, she stamped down on the unwanted excitement. "Are you insinuating that I am a corruptive force?"

Charlotte did not even have the grace to look abashed. "You know I didn't mean anything disparaging, and you cannot deny that you had a powerful effect on the man. He bowed. To. A. Parrot."

That bit of whimsy had charmed Hannah—and blast Malbarry for beguiling her. An heir to a dukedom had no right to possess such an impressive array of muscles. His height and broad shoulders were entirely lost on a man who never had to do a lick of physical labor. In his rough attire, he'd looked exactly like a prizefighter... and precisely the type of man who appealed to Hannah. But it turned out he was just a damn nob in a laborer's linsey-woolsey.

"I do not wish to speak of it anymore," Hannah said tartly. "May we please return to the original conversation?"

The teasing glint immediately vanished from Charlotte's grass-green eyes as she obliged Hannah's request. "What have you learned about the Aucourtes from your own inquiries?"

Hannah sighed, but the expulsion of air did little to alleviate the frustrations building inside her. "Nothing. Absolutely nothing."

"Every so often, we ask our contacts in the stews if they've heard a new rumor, but nothing is ever reported," Sophia explained further.

"Perhaps because there is nothing to discover?" Charlotte said softly, but her understanding tone didn't feel like a balm to Hannah. It only aggravated her.

"No." Hannah released the mug she was washing into the tub and slammed her fist into her other palm. "The Aucourtes are hiding something. I feel it in my bones."

Sophia gave her a friendly nudge with her hip. "I didn't know your bones were prophetic."

Hannah delivered another one of her best glares, this time in Sophia's direction. Her cousin ignored the look entirely as she dried off a saucer and handed it to Charlotte.

"I am not soothsaying," Hannah said defensively. "Don't you find it suspicious that there is not a single murmur about the Aucourtes—not even about what brothels the men visit?"

"I doubt Malbarry ever visited one," Charlotte piped up. "He's much too somber and pious."

"But his uncles surely have," Hannah countered. She did not believe that Malbarry was particularly saintly, but she did not want to think of him engaging in *that*. Because if she did try to picture him, then she'd imagine his muscles on full display, his biceps extending as he held his body above...

Bloody hell!

"My point," Hannah practically shouted, her voice so loud that it startled Sophia into almost dropping a dish. When Hannah spoke again, she lowered the volume considerably. "My point is that the very lack of noise indicates that there is a great deal of clatter that a powerful person is suppressing."

"As much as I teased Hannah, I do agree with her reasoning," Sophia said. "Rumors about the Aucourtes are too hushed."

"Hmmm," Charlotte said thoughtfully as she nestled a cup inside another. "Perhaps instead of investigating the Aucourtes in the back alleys, you should try the ballroom. With their public scandals, they have little clout left to stop gossip there."

"It is not as if Sophia and I can just don a gown and stroll into a nob's house," Hannah grumpily pointed out.

"My brother and I would be happy to collect rumors," Charlotte said.

"That would certainly be helpful, but I want to look into the Aucourtes myself," Hannah said.

"Well, one option may be…" Charlotte suddenly trailed off and whirled to focus on the stacks of dishes. "Never mind. That is an ill-advised plan."

Hannah narrowed her eyes on her cousin's back. "Often ill-advised plans turn out to be the best. What were you thinking?"

"Nothing," Charlotte said quickly. Too quickly.

"Please tell." Hannah gently released the dish that she'd been scrubbing and turned to advance on her cousin.

"Hannah, it might be best not to press Charlotte," Sophia said in that calm, logical manner of hers.

Through the years, Hannah had learned to listen to Sophia's thoughtful advice, but right now she couldn't. Not when it came to the Aucourtes. Hannah had spent too much time solving other people's mysteries. It was time to delve into her own.

"Charlotte, this is a matter of grave importance to me. If you have thought of a scheme—no matter how outlandish—you must tell me."

Charlotte worried her lip, and Hannah grabbed her hand. She plastered on her most pleading look, and she could visibly see when her cousin relented.

"I've never seen Lord Malbarry interested in anything before. He's always terribly aloof. But in your presence, he was like a tightly wound bobbin that had finally unspooled," Charlotte said cautiously.

"You want me to seduce the man into

spilling family secrets?" Hannah asked, not knowing if she should be aghast or intrigued.

Her cousin's face turned almost as red as her hair. "I did not mean for you to be that, uh, bold. If you just befriend him, and perhaps flirt a smidgen, Lord Malbarry would confide in you at least a trifle."

"No," Sophia said emphatically as if that one word ended all discussion.

Hannah stiffened. She detested being told that she couldn't do something. It was a flaw that had landed her in more than just a spot of trouble, but she'd never been able to resist the roar that surged through her.

"And why not?" Hannah demanded.

Sophia arched a single eyebrow. "Do you really think such subterfuge fits your temperament? You're too honest. We need to proceed cautiously if we're to tangle with a noble family, even one with a tarnished reputation. The Black Sheep has already brought down one peer. If we make a misstep, there's many who'd like to see that our doors are permanently closed."

Hannah harrumphed. Sophia raised excellent

points, but Hannah was utterly tired of caution. "What if Malbarry approaches me?"

"Did somebody say Malbarry?" Alexander, Charlotte's twin and the soon-to-be Duke of Falcondale, burst into the room. His sister had given him a key, which Hannah had fully endorsed at the time. Now that Alexander had failed to disclose Malbarry's identity, she was less sanguine about his unfettered access to the coffeeshop.

"Does that mean you've heard or that you haven't heard?" Alexander continued to talk as he sauntered over to the counter. "Ah, no coffee brewing yet? It is a shame. Any conversation goes better with a drink."

"Shouldn't you be planning your wedding rather than plaguing us?" Hannah asked.

"Haven't you forgiven me yet?" Alexander delivered his best sorrowful look.

Hannah was not swayed.

"No."

"What is the news?" Sophia asked Alexander.

"Lord Malbarry is no longer the viscount—or Malbarry for that matter. He's Foxglen now. The old duke died two nights ago."

"*What?*" Hannah felt like a hole had been drilled into her gut. Her family had waited too long for their revenge. The main perpetrator was gone.

"Pastry?" Alexander pulled a savory-smelling one from the sack that he'd carried in.

"How can you think of food right now?" Hannah demanded.

Alexander shrugged. "I'm famished. I was purchasing these for a snack when I heard the news, and I came here straightaway. I didn't want to anger you by failing, once again, to promptly disclose information pertaining to the Aucourtes. The sausage in them is delicious, by the way—in the pies, I mean, not in the Aucourtes."

"Does your fiancée ever accuse you of making her head spin?" Hannah asked, although she had to admit that the meat and onion mixture did smell divine. But she didn't want to be distracted either by her cousin's roundabout delivery of the news or by the food he was currently demolishing.

"No," Alexander said cheerfully between bites. "She finds me endearingly charming."

"The Duke of Foxglen didn't look well the last time that I spotted him at a ball, but I still cannot believe he's dead. He seemed as if he could just scowl death away," Charlotte said.

"I'm honestly relieved," Sophia said. "It feels like at least one tragic chapter in my family's history is closed."

"Well, I am not," Hannah disagreed. "I'm upset that we dawdled too long on seeking revenge."

"Malbarry—well, I mean the new Duke of Foxglen—is a good chap. Look how he came to our aid a few weeks ago," Alexander said in his typical happy-go-lucky manner.

Hannah, however, was anything but cheerful. Yet she felt a glimmer of some dark hope. Perhaps there still was a way to avenge her family. "The old Duke of Foxglen was forever prattling on about his family's reputation, correct?"

"Yes," Charlotte said slowly as if reluctant to give an answer, "but Sophia has the right of it. The perpetrator is dead—"

"But his precious legacy is alive and healthy," Hannah said, "and I aim to utterly destroy it."

# Chapter Three

"It's a shame that the new Duke of Foxglen isn't here although I suppose he is in mourning."

It had been a wonderful wedding breakfast celebrating the nuptials of Alexander and his bride at the Black Sheep. *Had been.*

But then the notoriously obtuse Lord Percy had just made the most flibbertigibbety observation possible, at least in Hannah's esteemed opinion. Why would the dratted man even think about the recently ennobled duke, let alone wish for his presence?

"We do not mention either the name Malbarry or Foxglen in this establishment." Hannah pierced everyone gathered around the table with a dark look. "I shall never forgive you all for not telling me his identity immediately. You let me lust after a bloody duke!"

"Well, technically, he was a marquess when you met him." If Lord Percy's statement wasn't galling enough, he had the audacity to punctuate it with an absurdly cheeky grin.

Hannah whirled on the irredeemable rogue. "That is not the point!"

"Blackguard!" Pan cried from his perch in the rafters, using the insult that he'd hurled at Malbarry when the parrot had met the nobleman in disguise.

Hannah glanced up at her pet, thankful that someone comprehended her frustrations. "That's right, Pan! I should have listened to you from the very beginning."

At Hannah's praise, Pan gleefully launched himself into the air. Unfortunately, the chaos-loving creature did not choose to return to his favorite rafter. Instead, he landed on the back of Ruffian Caesar, a dog of indiscriminate terrier origins. Although the little mutt seemed less excitable than many small pups, he clearly did not appreciate a parrot alighting on his back and screeching.

The dog scurried forward in an obvious attempt to dislodge the parrot. However, Pan merely whistled and hung tightly to the wiry fur. Everyone gathered for the wedding breakfast stood in an attempt to rescue the beleaguered canine.

"Gee-up! Gee-up!" Pan croaked out louder than any teamster.

Hannah lunged for the dog and the parrot. Unfortunately, Ruffian Caesar swerved sharply at just the wrong time and careened into her path. She narrowly avoided stepping on him as she stumbled. Her heart thudded as she pitched forward. Not wanting to fall and crush the pets, Hannah grabbed wildly for anything to stop her fall. Burlap scraped against her palms, and she desperately clutched it.

Small grains shifted beneath the rough material, and she realized that she was clutching the rice sack that she and Sophia had hung by the door to toss at the newlyweds. Before she could release her hands from the bag, it slipped off its hook. At just that precise moment, the door to the Black Sheep opened.

Hannah stumbled forward, desperately trying to maintain her balance while keeping the satchel upright.

Unfortunately, she only managed to stay on her feet. The sack slipped from her hands, and its entire contents poured like a white waterfall straight into the silk-cladded midsection of the newcomer.

Mortified that she'd just pelted a customer with at least two pounds of rice, Hannah slowly lifted her gaze to the man's face. If she hadn't spent her life immersed in the unpredictable chaos of the Black Sheep, she would have gasped. Even with her unflappable constitution, her jaw dropped the teeniest bit. For there, in the doorway, stood the new Duke of Foxglen—his finely tailored suit an elegant contrast to the white grains cascading down the lower half of his body.

Hannah did not know if Foxglen being the hapless victim of the ricing made the situation better or worse. She certainly did not give a fig if she'd just offended the man, yet she also didn't want him anywhere near her precious Black Sheep. She also didn't like how her body instinctively heated at the sight of his muscles. Although she would never admit it aloud, the cut of his coat and his tailored breeches showed off his form even better than the linsey-woolsey clothes he'd worn when they first met.

The massive nobleman seemed unperturbed by either the deluge of grain or the dog-riding parrot careening in his direction. He calmly reached down and grabbed Ruffian Caesar around his belly.

Hoisting both pup and bird into the air, Foxglen carefully disentangled Pan's claws from Ruffian Caesar's fur. The nobleman seemed utterly oblivious to the rice pouring from his silk breeches and running down his stockings.

Pan, however, was not so cavalier. Hissing out his indignation, he released the terrier, only to alight on top of Foxglen's head.

The duke ignored his feathered passenger and bent at the waist. Despite the fact that he still held the dog, he executed a perfect bow. Pan clung to his head like a diabolical, living hat. More rice rained from the folds of Foxglen's waistcoat before he straightened with a solemnity that contained no hint of irony.

"I do beg your forgiveness for interrupting this celebration, but I wished to speak to all of you privately. I deduced you would be gathered here today," Foxglen said in a calm, steady tone, which instantly irritated Hannah. How dare this man remain so placid when he made her feel like a top spinning on a string?

"I come to humbly ask for your assistance in locating my mother and older sister. They've been in hiding from the late duke since my father's death when I was six years of age. Now that he's dead, I want to reunite with my family." Foxglen spoke the words without a hint of emotion. Yet despite the staid delivery, or maybe in part because of it, Hannah felt an unwelcome tug at her heart.

Family had always meant everything to Hannah. When her parents had retired to the Caribbean, she'd missed them sorely. But she'd been an adult, and they kept in constant correspondence. From time to time, they even visited London. And Hannah had

Sophia—her cousin who'd grown up surrounded by the crystal blue waters of the tropics, but who'd decided to move to gray, foggy London to provide a place of refuge for people who society judged unfairly.

But what would it have been like to be ripped away from her parents at the tender age of six? Had Foxglen felt abandoned? If his mother and his sister had fled from the former duke, the old sot must have even terrorized his own relatives. Yet he'd been the one to raise the man standing before Hannah, who was all dignity despite the ridiculousness of the situation.

But Hannah didn't want insight into Foxglen's past because it would make it all the harder to destroy his family.

"Why did you come here?" Hannah asked, her voice sounding cantankerous even to her own ears.

"Because the members of the Black Sheep have unraveled at least two mysteries—one of which I personally witnessed being solved," Foxglen said, his voice perfectly calm with just enough inflection to prevent it from becoming a monotone. He was the epitome of dukeliness.

"What my dear cousin meant to ask is why are you turning to us for assistance?" Sophia stepped forward, a conciliatory smile on her face. "With your new powers as duke, surely it would not be hard to locate your relations."

Foxglen's bearing remained stiff as he regarded the room. "My mother has likely made a life for herself in the lower rungs of London society where my grandfather held no influence. If I poke around in those corners, my title will only seal lips, not open them."

Hannah vaguely recalled that Foxglen's birth had been a scandalous one—not because he was a by-blow but because he'd been legitimate. His rebellious father had married an Irish tavern maid in a Catholic ceremony. But no matter the blood of Foxglen's mother or the church where the vows were exchanged, the laws of primogeniture were clear, and even the late duke couldn't disinherit his grandson.

"Will she not come and find you of her own accord when she hears of your grandfather's passing?" Sophia asked.

Foxglen shook his head. "She may believe that I would threaten her like the former duke in order to suppress renewed gossip about my humble origins. Everyone says that I'm my grandfather's shadow."

"Are you?" Hannah couldn't help but inquire.

"Am I what?" Foxglen asked.

"His shadow."

Foxglen's lips twitched, but then they smoothed back into an expressionless line. "I am not sure what I am, but I would not harm either my sister or my mother. They are crucial to discovering just who I am."

Hannah had not expected honesty, especially when the truth made Foxglen look vulnerable. Once again, she felt herself softening. But Foxglen hadn't denied being a new version of the old duke. Hannah reminded herself that he'd only vowed not to hurt his own blood.

"What will you do when you find them?" Hannah asked.

"I'll confirm that my mother and sister aren't suffering. If they are, I'll immediately redress their afflictions to the best of my abilities. Any interaction beyond that would depend entirely upon their wants—although I will provide them with a largesse regardless." Foxglen spoke pragmatically, as if he was simply reciting from Samuel Johnson's dictionary. Yet surely the man felt...something. He couldn't possibly be that bloodless.

It was clear, at least, that Foxglen would do right by his mother and his sister. Moreover, he seemed to have no desire to uproot their world. In short, if Hannah helped him, she wouldn't be subjecting two innocent women to more heartache.

Because Hannah had a plan.

It could be brilliant or brilliantly disastrous. Foxglen had just presented her with the perfect opportunity to penetrate his sphere. She would indeed help him locate his mother and his sister, but she also fully intended to root out what his paternal side was hiding.

"I will compensate you handsomely for your time," Foxglen added. "Even if the search proves fruitless in the end."

"Before we can agree to help you," Sophia began, "allow me to talk to Hann—"

"We'll do it. Or at least I will," Hannah broke into her cousin's statement. She would not risk giving Foxglen a chance to reconsider.

"You will?" Sophia asked, shock drenching her tone.

"Yes," Hannah answered crisply before she turned back to Foxglen. She tried not to notice how far she needed to crane her neck to meet his eyes. "You said that you would pay. Would you be willing to give coin enough to hire another coffeehouse worker?"

"Yes," Foxglen said immediately, although his gaze bored into her as if she were a trick box that he couldn't figure out how to open.

"Good. It's settled then. The Black Sheep will employ someone to fulfill my duties while I take up residence in your home."

## Chapter Four

"Take—take up residence in my—my home?" Eoin was sputtering, something he never did. His grandfather had taught him to speak emphatically with no hesitation.

But Miss Hannah Wick had a way of disrupting Eoin in a way that no one else could ever manage. Warmth crept into his cheeks, and Eoin was sorely afraid that he was blushing.

"Yes. That is the best way to execute my grand idea."

But why would Miss Wick go to such lengths as to temporarily uproot her life to assist him? Normally, Eoin was very good at deducing ploys and determining other's motivations. But he simply could not divine Miss Wick's intentions. She'd seemed icy when he'd first entered the Black Sheep and nothing like the coquette he'd met on the road to London. Yet now she was offering to live with him.

"And what plan have you devised, cousin?" Miss Sophia Wick demanded. She sounded strict, but Eoin could easily hear the underlying thread of worry in her tone. By the way she kept sneaking subtle glances in his direction, he could tell the woman did not trust him.

"If I am to help His Grace, then I will need an excuse to be by his side."

Something about Miss Hannah Wick's words sounded hollow to Eoin, but before he could deduce why, she shot him a smile. It was the precise opposite of a guileless one. It contained secrets and heat...and more than a little challenge. Eoin's normally stalwart heart suddenly thumped madly. A strange whoosh of energy swirled through him, and he felt an elation that was disproportionate to witnessing a single grin.

"Uh—" He—who always had a short, succinct response to almost every situation—could think of nothing.

"If I am to find your relatives, I will need to be able to search for clues. Perhaps your grandfather left records in his study. Maybe servants who have worked with your family for years might know of something," Miss Hannah Wick said.

"Can't Malbarry—I mean Foxglen—just discover those clues himself?" Lord Percy pointed out, surprising Eoin with his insight. He'd always found the man to be rather vacuous.

Although Miss Hannah Wick had shifted her body toward Lord Percy when he'd begun speaking, she rapidly turned away from him. Had the nobleman's comment irritated her?

"If he was able to unearth evidence on his own, he wouldn't be asking for our assistance." Hannah's tone was decidedly clipped.

Eoin swallowed to wet his throat as he debated his next words. He hated revealing anything about himself, especially his treatment in his own residence. Yet his past and even current experiences were pertinent to the search. "Miss Wick is not entirely incorrect. The servants remain loyal to my grandfather and will not confide in me. I also cannot easily ask my own family for information."

"Why not?" Hannah asked, and Eoin appreciated her directness. It made it easier for him to answer in kind.

"My grandfather made their inheritance contingent upon me *not* reuniting with my maternal relatives."

Something shifted in Miss Hannah's grass-green eyes. Thankfully, it looked more like compassion than pity.

"Well, that's a miserly dictate," Lord Percy observed, and it took all of Eoin's training to maintain his stoic expression. The man clearly meant to commiserate with Eoin, but his words only cut.

"That presents a problem with my original plan," Miss Hannah said quickly.

Eoin wondered if she was simply returning the conversation to its initial course or if she'd detected his discomfort. If so, it was kind of her to offer a distraction.

"How?" Miss Sophia asked. "I think it is time you elaborate more."

"Well, I planned to pose as a maid. That way, I would have an excuse to poke around various rooms and to converse with the staff. But if I also need to pry information from Eoin's relatives, I require a more elevated position."

"What if you posed as a relation?" Lord Percy suggested. "My parents always have visitors popping by, and I always forget who's who."

"That would not work," Eoin said, his voice sounding stilted even to his own ears. He wished to stop talking about his strained relationships. Moreover, he did not like the concept of Miss Hannah posing as a family member, not with the way his heart pounded just by standing near her. "My paternal side is not large, and even my uncles would notice if a new relative suddenly appeared. For obvious reasons, I cannot claim that Miss Wick is from my mother's side."

"A governess, then?" Lord Percy tried again. "They do occupy that odd in-between sphere between family and staff."

"There are no children in my family." Eoin kept his tone modulated and hoped that he wasn't showing any signs of irritation. The man was only trying to assist.

"Perhaps a companion to one of your aunts?" A new voice spoke up. Eoin turned toward the speaker and instantly recognized

Lady Calliope, a daughter of a duke herself and a renowned poetess.

"I am not sure if my personality would fit that of a companion," Miss Hannah said slowly. "But I suppose I could try."

Eoin gave a quick shake of his head. He couldn't fathom this bold woman demurely fitting into the ducal household. "My Aunt Joan would not accept a companion chosen by me, and my Aunt Eliza does not tolerate strangers well. New people make her exceedingly nervous, and she spends most of her days locked away in her room."

"What if you invited houseguests over and included Hannah?" Lord Percy offered excitedly.

"He is still in mourning," Lady Calliope pointed out.

"Not to mention that the servants would not be inclined to share information with me if they thought I was a nob," Miss Hannah said.

"It would also be suspicious in other ways," Eoin added. "My aunts and uncles are well aware that I only associated with my grandfather's contemporaries."

"Perhaps we're trying to think too

conventionally." Miss Hannah began to rapidly tap her foot as a decidedly mischievous expression spread across her lightly freckled face.

"What are you considering?" Miss Sophia's voice carried an almost palpable wariness.

"What if I posed as Foxglen's mistress?" Miss Hannah asked as she shot him a decidedly wicked smile.

Wanton fire blazed through Eoin's body, and his mind immediately filled with images of Miss Hannah, her luxurious red hair unbound, her chemise slipping to expose a creamy white shoulder, her hand reaching to stroke his face as she lay beneath him on a feather mattress, her kiss-swollen lips parting…

Egad! What was he thinking?

The woman had said *pose* as his mistress, and he was already undressing her in his mind. He'd never considered himself a scoundrel, but perhaps he'd never faced temptation.

"Did—did you just say my mis-mistress?" Eoin was stammering again, but he couldn't help it. Miss Hannah had a knack for upsetting his internal balance.

"Yes. Your mistress. I know I'm not a

typical courtesan for a duke, but that only plays into my scheme," Miss Hannah said as if she were discussing dinner ingredients rather than debauchery. But then again, she wasn't proposing an actual illicit affair—just the trappings of one. "You needn't look so pole-axed, though. I am sure a man of your status has had mistresses before—"

"No." The single word squeezed out of Eoin as the last of his iron-clad composure rusted away under Hannah's spell.

Eoin heard a few smothered chuckles from the folks gathered along the long tables. The famous playwright and theater owner Alun Powys seemed particularly amused by the exchange.

"Truly?" Miss Hannah Wick looked astounded by his inadvertent confession.

"He's telling the truth." Lady Calliope must have taken pity on him...or perhaps not. Eoin didn't trust the slight smile playing at the corners of her lips. "In fact, I don't believe he's even flirted with a woman, although I suppose he did when he first met you. But he isn't normally like that."

"That fact may actually help my plan," Miss Hannah said. "As I will be his first lover—"

Eoin coughed... or maybe he wheezed. Whatever it was, it was a strangled sound.

Miss Hannah shot him a brief look and then continued. "As I was saying, if I am his first lover, it will make sense why he is so terribly infatuated that he cannot bear for me to leave his side."

"Do—do you plan to be with me constantly?" Eoin asked, his voice still a trifle hoarse. Yet despite his shock, he found the proposed charade appealing... perhaps exciting even. Life would certainly be less boring with Miss Hannah in it, and he certainly wouldn't be able to slide back into the grooves that his grandfather had carved for him.

"Yes. It will be the best way to glean information. Perhaps I can goad something out of your aunts and uncles, or they might let something slip in my presence."

"You wish for me to introduce you as my mistress to my relations?" The words escaped him before he could think of a more judicious response.

"Why, yes." The slight upward tilt of Miss

Hannah Wick's lips told Eoin that she was enjoying his bafflement.

Eoin lost the ability to speak any words at all. He merely stared at her as she smiled at him rather triumphantly. The sliver of his mind that was still capable of rationality hazily noted that her grin was sadly not of the flirtatious kind.

"Hannah, it would be difficult for His Grace to open his home to a courtesan," Lady Charlotte said in that soft gracious way of hers that had made her an esteemed hostess of her mother's salon.

"Oh, I am well aware that men don't set up their lovers in their familial abodes, even ones with more polish than a coffeehouse proprietress. Although I suppose that my mother is a legitimate daughter of a marquess, but that certainly doesn't offset the fact that my father is a pirate."

Despite the harshness of Miss Hannah's words, Eoin could detect her defiant pride. She clearly loved her father.

"But my low status doesn't signify for what I have planned. It only supports it," Miss Hannah Wick continued. "If you're enamored enough to allow me to live in your home, then it won't surprise people if I brazenly ask personal questions. Nor will it be as shocking when I drag you to disreputable establishments that you would normally disdain."

Hannah paused and winked at Eoin rather saucily. "And there's another advantage to cooking up a plump, juicy scandal for the ton to feast upon."

He blinked. He felt like he was drowning from a spinning sensation even though his body wasn't moving at all. Had anyone ever winked at him before? He didn't think so…and certainly if they had, they wouldn't have done it saucily.

"There's another advantage?" he parroted rather dully.

"I'm curious as well," Lady Calliope said.

Hannah sighed dramatically. Eoin was beginning to realize that the firebrand did nothing in half measure.

"I'm not even a part of Society, yet how is it that I understand how gossip works better than the nobs in this room? Especially you, Lady Calliope. Your family thrives on creating tittle-tattle."

"Because they're so far up in society that they're like untouchable clouds," Alun Powys interjected.

"Are you inferring that I have no substance?" Lady Calliope whirled on the Welsh playwright.

The actor only grinned broadly. "Your words, not mine, my dear Lady Calliope."

"This is no time for you two to trade barbs," Hannah said.

"You are forever telling us that," Mr. Powys pointed out. "I cannot believe we are that disruptive."

Hannah simply glared the man into silence, which Eoin found impressive. Although he'd only seen Mr. Powys perform onstage, the playwright had a reputation as a shrewd business owner who would not typically be cowed by a single look.

"Now," Hannah said with a compelling command to her voice, "as I was trying to explain, if the ton gorges themselves on tidbits about Foxglen and me, they should pay less attention to the news that he's reunited with his mother or sister. If the two of them wish to take their rightful place in Society, they won't face as much scrutiny with me as a more interesting target."

"Ooooh, Hannah. You are a devious schemer." Lady Calliope gave a little clap.

"I grew up in a notorious coffeehouse that caters to former and not-so-former criminals. Do you really think I wouldn't be able to handle the feeble machinations of tea-sipping matrons and fat lordlings?" Miss Wick jammed one of her fists against her side as she smiled broadly.

Watching her bask in triumph caused a rather odd sensation in Eoin's chest. He felt like he'd run a mile, even though he'd been standing in one place.

Prudence demanded that he should carefully consider Miss Wick's proposal before making any commitments. But he was tired of waiting. Tired of always analyzing. Tired of forcing himself to become the perfect courtier to achieve his grandfather's political dreams for the Aucourte family.

He wanted to be bold. Adventurous even. And most of all, he wanted to discover himself.

"I'll do it. I'll make you my mistress."

## Chapter Five

Except for a single masquerade at the Duke of Blackglen's townhouse, Hannah had never darkened the doors of a mansion. And even during that particular visit, she'd gone straight to the ballroom, which had been so stuffed with costumed partygoers that the architectural splendor had been obscured by drunk dairymaids, naughty knights, perspiring pixies, and raucous Robin Hoods.

Now it appeared that Hannah would be living in the impressive building looming in front of her... at least until she managed to discover the dirtiest secrets of the Aucourte family. Like all Mayfair homes, the stately edifice with its row of Corinthian columns had been designed to impress with its attention to symmetry. Each sash window was balanced by another, their brilliant white trim contrasting perfectly with the rose-colored brick.

Nothing much daunted Hannah, but her stomach fluttered as she ascended the impressive steps. Her mother had grown up sweeping boldly through arched doorways like the one before Hannah, but Mama had left that world behind when she'd eloped with a pirate. And Hannah—Hannah was meant for side doors. At least that's what Society claimed.

Sucking in her breath, Hannah lifted the brass ring attached to the lower jaw of a snarling lion's head. It was not the most welcoming sculptural choice. Clearly, the Dukes of Foxglen wished to intimidate their guests. But Hannah refused to be cowed.

With her confidence renewed, she stuck the metal piece hard against the back plate. It produced a jolly clang, and Hannah's lips tugged into a smile.

The whitewashed wood slowly opened to reveal a delightfully dour-looking man. He possessed the thin, ghoulish appearance of a butler in an overwrought novel, and Hannah couldn't have imagined a better greeter for the home of the late Duke of Foxglen.

The man's pale-blue eyes swept over her mobcap and simple serviceable dress. Foxglen had offered to purchase her a gown—and Calliope or Charlotte would have readily lent her a fashionable one. Hannah, however, thought it would be most effective to show up in her normal attire. She wanted both his relatives and the servants to underestimate her. Best they think her a vapid, ineffectual harlot than a shrewd, calculating one.

"May I ask—" the butler began to intone, his voice a hearty, booming sound that shouldn't have come from so thin a chest. Before the servant could finish, the current Foxglen strode into view. Despite his commanding, measured walk, he exuded an eager energy that reminded Hannah of an excitable puppy. She hadn't known that Foxglen could act so well. One would think he was actually rushing to meet a lover instead of a fellow schemer.

"You're here," Foxglen said in a pleasant, steady rumble. Like his walk, his tone was carefully controlled, yet Hannah thought she detected an underlying warmth. "Come in, my darling."

Hannah thought she detected the smallest of coughs from the butler. Interesting. She thought he'd be thoroughly staid.

Hannah flounced inside, and she didn't have to fake her reaction. The ceiling above her rose to a glorious height, but the most astonishing thing was that she could see the sky—not a painted facsimile but real puffy clouds. She'd heard about buildings having glass in their roofs, but she hadn't expected a private dwelling to offer such a surprising view. Now it appeared she could be temporarily living in such a palace.

Forcibly, she dragged her eyes back to the floor. But she was only met with more splendor. A veritable flower garden had been meticulously woven into the carpet at Hannah's feet. Peach hollyhocks brushed against pink roses and purple morning glories. And this masterpiece that she was stepping upon was simply in the foyer, not a drawing room. The Aucourtes certainly had wealth funded in part by enclosing the lands her ancestors had tilled for years.

"You must be tired after your journey from Covent Garden." The corners of Foxglen's lips had tilted almost imperceptibly upward in what appeared to be his version of a welcoming smile. "Would you like any refreshments?"

"Oh, most definitely. I am utterly famished." Hannah didn't have to feign boisterousness. After all, it was her natural state. "I could eat an entire goo—"

"You may not want to finish that sentence," Foxglen said with the same even-keel inflection that he'd been using. His sea-colored eyes flicked briefly to a spot of yellow and black fluff that Hannah had overlooked.

"Is that a gosling?" she asked, bending over to inspect the little bird. The small creature immediately darted behind one of Foxglen's buckled shoes. Its stubby wings flapped uselessly in the air as it squeak-chirped its distress.

"I am afraid so," Foxglen sighed. "The creature seems to have attached itself to me. It refuses to leave my side."

Hannah laughed in delight at the idea

of such a tiny bird faithfully shadowing the enormous and rather expressionless duke. "Why, it must think you're its mother! How utterly charming!"

Foxglen didn't deny her words as he also leaned down to stroke the fledgling's downy head. "I was unfortunately holding its egg when it broke through the shell."

"I didn't expect you to engage in any animal husbandry." Hannah turned to Foxglen. His head was closer than she'd realized, and an unstoppable warmth flooded her as she met his gaze. As stiff as the man outwardly acted, his eyes seemed to hold the beckoning waters of the tropics. And just as Hannah had plunged into the aquamarine surf as a child when visiting her aunt, part of her wanted to dive into Foxglen's depths—a perilous proposition. Although Hannah generally didn't mind danger, this was one hazard she'd avoid.

"I am not in the habit of breeding fowl. The gosling's mother belongs to my Aunt Eliza," Foxglen said as if that explained the unexpected presence of the barnyard bird in one of the stateliest houses in Mayfair.

"Is she preparing absurdly early for Christmas dinner?" Hannah asked, and she thought she heard another muffled sound from the butler, who was otherwise doing a remarkably good job of fading into the mint-green walls.

"The goose was a rather unkind bequest from my late grandfather to my aunt. I would not recommend mentioning the creature when I introduce you to my family. They are currently breakfasting. Would you like to meet them now?" Foxglen straightened with great dignity and gently inclined his head toward a corridor, which Hannah assumed led to the dining room.

Remembering her purpose for being in such a grand house, Hannah immediately snapped upright. She'd arrived purposefully at this unfashionable hour to interrupt their meal.

"I would love to speak with them!" Hannah injected more naïveté into her voice than she'd ever possessed in her entire life.

"Anything for my darling." Foxglen amazingly made the overly trite words sound serious instead of nauseating.

The butler didn't cough this time, but he did react... or at least his eyes did. Their cool, icy blueness seemed to warm ever so slightly.

Was Foxglen perhaps liked by his staff? As Hannah marched past the manservant to follow the duke, the fellow's thin lips curled at the ends in a small, but definite, smile.

Foxglen led her quickly through a spacious drawing room filled with so many wonders that she could scarcely take them in. A huge mirror hung over a wooden mantel that had been carved into two columns matching those on the outside of the house. The walls were covered in paper filled with birds of paradise displaying their colorful feathers. Even the ceiling contained a feast for the eyes with the plaster intricately molded into peacock feathers.

The dining room was more austere in comparison but no less impressive. Huge windows allowed sunlight to flood into the bright space painted in a pale sage green with white trim. The ceiling above the mahogany table also had plasterwork but only around a fashionable crystal chandelier. The glittering centerpiece threw shards of rainbows around the clean, airy room. Hannah had never seen the like, and she wanted to keep staring at the beautiful shapes, which looked like huge droplets of water frozen in time.

Unfortunately, she hadn't come to ogle but to investigate. And that meant concentrating on the people, not the furnishings. Dragging her eyes from the magnificent glasswork, she focused on Foxglen's relatives. None of the four looked anything like him. Their hair ranged from silvery blond to honey-toned, and although they possessed blue eyes, theirs were lighter shades than Foxglen's azure irises.

His aunts were dainty, diminutive women who seemed to have more in common with porcelain dolls than with living humans. His uncles were of middling height. Although they were not as slight as their sisters, they certainly did not possess anywhere near the impressive array of muscles that Foxglen had. All four were extremely pale—almost to the point that their skin appeared translucent—and Hannah wondered how often they ventured outside. They were all attractive but in a gilded, superficial way.

"What brings you here, nephew?" one of his uncle's asked, his voice fluctuating between casualness and annoyance. It was clear even to an outsider like Hannah that the fellow was trying very hard to appear congenial but couldn't completely mask his rather intense irritation.

"Goodness, who is that sorry creature behind you? Why is she not properly fitted in a maid's uniform?" His aunt did nothing to hide her own distaste as her upturned nose crinkled.

Foxglen's other two relatives kept eating, clearly content to let their siblings address the disturbance. His other aunt did not even glance up from the scandal sheet that she was reading. It was certainly not the warm greeting that Hannah would have received at her own paternal uncle's table—although she supposed she would have received a much chillier reception if she'd ever attempted to visit her maternal aunt.

Had Foxglen faced this dismissiveness since childhood? Is that why he acted so distant?

A pang of sympathy struck Hannah's heart,

but she promptly ignored it. Those weren't the questions that she'd come here to answer, and she had enough to ferret out already.

"Uncle Francis. Aunt Eliza. Uncle Hugh. Aunt Joan." The duke regally inclined his head to each relative as he spoke. "This is Miss Hannah Wick. She will be staying with us as a guest."

"A—a—a *guest*!" gasped Lady Joan, who'd been the one to inquire about Hannah's presence.

Lord Hugh, who had been in mid-bite, seemed frozen with his forkful of kippers jammed halfway into his mouth. "A what?"

"Oh my!" The startled cry came from Lady Eliza as her thin hand fluttered toward her neck.

"Surely you do not mean—" Lord Francis grumbled.

"I am his mistress!" Hannah cried happily as if this were a perfectly normal announcement to make in the dining room of an old noble family.

Lord Hugh's fork clattered to his plate as pieces of fish flew onto the table. Beside him, his sister Eliza gave a start, her sky blue eyes wide with shock. Her gossip rag flew into the air, and sheets floated down onto the expensive rug. Lord Francis attempted to look composed, but his lips kept twitching into a decided scowl. Lady Joan's eyebrows drew down, and her mouth popped open. However, before she spoke what would likely be damning words, she glanced over at Foxglen and promptly snapped her jaw shut. Resentment shimmered in her pale-blue eyes, but she did not speak.

Interesting. It was clear that Foxglen's relatives spared him no affection, but they were also loath to gainsay him. Given that their father had allegedly cut off their allowance and made their future inheritance contingent on Foxglen not finding his mother and sister, then perhaps they were at the mercy of the new duke's good graces.

"I am sorry to leave you alone so soon after your arrival, but I am afraid that there is business that I must attend to," Foxglen told Hannah in that stiff, perfunctory manner of his. She pretended to pout, but they'd actually planned this. The surprise, after all, would loosen their lips, especially if he wasn't around. Foxglen had worried about abandoning her, but Hannah had plenty of experience dealing with unruly customers. She could handle four nobs at a breakfast table.

Foxglen pivoted to leave, and Hannah grabbed his sleeve. If they were to convince people that she made the duke daft enough to install her in his London mansion, he needed to show her some form of physical affection.

"A kiss before you go!" Hannah said, with enough sugary enthusiasm to make her sick to her stomach. Puckering her mouth, she prepared just to buss the air near his cheek. It seemed, however, that Foxglen was bolder and more dedicated to their act than she'd anticipated.

His warm lips brushed against hers. She didn't even have time to close her eyes before he pulled back. Yet despite the quickness, that simple, soft kiss disrupted her body in a way that no other embrace had. Her skin tingled, and a pleasant heat billowed inside her. She wasn't some virginal miss who'd only experienced a quick, clandestine peck on the cheek. But Foxglen—Foxglen made her feel as if all her firsts were still before her.

His face had reddened into a shade deeper than the New World tomatoes that her Aunt Mary grew on her Caribbean island. He stepped back awkwardly, and he inclined his head toward her with a rapidity at odds with his normal measured motions.

"I will be sure to make time for you this afternoon, darling." Even his words sounded rushed as he turned and disappeared from the room.

"Now that is a juicy tidbit of gossip," Lady Eliza said as soon as Foxglen's footsteps faded. "Much better than anything in my favorite scandal sheets."

"I do believe this occasion calls for our special coffee," Lord Hugh said. "Right, brother?"

"Indeed. Indeed." Lord Francis's blue eyes were as round as two lakes.

*Special coffee?* Hannah would need to try some of that. Perhaps it was something that they should try serving at the Black Sheep. Not that any brew had much of a chance of competing with the delicious concoctions that Sophia dreamed up.

"I half expect Father to rise up from his grave to discipline that scamp. To think that he's turned out just like our brother," Lady Joan huffed out. "He's taken up with a woman just like his mother."

And this was just the opportunity that Hannah wanted.

"I possess similarities with the duke's mother?" Hannah asked. "Am I akin to her in looks?"

"Heavens, no," Lord Hugh scoffed as he took a huge swig of coffee, which looked rather thin to Hannah's eyes. "That's like calling a sapling an oak tree."

Hannah blinked. She was not exactly a small woman by any measure. In fact, she had several inches over both ladies and was probably a stone heavier too.

"Is she a redhead?" Hannah asked.

"No." Lord Francis paused to tip back his coffee cup and drain it. He placed it back down onto the saucer and poured more before he finally continued speaking. "Her coloring was like John's. They have the same mousy brown hair. Eyes are the same too."

John. Lord Francis must be referring to the duke, but Hannah would never describe his hair as mousy. It was too rich a color—like well-steeped coffee mixed with the barest hint of red.

"Because you're both tavern wenches," Lady Joan spit out.

"I'm not a tavern wench," Hannah contradicted.

"You certainly dress like one," Aunt Eliza pointed out.

"I am a proprietress of a coffeehouse." Hannah had no intention of hiding her identity. If it became known that a duke's mistress—or former mistress—operated the Black Sheep, it would only increase sales. She wasn't some noblewoman with a pristine reputation to safeguard. "Did His Grace's mother own the tavern?"

"That *Irish* woman? Own the *Horse and Hen*?" Lord Hugh's response was a trifle too loud and perhaps a tad slurred. Hannah was beginning to wonder if that special brew contained some sort of alcohol.

Lord Francis joined his brother's cackling as he topped off his brother's cup. The two were definitely in unfashionably high spirits.

"Why? Was the Horse and Hen in a place like Mount Street?" Hannah asked, naming the fashionable boulevard of shops in Mayfair. She highly doubted that Foxglen's mother had worked at an establishment there, but she wanted to ferret out the vague location of the Horse and Hen.

Lord Francis snorted loudly and for some reason that made him laugh. His brother joined in. Finally, when Lord Francis quieted his guffaws, he said, "Hardly. It was a smelly, dark little hole in Covent Garden."

"Was? Is it gone now?" Hannah asked, hoping that she didn't sound too interested.

"How the hell would I know? It was my dead brother who frequented the establishment, not me. Bloody place was filled with damn reformers," Lord Francis said defensively, his good humor all but vanished.

"Perhaps we shouldn't say more," Lady Eliza said in a shaky voice, her white hands flapping like nervous white moths.

"Whyever not?" Lord Hugh demanded. "You're the one always entrenched in gossip."

"Father wouldn't like it." Lady Eliza glanced around as if she expected the late duke's ghostly form to emerge from behind the cream silk curtains.

"And do not forget the bequest," Lady Joan added.

"Father isn't here anymore, and I am talking about events that happened over twenty years ago. It is hardly noteworthy." Lord Francis sounded a bit like a petulant and defensive child caught stealing candy.

Lady Joan ignored her brother's response and turned to Hannah. "Why are you asking so many questions? You have no place in this household."

"I want to learn everything there is to know about my darling duke." Hannah managed to sound perfectly lovesick.

"A duke won't marry a nobody like you—especially one as cold and calculating as John." Lady Joan leaned over the table, most likely in an attempt to appear fierce.

As Hannah had dealt with actual pirates,

she was not precisely impressed by this attempt at intimidation. She had an arsenal of pointed quips that would perfectly skewer Lady Joan, but Hannah didn't want to appear quick witted.

"Oh, I would never describe the duke as distant—at least with me." Hannah smiled brightly, feeling like a right flibbertigibbet. "And I would never dare to imagine that he would wed the likes of me. I'd make an absolutely dreadful duchess, don't you agree?"

Lady Joan blinked, clearly not expecting her target to so readily acquiesce to her station. "Well, I mean, you do admit to it yourself."

Hannah grinned broadly as if she hadn't a single thought in her vapid head. Playing into prejudices was deliciously easy and more than a trifle fun. Who would have suspected that she'd actually enjoy investigating the Aucourtes?

"I am very parched from my journey here." Hannah turned toward the uncles. "Could I try your special brew, my lords? I am always intrigued by different ways to prepare coffee."

Lord Hugh wasn't subtle as he pulled the

teapot against his chest. "I am afraid I poured the last drop."

"Oh, what a shame." Hannah pretended to pout but then instantly brightened. "Well, I'm famished as well. It's a wonderful spread you have. I've never seen the like."

Which was true. She typically ate a simple breakfast of bread and cheese. And if she was going to live in a grand home as a fake mistress, she might as well take advantage of the luxuries. Jumping to her feet, she flounced over to the sideboard and found it heaping with sausages, tongue, omelets, and kippers. Picking up a bone china plate painted with delicate roses and rimmed in gold, she piled on the food until the pattern was no longer visible. She plopped back into her seat without ceremony and dug into the victuals as if she were seated at her own table.

Her mother, who had at least tried to instill proper table manners, would be aghast at how she shoveled meat and eggs into her mouth. But Hannah wasn't here to impress but to disgust.

Her ploy worked. Within minutes, each

Aucourte sibling excused themselves. As soon as the last one had left the room, Hannah reached for the pot of coffee. Lord Hugh hadn't been fibbing. There were only a few drops left.

Curious, Hannah sniffed at the shallow brown liquid now lying on the bottom of her cup. She smelled the familiar, warm scent of coffee, but there was definitely something else: a pungent alcoholic note mixed with a strong floral bouquet. Gin? But it had never been a favored drink of the rich, and even the lower classes were eschewing it after the rise in grain prices.

Hannah took an experimental sip. Although she preferred ale, she'd drunk gin once or twice before. Even among the nutty bitterness from the roasted coffee beans, it wasn't hard to recognize the burst of juniper on her tongue.

Curious, Hannah glanced toward the sideboard again. Sure enough, there was a decanter situated there. She got up and poured herself just enough to take a sip or two. Amber liquid splashed out. Lifting it to her lips, Hannah tasted the sweet liquor. She'd never tasted brandy this smooth and complex, and she would wager that it came from France. If the brothers had access to this, why would they swill poor man's rotgut?

Was it akin to how some nobs toured Bedlam or the Foundling Hospital for a lark? Or had Lord Hugh and Lord Francis acquired the taste for the spirit after their father virtually cut off their allowance? Whatever the reason, Hannah found it deuced peculiar.

She wished, suddenly and very strongly, that Sophia were here with her. Hannah knew she had the habit of obsessing over matters, while her cousin sliced straight through insubstantial fluff to arrive at the solid core of an issue.

With a sigh, Hannah returned to her seat. Alone now in the massive room, she slowly ate her breakfast as she contemplated what she'd learned. Once she had her thoughts straight, she'd pay a visit to Foxglen's study. As she pictured bursting in upon the staid man, the right side of her mouth cocked up. Flustering Foxglen was going to be fun.

## Chapter Six

Eoin sat in his grandfather's study surrounded by the late duke's possessions. Despite building a home in popular and modern Mayfair, His Grace had preferred the older, heavier Jacobean furnishings of a century before. The massive oak desk sprawled like a dark, foreboding ancient altar in front of airy sash windows. The bookshelves were enormous with thick carved columns, which served only to make the furniture feel more foreboding. The dark wood contrasted sharply with the delicate white molding and the cheery, sky blue walls. Yet this room perfectly embodied the old Foxglen, a man determined to drag musty traditions into a new, changing era.

Eoin had spent many an hour between

these walls, scribbling away at a small desk tucked into the far-right corner. His grandfather had wanted to keep an eye on him while Eoin had read account books instead of fairy tales.

He'd hated this place, where the only sounds were his grandfather's raspy breathing and the scratch of his quill against vellum. Yet this had been Eoin's nursery, then his schoolroom, and finally his apprenticeship. And now it was allegedly his own study.

But it still felt like the former duke's. Even the title rested unevenly on Eoin's shoulders. He'd spent most of his life preparing for this role, but now that it was upon him, he didn't know what to do with it.

A sudden loud rap at his door caused Eoin to start. On the floor beside him, the gosling stirred in the nest of blankets that Eoin had laid down, but the fowl did not fully awaken.

The servants, even his steward, would scratch quietly. But this. This was a bang to summon an entire Roman legion—a long dead one at that.

The insistent sound was the only warning

Eoin had before Hannah popped inside. She still wore a workingwoman's drab linsey-woolsey, and her floppy mobcap hid most of her red curls. Yet she still managed to appear like a whirl of color. Perhaps it was the pink on her lightly freckled cheeks or the twinkling of her green eyes. Or maybe it was simply that she always seemed to burst with life as if stone walls or perhaps even the sky itself could not contain her exuberance.

Hannah shut the door behind her and winked. And just like the first time she'd made that gesture in his direction, his heart clenched and then began to ricochet madly in his chest. Why did the mere sight of her make him feel like an adventure was about to unfold?

Hannah did not appear at all intimidated by the looming pieces of furniture. With nary a sidelong glance at her surroundings, she walked boldly to the high-backed chair on the other side of the old duke's desk. Before Eoin could offer her a seat, she'd already plunked down. During the few occasions that Eoin had been instructed to sit rather than stand at attention while listening to his grandfather, he had found the dratted contraption exceedingly uncomfortable. Yet somehow Hannah not only managed to sprawl against the unforgiving oak frame but also appeared relaxed.

The former duke would have been horrified. But Eoin was impressed.

"I've already learned several things about your mother." Hannah clearly did not abide by any form of ceremony as she immediately charged ahead without a single nicety. "First, I do not look like her. Rather, you do."

To Eoin's surprise, he felt his lips twitch, and a rare amusement bubbled up inside him. "Which is a relief since I am her son."

"So bowing to Pan wasn't an aberration."

"Pardon?" Eoin asked in utter confusion.

"When we met on the road to London, you acted like a courtier greeting the king when I introduced you to my parrot," Hannah breezily explained her non sequitur. "I thought you must be a man of humor, but you've otherwise proved to be exceedingly stiff. Clearly, though, you are capable of a quick rejoinder."

Was he a man of humor? Eoin really didn't

know, but the idea suddenly appealed to him. Although he enjoyed reading the ribald satires by Willoughby Wright, he'd never considered that he, himself, could possess even a modicum of wit.

"Upon a more serious note, I learned that you share your coloring and size with your mother, and that she was Irish." Hannah ticked off each attribute on her fingers.

"Thank you," Eoin said, even though he'd either known or surmised all that.

"I suppose none of that is new information, but did you know that she was a tavern maid at the Horse and Hen in Covent Garden?"

Hannah's single question caused a rush of tangled emotions to barrel through Eoin. He almost clenched his fists at the onslaught. But Eoin was too well schooled to even twitch a muscle. Instead, he sat stiffly in his chair as he tried to absorb the news that they had not just another clue but a concrete lead.

Yes, his mother and his sister had probably long moved away from the tavern, but it was an actual physical place instead of the vague, mostly forgotten memories of a six-year-old.

For the first time since early childhood, hope flickered that he might actually see his loved ones again.

"It shouldn't take too long to discover more. I've already asked your butler to send a message round to Sophia. She'll send out one of our boys, and we should have an answer by late afternoon," Hannah said. "If you wish, the two of us can head to the Horse and Hen tonight—if it still exists—or we can visit whatever establishment took its place."

Eoin wanted to say yes, but he stole a reluctant look at the pile of ledgers sitting on his ink blotter. "I am afraid I have accounts to review. I cannot let my work suffer for a personal quest. Too many rely on His Grace's—I mean my—estates."

Hannah tilted her head. "Don't you have a steward or two who can help you with such matters?"

"I do," Eoin admitted, but they were all dour men whom he'd inherited from his grandfather.

"Then why aren't they assisting you? Do you mistrust their loyalty? Are they embezzling?"

Eoin stopped a sigh as he ran one finger over the leather binding of the top record. "I am afraid it is too much devotion, at least to my grandfather and his ways."

"Do you plan to run your holdings differently than he did?" Hannah was no longer slouching but leaning forward, her eyes the exact color of dew-kissed grass in the spring.

Eoin paused. He never shared his inner thoughts, and doing so felt odd—like he was trying to stretch a weak and underutilized muscle. "I—I believe so."

"You don't sound very confident." Hannah threw down her words like a gauntlet of old, but Eoin didn't want to spar. He desired a confidante, someone he'd never had even for trivial matters.

"I am indeed uncertain," Eoin admitted, even as he warned himself not to share too much. But he couldn't help it, not when Hannah was asking the perfect questions, echoing the thoughts that had been ripping through him since his grandfather's death. "I know what kind of duke my grandfather wanted me to be—he spent my lifetime making sure of it."

"But you don't want to be his version of a peer?" Hannah asked slowly, as if he were a particularly dense text that she was attempting to decipher.

"No," Eoin said, and an emotion akin to relief flooded him. It was freeing to admit that aloud, to confess that all his grandfather's efforts had failed.

"What kind of nob do you want to be?" Hannah asked in a straightforward way that should have grated. Instead, he welcomed the question.

"One that makes improvements to his lands," Eoin answered promptly because he knew at least that. "My grandfather resisted implementing the four-crop rotation system. He thought that turnips were unpleasant peasant food, and he didn't want them growing on his property. I'm considering replacing wheeled plows with newer, lighter ones. I've also been wondering if a short canal would improve transport. The Sankey Canal is a fascinating marvel, and I'm closely following the proposed Bridgewater Canal. There's also a possibility of hiring an expert to determine if there are any useful mineral deposits. And…"

Eoin trailed off as he realized that he'd started to babble. He didn't recall ever speaking so much at one time. His grandfather would have rebuked him after the second sentence. But these ideas... they'd been simmering in his mind for years. He'd never allowed them to boil over, yet now they seemed to spew from him.

"Are you going through the ledgers to see what you can invest?" Hannah asked, her gaze penetrating.

"Um, yes," Eoin admitted, slightly taken aback by how quickly Hannah had assessed the situation, but he supposed that she successfully ran her own business.

"You aren't the duke that I thought you'd be," Hannah told him, her expression hard to read but most definitely intense.

Her statement, though, bothered him. It almost sounded as if she knew him better than the circumstances warranted. But his thoughts immediately slammed to a stop when she smiled broadly.

"And I believe I like the difference."

Incendiary heat burst through Eoin, and

this time he did ball his hands into fists. It was either that or gulp like a landed fish. He should be wary of how easily this woman could turn him into an inferno, but instead he yearned to see what would happen if she continued to break through his legendary control.

"That is kind of you to say." Eoin's voice sounded strained to his own ears.

Hannah laughed, the sound rich and throaty. It seemed to rumble through Eoin until his body resonated with her mirth.

"You say the most perfunctory statements in the most unexpectedly charming manner."

"I'm not known to be charming," Eoin confessed. He was fully aware of his reputation for being "either a boring menace or menacing bore," as one debutante had quipped.

"Nor am I." Hannah grinned. "I'm much too bold."

"I—I like your boldness." Eoin stumbled over the words as a new, less pleasant heat washed over him. He'd never imagined uttering such a statement, and it made him feel unbalanced.

Hannah winked. "Well, then, I guess I'll need to employ even more cheekiness, won't I?"

This time, Eoin only managed to nod in response. He half hoped, half feared that she would continue this flirtation—confident on her part, awkward on his.

But she must have taken pity on him as she nodded toward the pile of books. "If I help you review those, would you be able to investigate later this evening?"

"You want to assist with the accounts?" Eoin asked in shock. When he'd agreed to Hannah living in his home, he'd never expected that she'd hole up with him in his dreary study and review ledgers.

"I am very good with numbers. I keep all the books for the Black Sheep. My mother—who used to handle them—was exceedingly happy to hand them over to me when I showed an interest. I started helping her when I was about ten or eleven."

"Are you certain that you wish to assist? It is not precisely a stimulating activity," Eoin said. He himself had never particularly minded it, but his grandfather had always viewed accounts as a necessary but irritating burden.

"Figures have always fascinated me. They can convey so much in a few short strokes of the pen," Hannah explained.

Eoin understood the sentiment, but he found people and their diverging motivations more intriguing. Perhaps it was because he was so restrained that he liked observing others' emotions.

"If you want to help, then this is what I'm looking for." Eoin turned the ledger he was reviewing in her direction. He explained how he was not just scanning expenditures and profits but searching for redundancies and other ways to cut expenses to free up funds for improvements. As Hannah had boasted, she understood the complicated task immediately.

A hush settled over the room, and just like when Eoin's grandfather was alive, the silence was broken only by the sounds of breathing, the flipping of pages, and the scratching of pens. But this was a pleasant kind of quietude—one free of all tension. It felt almost companionable as he and Hannah worked toward the same goal. When they paused for Hannah to report what she'd gleaned, Eoin was impressed by what she'd observed.

It was as if he had finally found a partner. But Eoin knew it was just a temporary façade. Once he reunited with his mother and his sister—or when it became obvious that they couldn't be found—this mirage of a connection would end, and Eoin would once again be left alone in his grandfather's oppressive study.

***

"The way your eyes keep darting to and fro, it's like you've never been to Covent Garden," Hannah said as they hurried down a narrow passage that reeked of smells that Eoin would rather not identify. Throaty laughter and raucous chatter poured from the hodgepodge of buildings stuffed together along the refuse-filled street where, according to Hannah's informants, the Horse and Hen was located. Judging by the scantily clad women and the ruffled men with coats and coiffures askew, many of the enterprises were brothels, but some were mere taverns.

"I've been to the Theatre Royal and, of course, the Black Sheep Coffeehouse," Eoin said as he pressed against the wall of a building to avoid a stumbling drunk. Eoin started to pull Hannah to safety, but she'd already nimbly avoided the bumbling human obstacle.

"Yet not a section like this?" Hannah inquired.

"No," Eoin admitted. "I have mostly just been to the two places that I mentioned."

"You haven't been in even a tavern in Covent Garden?" Hannah asked, her disbelief palpable. "Or another coffeehouse?"

Eoin shook his head, not blaming Hannah for her shock. It was unusual for a man of his wealth and age not to have visited at least one place of ill-repute. "I frequented the Elysian Fields Coffeehouse with my grandfather, but it's in Mayfair. And I think he only went there because it was so famous among his fellow antiquarians."

"I believe you may be as sheltered as Charlotte was before she invested in the Black Sheep," Hannah said, her words containing no malice but simply surprise. And since her observation carried no sting, Eoin felt none.

"Perhaps I am more closeted. Your cousin did help her mother run a salon, and according to rumor, she was very close to your mutual great-aunt, who was known for her frankness," Eoin said.

Before Hannah could answer him, Eoin felt a tug on his lapel. He turned to find a woman—with a bodice so low cut that she might as well have been bare chested—hanging half her body out a window. Her thin arm was extended as she held on tight to Eoin's workingman's attire.

"Come inside, lovey!" the woman hollered.

Another female popped out of a window from across the way. Due to the extreme narrowness of the passage and the breadth of Eoin's shoulders, her fingers also snared Eoin's sleeve. "Don't listen to her. I'm the better choice. I know how to handle a man of your girth."

"My apologies, but he's with me!" Hannah called out gaily as she snaked her arm around his middle. She nestled against him, and even through the layers of material that he wore, he could feel her warmth. She leaned farther into his side and gazed up at him with an expression that he could only call adoring. "Isn't that right, my love?"

His throat seized, and Eoin could only nod. He knew she was playacting to save him from a great deal of embarrassment, but he could not help reacting to her nearness.

The women pouted, but he knew it was also a charade. This was the London that reformers hoped to improve. If Eoin's father had met his mother while she was working in a tavern among such desperation, no wonder he'd advocated for change.

Eoin finally spotted a sign of a horse with a pair of chicken feet sticking out near its middle. He assumed at one time it showed a fowl nestled against an equine, but the paint had long since faded away. The weathered wood had cracked between the horse's ears and along its back. The building looked just as tumbled down—and certainly not as neat and trim as the outside of the Black Sheep. Daub had fallen away to reveal the wattle beneath it, and several shutters hung askew. Eoin had no idea what the establishment had looked like twenty-odd years ago, but his heart twisted at the thought of his mother working here. Yet what had he expected? He knew she was a poor Irish immigrant who'd somehow stolen the heart of an heir to a dukedom. Even more worrisome, how had she and Eoin's sister managed to survive after the death of Eoin's father?

He dreaded that answer most of all, but he still had to pursue it—even if there was only pain at the end.

"Oi!" Hannah's sharp voice broke through his reverie.

Blinking, Eoin turned to find Hannah holding the wrist of a slender waif. At first glance, Eoin thought the child to be about eight or nine years of age, but his features weren't soft enough. Although thin and undersized, the boy was more likely thirteen or fourteen.

"Give it back," Hannah demanded, stretching out her other palm.

The youth sighed and dropped Eoin's pocket watch into Hannah's fingers. The lad's gaze darted to Eoin. To Eoin's surprise, the urchin did not appear to be terrified of Eoin's immense size. Instead, the adolescent seemed to be carefully assessing how best to escape.

"I listened. Will you let me go now?" the lad demanded in the rough accents of the streets.

Instead, Hannah pushed up the boy's sleeve, revealing bruises. The child broke free of her grip and yanked down the soiled and ripped material.

"If you ever get tired of working for a kidsman, stop by the Black Sheep Coffeehouse," Hannah told the boy. "There's a benefactor there who will pay for small tasks like delivering messages and gathering information that isn't dangerous to obtain."

The youth jerked his head, but the nod seemed perfunctory. He feinted a move to the right but then ended up darting to the left. Within seconds, he disappeared down another alley.

"We should probably head to our destination before you suffer another mishap. It's a bit like I'm leading a lamb through the marketplace."

"I feel like one," Eoin freely admitted, as they drew closer to the raucous noise emanating from the tavern. Yet Eoin swore most of the sound was coming from below street level rather than from the open windows. He scanned the surrounding area and his gaze locked with the flat, cold eyes of a man guarding a set of sunken steps. The fellow was nearly as big as Eoin, and his smashed nose looked like it had been broken at least several times.

"That's likely not the entrance for us," Hannah told Eoin in a low voice. "I am curious, too, but we won't find answers by barging into places where we're not wanted. Our best chance of learning about your mother is to talk to one of the older serving maids."

"What do you think is happening down there?" Eoin asked, as a vague unsettled feeling took up roost in his chest.

"On this street?" Hannah said. "Any number of unsavory things. It's best not to think too much on it and to focus on our mission."

Yet how could Eoin not be concerned? Over twenty years had passed since his mother had worked at the Horse and Hen, and perhaps this street had been more presentable then. But Eoin couldn't help worrying that she might have been forced to participate in whatever required a fearsome-looking sentry.

## Chapter Seven

For a man who was allegedly stoic, Foxglen was very emotive, at least around Hannah. She could easily read the anguish in his eyes as he gazed around the narrow alleyway. Unlike many of his class, he wasn't judging or even pitying the destitute folks around him. Instead, he seemed to keenly feel their desperation, perhaps because he was imagining his own family suffering in the filth and squalor.

Hannah wanted to reach out and squeeze his arm like she would one of her cousin's. But although she'd cuddled next to Foxglen to dissuade the two prostitutes, she didn't want to physically soothe him. She must remember that he wasn't her ally, even if they were temporarily working together.

Unfortunately, the wretched man kept

inadvertently endearing himself to Hannah. Foxglen might look like a tough prizefighter, but he bumbled around Covent Garden with the shyness of a schoolboy. Although the women in the windows had clearly embarrassed Foxglen, Hannah hadn't detected rage, disgust, or even prurient interest rising from him. More surprisingly, he hadn't exhibited a modicum of anger when that street urchin had picked his pocket. Foxglen had simply allowed Hannah to deal with the matter instead of hollering for the youth to be shipped off to the Colonies.

Yet the duke was determined. It showed in the way he boldly pushed open the door to the tavern—even though he didn't know if he would find painful answers inside.

What greeted them, instead, was ominous silence. As soon as the patrons' eyes fell upon them, they immediately stiffened and stopped their conversations. Even the servers froze despite their heavy-laden trays. The entire place reeked of stale beer interspersed with the sharper scents of juniper. Evidently, the Horse and Hen still sold the aromatic swill.

It could be that the duke's massive build had quieted the crowd. The men were definitely sizing him up over their brimming tankards. Yet they were watching her with almost equal suspicion. A weighty wariness hung in the air and, with it, a tinge of danger.

Hannah was suddenly glad that Sophia knew of their destination. She hadn't thought searching for a duke's mother would be perilous, but apparently, she'd been mistaken.

"Do you wish to turn around?" Foxglen asked in a low tone that only she could hear.

"No," Hannah told him at the same volume. This wasn't the first hazardous situation that she'd faced.

Slowly, Hannah and Foxglen stepped into the dark, malodorous tavern. Even though it was still light out, no sun penetrated the dark, almost cave-like room lit by only a few tallow candles. Given the stench wafting from the tapers, the fatty wax had gone rancid.

As Hannah and Foxglen slunk in the direction of an empty table, every single patron glared. The tavern maids ignored them, but the man behind the locked bar glowered the most. Although Foxglen always walked with his back painstakingly straight, he seemed to somehow make himself even more unrelentingly large.

When they reached their destination, Foxglen pulled out a chair that was as spindly as it was wobbly. He hesitated, likely trying to determine if the pathetic piece of furniture would bear his weight. With a sigh, the duke gingerly sat down. The wood creaked but thankfully didn't break.

Hannah sat too. Slowly, the customers' conversation resumed, but the discourse was still obviously stilted. Occasionally, hollering and shouting drifted up from between the cracks in the floorboards. Whenever it did, the occupants of the tavern slammed their drinks down or stomped their feet.

The establishment clearly wasn't just a place to grab food and drink. But even though it was patent that these folks were intent on hiding secrets, it was much less certain if the enigma pertained to Foxglen's kin. After all, more than two decades had passed since his parents had met, and this area of London was constantly experiencing deterioration, rebirth, and deterioration again.

But Foxglen's father had been a notorious reformer—one who'd plotted with Jacobites to overthrow the current King George to place a Catholic king back on the throne. Perhaps the Horse and Hen had been a haven for like-minded men. It stood to reason that the tavern might still harbor budding demagogues, but that explanation didn't feel completely right to Hannah.

A man dressed in rags shuffled in, and Hannah recognized him as one of the beggars that they'd passed in the alley. No one seemed perturbed by his presence as he headed over to a crowded table. The seated men shifted to make room for the older fellow, and a serving maid instantly walked over to take his coin and handed him a tall mug of ale.

"No one is coming to serve us." Foxglen once again pitched his voice so low that only she could hear.

"Yes," Hannah agreed as she glanced around the poorly lit room. Most of the women looked too young to have been contemporaries of Foxglen's mother.

Foxglen warily scanned the tavern too. "Perhaps I should come back myself. This establishment doesn't feel safe."

"And what would you accomplish? Having your pocket picked?" Hannah asked. "I'm more accustomed to London's seamier side."

Foxglen didn't try to deny her observation. He merely leaned forward and said even more quietly, "I thought about laying some coins on the table, but I think that would only serve to encourage robbers."

Perhaps the duke wasn't completely naïve. He'd had the good sense to don his laborer's attire without her asking. And he hadn't made the beginner's mistake of wearing expensive shoes. His footwear was appropriately worn and scuffed and nothing that a man with steady work couldn't afford.

"Our presence is indubitably making everyone anxious," Foxglen observed. "The chatter is increasing in volume, and not just to mask whatever is happening below. The shifting gazes sent in our direction are occurring at an even higher frequency than when we first arrived. The servers have also begun to chat among themselves, and their voices are pitched higher and higher."

Shock flooded Hannah. "How can you notice all that but not a child reaching into your pocket for your watch?"

Foxglen shrugged. "I read people—their facial expressions, their tones, the little movements that they make. Even sighs can yield insights."

Hannah watched him curiously. "What about me? What conclusions have you drawn about my character?"

The right side of Foxglen's normally straight lips twitched up a fraction. "In all honesty, I find you to be an unpredictable enigma."

An unpredictable enigma? Hannah did not know whether to be pleased or displeased. "In what way?"

"Well, the second time that we met, you offered to become my mistress," Eoin pointed out.

Hannah frowned. "You requested help. It was the best way for me to insert myself into your rarefied world."

"But still unconventional and more

consideration than I would have ever expected from a mere stranger."

Guilt flickered inside Hannah. Perhaps Foxglen was having trouble deciphering her character because her motivations were too convoluted.

The left corner of Foxglen's mouth now quirked up to join the right side in a true smile. "After flabbergasting the butler, you handled my aunts and uncles masterfully. Within one meeting, you learned more than I have in years. And then you helped me with the account books. I never know which actions are part of your scheme and which behaviors exhibit your true nature."

"Everyone calls me blunt. My personality shouldn't be difficult to unravel," Hannah said as she fought a wave of uncomfortableness.

"You were bold when we first met. No one has ever looked at me so brazenly, and I rather liked your gaze upon me." Foxglen's reply seemed void of any artifice, and Hannah realized that, for all his staidness, he might be even more frank than she was.

Hannah's heart thudded. She both dreaded

and wanted to hear his next words. She was not disappointed.

"Perhaps my attraction to you has muddled my mind."

"Your attraction… to me?" Hannah's throat felt as if all moisture had been wicked from it. She'd sensed that her appreciation of Foxglen was mutual, but she hadn't expected him to openly confess in a dissolute Covent Garden tavern. Even though she warned herself this was not the time for lust, prickles danced over her heated skin.

"This isn't the kind of establishment where folks just pop by." An annoyed feminine voice broke into their conversation. Hannah lifted her head to find an older woman looming over them. Silver threaded her ash brown locks, and her hard life was etched into the wrinkles and pockets carved into her face. Although she'd tried to hide the syphilis scars with black silk patches and white makeup that she could probably ill afford, she'd only drawn more attention to them. Yet it was her gray eyes—the color of granite and just as unforgiving—that most vividly testified to the harsh existence she'd led.

"You best find a drink elsewhere." The woman jerked her chin toward the exit and turned to leave.

"It's good, then, that we're here for information and not for ale," Hannah said.

The woman's steps faltered, but she did not swivel back in their direction. "We aren't serving that either."

"It's about my mother," Foxglen said in that solemn emotionless way of his. "Perhaps you knew her. She worked here over two decades ago. I'm told that I look like her."

The barmaid half twisted in the duke's direction. Although she didn't fully face him, it was clear that she was studying his features. Her gaze flicked up and then down before she paused and repeated the motion. Hannah swore that her flat gray eyes widened for just the barest of moments, but they went utterly blank again.

"Her given name was Sorcha," Foxglen pushed just as the woman's expression snapped back to normal. A muscle in her cheek twitched, but otherwise she didn't react.

"What makes you think that I've been

hefting trays in a place like this for over twenty years?" the woman called over her shoulder as she began to sashay away.

"Then is there someone who has?" Hannah called after her, even though she realized the question was likely futile.

"You best leave." The server kept her back to them, but the men shifted ominously in their seats. It was clear that Hannah and Foxglen's presence was not going to be tolerated for much longer.

"We should listen. They won't share more information, so there's no sense in risking a fight." Foxglen had returned to speaking in a low tone. This time, though, he didn't lean over the table. Instead, he sat stiffly as he monitored the room.

"Yes," Hannah agreed. She hated being chased away, but she would not face the brunt of the attack. Foxglen would be the target.

Reluctantly, Hannah rose. As she and the duke made their way through the frowning throng, Hannah noticed that the peer was trying to use his big body to shield hers. She hadn't expected an Aucourte to be so chivalrous to a mere coffeehouse proprietress, but she'd begun to realize that Foxglen's character might be as difficult for her to unravel as hers was to him.

Quickly, they moved through the shadowy interior and burst back into the narrow alley. Despite the closeness of the tall buildings, Hannah felt relief at being back outside. A delayed shiver ran through her as her entire body sagged. She hadn't realized how tightly she'd been holding herself.

"I'm glad to be free of that place." Foxglen's jaw was set as he glanced down the street. "Do you think my mother suffered while working there?"

"It could have been an entirely different establishment back then." Once again, Hannah had to battle the desire to physically soothe the duke. The man didn't need her clutching at his hand or arm—or at least that's what Hannah told herself firmly.

"Oi!" The loud male voice caused both Hannah and Foxglen to whirl around. Before Hannah could call out a warning, a fist came flying toward Foxglen's midsection. To

Hannah's relief, the duke dodged the blow, which was rapidly followed by another sharp jab. Foxglen's footwork was a tad clumsy, but despite his large size, he managed to dance away from the second hit too.

By the third strike, Hannah had recovered her wits enough to take stock of their attacker. It was the same raggedy man who'd entered the Horse and Hen after them. Despite his age, the older fellow moved with deadly precision.

Hannah reached inside the slit of her skirts for the knife that she always wore strapped to her thigh. Her father, her uncle, and her aunt had all taught her to wield it. She grabbed the mother-of-pearl handle just as Foxglen raised his arms to deflect the rain of blows. Next, he swung his own meaty fist, the strike a bit unwieldly but definitely powerful.

The ambusher easily avoided the punch, and an incongruously broad smile broke over his face, revealing a nearly toothless mouth. A few of the remaining stubs were badly chipped rather than merely rotting.

Suddenly, the man nodded, as if he'd confirmed something grand. Then his hands dropped harmlessly to his sides, and he stepped back.

His grin turned lopsided as he regarded Foxglen with steady brown eyes. He reached up and rubbed his chin as he continued his study. Arthritis and maybe something more swelled the skin around his knuckles, almost obscuring them entirely. His steady, unyielding expression seemed just as weathered as his leathery skin.

"Don't go chasing after spirits and secrets," the attacker rasped without ceremony or further explanation. Then, before Hannah could question him, he turned on his heels and ambled away.

For a beat or two, Foxglen stood apparently frozen, his body trapped between an offensive and a defensive position. But then he shook himself and took two large strides toward the retreating man. "What do you mean, spirits?"

But the strange fellow didn't answer. Instead, he simply turned down another twisty passage. Foxglen immediately started running. Picking up her skirts, Hannah followed suit.

When they reached the entrance to the

next alley, they unfortunately spied nothing but shadows. Foxglen started to push his way down the narrow squeeze, but this time, Hannah grabbed his elbow.

"It's no use. If he doesn't want to be found, you'll never locate him. And if he does wish for you to follow, it would only be to lure you into a trap." Hannah also wanted to trail the mysterious man, but despite her brashness, she'd learned caution over the years.

Foxglen glanced down at her, and raw emotions swam in the blue-green depths of his eyes. The older fellow's words had deeply affected him.

Hannah found that she could not release Foxglen's arm even though he was no longer intent on perilous pursuit. He just looked so terribly wounded.

"The man said not to chase after spirits. Do you think my mother's dead and my sister too? Is searching for them just a foolish whim?" Foxglen's voice—which was normally so measured—thrummed with anguish.

"I wouldn't put too much stock in one fellow's words. His behavior was erratic at best."

Hannah linked their elbows as she gently guided Foxglen out of the alley and toward his carriage waiting a distance away.

"I believe that the man was acting with a specific intent." Foxglen's tone fluctuated from pain to his normal stoicism then back again. It was clear that he was trying to employ logic in a situation involving his heart. Hannah could not help but feel her own pang of sadness. The duke truly did care for his family—a sentiment Hannah readily understood.

"He tried to punch you and then grinned like a nincompoop. Next, he muttered about secrets and the supernatural before finally darting away. Those are the signs of drunkenness, not lucidity," Hannah pointed out as they reached the ducal coach with its crest covered to hide Foxglen's identity.

"I can't help but think that, like Hamlet, there was a method to his madness." Foxglen climbed the steps like an automaton. When he sat down, he tugged Hannah with him. Hannah half fell into him, and she made a concentrated effort not to notice the firmness of his muscles... or the heat radiating from him.

"He seemed very deliberate when he followed us, and his gaze was clear and steady," Foxglen continued. "His eyes weren't bloodshot, and he didn't walk with the stiffness that my uncles do when they're trying not to stumble. His voice was natural, too, with nary a slurred word."

"He could have simply been trying to warn you away like the serving maid, or he could have been trying to lure you into danger. There is no reason to believe that he knows anything about your family or their whereabouts," Hannah pointed out. "We will try to locate him but on our terms. It will do us no good to madly dash through back alleys. I know how to defend myself but not against an ambush."

Foxglen nodded curtly, and she could see his emotions leech away as his stoic mask once again fell into place. Watching the duke deny his feelings caused an ache to spread through Hannah.

"Excellent points," Eoin said, his tone crisp and orderly. "I wasn't thinking when I almost dragged you after that man. It was dangerous enough in the Horse and Hen."

The logical Foxglen was back, and Hannah should feel at ease. But she didn't.

"I don't mean to reject your worries about what the man said or to dismiss your pain," Hannah told him quickly. "I just do not wish for you to give up hope. It is early in our search."

Foxglen swallowed but otherwise his expression did not change. "I have learned it is best to remain impassive, and I am generally not given to strong reactions. I suppose something about this endeavor makes me feel as if I was still a small child again, and it is hard to remain regulated. I do apologize for my outburst."

"There was no outburst, Your Grace," Hannah said as the dull pain in her heart seemed to break into something much more raw. She was certain that Foxglen did not realize how revealing his words were. It was clear that he'd been taught to act like a stiff mannequin.

"Eoin."

"Pardon?" Hannah asked in confusion.

"Would you use 'Eoin' rather than 'Your Grace'?" Foxglen asked. "It's been so long since anyone has called me by my actual given name."

"What were you being called by your grandfather and aunts and uncles?" Hannah asked as more unease flowed through her.

"Lord Malbarry or John—the anglicized version of Eoin." Foxglen rattled off the information as if it meant nothing to him, yet clearly it did. But Hannah wasn't going to force him to share his emotions. If he wanted to retreat into stoicism, then she wouldn't pry open his defenses.

"You may call me Hannah, then, Eoin," Hannah said, his birth name falling rather naturally from her lips—perhaps too much so. She told herself that it was simply that she wasn't one for ceremony, especially when it came to dealing with puffed-up peers. But there was an intimacy to given names even among laborers like her.

"Hannah." Eoin's voice contained a hint of warmth, which curled through Hannah. A flutter started low in her stomach, and try as she might, she could not completely settle it.

"We should visit the Black Sheep tomorrow." Hannah spoke the words hastily. Now she was the one longing for the return of pragmatism.

She and Eoin—no Foxglen—were only sharing this carriage ride because of his mission and hers. They were not real lovers, and they shouldn't be acting like ones when there was no audience.

"I'll send a message round to the men and women who helped uncover the plot against King George." Hannah was speaking more rapidly than normal, and she hoped that Eoin did not notice. "They might know something about the Horse and Hen."

"I'm sorry. I didn't realize that the tavern made you that anxious. We should have left earlier." Foxglen frowned at her with palpable concern.

The nob's worry had the irritating effect of softening Hannah. "I was a bit uneasy, but never truly worried. Why do you think I was?"

"Your cadence changed, and I thought it was due to pent-up fear," Eoin explained.

Damn the perceptive man. He had noticed. Fortunately, though, he hadn't divined the real reason for her rapid speech.

"I wasn't fashed. I am just intent on locating your family." There. That was a good excuse... and words that she should strictly follow.

## Chapter Eight

The Black Sheep bubbled with life. The front room was loud and noisy with men jostling for seats and shouting to be heard. But the back room was the perfect marriage of literary salon and cheerful pub. Chairs and divans—more comfortable than Eoin had ever seen—filled the space, along with gentlewomen in delicately embroidered gowns and female laborers wearing linsey-woolsey dresses. Likewise, there were some men in finely tailored silk jackets and others in carefully patched clothing.

The spurts of conversation that floated in Eoin's direction ranged from discussions about bawdy plays to the latest fashions to the war with France to news from the Colonies to an art exhibit and, finally, to visits to the Royal Menagerie.

The old Foxglen would have passionately detested this place. That Eoin knew immediately. It was more difficult to ascertain his own opinion.

But as he sat on a chair and watched Hannah bustling about, he realized that he felt something he had not experienced in a long time. Simple enjoyment. He liked sitting here, surrounded by enthusiastic folks whose conversation was bound by no restrictions.

And in the center of that brilliant chaos was Hannah. Excitement and exertion pinkened her cheeks, and when she stopped to speak with her customers, her green eyes sparkled with enthusiasm. Every now and then, he could catch snippets of her conversation—and no matter the topic, she always chatted away confidently. She was an intelligent one, Miss Hannah Wick.

And he liked that about her. He liked everything about her. Perhaps too much.

She had proposed to become his mistress only as a ruse. But their relationship had begun to feel more and more real...at least to Eoin.

For a long time, he'd carried a constant ache in his chest, but he hadn't noticed it until recently. And that was only because the yawning emptiness shrank when he was with Hannah. When she'd attempted to buoy his spirits in the carriage yesterday, he'd felt a comfort that was alien to him.

"Eoin, darling," Hannah called out as if she'd heard his thoughts, "how are you liking the brew?"

Eoin's heart flipped. Although he'd asked Hannah to use his given name, he hadn't expected her to use it publicly, especially coupled with *darling*.

Before he could recover, she leaned over him, her breasts grazing his back as she placed another cup of coffee on the low table in front of him. "You must try this one. It's one of Sophia's latest creations. Since it contains imported spices, we generally charge extra but consider it a little love token from me."

Hannah was playing a role. The flirty words. Her semi-embrace. Even the gift of the delicious-smelling concoction. They were all carefully crafted lies.

But Eoin was falling for each gesture.

"I am sure it will be delicious." His voice seemed blessedly normal, even though *he* didn't. Perhaps he, too, could act. After all, hadn't his entire life been a carefully scripted performance?

"Hannah," she whispered into his ear, and the gentle puff of her breath against his skin triggered a cascade of sparkling sensations. He'd never felt the like before. And he wanted more. Just not in a public place with many curious eyes turned in their direction.

"If I am openly employing your first name, you should use mine as well," Hannah quietly instructed. "We're not just lovers but shockingly affectionate ones, remember?"

"Hannah." He breathed out the word, and he felt deliciously rebellious. He'd always followed etiquette perfectly. Breaking the rules didn't just feel freeing but unexpectedly intimate. Sharing something private with her among so many people made him feel like they were an actual unit.

"Much better," Hannah praised him before she straightened. Then in a louder voice she said, "I'll keep the coffee coming. Anything to keep my darling happily ensconced."

As she sashayed away, Eoin sipped the piping-hot liquid. Bursts of cinnamon and nutmeg danced on his tongue while the cream tempered the bitterness. The rumors had been right. The Black Sheep had managed to make delicious brew.

When he placed the cup down, he could feel the stares. Most were being discreet but a few eyed him openly. A clandestine back room wasn't a place anyone would expect to find him, and his recent rise to the title already made him an interesting specimen for gossip. But even if Eoin understood the reason for the curiosity, it didn't make him any more comfortable. He'd never been on display, and he found he didn't like it.

The Black Sheep's patrons spoke softly enough that Eoin couldn't hear, but he could easily read their lips. Although Eoin knew that he should adjust his gaze downward, he found his eyes riveted to conversations pertaining to him.

"What is the Duke of Foxglen doing here?"

"I wouldn't think he'd ever deign to grace a place like this."

"People say he is even more rigid than the old duke."

"Did you hear Miss Wick call him *darling* and use his Christian name?"

"I know! It's terribly scandalous."

"I would have thought he'd try to send someone to the Colonies on false charges for taking such liberties."

"He's a cold one."

"Born a wizened old man."

"Yet it seems like he's begun an *affaire de coeur* with Miss Wick."

"Does he even have a *coeur*? I thought he was as heartless as they come."

"Bloodless too."

"Your Grace?" The new voice was quiet and cultured but not one that Eoin recognized. Unlike the others, it didn't drip with prurient curiosity.

Glancing up, he found Dr. Matthew Talbot standing across from him. Eoin didn't know much about the fellow beyond that he'd married Lady Charlotte, Hannah's cousin, and that he was the disinherited third son of a duke.

Eoin's grandfather hadn't approved of the physician who'd eschewed his noble roots to practice medicine, including working as a mere ship's surgeon. But was Dr. Talbot a radical man or just a compassionate one?

"Dr. Talbot." Eoin rose to greet the man who had helped expose his own brother's crimes as a masked highwayman.

"May I join you?" Dr. Talbot asked.

"Certainly." Eoin swept his hand toward the empty chair across from him and resumed his seat.

"I am a bit early for our group meeting." Dr. Talbot kept his voice low. "But I've never minded spending time at the Black Sheep, even before my wife's involvement. I have always found it to be a place where ideas can be freely exchanged."

Eoin studied every detail of Dr. Talbot's facial expressions. Was the man merely making conversation or was he testing to make sure that Eoin wasn't a covert foe? The physician's eyebrows were raised, which generally meant someone was interested in the conversation. But he was also tugging slightly at his throat, a sign that Eoin attributed to nervousness.

"Since becoming the new duke, I find it best to expose myself to all different schools of thought." Eoin tried to put Dr. Talbot at ease. He needed this man and his friends' assistance, not their suspicions. Thankfully, Eoin was well accustomed to soothing others' heightened emotions. "One area where I lack understanding pertains to the natural world. I've heard that you're well known for your sketches of wildlife both here in England and in the New World."

Dr. Talbot stopped playing with his neck. His hand dropped to the table, his fingers relaxed. "Animals are one of my passions."

Eoin asked a few more questions, and soon the man was chatting freely. Eoin felt his own muscles uncoil a fraction. It was good sitting with a companion, especially one near his own age. Even if Dr. Talbot did most of the talking, Eoin didn't feel like a shadow on the peripheries.

Eoin found himself surprisingly fascinated

by the plight of the vanishing Scottish wildcat. He almost didn't notice when the other patrons left or when the core members of their investigating group arrived and began drawing up chairs. But as soon as Hannah sat down, Eoin's senses crackled to life. Even though he was still looking at Dr. Talbot, his body seemed attuned to Hannah's every movement.

"Where's the new Duke of Falcondale and his wife?" Mr. Powys asked, his lilting Welsh intonation tempering the abruptness of his question.

"They're touring my brother's Lake District estate for their honeymoon," Lady Charlotte, who'd sat next to her husband, explained. "They hope to attend the next meeting."

Eoin felt a sliver of disappointment that Alexander Lovett would not be attending. It was, after all, Lovett's writings as Willoughby Wright that had first inspired Eoin to think differently than his grandfather. But he wasn't here to talk to his favorite satirist.

"I called this meeting because I was wondering if anyone knows about the Horse and

Hen," Hannah announced before she briefly explained Eoin's connection to the place.

"What if we discover that this tavern is still a cradle for reformist ideas?" Mr. Powys crossed his arms, his fingers balled into fists, as he openly studied Eoin. His mistrust was so palpable that even someone not versed in reading the sentiments of others would clearly detect his suspicion. "How are we to know that Foxglen won't report that information to the king? Perhaps this search for his mother is a ruse designed to ferret out royal opposition."

The playwright's words didn't bother Eoin. They made logical sense, and Eoin had done nothing to earn this man's trust. Swounds, how could Mr. Powys glean Eoin's true character when he had so much difficulty defining it himself?

"Foxglen was a crucial part of stopping the mass poisoning at Court, and he's never breathed a word about it," Lady Calliope pointed out.

"My point exactly. He saved you nobles and kept the king's secret." Mr. Powy's distrustful gaze had transformed into a full glower as he regarded Lady Calliope.

"You are the one with the bias," Lady Calliope shot back. Her sky blue eyes glittered with emotion, and like Mr. Powys, she clenched her hands. "We nobles are not a monolith."

"Nor are we commoners." Mr. Powys's response was swift.

Hannah broke in to the argument. "This is not productive. I am beginning to think that we cannot have meetings with both of you present."

"I still believe they're flirting," Lord Percy said.

"That is most assuredly not the case," Lady Calliope admonished at the same time Mr. Powys said, "Bollocks."

"Then prove your point by not exchanging barbs." Hannah spoke through her gritted teeth, clearly not afraid to reveal her frustration.

This was a particularly lively group. Eoin had never experienced so many sharp turns in a discussion, and he found he rather enjoyed being part of such chaos—even if he was the object of the debate.

"Mr. Powys's concerns about me are valid,"

Eoin admitted in his normally steady tone, even though his heart was vibrating. He did not want these people to reject him—and not just because he needed their assistance.

"Hear that…" Mr. Powys waved his hand in Eoin's direction as he addressed Lady Calliope. However, he trailed off in the middle as he probably realized that he was touting the word of the very man whose honor he'd questioned.

"I am aware of my reputation, but I have no desire to injure the folks who may have sheltered my own family," Eoin said. "That is why I waited to search for my mother and sister until after the duke's death."

Mr. Powys watched him closely. "You seem honest, but I know plenty of good actors."

"My talents do not lie in that area," Eoin admitted. "I can hide emotions but not feign them."

"I can attest to his sincerity." Hannah smiled broadly in his direction, and Eoin felt like he'd just emerged from the depths of a dank cave into the brilliant sunlight. He was not accustomed to anyone championing him, and he found he rather liked the unexpected support.

"Besides," Eoin said slowly, "I did not get the sense that the Horse and Hen is a place of political discourse—at least not anymore. The air was edged with violence, not subterfuge. It is likely a boozing or flash ken."

"How do you know those words for a den of thieves?" Hannah's green eyes widened as she leaned in his direction.

Eoin allowed just the corner of his right lip to tip upward. "Do I appear that naïve?"

"Well, you almost did get pickpocketed." Hannah nudged his arm, clearly to show that she meant only to tease. He would have realized her intentions just by the skin crinkling merrily around her eyes, an indicator of a true smile, but he welcomed the physical touch.

"I will confess to being sheltered, but I've read thousands of pamphlets and circulars—anything that could be useful to a potential advisor to the king," Eoin stated.

"You admit, then, to gathering information for the monarchy?" Mr. Powys interrupted.

"My grandfather wanted me to become a

courtier to win back the favor that my father lost. I have no such ambitions." There. Eoin had finally said it. A definitive statement about his own desires for his life.

"We keep allowing ourselves to be sidetracked." Hannah slapped her hand down on the table.

"I agree," Sophia chimed in. "If the Horse and Hen is flash ken, why didn't we discover that when we paid a lad to find the location? Surely, we would have heard something?"

"Maybe they do a good job of hiding their criminal activity?" suggested Mr. Powys.

Eoin shook his head. "It was obvious that something was amiss as soon as we entered the Horse and Hen. Pretending is not their strength."

Hannah nodded. "I agree. They would have been more welcoming. If they've kept things quiet, it's through intimidation, not stealth."

"Which means they must exert some degree of power." Sophia drummed her fingers thoughtfully against the table in front of her. "I haven't heard of any particularly powerful groups occupying the area around the Horse and Hen, though."

"Isn't that in itself odd?" Hannah said. "That there's a gap, especially for a back alley with so many illicit establishments?"

"Are there any shadowy organizations that you've heard whispers of?" Eoin asked, as he dutifully filed away each new piece of information. Although he'd read literature about spidery networks of thieves, this wasn't the world that he'd studied.

"No." Hannah answered the question too quickly, and she briefly sucked in her lips when she finished speaking—often a sign of dishonesty. Unease whooshed through Eoin. Was Hannah hiding something from him? And why?

"The Horse and Hen." Lord Percy spoke the words slowly as if he was testing each one out as he scratched at his temple.

"Is the name familiar to you?" Eoin asked, welcoming the distraction. He didn't want to suspect Hannah—the first person who'd ever really lent him assistance.

"Yes." Lord Percy made a frustrated grimace.

"But I simply can't place it. It floats tantalizingly at the peripheries of my memory, but then it dances out of reach like a will-o'-the wisp."

"Does the name stir up any vague sentiments?" Eoin asked, trying to gentle his normally clipped tone. It was hard for him, though, not just to speak in a virtual monotone. Only with Hannah was it easy to speak freely.

Percy stopped flicking at his overcoat as he sat perfectly still. "Negative, I suppose. But it is odd that I am the one to know about the Horse and Hen. Unlike you, I've never heard of a boozing ken. I would have thought that it was some sort of pub, but Hannah said it was a criminal hideout."

"That is right," Eoin confirmed.

"My morals are not the most upstanding. In fact, they are likely in need of good polish. But my illicit dealings are confined to drinking smuggled French brandy and attending a clandestine horse race." Lord Percy waved one of his gloved hands. "I am certainly not one to traipse into dark alleys for furtive business."

"Perhaps the name is similar to another place you frequent," Sophia suggested.

Lord Percy immediately brightened. "I say, that does make the most sense. I am a member of the Horse and Trot, a wonderful chocolate house dedicated to all things equine-related. Perhaps I was merely thinking of that."

"I can ask at the Grand," Mr. Powys offered. His voice was still surly, and his arms remained crossed over his chest, but at least his fingers were no longer balled into fists.

"I'll check to see if my older brother has heard rumors about the Horse and Hen." Lady Calliope smiled graciously at Eoin, causing Mr. Powys's glower to deepen. "If a lord is involved, he might have heard some rumors."

"The tavern was very run down. It didn't look like the secret haunt of a nob," Eoin pointed out.

"But we didn't see the basement or the upper floors, and there could be a hidden room like this one," Hannah pointed out. "No matter, it won't hurt to ask."

"My brother loves a good mystery," Lady

Calliope said. "It will be a grand lark for him to make inquiries."

"Why doesn't he ever join us?" Mr. Powys asked.

"When his paternal uncle died, he vowed never again to grace any respectable establishment," Lady Calliope explained.

Sophia laughed good-naturedly. "Never thought I'd hear the Black Sheep being called too respectable for a duke."

Hannah joined her cousin's mirth. "Perhaps we need to add some more debauchery."

"Boozy coffee!" Lord Percy called out, lifting his glass high.

"Doesn't that defeat the stimulating rush?" Dr. Talbot asked.

"Does it really matter as long as it tastes as divine as Sophia's other creations?" Mr. Powys asked.

"Just have Pan recite naughty lines from Shakespeare," Lady Charlotte suggested.

This awoke the lime-green bird, who'd been peacefully sleeping on the rafters above. Ruffling his tail feathers first, he stretched out his head and gave it a good shake. After several struts along a thick beam, he began hollering, "Beast with two backs! Beast with two backs! My tongue in your tail!"

Eoin felt his entire face flame like a furnace. Across from him, Dr. Talbot also turned a very vibrant red. Overhead, Pan produced a gravelly sound that seemed suspiciously akin to laughter.

Yet there was another warmth suffusing Eoin that had nothing to do with embarrassment. Eoin was enjoying himself. Immensely. For once in his life, he felt neither judged nor overlooked. Was this what people called companionship? If so, he rather liked it.

⁂

Eoin had just settled in bed to read a pile of gazettes when a knock startled him. His valet had long since gone to bed along with the other staff. The only other sound was the curtains rustling in the summer night's breeze. Even if a servant was awake, they would scratch softly. Only one person would knock so officiously.

An odd fluttering erupted deep within Eoin as he swung his legs off the feather tick mattress and padded over to the door. That cursed blush—the one that only Hannah and that wretched parrot could inspire—washed over him. Yet even as his body started to kindle, he firmly drew steadying breaths. He shouldn't get excited. Hannah wasn't his real mistress. There was no reason for her—

Swounds. It really was Hannah. And she wore naught but a nightgown; even her feet were bare.

Eoin's hand froze on the knob, and he stood like a wooden sentry. Hannah, however, pushed inside without a hint of embarrassment. As she moved close, he swore he could smell coffee, nutmeg, and vanilla.

She paused only a scant few inches from him. Though Hannah didn't even brush against him, his skin reacted to her nearness. Brilliant small pricks flared into larger sparks until he feared his breathing would grow uneven. When her warm fingers closed over his, he nearly jumped.

As if from a distance, he registered that she

was closing the door. When it snicked shut, they were standing with his body practically bracketing hers against the paneled wood. He knew little of embraces and even less about lovers, but he instinctively understood the intimacy inherent in their position. All he needed to do was to dip his head, and their lips would meet. Would she accept his kiss? Would her lips open under his? Would she sigh or perhaps even moan?

"I thought I should pay a visit to your chambers," Hannah told him blithely, her voice containing none of the strained excitement thundering through him. "It would be rather strange if a mistress did not stop by occasionally, especially since I didn't the first night. I made sure to tread extra loudly when I passed your uncles' and aunts' bedrooms."

"Oh," Eoin said as disappointment rushed through him. Although what had he expected? At least his tone sounded as neutral as hers.

"Should we take a seat?" Hannah asked. "On furniture other than the bed. No need to make this awkward."

"Of course." Was his voice pitched too high?

Thankfully, Hannah didn't appear to notice. She was striding in that economical manner of hers over to the heavy wooden chairs in front of the unlit fireplace. Like in his grandfather's former study, the bedchamber was filled with uncomfortably solid Jacobean pieces that felt more like squat monuments to the late duke's old-fashioned ways than functional furnishings. Eoin really should redecorate, but he still felt like he didn't have the authority.

Hannah, though, appeared to have no qualms as she plopped down on one of the thin cushions overlayed with a tapestry of a hare standing on its hind legs. She once again managed to lounge—a true feat since the back was not only straight but carved into a relief of a medieval hunt. Although the art piece was impressive, it was not exactly the most comfortable surface. There were too many raised hooves and dog noses that viciously poked into one's ribs.

"Aren't you going to sit too?" Hannah asked.

"Ah, um, yes." Eoin slowly lowered himself

onto a matching chair. He sat stiffly, careful not to press against any of the designs.

"I suppose we should pass the time talking about our plans."

Hannah's efficiency should please him. After all, he rarely indulged in pleasantries. But he found himself wanting to have a simpler, quieter conversation with her. One in which they shared tidbits about themselves—like whether they preferred butter to jam on bread or if they liked foggy days more than sunny ones. Small things that Eoin had never cared to know about another person but now seemed vitally important.

"Yes. Yes, I suppose we should discuss the investigation." Coward. All Eoin had to do was ask a simple question, and she could decide whether or not to answer. But apparently that was too difficult.

"It is good that the others are investigating, but you and I should—"

Hannah stopped as a round object suddenly sailed through one of the open windows. It crashed against the curtains surrounding his four-poster bed. The missile was hefty enough that it didn't bounce back but instead pinned the thick material against the feather tick.

"What was that? A rock?" Eoin blurted out as his heart thudded from surprise. Had someone been aiming to hit him? At this late hour, he was always abed, even if not asleep.

Hannah said nothing. Instead, she bolted upright and flew toward the bed. With a battle cry, she snatched up the projectile and whirled around. Her eyes frantically searched for something. When her gaze landed on his filled washbasin, she dashed over and dumped the pomegranate-shaped thing into the porcelain bowl. A thin trail of smoke wafted into the air.

"Was—was that on fire?" Eoin felt even more poleaxed. He'd heard of unattended candles setting bed draperies ablaze and quickly killing the sleeping occupant. If someone had tried to set his aflame, they weren't just aiming to frighten but to kill him. His limbs felt curiously weak as he slowly pushed himself from his chair.

"Yes," Hannah said. Even her voice didn't sound as confident as it usually did. In fact, he may have detected a very faint quiver.

"What was it?" Eoin asked, ignoring how his legs threatened to buckle under his weight. Instead, he forced himself to cross the room.

"A grenade." Hannah bit out the two words, her tone dark.

Eoin faltered before managing the last few steps. Swallowing, he stared down at the submerged metal ball. The wick sticking out of the cylinder was perilously short. A hairbreadth more and the entire incendiary device might have detonated.

"I've read about these types of munitions being used in the Battle of Killiecrankie," Eoin breathed out as he studied the sphere, "but I've never encountered them in real life."

"Most people don't unless they're soldiers." Hannah also watched the munition carefully. Eoin wondered if she felt like he did: that if he looked away for a moment, it would spontaneously reignite and explode.

"How did you recognize it so readily?" Eoin asked, as his normal good sense began to return.

"I saw them on my aunt's island in the Caribbean when I visited her stronghold as a child," Hannah explained. "Forty years ago, they were frequently used by pirates. She still has a few for when she boards ships to free slaves, child prisoners, or sailors impressed by force into the Royal Navy."

"Do—do you think it could have killed us?" Eoin's voice audibly shook, but he didn't care. Someone had clearly tried to murder him. Although he wasn't precisely a beloved member of Society, he wasn't that hated either.

"Yes, if shrapnel hit a vital organ or if we were standing too close and lost too much blood from our injuries," Hannah said. "The curtains catching on fire would have been another danger."

Eoin wobbled back and landed on the edge of the bed. He could hear the draperies tearing, but he didn't care.

"Thank you." He gazed up at Hannah in wonder. "Thank you for saving me. I never—I never would have reacted so quickly. You are truly a marvel."

## Chapter Nine

Hannah's heart was reacting in the most curious way. Aye, she was accustomed to the tug of physical attraction. She'd even indulged in the pull from time to time. One of those relationships had even lasted a year when she'd been seventeen. He'd been a sweet boy, but they hadn't been a perfect fit, and in the end, they'd parted ways.

But she'd never experienced this fiery, almost painful force. Eoin's teal eyes were filled with an undeniable admiration as he gazed up at her. His shoulders were slumped, and she could see him fighting back the shivers that were threatening to erupt all over his body. He was vulnerable right now—this huge, fearsome-looking man. Someone had very obviously tried to kill him in a horrific manner. By all rights, he should be erecting every defense that he possessed. He was indubitably capable of stoicism. But he was choosing to remain open to her—to let her witness his emotions, even his need for her.

Cautiously, Hannah laid her hand on his shoulder. When he didn't shake her off, she gently squeezed. It was either that or gather him close—and she wasn't sure if either of them was ready for that.

"I simply recognized what the device was. I am sure you would have reacted the same had you seen one before." Hannah's statement felt weak even to her own ears. It was so perfunctory with no emotion, no feeling. Yet he had called her the brave one.

Hannah, too, felt on edge. Facing death did that. She wasn't sanguine about the fact that she'd just carried a deadly device in her bare hands.

"I am trying to be logical about this attack, but my mind is just too cluttered," Eoin confessed. "I don't know how you're standing."

"I've locked my knees," Hannah admitted. Somehow that honest admission seemed harder than seizing the small bomb. Eoin was supposed to be the enemy—her enemy—but here she was admitting weakness.

Eoin huffed out a rough chuckle. "It is no wonder." Then he patted the mattress. "You should sit too."

That was a bad idea, sharing a bed—even innocuously—with a man who looked like Eoin. But try as she might, Hannah couldn't muster the volition to walk over to the chairs.

She flopped down beside Eoin with more devil-may-care confidence than she actually possessed. It was a strategic mistake. She slid, quite emphatically, against Eoin. When her thigh squashed into his muscular one, she was acutely reminded that she was not wearing her usual layers. There were no petticoats to provide a buffer. Only two thin sheets of linen separated their skin.

Hannah was a strong woman. She was accustomed to hefting trays of coffee, mopping floors, hoisting bags of beans, and then grinding them into powder. She had biceps that she was proud of—after all, she'd earned them. Yet pressed against Eoin's massive frame, she felt...delicate, not fragile but delicate. And that sensation thrilled her in an elemental way.

What had happened to her good sense?

"I suppose I should try to decipher who is trying to kill me." Eoin's voice sounded somber—and not in his usual stoic way. There was a sadness to his tone that caused an echoing pang of sorrow in Hannah's own heart.

"The most likely candidates would be my uncles," Eoin continued. "My Uncle Hugh has the most to win upon my demise as he is my heir presumptive. But Francis would likely throw in his lot with his brother. The two rarely do anything alone."

How devastating must it be to consider that your own family members wished to kill you? Hannah's maternal side had utterly rejected her, but they hadn't plotted to murder her. And she'd never known them. But Eoin had been raised in the same household as his uncles.

Hannah leaned a little closer to him. She wished she could dismiss his theory for his sake, but she couldn't deny its truth. And false hope wasn't just empty in this scenario but deadly as well.

"They could very well be the culprits, but it speaks to their villainy and not to your worth." Hannah could not believe that she was supporting the grandson of her familial enemy, but she realized how accurate her words were.

Eoin rubbed his hands over his face, and Hannah sensed a deep weariness welling up inside him. "I have oft wondered about my own measure. Since the age of six, my grandfather groomed me into the lord he wished me to be. But now that I have obtained the position, I am unsure of my role."

The stark honesty of Eoin's confession startled Hannah. She had never thought of a duke having doubts—although she supposed Alexander had plenty of them. But then, she'd never really thought of her cousin as a nobleman. He'd always just been Alexander.

And now she was starting to see Foxglen, not as his title, but as Eoin. And that...that was dangerous indeed.

"You are a newly minted duke," Hannah said, "and your first thought was to locate your mother and sister to ensure that they were living good lives. Your second has been to scour the account books to determine what funds are available to reinvest in improvements for your tenant farmers. I believe you have the makings of a fine gentleman, and I'm not given to complimenting nobs."

Eoin's fingers slid from his cheeks, and he shot her a shy grin, which immediately set her heart a pumping. Dash it all. This was not in her plans.

"Thank you. It's good to have the support of someone who's been managing a business for years."

Hannah could sense nothing but sincerity in Eoin's words. A pleased warmth suffused her, and she couldn't deny that she was being charmed. No other compliment would have melted away her natural defenses so quickly. She never thought a high-and-mighty duke would be the one to recognize her value when so many other men of every class dismissed her intelligence simply because she'd been born female.

Hannah suddenly found herself battling

the urge to place her head upon Eoin's exceedingly broad shoulder. She yearned to just sit in companionable silence, their bodies touching as they each drew quiet strength from the other.

But she wasn't in his bedchamber for sweet domesticity—or fiery passion. She'd come for a purpose, and the presence of the grenade still soaking in the washbasin was empirical proof of the urgency of the matter.

"Although we certainly cannot dismiss your uncles as suspects, they may not be the persons behind this attack." Part of Hannah hated breaking their fragile intimacy with talk of attempted murder. But it needed to be said—for more than one reason.

"Do you think we inadvertently stirred something up when we blundered into the Horse and Hen?" Eoin asked.

Hannah nodded. Although Eoin was surprisingly sheltered, he was also exceedingly keen. "The timing is suspicious unless there were other attempts against your life since your grandfather's death."

"This was the first," Eoin confirmed. His

voice was back to sounding dull again. Hannah hated that, yet she had no choice but to make these inquiries.

"Are you certain that there weren't other incidents—more subtle ones that you might have overlooked? A carriage racing in your direction as soon as you started across a street? An object seemingly dropped accidentally from a window just after you passed under it? The sense of someone trailing you?"

Eoin thought for a moment, his eyes focused on a distant spot that only he could see. Finally, he shook his head. "No. Not that I recall anyway."

"Then we cannot rule out the possibility that we stumbled upon a conspiracy yesterday." Hannah debated for a moment if she should confess that she suspected his family members of nefarious activities. It seemed unlikely that his uncles had any connection to the Horse and Hen. Although the two obviously frequented disreputable establishments, they would hardly choose places that shabby. Still, that did bring to mind another issue.

"If the attempt was triggered by our visit to

the Horse and Hen, it would suggest a more sophisticated operation than the condition of the establishment would indicate."

"I agree." Eoin rubbed his temple but the gesture seemed more thoughtful than weary, and at least he wasn't scraping his hands over his entire countenance. "I should have thought of it myself."

"Someone threw an explosive through your bedroom window in the middle of the night," Hannah pointed out. "Of course you're not thinking properly."

"But you are," Eoin pointed out.

"I was most likely an accidental bystander, and besides, this isn't my first brush with danger."

"It isn't?" Eoin glanced at her, his sea-blue eyes filled with palpable concern.

"Daughter of a pirate." Hannah held up her hand and laughed. But that wasn't the whole truth. It was her family's endeavors to save the downtrodden in London that put her in the most peril. But even if she was gradually warming to Eoin, she couldn't divulge secrets that would jeopardize not just the

Black Sheep but Sophia and her friends' personal safety.

"Ah," Eoin answered, but Hannah sensed that he knew that she wasn't telling him everything. "Then what does a piratess recommend for how to proceed?"

Hannah sighed. "First, I suggest we start with the nearest suspects. We should discuss tonight's incident at breakfast tomorrow with your aunts and uncles. Their reactions might be telling. I've also been meaning to talk to your butler. Servants always know more than they let on. As for the Horse and Hen, hopefully one of my friends from the Black Sheep will uncover pertinent information. If not, we may need to pay the tavern another visit."

"Thank you," Eoin said, his blue eyes shining in the flickering candlelight.

"For what?" Hannah asked. "My advice?"

"Yes." Eoin bobbed his chin but didn't break eye contact. "But more than that, I appreciate the fact you're here. By my side. It's nice, novel, I suppose—having someone's support simply because they wish to help me."

It felt like the grenade had exploded inside

Hannah... except she was being hit with shards of guilt instead of shrapnel. For the first time, Hannah began to realize how betrayed Eoin would feel when he learned the truth behind her less-than-altruistic offer to assist. Because Eoin had ceased being the enemy and was slowly becoming something more. A partner, perhaps? Yet that didn't fully describe the nascent feelings rattling around in Hannah's chest.

But even if she hadn't started this quest for all the right reasons, Hannah was determined to help Eoin locate his family. And now she had the additional duty to protect him from whatever scoundrel wished him dead.

✦

"You're joining us?" It was obvious that Eoin's Aunt Joan was attempting to keep her voice neutral. However, it rose just a bit at the end, exposing her displeasure at her nephew's decision to eat with the family.

"Yes. The lovely Miss Wick has convinced me that a more leisurely breakfast is better for one's digestion." Eoin shot Hannah a slight smile, which she found more convincing than if he'd suddenly changed his character and broken into a broad grin. His acting was commendable.

"I am not sure anything would improve his naturally dyspeptic humor," Lord Hugh whispered to Lord Francis. Hannah assumed that the man had meant to say the words under his breath, but he'd sorely misjudged his volume. Everyone, including Eoin, could hear him clearly. Eoin, though, never changed his expression. He merely kept shoveling eggs onto his plate from the sideboard.

Hannah decided her best strategy was not to pretend that she hadn't heard. She wanted Eoin's relatives shaken.

"Oh, but he has every reason to be upset this morning!" Hannah placed her food down on the dining table and then clasped her hands together in a dramatic sweep.

"Oh, I didn't mean—" Lord Hugh's gaze darted over to Eoin. It was obvious to Hannah that he was trying to judge if he'd upset the new duke. He seemed to lack any true contrition, though.

Hannah, however, ignored his stumbling attempts to smooth over his mistake. "I daresay, even a veritable saint would feel out of sorts this morning after what my dear Eoin endured."

Hannah paused and placed both palms on the table, as she bent forward. Dropping both the volume and pitch of her voice, she finished with, "Someone tried to kill him."

Hannah watched everyone's reaction. Lord Hugh smirked while Lord Francis shook his head, his expression a cross between annoyance and bemusement. Lady Joan rolled her eyes. Lady Eliza, who had been scouring the gossip rags, let the broadsheet flutter to the tablecloth.

"Did you say *kill*?" Lady Eliza's voice rose an entire octave at the end.

"Don't fash yourself, Eliza." Lady Joan leaned over to pat her younger sister's arm. "Miss Wick is just bamming us. Either that, or she's one for melodrama."

"Oh, but I am quite serious." Hannah shifted her gaze around the table, and she noticed Eoin doing the same. From her perspective, she didn't think any of them were acting particularly guilty, but perhaps Eoin was sensing a whiff of suspicion that she was overlooking. Her job was primarily to goad the four siblings. Eoin's was to watch.

Hannah turned to Eoin. "You found a—what was it, again, in your chambers?"

"A grenade." The two words rumbled from Eoin with little inflection. Gone was that man who'd looked so dejected and vulnerable last night. The stoic duke had returned.

"A pastry? Was it poisoned?" Lady Joan asked in confusion as she frantically pushed her plate away from her.

"No. It wasn't a dessert," Eoin said.

"It certainly sounds like one—a fancy French one made from white sugar." The more Lord Francis described the fictional sweet, the more excited his voice became. Hannah had no idea if the siblings were actually feigning ignorance or if they honestly had no idea what the munition was. It wasn't precisely common, and the troops who employed them were not generally from the elite classes.

"Your confusion is likely because the word

is French in origin, but it has nothing to do with—" Eoin began as if he was simply giving a scholarly lecture rather than describing a device that could have easily killed him.

"Oh, now I remember!" Lord Hugh sounded a bit like an excited schoolboy who'd finally figured out the lesson. "It's something thrown by soldiers."

"It's a hollow iron ball packed with gunpowder and connected to a fuse. When the flame reaches the residue, the entire contraption explodes, sending flames and metal shards everywhere." Eoin's emotionless delivery even caused Hannah to shiver, and she was well versed in a grenade's destructive force. Lady Eliza squeaked in dismay, and she immediately clutched at her throat. Her sister was a little less dramatic, but she did emit a loud gasp. Lord Hugh paled while his brother reached for his stomach.

"You wouldn't want to eat that," Francis observed, rather unnecessarily.

"Did we almost all die last night?" Lady Eliza demanded, her pale-blue eyes huge pools of frightened dismay.

"No," Eoin continued in the same bland tone. "It would have only killed me—unless, of course, the bed had caught on fire and burned down the house. Likely even in that case you would have had time to escape."

Lady Eliza emitted a strangled sound. Lord Francis reached over to pat her back. "Now, now. A sensitive thing like you would have smelled the smoke immediately and raised the alarm."

Lady Eliza sniffed. "I suppose you are right."

Hannah noticed that none of the four siblings seemed to be concerned about their nephew's near death—only about the danger that they'd personally faced. They did seem surprised, but perhaps they were better actors and actresses than she'd given them credence for.

Now that she'd shocked them about last night's events, it was time to launch an entirely different line of inquiry.

"Whatever happened to the Horse and Hen?" Hannah asked, keeping her voice light and airy. If the Aucourtes could act brainless and blithe about danger, then so could she.

"The Horse and Hen?" Lady Eliza asked.

"Why are you asking about that old place again? It was closed down years ago when it was discovered to be a den of traitors—our elder brother Henry included."

"Father played a role in seeing the owners hanged," Lord Hugh added. "He blamed the place for leading Henry astray."

"Pity. It was one of the best places to watch—" Lord Francis started to stay.

"Oh!" Lady Eliza burst out. "Why must we talk about that terrible place as if nothing happened last night? I almost died!"

Lord Francis heaved out a beleaguered sigh before he reached over to pat his sister's shoulder again. Hannah noticed that his hand moved more rapidly than last time. It was clear that Lady Eliza's outbursts annoyed him, but it was equally apparent that he'd rather attempt to soothe her than deal with her caterwauling.

"We're all perfectly safe, Eliza," Lord Francis reminded her. "Just go back to reading your tittle-tattle. Maybe you can even attend a ball soon to cheer you up."

"They aren't nearly as fun as they were

during my youth." Lady Eliza sulked. "I learn better gossip by reading the newspapers."

"What did you used to watch at the Horse and Hen?" Hannah asked, utterly refusing to allow Lady Eliza's fears to disrupt the entire conversation.

"There's no use talking about the past." Lady Joan speared her soft-boiled egg with a rather surprising ferocity, especially since she was using a spoon. A few droplets of runny yolk even ended up on the tablecloth. "Father would not approve."

"But he's gone." Eoin spoke again, and by the way his relatives jumped, it was clear that they'd half forgotten about his presence, despite his considerable size. "I am duke now, and I am interested in the answer to Hannah's question, especially as it pertains to my mother."

"Oh, they simply had the best tavern maids. It's no wonder that your father fell for one." Lord Hugh's attempt at a grin was both garish and more than a tad unsettling.

"Are you afraid of Grandfather's ghost?" Eoin asked.

"What? No. What in heaven's name are you blathering about?" Lord Hugh paused to take a healthy swig of his special tea and then a second. "I don't believe in spirits."

"Then why are you lying?" Eoin asked evenly.

"I am not fibbing." Lord Hugh swung a desperate look in his younger brother's direction.

Lord Francis took his own gulp of gin-laden tea and then cleared his throat. "It's no falsehood. The place had prettier girls than many a brothel."

"First, you should do well to remember that my mother worked at that establishment," Eoin said stiffly. "Second, you always tug your ear when you lie, Uncle Hugh."

"I don't!" Lord Hugh exclaimed as he simultaneously reached for his lobe. As soon as his finger had brushed against it, he realized his error. His pale-blue eyes grew huge, and he slapped his hand down on the table with enough force to send the silverware clattering.

"This entire meal is giving me indigestion." Lady Eliza shoved her plate away before she jumped up from the table. Clutching her stomach, she hurried from the room.

"Now you've done it!" Lord Hugh cried out as if his sister was truly suffering a dire malady. It was clear to Hannah, though, that Lady Eliza's dramatic exit had only provided her brother with the perfect excuse to avoid Eoin's questions.

"Once she gets into a state, she is inconsolable," Lady Joan moaned as she gently laid down her silverware. "It will take all three of us to calm her down."

"Most assuredly," Lord Francis chimed in.

The three then arose in unison and then just as quickly vanished after Lady Eliza. Eoin sighed when the pocket door slid shut behind them. "That was decidedly unproductive."

"Not entirely," Hannah disagreed. "There is something important about the Horse and Hen. Lord Hugh is acting cagey. It may be dangerous, but I think we may need to make another visit there. Perhaps after we talk to your butler."

Because it was clear that things were more complicated than Hannah had assumed.

# Chapter Ten

"You wished to speak with me?" Smythe asked in his booming voice as he stiffly marched into Eoin's office. Like most well-trained butlers, he didn't give as many visual clues to his emotions. His hands always remained clasped behind his back and his expression placid as if someone had carved it.

Yet Eoin had felt less coldness from the man than he had from the other servants. The others avoided him, especially the maids. Even when he was a young boy, they'd scurry from the room whenever he entered it, with the exception of his nanny. She had been exceedingly distant and regularly employed a switch when he did not behave as the duke dictated. She'd been replaced by an equally strict tutor, who also had not believed in sparing the rod either.

But Smythe hadn't entirely ignored Eoin's presence nor had he ever disciplined him.

"Oh yes!" Hannah replied to Smythe in that overly bubbly tone of hers. Eoin much preferred her real voice, but so far, her fake naïveté had worked in their favor.

Smythe solemnly turned in her direction. If he took umbrage to a mistress addressing him like she was the lady of the house, he did not betray a single hint of frustration.

"You see, I was asking my dear Eoin about his mother, and I was very distressed to hear he knows so very little. Are you privy to any details, Mr. Smythe?" Hannah asked and then belatedly waved her hand toward a chair. "Please sit, but I must warn you that these chairs are very uncomfortable."

Smythe glanced at Eoin, clearly asking for permission to accept Hannah's unorthodox offer. Eoin nodded. Smythe slowly settled his long-limbed body into the high-backed furniture.

"Do you wish to know about your mother, Your Grace?" Smythe's brown eyes studied him. Despite his solemn, almost sour, countenance, Eoin couldn't help but sense a kindness.

"Yes," Eoin said.

"I do not know much," Smythe said. "Your father had long left the household when he married her."

"Oh, there had to have been some absolutely glorious gossip discussed in the servants' halls and the kitchens," Hannah said.

"The former duke would have sacked anyone who mentioned it," Smythe said. "And he would have ensured that they could not find good employment elsewhere. The staff are still afraid to mention His Grace's parents even now."

"Are you fearful, Smythe?" Eoin asked as he resisted the urge to rub his hands across his face. It was so damnably frustrating that no one would speak of his mother and his sister, even with the previous Foxglen dead and buried.

A surprising wry smile burst over the man's face. "No, but as I said, I was not entrusted with much knowledge of her. I do know that your grandfather tried his best to prevent you from being exposed to anything remotely connected with your maternal side."

"Like changing my name from Eoin to John to obscure my Irish ancestry?" Eoin said. "Or his insistence that I attend daily Anglican services even though he did not in an effort to suppress any Catholic tendencies?"

Eoin's examples caused Hannah's heart to squeeze, especially in light of their conversation last night. *Since the age of six, my grandfather groomed me into the lord he wished me to be. But now that I have obtained the position, I am unsure of my role.* How many decisions had Eoin been deprived of?

"That is precisely what I meant, Your Grace." Smythe inclined his head.

Hannah pushed aside the pain she felt for Eoin. The best way to help him was to remain clearheaded. He needed her rationality, not her emotions. "Are you recommending that Eoin gather clues about his mother by considering what he was forbidden from doing as a child?"

Smythe's assessing gaze landed on her, and she realized that she'd inadvertently dropped her silly coquette act. The man, however, did not appear particularly surprised.

"Yes. His Grace, for example, forbade ale

from the house and would only serve brandy and sherry. Also after your father's death, he ordered all cats be removed from the stables, even those who'd proved to be excellent mousers."

So Eoin's mother loved cats—not a particularly useful clue. But by the way Eoin quirked his head, it was clear that he was hungry for any detail, no matter how trivial.

"Of course, some of the late duke's behavior could also be attributed to his son's treason. His Grace was adamant that we should immediately report if we ever saw the young lord engage in fisticuffs," Smythe explained.

Eoin grimaced. "He wouldn't even permit me to learn to sword fight."

Now it was Hannah's turn to tilt her head. "Isn't that a normal part of a young lordling's education?"

"The duke wished for me to remain even tempered and calm. I was allowed to learn the minuet but not the livelier country dances for fear they would be too full of vigor." Eoin spoke as if these bizarre rules were commonplace, and sadly, they must have been for him.

"Alexander said that you were familiar with

handling a pistol when you helped to rescue Lord Percy," Hannah said in confusion as she desperately tried to make sense of the odd set of rules that Eoin had lived under.

Eoin jerked his head in assent. If this conversation upset him, he betrayed nothing. "My grandfather regarded shooting as a more scholarly activity that demanded concentration rather than spirit. Moreover, the perfect courtier must have some means to protect his king."

"I—I am struggling to understand the old Foxglen's rationale." Hannah knew she was screwing up her face as she tried to unravel the idiot nob's reasoning, but she couldn't stop herself. It just beggared belief, and she couldn't imagine having to grow up navigating such convoluted and conflicting dictates. It had to have been disorienting to Eoin. Perhaps he showed so little emotion because he never knew what his grandfather wanted him to convey. Hannah's heart constricted, and pain shot through her.

"His Grace was…an eccentric man driven by fear that the family name would descend into ruin." The butler spoke haltingly, and it was clear that he was carefully weighing each word.

Eoin appeared unperturbed by his butler's less-than-shining assessment of the man who'd raised him. Instead of directly responding to Smythe's observations, he simply continued his previous line of inquiry. "I know the coachmen were told not to take me to certain establishments where I could face temptation. Do you recall any in particular?"

"Only that they generally involved bloodsport," Smythe answered promptly. "There was a list of businesses known for their Jacobite sympathies. I cannot recall each one, but I can give you a copy."

"Was the Horse and Hen on it?" Hannah asked, watching the butler closely.

Smythe turned to Eoin. "Are you aware, then, of the tavern's connection to you, your Grace?" the butler asked cautiously.

"We know that my mother worked there, yes," Eoin confirmed.

"The former duke arranged for the establishment to be closed," Smythe continued at a tentative pace. "But a few years later, I overheard your uncles discussing its reopening as a gin house. I do not believe your grandfather ever learned about the new iteration. He would have been furious. I suspect Lord Hugh and Lord Francis only frequented the reconstituted Horse and Hen as an act of secret rebellion."

A rather pathetic revolt but also an interesting one. Is that when the brothers began to drink gin? More importantly, was the juniper-tinged elixir the reason for the secrecy at the current Horse and Hen? The Gin Act of '51 and the rise of grain prices had been the death knell for the popularity of the drink, and it was no longer profitable enough to sustain clandestine establishments.

"Did Lords Hugh and Francis gossip about other illegal happenings there?" Hannah asked.

"No." Smythe shook his head. "I can inquire if the other servants have heard otherwise, but many have left the household's employ. This occurred fifteen years or so ago."

"Thank you for all that you've told us," Eoin said. "If you think of anything more, please let me know."

"That I will, Your Grace." Smythe clambered to his feet and delivered a very stiff and formal bow—a return to the normal social gap between duke and servant. He strode from the room, the perfect example of a proper English butler.

After Smythe shut the door, Hannah waited a few beats until his footsteps faded away. "I plan to return to the Horse and Hen. I will take Dr. Talbot with me—he's more formidable than he appears."

Eoin shook his head. "No. I will go. This is my search and my danger to face, not yours and your friends'."

Hannah frowned. "You may be exceedingly clever about reading people's expressions, but you know nothing of the inner workings of London's seamier side. You'll either be turned away or set upon by criminals—and with your large frame, it will be hard to hide your identity."

"Are you good at disguises?" Eoin asked.

"Fairly," Hannah admitted.

"Could you make my face look very bruised and swollen?"

"Pardon?" Hannah asked. It was not every day that a nob wished to appear like he'd been beaten to a bloody pulp.

"My grandfather was forever bemoaning

the fact that I am the very image of a prize-fighter," Eoin explained.

Hannah couldn't refute the similarity. She'd had the same thought herself—although hers came from a decidedly more appreciative place.

"If I look like a boxer, no one will recognize me as the chap who visited a few days ago," Eoin continued to reason.

"Your idea has merit," Hannah agreed. "And I could dress as a boy. I've done so in the past, and it makes it easier to slip in and out of places."

"You have led a much more adventurous life than I."

A smile—which Hannah could only describe as fond—stretched over Eoin's lips. She did not want to admit how much the sight affected her. Yet she couldn't deny that she liked the fact that Eoin seemed drawn to the parts of her that the rest of Society often condemned. They were, after all, the aspects that she took the most pride in, and the recognition felt good. More than good.

"I'm happy to share this quest with you." The words tumbled from Hannah's mouth before she had thought better. To her surprise,

Eoin didn't blush. Instead, he grinned—broadly and with a warmth that she didn't know the stoic man could generate.

"Could you apply paint or soot to my face and make it look like I've fought in a few bouts?" Eoin asked, his voice boyishly eager.

"I can't—at least not convincingly," Hannah admitted. "But I know someone—two someones, in fact—who can help. They might not get along, however."

---

"No! No!" Calliope cried, her normally sweet voice tight with frustration. "That is much too dark and untextured. This isn't for the stage!"

"I'll have you know that people rave about how realistic the blood and gore look at the Grand. It is one of the reasons that my theater does so well!" Alun waved a burnt piece of cork as he paused in placing smudges around Eoin's eye.

Hannah tried very hard not to jump into the fray. Her last attempt to enforce order had only worsened the situation. What had she been thinking to invite both the poetess and the playwright?

"*Hisssssss!*" Eoin's gosling flapped its stubby wings as it ran at Alun.

The actor leaped back, but the enraged ball of down was faster. Although the creature didn't possess its signature long neck yet, it still managed to close its short beak around the skin at Alun's ankle.

"Owwww! That hurt! Why does that menace keep nipping me?" Alun demanded.

"It is an impeccable judge of character?" Calliope offered tartly.

"I am exceedingly sorry." Eoin bent to pick up the vibrating animal. "As of late, it's become very protective of me."

"Whyever did you bring that fowl to the Black Sheep?" Alun glared at the bird as he bent to rub his injury.

"I am afraid that I am to blame," Hannah confessed. "It put up such an awful fuss when we were departing that I couldn't bear to leave it."

"Ninny!" Pan called from the rafters. He had been displeased when the gosling had waddled into the coffeehouse.

"Watch what you say, Pan." Sophia glanced up at the parrot. "The main reason you have a home is due to Hannah's abiding love for feathered beings."

"Is that true?" Eoin asked, and Hannah couldn't help but notice that his voice sounded more animated. His clear interest warmed her—much more than was sensible. Even if she wasn't investigating Eoin's family, she'd make an absolutely rubbish nob. Not that she was considering becoming Eoin's duchess.

"I was living in the Caribbean when my cousin rescued Pan," Sophia explained to Eoin. "But the way my uncle tells the story, he decided to take five-year-old Hannah down to the Pool of London to see the big seafaring ships. She spotted a sailor trying to shove Pan into a much-too-small cage. She broke free from her father's grasp, stomped over with hands on her hips, and called the fellow a bad, bad man. Uncle Jack said that the chap didn't know whether to be offended or to laugh. Little Hannah proceeded to lecture him on how to be nice to birdies. Uncle Jack finally caught up to her and tried to urge her along. Hannah refused, and Uncle Jack is secretly softhearted too. He ended up buying Pan at an exceedingly high price. And Pan has happily roosted in the Black Sheep's rafters ever since."

A flush of embarrassment washed over Hannah. She only remembered snippets of the actual event, but she'd heard her papa recount the tale over and over. As a girl, she'd loved the familiar story, but it was a mite awkward watching while Eoin listened to her misadventures. The fact that she was particularly concerned about his reaction was not something upon which she wanted to dwell.

"Enough about the past," Hannah said brusquely. "We need to make Eoin look beat up."

"Eoin?" Calliope arched a golden eyebrow.

"Oh, we decided to use first names to maintain our charade," Hannah said quickly, hating how her heart plinked inside her chest like a tightly wound harp string. She thought she did a fairly good job of obscuring her reaction, but Eoin flushed a deep scarlet. The stoic man really had more tells than Hannah had ever suspected.

"Never knew of a nob who wanted to look like a ruffian." Alun thankfully broke the uncomfortable spell as he once again lifted the burnt cork.

"Put that ridiculous charred thing away. Skin doesn't look like a sooty smudge when bruised. Flesh mottles." Calliope made a shooing motion with her hands.

"And how does a gentlewoman such as yourself come to obtain such a breadth of knowledge about contusions?" Alun demanded.

Calliope rolled her eyes. "I have four brothers who are constantly getting into scrapes, and Blackglen is the worst of them all. It's not as if my sisters and I are particularly sedate. Do you seriously think that we've led such rarefied lives that we haven't even bumped our shins on heavy furniture?"

"Do you really wish for me to answer?" Alun's voice perfectly matched the smirk on his face. Even Hannah, who tended to agree with him about the nobility, wanted to scrub away his pleased expression.

"Your bickering is not productive." Hannah wished she could bash something—preferably

Alun's and Calliope's heads together. It was likely the only way for the two to see eye-to-eye.

Alun sighed heavily. "Fine then, Princess Poet. How do you propose that we make a bruise look realistic? I have ochre powder that works for faded contusions, but if we're hiding Foxglen's identity, we need something darker. I don't have any blues, though, which we'd require for purple hues. That pigment is too damn expensive even for the Grand."

"As it so happens, I do." Calliope opened an alabaster box covered in images of the Muses. Inside were smaller circular containers inlayed with decorative pieces of mother-of-pearl. She unscrewed one of the wooden boxes to reveal a vibrant blue powder. As far as Hannah knew, such a color could only come from pulverized precious stones.

Although Calliope had been coming to the Black Sheep for half a year now, Hannah still was not accustomed to her casual displays of wealth. It was clear that Alun wasn't either.

"You do realize that is a crushed gem," Alun scoffed.

"Of course," Calliope answered, her voice

sounding deliberately blithe as she was clearly intent on baiting the playwright. "It's high-quality lapis lazuli. My sister, Clio, is an artist, and I borrowed her supplies. Clio suggested that we mix some of her lapis and vermillion with a touch of oil of myrtle and gum arabic. We both think that will produce a good paint."

"I agree," Eoin said.

"Calliope will mix the ointment, and Mr. Powys will apply it." Sophia broke into the conversation, clearly trying to stave off another dispute. Not for the first time, Hannah was thankful for her cousin's levelheaded foresight.

"A capital idea," Calliope cheerfully agreed as she set about pouring the crushed minerals into oil.

"Do you acquiesce to my unparalleled skills in stage cosmetics?" Alun asked, his voice once again punchably superior.

Calliope rolled her eyes. "Hardly. I've had plenty of experience painting my siblings' faces for my brother's masquerades. I simply don't wish to be bitten by that goose!"

"So I must sacrifice my ankles?" Alun demanded as Calliope handed him the solution.

"Aren't you always accusing me of being a hothouse flower?" Calliope asked archly. "How would my delicate skin endure such an assault?"

"She makes an excellent point," Sophia pointed out.

Alun started to open his mouth for a rebuttal, but Hannah gently pushed him in Eoin's direction. "Work your artistry!"

"While he's still holding that menace?" Alun asked, glowering at the goose.

"Perhaps the gosling will allow me to hold it," Hannah said.

Eoin handed her the goose. To Hannah's surprise, the bird didn't protest too much as long as Hannah stood close to Eoin. Thankfully, Alun and Calliope stopped spatting long enough to create rather convincing bruises.

As the fake welts blossomed over Eoin's countenance, an ominous feeling swelled inside Hannah. Something was clearly amiss at the Horse and Hen, and she had no idea what she and Eoin would encounter. But Hannah had never been one to shy away from danger.

## Chapter Eleven

~~~~~~

Eoin had always preferred the country air to the smells of London, but he'd grown accustomed to the scent of manure from the endless stream of horse-drawn carriages. And even in the nicer sections like Mayfair, odors lingered in the air from the refuse of city living. But this particular area of Covent Garden possessed a uniquely terrible stench. Sourness mingled with desperation, and the tight weave of buildings trapped the oppressive atmosphere, distilling it into a potent brew of discontent.

Or perhaps it only felt that way to Eoin, and the alley was really no different than any other cobblestoned close lined with disreputable businesses. Eoin had little occasion to visit unsavory establishments, and moreover, he had no personal ties to those grim passageways. Yet at the end of this dark, twisty corridor, his parents had met, and after his father's death, his mother and his sister had likely been forced to live on a similar sordid street.

*Don't go chasing after spirits and secrets.* Those hoarse, foreboding words whispered through Eoin, and he couldn't suppress the shiver that racked him.

"It will do no good to think about that beggar's cryptic words. If we have any hope of learning the Horse and Hen's secrets, we must keep all our wits about us." Hannah gently bumped Eoin's arm with her fist, and he suspected that she would have linked elbows with him if she wasn't dressed as a lad. It amazed him how quickly she'd deduced the reason for his shudder.

"Wits! Wits! Wits!" Pan cried from Hannah's shoulder. She'd insisted on bringing the noisy pet in case they required a distraction. Even the levelheaded Sophia had recommended taking along the bird.

Ignoring the grating cries, Eoin jerked his head in assent to Hannah's advice. He couldn't think of his mother and his sister as ghosts or even as shadowy figures from his own faint memories. No. He had to retain the hope that he would meet them and offer whatever assistance they needed. He could never change what they had endured, but he could improve their futures.

If they were alive...

This time when they passed the bawdy houses, Eoin made sure to stay to the center and keep his head down. It wasn't as if Hannah, dressed as a lad, could save him as easily as she had last time—and he had little faith in a parrot flying to the rescue despite Hannah's and Sophia's assurances of the feathered creature's skills.

Eoin glanced surreptitiously toward the set of stairs leading to the Horse and Hen's cellar entrance. Sure enough, a large man loitered at the bottom, his gaze flicking not-so-subtly over every passerby. Short of storming the door, it didn't appear as if they could manage to get inside. Hannah had been right to suggest that they once again try their luck on the main floor and hope that their current disguises and ripped, soiled clothing made them look like regular patrons.

Eoin shifted his gaze away from the fellow. Hunching his shoulders, he slunk forward. How he wished he could compress his body into a normal size and blend in. With any luck, people would be more focused on the lime-green bird perched on Hannah's shoulder.

"Oi!" The deep voice boomed down the alleyway, echoing off the cracking plaster of the half-timbered buildings.

Eoin's muscles tightened, and he sorely wished he'd learned how to use his considerable bulk to defend himself. Luckily, he was a handy enough shot, and he'd hidden a pistol under his workman's clothing.

"You! There! You're late!"

Eoin whirled around to find the burly fellow waving him over to the cellar steps of the Horse and Hen. Eoin started to glance around to confirm, but Hannah tugged his sleeve.

"This is our chance," Hannah whispered softly so only he could hear. "Just play along."

Eoin started cautiously walking forward,

but Hannah poked him gently in the ribs. "Swagger. Look confident. You must appear tough. Live up to those bruises."

Eoin tried his best to strut. He even clenched his fists in order to swell his biceps. Unfortunately, he felt utterly ridiculous and not the least bit intimidating. He half expected the guard to burst into guffaws.

He didn't. Instead, the sentry's light brown eyes flicked assessingly over Eoin. Then he glanced over at Hannah, his gaze dismissive. "Who are you? The young lads are almost done. And why the bird?"

"The youth's with me," Eoin said gruffly, immediately sensing that this brute wouldn't pay Hannah much mind. He didn't want a squabble to erupt when they were so close to their goal.

"And the parrot? A good luck charm?" The left corner of the man's lips turned up into a sneer.

"Yes," Eoin said with more confidence than he had. He could tell that the man found Pan's presence absurd, but then, so did Eoin. He couldn't think of a legitimate reason to drag a talking bird into whatever situation they were about to encounter.

"Balderdash. You either have skilled fists or you don't."

What the blazes did fists have to do with anything? Hopelessly confused, Eoin grunted. Beside him, Hannah shifted. She clearly wanted to speak, but she must have thought better. She didn't even huff out an annoyed sigh.

"Argh. I suppose it doesn't matter much to me," the sentinel ground out. "Just bring the bloody creature. There's no rule against it, although Ursus might not be so welcoming."

Ursus? The Latin word for bear? That was an unusual name, especially in a derelict alley. Did thieves employ nicknames from dead languages?

The sentry chortled as if he'd made a grand joke. Eoin simply grunted again, and Hannah remained silent.

Still chuckling darkly, the fellow opened a surprisingly thick door, which seemed more suited to a castle's keep than the entrance to a tumbledown cellar. The metal hinges groaned, only adding to a faint sense of doom.

Eoin stiffened his shoulders as he ducked under the low-slung doorframe. He wasn't typically a fanciful man. Screeching metal shouldn't send shivers skittering along his spine, but it did.

"Something's wrong." Hannah spoke in a low tone as she followed him.

Eoin nodded as he reached down to touch the handle of his pistol. This time, he was grateful for his bulk. If trouble arose, he could shield Hannah.

The outdoor steps had been stone, but those beyond the door were wooden. The oak creaked beneath Eoin's feet as the scent of stale ale and body odor wafted through the air. Another scent tickled Eoin's nose—a metallic one. Eoin didn't recognize it, but his body did. The hairs on his arms rose, and his heart pounded.

"Blood." The ominous word hung in the air as soon as Hannah spoke it. Eoin's nerves weren't helped when the guard shut the door behind them, plunging them into darkness. The thud of the wooden bar echoed down the gloomy, rickety staircase.

They were locked inside with only their firearms and a foul-mouthed parrot for defense. Shouts and jeers arose from the darkness below. A crowd—and a barbaric one by the sound of it—was gathered.

Panic shredded Eoin's gut, but he forced back the fear. If ever his levelheadedness was imperative, it was at this very moment.

"Did you say blood?" Eoin asked, hoping that he'd heard incorrectly, even as more ferocious cries surrounded them.

"Unfortunately, yes. Don't you recognize the scent?" Hannah asked as though the smell of gore were a common perfume like rose water.

"No." Eoin gripped the roughly hewn railing and ignored the splinters digging into his flesh. Cautiously, he dipped his foot to find the next uneven step. Once he'd found purchase, he continued, "I haven't had the occasion to be around blood."

"Not even during a boyhood brawl?"

"Books tend not to punch," Eoin said wryly, even as he hated to admit, once again, how sheltered and lonely his existence had been.

"I suppose not," Hannah said with a gentle

laugh that contained amusement at his turn of phrase. "But if they did, I am not sure if pugilistic tomes would make learning more or less appealing. Studying would definitely become a more physical endeavor."

Eoin's eyes had finally begun to adjust, and he realized that they were not surrounded by pitch blackness after all. At the bottom of the stairs, he could spy a faint, golden flicker—torchlight perhaps.

"There's a glow ahead," Eoin said as he heard more enthusiastic yells. Before he could continue descending, Hannah pressed against his back and peered over his shoulder. Instantly, a flush suffused Eoin, followed by those peculiar sparks of energy that only Hannah could elicit.

"Do you think they purposely made the staircase as deadly as possible?" Hannah asked. "They're exactly the kind that a villain in a play would push a victim down."

Despite the circumstances, a small huff of laughter escaped Eoin. Hannah had a remarkable way of making him feel lighter. "That is very apt."

A new roar rumbled toward them, and Eoin swore he felt the vibrations in his heart. He faltered, and Hannah bumped into him.

"That—that sounded like a b-beast." The quaver in Eoin's voice would have embarrassed him if he'd been accompanied by anyone but Hannah. Yet even with his blood pumping furiously, he trusted Hannah not to judge him too harshly.

"A bear!" Hannah practically shouted the words in his ear. "That was definitely a bruin. I've heard them growl at my friend's menagerie for rescued animals. Do you think a bearbaiting is happening right now? They've become more and more rare."

"Do you think they conduct a bloodsport like that underground?" Eoin asked as he stared into the torch-lit gloom. Outrage and disgust filled him as he thought about animals being forced to battle for the perverse enjoyment of humans.

"It happens, but I don't hear dogs barking," Hannah added, her voice full of anger. "It is despicable. Torturing animals for pleasure."

"I plan to use my seat in the House of

Lords to advocate for a ban on animal bloodsport," Eoin said as he continued his descent into the cacophony of sounds. "I've dreamed of championing such a law ever since I read a Willoughby Wright essay on cockfights."

"Willoughby Wright? I've never heard of him," Hannah said, and Eoin realized that she had no idea that her cousin was the author of cutting satires.

But he had no time to consider the revelation as he finally set his foot on the ground. Immediately, a great rattle exploded next to his right ear. Eoin turned swiftly and found himself facing a large, massive paw. His customary calmness fled. Yelping, he surged forward. In mid-leap, he realized belatedly that his dodge could potentially leave Hannah vulnerable. He tried to halt his jump, which resulted in a rather awkward pirouette. Somehow, he managed to land upright with his massive frame still shielding Hannah but with his face tilted away from the bear.

Breathing heavily, he felt Hannah's warmth as she once again peered over him from her vantage point on the steps. To his shock,

Hannah gently patted Eoin's shoulder instead of gripping him in terror.

"Poor bear. It's in such a small cage." Hannah clucked her tongue. "I must tell Matthew about the dear creature."

Although Eoin was most assuredly against any form of animal bloodsport, he was not particularly ready to call the owner of that lethal paw a "dear creature." However, Hannah's statement did cause his pounding heart to slow... a fraction.

"The beast is restrained?" Eoin cautiously swiveled, his hands raised in rather useless fists. Even with his bulk, he highly doubted that he would win a boxing match against a bruin.

"Yes. It can reach through the bars but not far."

Sure enough, a scarred and scruffy bear was staring through wrought iron rods. Its dark gaze seemed aimed not at Eoin but at a point above his head. Eoin's blood started flowing madly as his muscles tensed even more. Was the animal fixated on Hannah?

"Not dinner! Not dinner!" Pan screeched.

Hannah reached up to calm her pet. "It does

seem rather focused on Pan. We should move quickly. I don't want to taunt the poor dear."

"Not dinner! Not dinner!" Pan repeated.

As a degree of calm returned to Eoin, he marveled at Hannah's innate compassion. Where others only saw its massive size and enormous paws, she observed the bear's pain.

Calmer now, Eoin studied the animal. Bits of its fur were missing, and healed gashes marred its muzzle. Although its feet were about the size of Eoin's face, the vicious claws had been filed down. Its teeth had likely received the same treatment.

"Ursus," Eoin said as the sentry's words replayed in his mind. "This is who the guard was referring to when he said that Pan might not be welcomed."

"Not dinner!" the parrot screeched again.

"Why don't you walk on the other side of me when we pass Ursus," Eoin suggested. "It might calm both bear and bird—or at least not excite them more."

"I'm happy for you to play the gallant gentleman this time," Hannah admitted as she again reached up to stroke her pet.

Eoin nodded, not wanting to admit that he also wished to protect her. There was likely no danger, but it was still unsettling to pass so close to a predator. Eoin wished he could sling his arm around Hannah's shoulder and curl his form over her smaller one, but he had no idea if someone was watching them in this dark corridor. Such a gentlemanly gesture could damage Hannah's disguise as a lad. Moreover, Eoin didn't want to trample her independence. In many ways, she was more capable than him of defending herself in London's underbelly.

Ursus thumped his big body against the bars as they rushed by. Roaring his displeasure, he stomped his feet. The dirt floor shook under the beast's impotent rage, but the cage otherwise held firm.

"It's telling that this establishment forces its patrons to pass by Ursus," Eoin said.

"Not dinner!" Pan flapped his lime-green wings. Thankfully, the ornery bird didn't take flight. It seemed even he could be cowed.

"The bear is definitely a warning," Hannah agreed, her voice so low and dark that Eoin had to bend even more to hear. The cries from the bowels of the Horse and Hen had grown louder. Their frenzied tone worried Eoin even more than the trapped bear to his side.

As soon as they passed Ursus, Pan—the cheeky imp—swiveled his head so that he faced back toward the bear. With his one beady eye fixed on the bruin, the parrot opened his gray mouth wide and then roared.

Ursus, however, was not impressed by the mimicry. He snarled, but that only seemed to amuse Pan, who danced happily on Hannah's shoulder.

"Shhh!" Hannah admonished. "Don't torment Ursus."

"How does a parrot sound so much like a bear?" Eoin asked, trying to focus on anything but his own mess of misgivings.

Hannah sighed. "He's visited my friend's menagerie and has listened to the bears and the resident lion. Pan discovered that his mock-roaring annoys Sophia and me, so the little devil likes to repeat the sounds."

As if to prove Hannah's statement, Pan bellowed even louder. The sound bounced around the narrow space that they were traversing. The passage seemed to be a purposefully squashed affair—with a crude wall to the right and the building's foundation on the left. It reminded Eoin of a castle's narrow circular staircase—a structure designed to make an invasion difficult. Were the owners of the Horse and Hen expecting an attack? And why?

An incongruously pleasant glow beckoned at the end of the torch-lit hallway, yet part of Eoin wanted to stay in the darkness with the snarling beast. He didn't know what he would discover in that light, and what it would mean about the fate of his mother and his sister.

A cool hand briefly touched his, and Eoin turned to find Hannah smiling at him. "I will stay by your side, Eoin. No matter what we learn."

Eoin swallowed as a bolt of warm emotion slammed into his heart. Since childhood, Eoin had faced everything alone. Yet leaning on Hannah, trusting her, came easily. Perhaps too easily.

Eoin couldn't help but give her fingers a quick nudge back. Then he drew in his breath and marched in lockstep with the woman beside him.

## Chapter Twelve

Hannah could not shake a sense of utter doom as she and Eoin entered a surprisingly extensive chamber. Men crowded shoulder to shoulder, forming an almost impenetrable wall around whatever they were watching. A few of the coats were of fine silk, while others were serviceable linen, and still others were threadbare with patched holes.

The place reeked. Of mold. Of sweat. Of stale ale. Of old gin. Of blood—fresh and long dried.

The atmosphere was stifling and not just due to the putrid odors. Desperation, greed, violence, and unholy excitement hung like an almost palpable miasma. Hannah had experienced unsavory places. She'd grown up in Covent Garden after all. But she'd rarely sensed a darkness this cloying.

Hannah was suddenly very glad that Eoin was standing next to her. She'd never thought a man—a nobleman at that—could offer her fortifying comfort by his mere presence. Yet she felt buoyed by his nearness and not just because of his massive build.

"This room is too large to fit under the Horse and Hen." Eoin practically shouted the words near her ear, but the din was so great that she still struggled to hear. "It must extend under several buildings and even across the alley itself."

Hannah nodded. She'd been thinking the same. The tavern was smaller than her coffeehouse, yet her cellar was nowhere near this size. The ceiling was propped up by rickety, improvised pillars that appeared to be constructed of whatever scraps were handy at the time. The results looked akin to a child heaping a bunch of twigs together to make a tower. Those haphazard structures held up equally crude wooden beams that looked nothing like the sturdy rafters of the Black Sheep. Between the questionable supports were wooden planks where men sat, their legs dangling in the air, their faces red from drink or excitement or both. Their mouths were contorted in angry shouts and jeers. Below them were the heads of other spectators, who peered around or through the slapdash columns to watch whatever entertainment was holding them in thrall.

Hannah shivered. It was as if someone had moved the St. Giles rookery indoors and underground. The whole building was one spark or push away from an inferno or devastating collapse.

"Do you think this place existed when my mother worked at the Horse and Hen?" Eoin asked, and Hannah had no trouble detecting the worried pain in his voice.

"I don't know," Hannah admitted. The mess of uneven wooden stakes, poles, planks, and logs could have been built ages ago and shored up over the decades, or it could be a new construction. "But we can't hover here in the shadows if we wish to learn more. Do you think you can make a path through the crowd?"

Normally, Hannah would just slip through,

but with Eoin's size, that wasn't a possibility. Thankfully, due to his hulking frame, he was the type of fellow that other men quickly sidled away from.

Eoin nodded and quickly began shouldering through the smelly, sweaty mass of humanity. Hannah followed him closely, and she doubted that anyone noticed her even with a parrot perched on her shoulder. Every gaze was riveted to Eoin's massive form and huge fists.

Within a few seconds, they reached the crowd's nexus. Eoin halted abruptly, and Hannah smashed painfully into his back. Yelping, she rubbed her nose. She would have much preferred a more pleasurable way to discover just how firm Eoin's muscles were. Still wincing, she peeked around the duke and then froze too.

Two lads were clobbering each other in a thirty-by-thirty-foot pit a few feet below Hannah's toes. Although she had witnessed plenty of street fights and even attended a few matches while dressed as a boy at Championess Quick's amphitheater, she was stunned by the particular cruelty that the youths displayed. Viciously, they tore each other's hair and skin as if their only goal was to inflict the most pain on the other.

When a bigger adolescent slammed the scrawnier one to the ground, Hannah gasped, not bothering to suppress the noise. She couldn't even hear her own exhalation over the enthusiastic shouts encouraging the juvenile to keep hitting his prone opponent's face.

She knew the fallen boy—or had at least met him. He'd been the young pickpocket who'd tried to steal from Eoin only two days before. Back then, she'd spotted bruises and welts on his arms, but she'd thought he'd received them from a kidsman or from encroaching on another urchin's hunting grounds.

Blood sprayed from the boy's nose, and the other fighter turned to kicking his ribs. Hannah tensed, ready to jump into the ring herself—even though she realized she would likely only get beaten. Beside her, Eoin shifted his body in obvious preparation to assist the lad.

But before either of them could react, a man dressed in a tattered silk coat stepped into the ring. He pointed to the dominant competitor. The youth climbed out of the pit to cheers and slaps on the back. The fallen boy was hauled up by his collar and half tossed, half forcibly guided up the wooden wall. He landed at the feet of a burly man standing next to Eoin and Hannah.

The fellow raised his foot. Although Hannah couldn't hear every screamed word, she caught a few. "Worthless cur." "Lost...three shillings."

Hannah almost dove to cover the boy's body, but Eoin was faster. He simply moved in front of the prone lad. "Will you stop if I pay you that amount?"

"Eh?" the man asked as he bobbled a bit, likely from drink and pent-up ire.

"If I give you three shillings, will you leave the child alone?" Eoin asked.

"What child?" the man sneered.

"The one behind me." Eoin's eyes blazed, but still he made no move to attack even though he could have easily defeated the smaller, drunk fellow. Instead, he calmly withdrew the coins.

"That's no child. He's just a fighting mutt from the streets."

"Will you take the money and stop hurting the boy? I won't ask again." Eoin's voice had become cool—deadly cool.

Even the inebriated man registered the chill. His mouth flapped closed, and he snatched the money from Eoin's outstretched palm. Then he slunk a few feet away, glancing back once or twice as if making sure that Eoin wouldn't follow.

Eoin bent to help the lad, but the adolescent half lurched and half stumbled to his feet. He clutched his side and glared. Hannah could see a flicker of surprise in Eoin's blue-green eyes, but she understood the boy's venomous reaction. The child had to fend for himself, and he'd probably learned early that nothing came without cost. Hannah's parents might have shielded and loved her, but she'd grown up close enough to the edges of society that she could comprehend what the lad had endured.

"What do you want?" the boy demanded

as he wiped his bloodied lip with the hand not gripping his ribs.

"Just to help. That's all. You have nothing to fear from me." Eoin's measured voice was tinged with kindness.

The boy didn't stop glowering, and his slight body remained tense, clearly poised to bolt. But he didn't dart away. Perhaps he expected others who lost their bets to retaliate against him. It might be common in the vicious hellhole. For whatever reason, though, the lad lingered near them like a hunted deer huddled below a rock shelter.

The fellow in tattered finery announced the next fight—this one between two women, who were naked from their waists up. This wasn't about boxing talent. It was about the prurient interests of the onlookers.

"I—I think we know what happens underneath the Horse and Hen." Eoin's normally even voice was shaky and hollow. "There's no need to stay for another match."

Eoin was clenching his jaw so hard that his cheek muscles had dented. His big hands flexed as he stared at the fighting women. It was clear to Hannah that he was imagining his own mother in that ring. Had she participated in catfights in this subterranean room before she'd married Eoin's father? What about after? Had she found herself forced back into this brutal life in order to feed herself and her daughter?

No wonder Eoin's aquamarine eyes had gone dark. Hannah knew the pain she experienced when she thought about what her father and uncle had endured when they'd been shoved into a dark hold of a ship along with hardened adult criminals.

"I agree that we should leave," Hannah said quietly. Eoin's sorrow wasn't the only reason for an immediate departure. "I think I know why that guard allowed us to enter."

"He thought I was a fighter," Eoin said grimly, tapping at one of the fake bruises on his face.

Hannah nodded. Eoin wouldn't survive long if forced into that ring. Even his bulk couldn't compete against the skill of a hardened prizefighter.

Before heading to the exit, Hannah gave one last glance toward the ring. The women were both yanking each other's long locks and shuffling in an agonizing circle.

Hannah was just about to turn when the master of ceremonies jumped into the ring, his tattered coattails flapping from the effort. He raced toward the women and started shouting, "Break it up! Break it up!"

Protests erupted, and the screaming caused pain to explode inside Hannah's head. The pressure swelled with the ferocity of the crowd's ire. Gnawing unease swept through her. Something wasn't right. The women ignored the command as they each tried to force the other to the ground.

The silk-clad announcer did not seem deterred as he waved to four burly fellows. After leaping into the pit, they broke into two pairs and pulled the fighters apart. The women rained blows upon each other and their captors. Finally, they were separated—their fists still swinging. One of them even clutched a chunk of the other's hair.

"The Purveyor has spoken. The Purveyor has spoken," the master of ceremonies solemnly called out, as if this were akin to a proclamation by King George. At the name, the unruly crowd miraculously settled. Whoever the Purveyor was, he held sway.

"The Purveyor wants the first prizefighter match to begin!" the announcer bellowed.

Dread burst through Hannah as the man swung with a flourish in Eoin's direction. Desperately, Hannah tried to scramble to stand in front of Eoin—even as part of her recognized the futility. It was not as if her slender frame could obscure Eoin's massive one.

"You!" The master of ceremonies pointed a finger in Eoin's direction. "You! Come down here now. Show us what a fight really is."

Eoin stepped backward, but to his stoic credit, he managed not to look like a hunted hare. Hannah was fairly certain that she was the very picture of a prey animal as she swiveled her head around to locate any exits.

"Why are you backing away?" the announcer sneered. "Do we have a cowardly jackanapes here? Don't let him run, fellows!"

The crowd behind Eoin shoved him forward, and he stumbled into Hannah. Before he mowed her over, he picked her up and plopped her down to his side. Hannah watched in utter horror as Eoin was forced to leap into the pit. Cheers and jeers rang through the chamber. Hannah's stomach clenched so violently that bile burned her throat.

How was she to stop this? She could fight, but not at the level of a prizefighter. She had no prayer of helping him.

Pan paced nervously on her shoulder, but he did not fly into the air. It was as if the slender bird was trying his best to protect her even as she was trying to save Eoin. Pan had been trained to provide distractions during times of danger, but normally he screamed about ghosts and murder. Hannah doubted that either of those cries would terrify this crowd. In fact, they'd probably want to witness a killing. What could instill fear?

The bear could. Obviously, it was at the entrance to intimidate. And all these men had witnessed its frustrated anger.

And Pan. Pan could roar.

Perhaps not well enough to fool a calm and rational gathering, but this was a crowd on edge. It wouldn't take much to stir up a panic.

## Chapter Thirteen

Eoin—who had lived so many years numb—felt shredded by emotion. Fear. For himself. For Hannah. Even for their bloody parrot companion. Guilt. Over his mother. Over his sister. Disgust. With the violence. With the blasted, depraved crowd. With his own weakness.

Nothing made sense. Not this hidden, massive underground space. Not the secrecy surrounding this entertainment—which, although abhorrent, wasn't illegal. Not the Purveyor's demand that Eoin, a random person in the crowd, fight in the middle of the female bout. Swounds, even the existence of a mysterious, powerful figure named the Purveyor was absurd and unsettling.

Eoin knew that he'd blundered into a trap,

but why was someone trying to ensnare him and why here? Was his mother still connected to this place? Had she fought…and bled… in this very ring?

A roar ripped through the air, and Eoin froze. Every hair follicle stood at attention as a bone-deep chill washed over him.

Hell. Was he to fight the bloody bear? Did they think this was the Roman Empire and this dank hole the Colosseum? Of all the ways Eoin thought he would die, he'd never thought it would be as a modern-day gladiator fighting in a venatio.

"The bear's escaped!"

Was Hannah speaking? Even though she was attempting to sound more masculine, he'd recognize her voice anywhere. So many aspects of her seemed embedded upon his very soul.

*Rawrrrrrrrrrr!*

How was that rumble coming from overhead? Eoin vaguely recalled that bears could climb, but he doubted that the rickety wooden pillars could hold even his weight, let alone an angry bruin's.

The crowd quieted, and heads bobbed. It was clear that everyone was trying to determine the extent of the danger.

*Rawrrrrrrr!*

The second roar triggered pure chaos. Yells and screams erupted throughout the chamber. The throng was no longer focused on the ring or on Eoin but on their own safety. Some of the shouts floated down to Eoin as he desperately tried to assess the situation. How was he supposed to get Hannah and himself to safety if there was a bear on the loose...or if the gathered mass stampeded in the tight, cramped quarters? They could literally bring down the entire building if too many people pushed against the poorly installed supports.

"Shite!"

"That's sounds like Ursus!"

"He's escaped!"

"I hate that bear."

"Get away from the exit!"

"But how will we flee?"

"I won't walk straight into its open maw!"

"I don't want to be eaten!"

"Not dinner! Not dinner!"

Was the last cry... Pan's? Eoin craned his neck toward the ceiling, and he thought he saw a streak of green.

A thud sounded behind him. Eoin whirled, reaching for his gun with one hand and fisting the other. He relaxed a fraction when he spied Hannah.

"Say you'll capture the bear!" Hannah shouted in his face.

"What?" Eoin asked, his voice sounding distant even to his own ears. His normally fast-paced mind could not keep up with hers. It was clear that she had a plan, but what?

"Quick! Before this throng turns into a completely mindless mob!"

"You want me to catch a bruin? With just my hands? Not even a rope?"

"It's Pan."

"What?"

"Pan's the bear," Hannah explained. "It's the only scheme I could devise. Quick! Before it's too late to calm the crowd."

Pan was the bear?

"Look up!" Hannah commanded.

Eoin did as he was told. This time, he

definitely did catch sight of the rascal. As the feathered menace swept through an opening in one of the precarious supports, it opened its beak. A distinctive roar followed.

Swounds, Hannah was a genius—a reckless and unpredictable genius—yet a genius nonetheless. Eoin had no time, though, to process his growing swell of gratitude and pride. He'd have time to feel impressed by her quick thinking once they were safe and they'd stopped the potential disaster of their own creation.

Already the crowd had begun to jostle toward the exit. The master of ceremonies had disappeared—presumably slinking toward an escape route rather than attempting to quiet the crowd that he'd whipped to the edge of a frenzy. To Eoin's horror, he saw the boy that he'd helped earlier get knocked to the ground near the lip of the pit.

"I will wrestle the bear back into his cage!" Eoin cried as loudly as he could, the force of his scream already burning his throat.

It was a rather absurd statement, and it felt even more ridiculous by the theatrical way in which Eoin shouted. Mr. Powys, Eoin was not. He definitely should not be treading the boards on any stage.

But his shout worked. Those around him heard, at least.

"The new fighter is going to battle the bear!"

"Let him through!"

"What's going on?"

"A boxer will take care of the bear! Make way for him!"

"Make way!"

Eoin helped Hannah from the pit before scrambling out himself. He only paused to snatch the scrawny youth around his middle and hoist the boy over his shoulders. Given the lad's last reaction to Eoin's help, Eoin was grateful that the youngster didn't fight him. The adolescent must have realized he'd be crushed otherwise.

Hannah pressed close to Eoin's side. He wished he could sling his arm around her to add more protection, but he had his hands full. A small gap had opened in the crowd, but Eoin still needed to shoulder their way toward the exit. As news of his promise to contain Ursus spread, a path began to clear. Eoin felt like Moses parting the Red Sea as he strode through the mass of milling men.

In a surprisingly short amount of time, Eoin and Hannah reached the narrow hallway leading to the exit. Eoin angled his body so that he didn't knock the adolescent's head or feet against the walls. No one followed.

Well, no one except the parrot.

Pan flew gracefully into the passage and landed on Hannah's shoulder. He began preening himself in a manner that could only be described as extremely self-satisfied. The bird was a fiend—a useful, life-saving fiend—but a fiend nonetheless.

When they had gone a few feet down the tunnel, Eoin lifted the youth off his shoulders and set him on the ground. The adolescent gripped his side, his brown eyes wide in his pinched, too-thin face.

"Are you really going to fight and catch Ursus?" the boy asked.

"Stay here, lad," Eoin said, not trusting the boy with their ruse. "I'll return in a moment."

As much as Eoin wanted to immediately flee with Hannah, simply disappearing could retrigger the terror. The only way to avoid disaster was to mock-fight Ursus and then announce his "victory."

"You're going with him?" the youngster asked Hannah as she started to follow Eoin.

"Oh, I'm very good at corralling animals." Hannah winked, and Eoin couldn't help but marvel at how she kept her humor even in a circumstance like this.

"How do I pretend to battle a bear?" Eoin asked Hannah as soon as they were out of earshot.

Hannah lifted the shoulder not serving as a parrot-perch and let it drop. "Make a lot of noise, I suppose. Pan will also be happy to assist. As I said, he adores mimicry."

Hannah glanced over at her passenger. "Pan, can you be a dear and roar again?"

Pan happily obliged. Tossing back his lime head with a flourish, he emitted a rather terrifying growl.

This, of course, displeased Ursus, who was already watching their approach with undisguised loathing. The bruin's snout shot into the air as the beast let out his own battle cry. Pan snarled right back. Ursus slammed against his cage, the noise echoing down the hall.

Hannah nudged Eoin. "Yell. Pretend you're grappling with Ursus, but make sure it sounds like you're winning."

"Take that, bear!" Eoin shouted, and a blush heated his face even though Hannah was the only witness to this utter farce.

Pan flew into the air as he cackled evilly. Swooping near the beast's caged head, he emitted a taunting roar—almost as good as the bruin's own.

Ursus lunged, rattling the wrought iron, his back paws thudding on the ground. His trimmed talons scraped against the metal.

"What's *that*?" someone cried from the arena.

"In you go, you great brute!" Eoin shouted like an extremely bad stage actor.

"Has he already caged the bear?"

"I wish I could see the fight!"

"Yes! Why are we all hanging back?"

Hannah tugged on Eoin's sleeve. "We best run. Ursus has suffered enough. And those blighters out there are liable to force you into the pit again instead of thanking you."

Eoin heard a shuffling sound. He glanced over to find the adolescent standing in the gloom, his brown eyes solemn and guarded. Eoin had no idea how much the boy had overheard, but he suspected that the boy realized all their lies.

"The bear's been caught!" the youth cried out loudly as he motioned for Eoin and Hannah to flee. "The bear's been caught!"

Eoin nodded his thanks, touched that the distrustful youth had come to their aid. Then he stepped back to allow Hannah to pass.

"You set the pace," Eoin instructed. "Your stride is shorter."

And Eoin wanted to protect Hannah. Luckily, she didn't protest. She only nodded curtly and bolted up the rickety stairs. Eoin waited for a few minutes, watching the tunnel to make sure no one was close behind. Then he turned and took two steps at a time. He easily caught up to her, but he could hear the voices coming closer. When they reached the top, Hannah pounded on the door. Eoin leaned over her to slam his own fist against the oak.

There was the scrape of wood knocking against wood, and then the guard's face appeared. "Done already? It must have been a good but short fight. It's been awfully noisy today."

Eoin squeezed around Hannah and used his bulk to shove the door fully open. The sentinel stumbled back, too shocked to protest. Eoin pressed on the oak panel, pinning the man against the wall. Hannah darted through the opening that Eoin had made. As soon as she had a head start, Eoin tore after her.

"Oi! What was that about?" the sentry cried after them, but Eoin and Hannah didn't stop moving until they'd reached the main road, where Eoin's carriage stood. He waited for Hannah to climb in and then bounded in after her, slamming the door shut.

"Tell the coachman to head to the Black Sheep," Hannah instructed. "We must speak with the others. Nothing makes sense about what just happened."

"I agree," Eoin said as disparate thoughts and emotions whirled inside him like an unstoppable hurricane. But for once, he wasn't alone. Not only was Hannah by his side, but she'd promised to stay there. And others were willing to help with Eoin's quest. After a lonely life, companionship was a wonderful, wonderful thing—even if the rest of him felt bruised and battered after witnessing the horrors underneath the Horse and Hen.

---

"Do you wish to talk about it?"

Hannah's voice broke the silence that had descended upon them as Eoin's carriage painstakingly wound through the thick London traffic. Although both the Horse and Hen and the Black Sheep were in Covent Garden, they were at opposite ends, and the snarl of coaches, wagons, and carriages seemed especially slow.

"I am trying too hard to unravel what this

all portends," Eoin admitted. "I should allow time for my thoughts to settle before any serious analysis. Unfortunately, while we're trapped in this carriage, there's not much else to do but overthink."

"Would you like a distraction?" Hannah asked as she shifted closer to him on the seat that they shared.

Eoin looked down to find Hannah staring at him, her green eyes glittering so brightly, it was as if they could generate their own source of light. His heart pounded just as hard as it had during their dash to safety...but this time it wasn't beating from fear.

Eoin wanted to dip his head and capture Hannah's pink lips. But surely she hadn't meant that particular type of distraction.

Not that Eoin had ever indulged in passion of any kind. He couldn't, with his grandfather monitoring every aspect of his life. Romance—considering his own parents' disastrous love story—was particularly forbidden.

"Beast with two backs! Beast with two backs!" Pan cried out happily.

Swounds. Was the damnable parrot a seer?

Although Eoin hadn't progressed quite that far in his imagination. Yet now he couldn't help but think of undoing the buttons on Hannah's linen shirt and slipping his hand inside to capture...

"Pan, hush." Hannah turned to glare her bird into submission, but the bird did not seem impressed by his mistress's dark looks.

"Not dinner! Not dinner!"

Hannah arched an eyebrow. "That can be rectified."

Pan hopped along the cushion across from them, his chest puffed out in offense. However, it seemed that perhaps the threat worked, as the bird fell to silence.

"What manner of distraction?" Eoin asked. His cursed blood rushed to his face as he realized how the question sounded after Pan's crude suggestion.

Hannah tilted her chin at a coquettish angle. "What kind do you desire?"

Eoin's throat went utterly and completely dry. Was he just imagining the flirtatious head cock and the throaty quality of Hannah's voice?

"I—um—I."

Eoin was articulate. Generally. But now the words that usually flowed so easily wouldn't come, but the feelings did. A frothy energy had bubbled inside Eoin ever since their desperate escape from the bowels of the Horse and Hen. Now that vigor surged forward with a brilliant, shining force. And for once, Eoin allowed himself to be carried away by emotion.

He gently cupped Hannah's face. Surprise flared in the grassy green depths of her irises. Perhaps she'd only been gently teasing, but even if she had, she didn't pull away from his touch. In fact, she leaned forward. And her eyes...her eyes fluttered shut.

Eoin might not be a man of passion, but he instinctually recognized her wordless encouragement. Yet even so, he wished for no misunderstandings.

"May I kiss you, Hannah?"

One of her eyes snapped open, and her lips spread into a decidedly saucy smile. "If you don't initiate one forthwith, then I will."

Eoin couldn't help but grin in return.

Nervousness rushed through him but so did desire. Before anxiety overcame his rare daring, he lowered his mouth. Her tongue teased the seam of his lips, and sensation ricocheted through him. When he gasped, Hannah deepened the kiss.

How could friction feel so absolutely marvelous? The mere glide of mouth against mouth shouldn't produce such intensity. But it did. And Eoin reveled in it.

He groaned, wanting more, needing more. Hannah must have understood his silent pleas—even when he, himself, couldn't fully grasp his needs. She climbed onto his lap, her legs straddling his, her knees pressed into the cushion at his sides. Somehow, she never broke their kiss as her body slid against his.

Eoin's hands instinctually wrapped around Hannah's back—both to ensure she didn't topple backward in the swaying carriage and to simply touch her. He could feel her delicate shoulder blades underneath her thin coat and shirt, but when his fingers inched downward, he felt lumps from successive bands of fabric. He was so engrossed by desire that it took him a moment to realize that she'd bound her breasts.

Hannah's mouth left his, and he moaned in protest. But then she placed her lips near his ear, and his whole body shivered.

"Are the bindings making you grumpy?" Although Hannah's voice was husky, her words themselves were light.

"No," Eoin said quickly, embarrassed by how much he wanted to remove those interfering strips of fabric. He yearned to feel Hannah—all of her.

"Liar." Hannah gently nipped his earlobe. Sparks spiraled down Eoin's spine, which turned into veritable fireworks when Hannah sucked the very spot that she'd nibbled. And if that wasn't enough of a bolt of lust, Hannah then leaned back, shucked off her coat, and swiftly undid the laces of her shirt. Maintaining eye contact, she reached inside her clothing and slowly withdrew the long band of muslin. When the end of the cloth finally popped free, Hannah casually dropped the material to the floor of the carriage. She watched Eoin with an impish smirk on her kiss-swollen lips.

Eoin didn't just forget to breathe. He forgot everything, except Hannah and her estimable boldness.

"Let's rid you of some layers, too, shall we?" Hannah asked coyly as her quick hands unbuttoned his linsey-woolsey coat. As she tugged at the rough, serviceable material, he leaned forward, allowing her to divest him of the garment.

No sooner had it found its way to the bottom of the coach than Hannah's mouth once more descended over Eoin's. He pressed back against the squabs as she moved against his chest. This time he could feel the full softness of her breasts. He gripped her body, only to discover that her shirt had ridden up, exposing the small of her back.

The satiny smoothness of her skin enthralled him, and he could not help but run his fingers gently along her flesh. And this time... this time, Hannah was the one to shiver.

Heady pleasure shot through Eoin, and he stroked up her spine, feeling each delicate bump. Hannah quaked in his arms, but her mouth still moved in a hungry demand against his.

Eoin had lived his life as a series of thoughtful deliberations—all calculated to meet his grandfather's exacting standards. He'd never been allowed to simply feel and to permit his instincts to reign.

But for once, Eoin wasn't driven by reason but by unmitigated passion. His fingers dipped around Hannah's side until they slid across the swell of her breasts. Hannah didn't push him away as she moaned into his mouth.

Sweet fire erupted, setting every fiber of Eoin's body ablaze. Hannah's lips left his to trail down his neck as her hands slipped under his shirt. The coolness of her fingertips was a delicious contrast to his heated flesh. He wanted her tender ministrations as badly as he wanted to attend to her needs.

Swounds, he simply couldn't get close enough to Hannah. It was as if he wanted them to absorb each other's essence or merge or... he couldn't think of the right term... he just knew that he needed to connect with her in the most elemental of ways.

Her lips left his and trailed down his neck as she pushed her bosom against his curious fingers. Understanding her wordless command, he palmed each breast, massaging gently as his thumbs swirled around her nipples.

She gasped, her mouth leaving his body as she arched her back. This time, it was he who placed his lips against her exposed neck. He slid one hand around her, bearing her weight so she could lose herself in pleasure.

His body trembled at the onslaught of sensations, yet he felt like he could support Hannah forever. He'd never allowed himself to be so vulnerable in the presence of another, yet then again, he'd never felt so secure. Hannah, he realized, felt like home to him.

# Chapter Fourteen

Hannah was not precisely a stranger to passion, and she certainly was no sheltered miss. But no one had ever made her feel like she was as powerful as the sea...until now. With Eoin, she didn't just feel like she was skimming along brilliant, sunlit waves. Instead, she was part of the incredible force—surging, strong, and unstoppable.

He'd been tentative at first, sweetly so. Very quickly, though, his raw hunger had matched hers, and she wanted it, wanted him and his need.

When Eoin's lips found a particularly sensitive spot at the base of her neck, Hannah whimpered. Actually whimpered. Never in her life had she thought she would allow such a sound to escape her lips in front of another human being.

But with Eoin, it didn't seem like a weakness. It simply felt right as his large hand slid in a seductive rhythm over her breast while his thumb toyed devilishly with her nipple. There was a certain thrill to hanging half in the air, her body bonelessly draped against Eoin's muscular forearm as he bent over her, his mouth practically devouring her neck. Each sway of the carriage bounced their bodies together in the most wonderfully erotic way.

Why had Hannah never attempted this in a coach before? But then again, she'd never ridden in one of these rarefied equipages until she'd met Eoin.

Suddenly, a very unwanted spike of reality drove through Hannah's glorious haze of pleasure. She gasped and not from delight.

Eoin immediately jerked them upright, his blue eyes studying her closely. She had never known another person so attuned to her emotions.

"I am fine. Just a stray thought," Hannah said, silently adding to herself, *but not a very pleasant one.*

What was she doing, kissing Eoin so

fervently? She'd only meant to tease away a few of his worries. She hadn't expected him to actually accept her bold offer.

Or maybe part of her had. She'd felt an explosive attraction to him since their first meeting.

But then she'd discovered Eoin's identity, and she hadn't been able to indulge in that intense yearning. That was the crux of the problem.

It wasn't just because he was her family's enemy—or perhaps their intertwined past was no longer a reason for Hannah to avoid intimacy with Eoin. After all, Eoin was nothing like his grandfather, who'd sent two boys to the Colonies for trying to feed their families. Instead, Eoin was the type to step in and save a street urchin.

Eoin possessed a sensitive side, a part of him that Hannah suspected was revealed only to her. And she was afraid of injuring him—for he trusted her, while she was keeping secrets.

Nay, not just secrets.

Hannah had entered into this partnership with the intent of destroying Eoin's family. But even as she'd begun to realize that Eoin would willingly help uncover his relatives' perfidy, she also knew for certain that he'd be sorely wounded that she'd tricked him.

And then she'd gone and kissed the man. Or rather devoured him.

She really needed to confess the truth. But how could she at this moment? Eoin was still reeling from the brutality of what they'd witnessed at the Horse and Hen. He believed his mother to be dead, perhaps even from a fight in the ring. And she—Hannah—was his main support in the dark world that he'd just discovered. Could she leave him with absolutely no foundation?

Damn it. She'd made a bloody mess of things.

"A stray thought." Eoin tapped Hannah's forehead lightly and brought her from her stupor. To her surprise, an adorable half pout touched Eoin's lips. She hadn't thought the stoic man capable of such a petty emotion. "And here you have utterly destroyed my capacity for reason."

Oh, she was the very devil. The truth behind her original motivations would utterly crush this sweet mountain of a man.

"Perhaps I need to try harder." Eoin

attempted to wink, but he didn't quite succeed. It was more like a lopsided blink. But his failure only made the gesture more lovable.

Hannah's mind scrambled for how best to proceed for Eoin's sake. She did not want to reject him, but she also didn't want to engender more closeness until she could tell him the truth.

Eoin's expression seemed to deaden, and Hannah realized the astute man had noticed her hesitation. "Eoin, I—"

Thankfully, the carriage drew to a stop, and the coachman rapped on the ceiling—the signal that Eoin liked his footmen to give upon arrival at a destination. Hannah nearly catapulted off Eoin's lap.

"We best put ourselves to rights," Hannah said as she tugged on her shirt and patted her shoulder as a signal for Pan to return to her.

At the Black Sheep, it was no secret that she sometimes donned boys' clothing, so there was no need to rebind her breasts. She just needed to look…well…untumbled. Not that there had been any actual tumbling, which was probably for the best—but oh, what an intense tumbling it would have been.

Eoin nodded and stiffly donned his simple coat. "I hope I did not offend you with—"

"Not at all," Hannah reassured him, resting her hand on his arm for a few brief seconds. She wouldn't have risked even that contact if they hadn't been about to depart the carriage. She didn't trust herself around Eoin—not with how incendiary their kisses had been.

"I've never experienced an intensity like that," Hannah admitted.

Eoin's eyes heated, and when he spoke, his normally even voice sounded like a growl. "Nor have I."

Hannah sucked in her breath. *Calm. Now is not the time. You can be calm.*

"We'd best go inside." Hannah turned and pushed on the carriage door. "I'll send a boy around to collect our friends. Once the Black Sheep closes, we need to discuss what we learned."

"I am afraid of the conclusions," Eoin admitted grimly, and then a shadow of a smile touched his lips. "But I am glad you will be next to me."

Hannah's remorse skewered her, but a

confession now would only ease her guilt and make Eoin feel worse. So she squeezed his arm and nodded.

"I'll stay at your side, Eoin," Hannah promised, while silently adding, *until you chase me away.*

---

"None of this makes sense." Sophia tapped an elegant finger against a low table in the back room. They were all gathered on the comfortable furniture, and Hannah and Eoin had just finished recounting what had happened in the bowels of the Horse and Hen.

"Nothing you described is illegal," Sophia pointed out. "Why would they position a guard at the entrance?"

"And a bear!" Charlotte said, shaking her head. "That poor creature."

Her husband reached over and patted her hand. "Don't worry. I'll either buy it or figure out another way to rescue it. There's plenty of room at our friend's menagerie."

"Illegal operations must be occurring at

the Horse and Hen," Sophia sighed, her fingers beating out an even faster tattoo. "But none of our patrons know anything about it."

"I haven't learned anything specific either," Powys added with an especially theatrical sigh, a hazard of being an actor.

"But you have heard something?" Hannah leaned forward. Beside her, Eoin stiffened. She wanted to reach out and comfort him, but she had no idea what their relationship was… or would become. And it didn't feel fair to expose him to the scrutiny of her friends.

"Just about the street in general. It was known for being a hotbed of pro-Catholic activity and then as a center of the gin trade," Powys explained. "But it was curiously difficult to obtain even that much information. No one seems to want to talk about the Horse and Hen."

A shivery sensation slipped through Hannah. Powys's description sounded similar to her search for information about the Aucourtes. But she shouldn't make connections between two separate investigations simply because they were occurring at the same time. There was no link—other than Eoin himself.

"I'd suspect that they were still distilling, but since the fall in popularity in gin, they must have acquired another means to earn enough blunt for an underground lair," Eoin said, his voice neutral as if the discussion had nothing to do with him. But despite his ability to hide the pain, Hannah knew he was hurting.

"The name still feels deucedly familiar." Lord Percy rubbed his forehead. "But I've never had anything to do with gin. I can't stand the vile stuff. It's like drinking a bouquet of flowers."

"Were any members of your family Jacobite sympathizers?" Matthew asked.

Lord Percy shook his head, and it was clear that he was only half listening. "My relatives have always been staunch royalists—or at least staunchly in favor of what lines their coffers and keeps them from troubling situations."

"At least we know the nom de guerre—the Purveyor," Eoin said before he turned to address Powys. "Would you be comfortable making inquiries into the name?"

Powys nodded. "Although I am afraid the results might be the same as when I've asked about the Horse and Hen."

"If people fall silent at the mere mention of the Purveyor, that is telling in and of itself," Sophia pointed out.

Hannah glanced over at Eoin as she thought about how the master of ceremonies had practically dragged him onto the stage. That image plagued her, along with a worry that she'd missed something vital.

"The Purveyor seems to know Eoin," Hannah said slowly, "or at least, Eoin attracted the fellow's attention."

Eoin shrugged. "It could be my size. It's not unusual for folks to espy my stature and wonder how good I am at fighting."

"But to stop the match between the women?" Hannah pointed out as she worried her bottom lip. "That's a way to anger customers and lose money. You were already presumed to be a contestant, so why rush matters?"

"I was turning to leave," Eoin said slowly, and Hannah could tell that he was reviewing the details in his mind. "But I agree that it was unusual to halt a fight. Yet I have no dealings with the Horse and Hen. Even though my mother worked there, it was over two decades ago. Would someone harbor that much animosity against her son?"

"But what if the Purveyor is someone you know?" Hannah asked, thinking once more about her suspicions that one or both of his uncles were involved in some underhanded business.

"Doubtful, although I suppose not entirely impossible," Eoin said. "I mainly associate with my grandfather's friends."

Calliope snorted. "I can't imagine any of those boring ancients venturing into the bowels of London to conduct nefarious business. They can barely bestir themselves to attend a ball. Their only pastime appears to be griping about the younger generations."

"She is not incorrect," Eoin agreed but more judiciously.

"But…" Hannah trailed off as she realized that she was about to reveal her suspicions about his uncles. Perhaps Eoin was right, and the Purveyor just wished to witness a fight between a mountainous fellow and one of the establishment's regulars. On the other hand, it had felt targeted, perhaps even personal, when Eoin had been forced into the ring. And Eoin needed to understand all the facts, so he could apply his own astute reasoning.

Hannah couldn't reveal the rumors about the Aucourtes in front of an audience, though. Even if Eoin was not close to his uncles, he needed privacy to grapple with his relatives' potential perfidy.

Lord Percy suddenly slammed his hand down on the table, pulling Hannah from her dilemma. When he spoke, his voice was loud and edged with frustration. "The fact that I've heard about the Horse and Hen must have something to do with boxing. It is the only possible link that I can deduce."

"Do you think you attended a match there?" Eoin asked.

Lord Percy's face screwed up. "Certainly not. I may be a rogue, but I don't like fights where the sole purpose is to watch the pulverization of a weaker opponent. There's no sportsmanship in that."

Both Cousin Alexander and Lord Percy were boxing enthusiasts, but Hannah couldn't imagine either of them attending a catfight.

And they certainly would never condone a brutal bout between youths.

"I wish Alexander was back from his honeymoon." Lord Percy sighed. "He is the one with all the knowledge about prizefighting."

"I can write to my brother. I'm sure he'll respond promptly," Charlotte offered.

"Surely there is someone else that we can ask? It is not as if boxing is an obscure pastime," Powys pointed out.

"We could head to Championess Quick's establishment," Hannah suggested.

Lord Percy nodded enthusiastically. "A brilliant plan! I can even introduce Eoin to the proprietress herself. She knows everything about London's boxing world—even the more unsavory parts. There's even a match tonight—one of the special late-night bouts that she holds for those bored with the ballroom."

"If that's the case, you two should leave immediately," Powys advised. "It starts soon, and traffic will be a snarl."

Eoin stood, and Hannah scrambled to her feet to join him. Percy was a bit slower, but he, too, rose.

"I'll tell my coachman to hurry," Eoin said.

———⚜———

The trip to Championess Quick's was starkly different from the journey to the Black Sheep. However, given Hannah's resolve not to further pursue a romantic relationship with Eoin until he knew the truth, the change in atmosphere was a very good thing... even if she might have yearned to return to that intimate ride.

The other major difference was the presence of Lord Percy, who Hannah discovered was an absolute prattle basket. The man never stopped chattering about the most inane things—the best wig maker in London, last week's horse race, the best of shoe buckle fashion, and countless other subjects that Hannah simply blocked out.

It was as if the man could not abide any silence, and since neither she nor Eoin seemed inclined to fill it, Percy clearly took it upon himself to prevent any gaps. Hannah knew she should be grateful. His presence prevented her from telling Eoin about the Aucourte mystery, and that, in turn, gave her a reprieve from revealing her own duplicity in agreeing to help Eoin search for his mother and his sister.

But the constant stream of stories never ended! Hannah's head was nearly pounding. Although Percy had always been on the glib side, Hannah didn't recall him being quite this loquacious.

"Oh, we're here!" Percy called out with more joviality than the situation merited. "I thought we'd never arrive."

Hannah—who was not exactly reticent herself—only managed a nod. Poor Eoin seemed poleaxed.

Percy practically bounced from the carriage. Hannah noticed that Eoin followed much more sedately, but there was a suppressed eagerness about his motions. It was as if he wanted to bolt at any moment but kept checking himself.

Hannah wished she could grab Eoin's hand, but she still wore male clothing. With her breasts rebound, she looked like a lad. But even if she were wearing female garb, she wouldn't have linked fingers with Eoin—no matter how badly the man needed the reassurance. She did not want Lord Percy detecting her and Eoin's mutual attraction. In the nob's current chattering state, Percy would likely reveal their nascent feelings to all and sundry, and that would be the opposite of comforting for Eoin.

"Is that Championess Quick's?" Eoin pointed his gloved thumb in the direction of a round Palladian building made of white-gray Portland stone. Doric columns arose around the entire structure, and Hannah had heard from Alexander that it was reminiscent of a small, modern version of the Colosseum.

The arched windows glowed a warm, welcoming yellow against the black sky. Such illumination would require a scandalous amount of candles—as much as would be burned during the grandest balls. The fact that Mistress Quick could afford to light so many spoke to her success.

Her amphitheater's preeminence was also made obvious by the throng gathered outside the massive doors. Like at the Horse and Hen, the men's clothing represented varying degrees of wealth. But at Championess Quick's, there were significantly more finely tailored silk coats and powdered wigs. Despite the different classes, they all mingled on the street as they waited their turn to file into the massive structure.

"This is a crush!" Percy said as he bounced on the balls of his feet. The jewels embedded in his gold shoe buckles glinted in the light pouring from the windows. "At least with this crowd, we have something interesting to discuss while we wait. Did you see Lord Polcenby's waistcoat? There must be an entire mine's worth of silver covering it!"

"It is, uh, very noticeable," Eoin said, clearly much less enthusiastic about the peer's choice of attire than Percy. His lackluster response, however, didn't prevent Percy from babbling about the quality of another man's wig.

Hannah was suddenly glad for Percy's constant stream of observations as she sidled closer to Eoin. He'd snapped his emotionless mask into place, but Hannah knew he was currently anything but stoic.

"Anxious?" Hannah asked Eoin softly when

Percy turned his head to study more of the crowd.

"Yes."

It touched her that Eoin trusted her enough not to prevaricate. Yet it also triggered a fresh stab of guilt.

"I wish I could squeeze your hand," Hannah admitted.

Eoin glanced down at her, the slightest of smiles gracing his lips. "Just knowing that is a comfort."

Hannah swallowed against the lump now occupying her throat. She wanted to assure Eoin that everything would be all right. But they both understood that his search could lead to nothing but pain.

"I realize decades have passed since my mother worked at the Horse and Hen, but I cannot help wondering if she ever encountered the Purveyor." Eoin held himself stiffly, but Hannah noticed that he was discreetly rubbing his thumb and his forefinger against each other. "During our first visit, I did mention to the tavern maid that I was looking for her. Mayhap you are right, and the Purveyor had another purpose behind ordering me to fight. I also haven't forgotten that older chap who stopped me in the street to warn me. Could everything be linked?"

Hannah glanced over at Percy to see if he was listening. But Percy had begun nattering to a gentleman nearby, so the fellow wouldn't hear Hannah and Eoin over Percy's commentary. Other nearby groups of young bucks were likewise engrossed in their own conversations.

Perhaps now was the time to confess—or at least partially reveal what Hannah suspected about Eoin's family. It was not ideal, but there never would be the perfect time to reveal the truth to him.

"Eoin, I should tell you that—"

"Lord Percy! What brings you to the bout tonight?" A woman's deep, throaty voice interrupted Hannah's statement.

Hannah turned to find Championess Quick warmly greeting their companion. Although the fifty-year-old no longer boxed competitively, she'd retained her athletic build. She was a tall woman who towered several inches above the average man, and she always wore clothing that showed off her muscular legs and arms. It was not salacious attire, though, and nothing like the bare-breasted women at the Horse and Hen. Championess Quick's freshly laundered Holland trousers and tightly laced navy blue corset bestowed upon her a neat, officious appearance. She always wore her brown and silver hair in a braided crown about her head, which Hannah found to be a clever nod to her legendary status in the ring. Standing bathed in the light pouring from the establishment that she had single-handedly built, Championess Quick seemed like an ancient Amazon warrior standing guard over her domain.

"And you have come, too, Mr. Wick." Championess Quick winked at Hannah as she was well aware that she was a miss, not a mister. It was the woman's usual greeting to her as Hannah occasionally frequented the establishment with Alexander.

But her prior visits weren't the reason why Championess Quick's blue-green gaze was so agonizingly familiar. It was because Hannah had spent a good portion of the afternoon staring into irises of the same tropical azure hue.

"And who is your companion…" Championess Quick's husky voice trailed off, and the woman—known for taking a male prizefighter's blow to the stomach with nary a blink—visibly flinched. Her bronzed cheeks drained of color, and those lagoon-colored eyes went hazy.

Eoin's voice—raw with hope and pain—filled the sudden silence with a single, hoarse word. "Mother?"

## Chapter Fifteen

Eoin sat across from his mother in the private sitting room located above the amphitheater. She had immediately ushered him to her living quarters when he'd blurted out their relationship on the crowded stairs. He doubted anyone had heard other than Hannah and Lord Percy. Still, he shouldn't have been so careless.

He had no idea if his mother even wanted to form a relationship with him—public or private. After all, she was the proprietress of one of London's premier entertainment facilities. She most certainly had heard about his grandfather's death, and she'd known exactly where to find him.

But she hadn't visited, hadn't even sent a missive.

It was highly likely that she didn't want Eoin intruding upon the life that she'd so carefully built. If he'd been thinking logically, he would have taken the proper precautions and not shouted out "Mother" like a lost six-year-old.

But in that moment, he'd felt like the child that he'd been—the boy who'd wept every night into his pillow, wanting his mama and his dear papa and even his treat-stealing older sister. Eoin had taken one look at his mother's face, and his hazy memories emerged from the fog to form into images with brilliantly sharp edges. Her hair was now threaded with silver and lines crinkled around her eyes, but Eoin had no trouble recognizing her as the woman who'd hovered just out of reach in his dreams.

But now she was before him, her face blank, her body stiff. Eoin supposed he'd inherited his stoicism from her. And like him, there were small tells attesting to her inner nervousness—the way she rubbed her thumb and her forefinger against each other, the slight unevenness to her breathing, and even the storminess deep within her eyes.

"Your sister should be here soon." Mama's voice wasn't as he'd remembered. Back then, she possessed an Irish lilt...or at least he thought she had. Perhaps his recollection was faulty or maybe she'd purposely hid her accent when she'd become Mrs. Quick.

Eoin gave a curt nod, afraid what his voice would do if he tried to speak. It might sound hoarse or high or maybe a combination of both. He had so much to say, yet he was afraid to speak any of it.

At least his mother had sent a servant to fetch his sister, Elizabeth. It meant she wasn't trying to obscure their blood connection—at least that's what Eoin hoped. He yearned to read her as well as he could others, but he was too nervous. His mind wouldn't focus, and it hurt to study her facial features.

He wished he'd brought Hannah with him to this sitting room. He longed for her support. But he hadn't wanted his mother to feel ill at ease or cornered. Instead, Hannah and Lord Percy were downstairs watching the match.

"I am sure you have many questions." His

mother's words were clipped, officious even. Did he sound like that? No wonder people called him unfeeling.

"Are you doing well?" Eoin glanced around him. Her salon was not as luxurious as those at his Mayfair residence, but not many could afford a separate room for entertaining. There were two comfortable-looking chairs by the fire, and he wondered if his mother and his sister sat there during the winter. There was a single figurine of a small boy on the mantel, but otherwise the place contained little ornamentation. A few books with half-broken spines lay on a simply carved side table, which was entirely functional. Except for a few samplers that Eoin assumed his sister had completed in her youth, there was no artwork. The walls, however, were painted a pleasing blue and decorated with a plain white trim. Someone, his sister most likely, had embroidered flowers on a fire screen.

The room was a snug, wholesome space—a family domain. And Eoin sorely wished this had been his home instead of a townhouse stuffed with formidable furniture from a long-ago era.

"That is the first question that you ask me?" His mother's voice no longer sounded steady.

At the hitch in her tone, Eoin jerked his attention back to his mother. Her green-blue eyes seemed shinier than before, and Eoin's heart ached. Were those unshed tears? And were they for him?

"It is why I looked for you and Elizabeth as soon as I inherited the title." Eoin thought that his own voice sounded shaky, but at least it wasn't cracking like a green lad's. "I wanted to ensure that you both had good lives."

His mother swallowed, and the sheen in her gaze only intensified. "As your parent, I should be the one asking about your well-being. I—I never wanted to allow your grandfather to take you, but the law was on his side."

"I remember you arguing and pleading with him," Eoin told her, somehow managing to speak despite the tightness of his throat. "Many other details faded from my memory but not that one."

But why hadn't she written to him after his grandfather's death? That haunted him, yet he could not bring himself to ask the question. He was too afraid of her reasoning.

"I didn't know if you would want to hear from Lizzie and me." His mother blurted out the answer to his unspoken inquiry. "I feared I would disrupt your life. I knew your grandfather would have tried to poison you against us."

A bitter relief poured through Eoin along with a sharp ire toward the late duke. Rage had festered inside himself for years, but to survive, he'd had to ignore the burning animosity.

"He did attempt to sever any connection that I felt toward you and Lizzie," Eoin said cautiously as he realized what he was admitting and how it made him vulnerable. But Hannah had been teaching Eoin to open up, and he didn't want to stay estranged from his mother and his sister. Eoin sucked in his breath and continued. "However, Foxglen never succeeded. But I…I am not demanding anything of you or of Elizabeth."

"You're not demanding anything of me?" There was a hollowness to the way his mother repeated his words, and her naturally red cheeks paled.

Eoin couldn't decipher precisely why his phrasing had upset her. Had she interpreted his statement to be an oblique threat?

"I know that my grandfather cast you aside with nothing." Eoin spoke tentatively at first, realizing that everything he was saying was an understatement. The old sot had tried to destroy any evidence that his son had sympathized with the Jacobite cause, and Eoin knew that the peer's purge had extended to Eoin's mother and sister.

Yet after Eoin's first cautious statement, the words that he was normally so judicious about flowed freely. "I was worried about the life that you may have been forced to lead. I am willing to give you and Elizabeth a generous allowance. I was going to offer to set you up with a house if you desired, although it is clear to me now that you are not in need of shelter. You have, quite remarkably, built your own empire. There is no obligation for you to have a relationship with me or to assume the duties of a duke's mother. But I am willing to welcome you both into my life and home if that is what you desire. If Elizabeth wants to reclaim her birthright as a noblewoman—"

"Me? A bloody nob?" A new voice rang through the room, and Eoin turned to see a younger version of his mother standing between the open pocket doors.

Elizabeth. He had a vague memory of a little girl with wildly curly hair; an impish, dimpled smile; and eyes as blue-green as his and his mother's.

Her gaze was the same and so were the dimples. Her hair had been tamed in a crown braid that mirrored their mother's—although Elizabeth's dark brown locks weren't threaded with shiny silver. And she was no longer a slip of a girl. She was an inch or two taller than their mother, although Eoin still towered over her. As a pugilist, she had an athletic build. Eoin knew little about her, but Hannah had whispered before he'd left with his mother that Elizabeth had become an expert with the quarterstaff.

"You grew up, little brother!" Elizabeth crossed the room in four giant strides and immediately enfolded him in her arms.

He stiffened, unsure of how to accept a familial embrace. Elizabeth, however, didn't seem to mind as she gave him a quick squeeze before stepping back. Her grin remained broad as she openly studied him.

"You look like a prizefighter," Elizabeth announced with a pleased nod. She smiled so broadly that Eoin felt his lips tip upward in an instinctual response. He was so accustomed to his relatives criticizing his physique that he barely understood how to react to her praise beyond that ghost of a grin.

"See, I told you we should send Eoin a missive when that old bastard was finally put to bed with a shovel." Elizabeth turned to her mother, who was still standing at attention. Elizabeth whirled back around and clasped his hands. "We have missed you sorely, especially Mama. With my first prize money, I bought that little boy figurine for her, so it felt like we had a little bit of you in our home."

Tears stung the backs of Eoin's eyes, and his knees weakened. For a moment, he very much feared that he would collapse on top of Elizabeth. Although she clearly possessed muscles, she wouldn't be able to hold up his massive weight.

"May I... may I sit?" Eoin asked.

"Of course," his mother said, instantly rushing to his side and leading him to the small settee across from the fire. As soon as he was seated, she lowered herself into one of the chairs by the fire. Elizabeth, though, plopped down next to Eoin. He was quickly learning that what his sister lacked in grace, she made up for in exuberance.

"I am so happy you came." Elizabeth scooched against him. "Mama was afraid you wouldn't want to see us."

"I did not want to intrude on your life or make you think that I was after your blunt," his mother said, her voice a quiet, calm contrast to Elizabeth's.

"She made her own fortune, you know." Elizabeth squared her shoulders and beamed proudly over at their mother. "It wasn't easy living under fake names, knowing that the duke would have her transported to the Colonies and me tossed into the workhouse if a single whisper of us ever reached his ears."

Eoin's stomach sloshed uncomfortably, and for a moment, he thought he might be ill all over his mother's neatly swept floor. But he managed to force back the nausea.

"Lizzie," their mother admonished her, but Eoin raised his hand.

"No," he said hoarsely. "I want to hear. I want to know. That's why I've been searching for you."

Elizabeth slung her arm around his shoulders and pulled him into a rough hug. "You were always such a sweet baby brother, even if you could be annoying at times. I knew Grandfather couldn't change that."

Eoin glanced over at his mother, wishing she wasn't trying so hard to protect him. "Did you fight at the Horse and Hen? What I saw there…"

"You were at the Horse and Hen?" His mother—who was already sitting stiffly—nearly bolted from her seat.

Eoin nodded. "With Miss Hannah Wick. I was searching for you, and it was the only clue we could discover."

"Don't darken those doors again!" The

words were obviously an instinctive maternal command, and Eoin literally basked in her scolding tone as if she'd praised him. Unfortunately, she instantly realized that she'd been rebuking him, and she retreated back into anxious politeness. "What I meant to say is that the Horse and Hen is a dangerous place. I would not be so bold, however, as to give you commands."

"I am your son," Eoin said, and a whoosh of emotion rushed through him at the statement. "You never abandoned me. I want you to fuss over me, to act as my parent."

His mother managed to execute a curt nod, and then her face crumpled. She quickly glanced away, and her shoulders heaved in silent sobs. The sight rooted Eoin to his seat until Elizabeth nudged him.

"Go. Hug her. You both need it."

Eoin capitulated immediately. He bolted from the settee. When he reached his mother's side, he bent over and enfolded her in his arms. She shifted, clinging to his shoulders. When he felt her tears through his layers of clothing, something broke loose inside him. A sob tore from him—and for once, intense emotion didn't shame him. All his bottled-up fear and anger and pain came tumbling out from where he'd buried them. He became a lost little boy again, and he and his mother hung on to each other. Together, they poured out the grief that had been stolen from them too.

---

"You two should be wary of the Horse and Hen, and anything to do with it," Eoin's mother warned him and Hannah as they sat next to each other on the settee.

After Eoin and his mother had sobbed together, she and Elizabeth had demanded to know more about his misadventures. He'd asked if Hannah could join them for the recounting, and his family had readily agreed. Elizabeth, though, studied them closely. Her scrutiny had started when Hannah had squeezed in next to him rather than taking one of the chairs.

"Were you a fighter at the Horse and Hen, Mother?" Eoin asked again, wishing that he could hold Hannah's hand. However, Elizabeth would absolutely notice.

"Not under the current establishment," his mother explained. "But I was a participant when the tavern was operated by those sympathetic to reform. The money was good, and there were rules in place to promote sportsmanship. Eye gouging and hair pulling were banned, and we fought fully clothed. Moreover, some of the pot was given to charities that helped the Irish community in St. Giles."

More relief filled Eoin. Although he didn't like imagining his mother or sister absorbing blows in the ring, at least they hadn't suffered the depravity that he'd witnessed at the Horse and Hen.

"How did you become Championess Quick?" Eoin asked, hoping that the question would not cause her more pain.

"After your father's death and your grandfather's threats, I needed a way to earn coin to support Lizzie and myself. Most of my friends were dead, in prison, or deported. I started fighting again. But what ended up saving me was that your father had taught me to read. I saw an advertisement for women fighters from John Pippen. He mostly organized professional prizefights for men, but on occasion, he arranged matches featuring his wife, Alice, and other women. He wanted a contender to replace Alice as she was getting too old for sparring. I showed up and impressed both Jane and John with my skills. Alice had a soft spot for Lizzie, and the Pippens ended up training me not just as a fighter but as a promoter. I had a knack for advertising bouts, so I took over the business when they retired."

"So you and Elizabeth...you both have had a good life?" Eoin asked haltingly as the wretched tension in his stomach began to uncoil.

"Aye," his mother said.

"Much better than if I'd been raised as the granddaughter of a duke," Elizabeth said, punctuating her words with a hearty laugh. "I'm much more suited to the ring than the ballroom. Dancing is boring if you're not using your footwork to dodge a well-placed blow. I don't think nobs would take kindly to me landing a facer on one of them. Oh, and

I haven't been Elizabeth for years. Call me Lizzie."

"You're not interested in assuming your position in Society, El... Lizzie?" Eoin asked, and disappointment flickered inside him. He'd told himself he'd be content if his mother and his sister wanted nothing from him, yet part of him still had hoped for some sort of a relationship. Although he was fairly certain that he'd masked the sliver of hurt, Hannah surreptitiously stroked his pinkie finger with her own.

"I want to be your big sister again, but I've no interest in becoming a lady. Too many rules and even more yards of fabric." Elizabeth—no, Lizzie now—pretended to theatrically shudder. "But I'll even endure uncomfortable dresses if it means being part of your life."

"I promise that I won't try to change you. Either of you." Swounds, tears were burning in Eoin's eyes once more. He had a sister who was willing to fit into a world that she despised just to be close to him. But Eoin meant what he'd said. He knew the pain of being molded into someone else's image, and he'd never force that upon Lizzie or his mother.

"There will be a scandal if it becomes known that Championess Quick is the mother of the Duke of Foxglen, especially if I do not close the establishment permanently. If we are to have a relationship, it will be necessary to shutter or sell the amphitheater." Nary an emotion showed in his mother's voice, but Eoin understood how much the words cost her. His heart squeezed as he realized how much she loved him. She was prepared to walk away from the culmination of years of hard work just to protect his reputation. And as much as his mother's sacrifice touched Eoin, he would never let her destroy her amphitheater.

"You, Lizzie, and I have already lost too much to protect the Aucourte legacy. We should not ransom anything else precious to us to protect an empty title," Eoin said, and he felt Hannah jerk beside him. Had she thought he'd order his mother to terminate her business? Hurt pricked at Eoin. He did have a reputation for callousness, but surely Hannah comprehended his motivations. After all, he'd explicitly explained them to her. But perhaps he was the one misunderstanding her reaction.

"But there will be rumors—vicious ones." This time emotion seeped into his mother's voice. Her worry for him was palpable.

"I am the Duke of Foxglen. I can weather tittle-tattle if you and Lizzie are able to bear it too," Eoin promised.

"Oh, I like causing scandals," Lizzie said. "Remember when I challenged the Duke of Blackglen to a bout and then beat him soundly? The caricatures of me were fabulously hilarious. I looked like a cross between an Amazon warrior and a living mountain."

Eoin failed to see the humor. Although he was not generally prone to physical violence, he found his fingers clenching, almost of their own accord. What print shops had dared to produce such drivel against his sister? She might be a modern Amazonian, but she did not look at all like a giant land formation.

"You fought Blackglen?" Hannah piped up, respect lacing her voice.

"Oh yes. It was years ago when we were both nineteen. He made disparaging remarks about women prizefighters that I simply would not let stand. Hedonistic, conceited nob.

Handsome devil, though." Lizzie laughed again, and another old memory burst back to life. Not of Eoin's sister, but of his parents gathered around the fire. Papa had said something witty, and Mama had chuckled just like that.

"But we have plenty of time to catch up and even to discuss the future," his mother said. "What I need to know now is that you're done visiting the Horse and Hen."

"Why are you so insistent that we don't return?" Eoin asked as his alarm reawakened. Was his mother hiding from someone other than his grandfather? "Does it have something to do with the Purveyor?"

"Who?" His mother's voice was back to being even, but she was rubbing her fingers together. Was she only pretending not to know who the person was? Or did this entire conversation make her nervous?

"We only know the nom de guerre and that this Purveyor holds sway in that part of Covent Garden," Eoin explained.

Hannah was staying unusually quiet, and Eoin realized she wanted to be as unintrusive as possible for his sake. His whole life, he'd been the one forced to adjust to others' needs. But Hannah...bold, intrepid Hannah...was considerate of him.

"I only know pieces of what happened in the aftermath of your father's death," his mother explained. "The Duke of Foxglen was ashamed that his son was involved in a pro-reform, anti-Hanoverian movement. He and others called us Jacobites—and although we wanted to restore the Catholic-sympathizing Stewarts to the throne, we were not traditional conservatives. We simply wanted better treatment for the Irish, Scots, and common folks. But that mattered little to Foxglen and the Royalists. With Foxglen leading the charge, our entire organization was rooted out. The Horse and Hen was a large complex of buildings—all operations for our political and charitable endeavors. When the warren of buildings fell to disuse, a shadowy figure claimed the entire complex—at least from the rumors that I heard. I tried to avoid any whispers about the Horse and Hen. It hurt too badly, and I wanted to avoid any connection with that place. I didn't want Foxglen to hear anything about me, or he might have carried through with his threat."

"Do you know why the Horse and Hen was taken over by another party?" Eoin asked.

"I assume for gin making. It was profitable at the time, and there are many rooms that are only accessible through the cellar of the Horse and Hen. Some of the passages twist through the entire length of the close, and the rooms are walled off from the actual buildings that they're situated inside of. It is akin to a spider's web. The leader of our reform movement trusted no one—rightfully so, as it turned out. An ideal sanctuary for dissidents would also suit criminals. There were plenty of places where stills could be set up entirely unnoticed." Although his mother's voice remained neutral, she had begun to rub the base of her neck—a clear sign of her distress.

Eoin wouldn't press her further. At least for now.

An enigma still remained. The underground boxing ring was likely an elaborate blind to hide illegal activities. Somewhere in the network of interconnected rooms, something nefarious was occurring.

Now was not the time for Eoin to unravel the mystery, though. His mother, sister, and Hannah needed to be his priority. He had to make sure they were well protected before taking any more action. And why would this specter wish to haunt him, especially if Eoin avoided that stretch of Covent Garden until he had adequate defenses in place?

Still, Eoin couldn't completely stamp out a nascent feeling of misgiving that perhaps he should not delay further inquiries. After all, he had attracted the attention of the Purveyor.

## Chapter Sixteen

"Could I speak with you privately, Miss Wick?" Lizzie asked.

Hannah noticed that the prizefighter had lowered her voice a few notches, and perhaps she thought she was whispering. She was not. Her words boomed through the Quicks' sitting room, but fortunately, Eoin and his mother did not seem to notice. They were huddled together on the settee, exchanging stories, and Hannah had been wondering how to politely extricate herself.

"Most assuredly," Hannah told Lizzie. She thought she did a better job at softening her voice than the prizefighter, but then again, she'd been accused more than once of being overly loud.

Lizzie nodded and led Hannah down a

short hallway that seemingly terminated at a wall lined with two bookcases. Lizzie moved in front of the tomes and curios, using her tall body to shield her motions from Hannah's view. Within a few seconds, the shelves shifted, revealing a hidden door. Clearly, Championess Quick had retained a few tricks from her dissident past.

Hannah followed Lizzie into a narrow room that ran parallel to an intriguing wall containing four deeply recessed arrow slits shaped into tulips. They reminded Hannah of illustrations of medieval towers, but the windows were not perches for archers. Each had a comfortable cushion, roomy enough for one person to sit comfortably upon. Lizzie waved for Hannah to slide onto one, and she eagerly complied. She found herself staring down into the boxing ring.

"I never knew this place existed!" Hannah cried out excitedly.

"That is the point," Lizzie said without any attempt to temper the bluntness of her words. Hannah, who also had a reputation for frankness, found that she didn't mind Lizzie's.

"It is a fabulous view." Hannah peered down at the two female prizefighters. They were not boxing with their fists but instead were using quarterstaffs. The weapon was both Championess Quick's and her daughter's specialty. The wooden rods whistled through the air until they cracked together, the sound echoing around the roof of the circular amphitheater despite competition from the crowd's roar. The women dodged and spun, always staying on the balls of their feet like expert dancers. Each strike came with swift precision. There was no flailing and wild strikes at Championess Quick's. All of her contestants—male or female—possessed a keen, practiced edge.

"Impressive. Is it not?" Lizzie asked as she stood behind Hannah, rather than sitting in her own arrow slit to watch the action.

"Yes. It is always a grand spectacle when I come to Championess Quick's." Hannah pressed closer to the opening as she watched the action below her. Although her focus primarily remained on Jane and Anne, she could see most of the gathered throng. She even spotted Lord Percy cheering from one of the higher seats. Nearer to the stage, the poorer folks stood in a pit, gesticulating enthusiastically with each clunk of the staffs.

Energy crackled through the air, but it felt remarkably different from the danger-tinged frenzy at the Horse and Hen. This crowd wanted skill, not blood.

"You have been to our establishment before?" Lizzie asked. Unlike her mother, she didn't greet their patrons, and perhaps she also hadn't inherited the Championess's uncanny ability to recognize and name each and every customer.

"Yes." Hannah nodded. "I am a cousin to one of your most ardent patrons, Alex—I mean the new Duke of Falcondale."

"You are a nob, then."

Hannah's neck began to tingle, and she turned to discover Lizzie regarding her with extreme intensity. Although Hannah generally didn't mind scrutiny after spending her childhood in a crowded coffeehouse, a sense of awkward unease slipped through her. She felt judged.

"Hardly. My mother was the daughter of a peer, but she ran off with a pirate—my father.

I'm a proprietress of a coffeehouse along with my cousin Sophia Wick," Hannah explained, feeling a deep-set need to defend herself.

"Oh. I have heard about you. Your story reminded me of my own family's." Although Lizzie was pointing out their similarities, Hannah still felt that the woman was purposely maintaining a distance. Perhaps it was just a trait of a prizefighter—always sizing up opponents.

"Yes, our pasts do bear a resemblance to each other," Hannah agreed, deciding that it was best not to point out the significant difference between their tales. Lizzie, as the lawful issue of a man holding the courtesy title of marquess, was rightfully Lady Elizabeth. Although Hannah was also legitimate, she was the child of a disgraced gentlewoman and therefore not considered part of the nobility at all. Given that Lizzie did not appear particularly enamored of her rightful position in Society, Hannah didn't think that the prizefighter would appreciate being told that she was actually a nob herself.

"Have you watched me spar?" Lizzie asked, her voice deceptively casual, but Hannah sensed an underlying tension.

"I have," Hannah admitted cautiously as she hung on to the last syllable perhaps a beat too long.

Lizzie, however, continued to plow through the conversation the same way she boldly strode across the ring at the start of a match. "You are aware of my talent, then?"

"I am," Hannah admitted as the unsettled feeling inside her began to churn. It almost sounded as if Lizzie wished to challenge Hannah to a fight. Although Hannah had been taught to defend herself, she could never hold her own against someone of Lizzie's caliber—no matter if they fought with their fists, quarterstaffs, or another weapon.

"What is your relationship with my brother?" Lizzie crossed her arms, and Hannah could see her biceps flex under her shirt's pristine white linen. Hannah sucked in a breath, and the air tickled her suddenly dry throat.

"We are—" Hannah began and then paused. She had no idea how to define her relationship with Eoin. It was not as if they'd discussed it. Something was developing between them, an affection and comradeship that Hannah would never deny. But she should be having this conversation with Eoin instead of his sister.

"We are friends," Hannah finally concluded, pleased by how confident she sounded.

Lizzie, however, was clearly not impressed.

"I would not categorize what I have witnessed between you and my brother to be merely comradeship."

Lizzie's brow drew downward, and Hannah suppressed a shiver. Is this what the prizefighter's opponents experienced before a match? Hannah suddenly felt very trapped, wedged inside the recessed alcove with Lizzie glowering over her.

"Eoin and I grew close during our search for you and your mother." Hannah nearly squeaked out the excuse, and Lizzie's mouth twitched.

"Why did you agree to help my brother?"

*Because I want to destroy your paternal family.* The truth was probably not the best answer. Although Hannah doubted that Lizzie cared about her aunts and uncles, she certainly treasured her long-lost sibling.

"Eoin came to the Black Sheep for assistance."

"Why would he do that?" Lizzie asked.

"Because he was alone and had no one else to help in his search for you and your mother." And Hannah had taken advantage of Eoin's need. "He was aware that members of the Black Sheep had solved other mysteries, so he visited our establishment."

"Did you agree to aid him for a sum of money? My brother is exceedingly wealthy now that Foxglen is dead." Lizzie cocked her head, and Hannah fought the urge to instinctively duck. It felt like the woman could throw a facer at any time.

"My coffeehouse is successful." Hannah resisted the urge to cross her own arms. She didn't want to seem as if she was challenging Lizzie. Still, she couldn't help a swell of defensiveness. "I have no need to become a man's mistress."

"Yet judging by the tale that Eoin told my mother and me, you inserted yourself into my brother's household rather quickly." Lizzie leaned forward a smidgen more.

Hannah sank her fingers into the cushion and did her best not to scoot backward.

Although she couldn't move very far, she did have a few inches before she would collide with the wall.

"Masquerading as his mistress was the most efficient way to gather information. You cannot deny that my ploy worked. We found you and your mother very rapidly all because we pursued a clue that I learned from breakfasting with your aunts and uncles."

"They are not my relatives," Lizzie said stiffly. "They never claimed me, and I certainly do not claim them."

"Your brother does not have that luxury." Hannah knew that it was not Lizzie's fault that her brother had endured his paternal family's hatred, but she was tired of Lizzie's half-veiled accusations. The woman was striking at the heart of Hannah's guilt. And if Lizzie wanted to interject herself into Eoin's life, then she needed to deal with their horrible relatives.

"Do you care for my brother?" Lizzie asked.

Hannah had no difficulties answering that. "Very much so. He is kind and thoughtful even though his grandfather tried to teach him to be cool and distant. I never had much use for nobs until I met him."

"As a young child, he was a sensitive sort—always making presents out of scraps of cloth and twine for my parents and me. Mother constantly worried about him being under the tutelage of Foxglen. Even though we were forced to leave him, he was and is very precious to us."

And he was very precious to Hannah too. "You should tell Eoin those very words. He needs to hear them."

Lizzie visibly relaxed a fraction—but only a fraction. She still loomed over Hannah, although Hannah had begun to wonder if looming was Lizzie's natural state.

"I shall tell my brother how much I care for him. I may not like the world he inhabits, but I will not abandon him now that I have a choice to be in his life."

Hannah nodded. It seemed as if they'd reached some sort of understanding. Yet Lizzie still stood close... too close.

"You should watch the bout again. Jane is about to defeat Anne."

Hannah glanced toward the contest below.

Even though she tried to lose herself in the action, she could feel Lizzie lurking behind her. Prickles rose over Hannah's flesh, and she tried to ignore them. It was apparent that Lizzie was acting in the same protective manner that Hannah did when a man showed interest in Sophia. Yet even if Hannah recognized the sentiment, it was uncomfortable being on the receiving end.

"Jane seems to be flagging. Is that part of her strategy?" Hannah asked, more from uncharacteristic nervousness than from true interest.

"Aye. She's clever, but she's never managed to fool me."

As Anne struck out, Jane suddenly burst back with renewed vigor. Her staff clipped the edge of Anne's, and the clack reverberated around the room. Anne's rod flew into the air. She pirouetted gracefully, narrowly missing a strike from Jane. Incredibly, Anne caught her weapon before it hit the ground. Bending half over, she snapped back up to block another blow. But she was on the defensive now, and Jane was clearly in control. The end was a whirlwind of motion, their quarterstaffs nothing but whistling brown blurs in the air, their feet bouncing in an intricate dance. Anne fought hard, but Jane ultimately outmaneuvered her. As Jane raised her fists in triumph, the crowd roared.

"They are both very talented, are they not?" Lizzie asked, leaning over Hannah's shoulder.

"They are."

"I am more skilled than both of them put together." Lizzie's claim was not spoken as a boast but as a simple matter of fact.

"I am aware." Hannah very slowly swiveled in Lizzie's direction.

The prizefighter was smiling. It was not a friendly one.

"Good. Then you know how swiftly I can mete out justice."

"Are you…planning to…mete out justice?" Hannah's throat went tight, and her normal bravado seemed to have woefully fled.

"That depends if it's needed." Lizzie's grin had grown to ominous proportions. "Will it be?"

"Pardon?"

"Will the meting out of justice be required? It is, after all, your choice." Lizzie's lips tipped upward into even more chill-inducing heights.

"My choice?"

"Do not hurt my little brother. If you treat him properly, I believe we may become fast friends. However, don't even consider playing with his emotions. If you do, I will be the one toying with you."

---

"It should be dawn soon." Eoin broke the silence that had fallen over the carriage ever since they had dropped off Lord Percy at his home.

Eoin drew back the thick curtains to reveal a still darkened London. Only the moon and the light from a few open establishments illuminated the way.

"Yes," Hannah said, although she only half heard Eoin. She was steeping in her own guilt and debating if she should tell Eoin the truth about her connection to the Aucourtes. After all, he'd found his family and obviously had their support.

Yet should Hannah puncture Eoin's joy so soon? Shouldn't she allow him to bask a bit in this triumph?

*However, don't even consider playing with his emotions. If you do, I will be the one toying with you.*

Lizzie's threat echoed in Hannah's head, but the memory of his mother's words gave her the most pause. Championess Quick had pulled Hannah aside before she'd climbed into the carriage with Eoin and Lord Percy. The woman's implacable mien suddenly crumbled, and Hannah had witnessed the decades of heartache. *Thank you, Miss Wick, for helping my son. I sense you mean a lot to him. Please continue to keep watch over Eoin. I am afraid these next few weeks will be challenging ones indeed when the truth of our relationship is revealed. I am glad you will be by his side.*

"I do not feel like retiring to bed," Eoin said as the hackney drew up to Aucourte House. "Perhaps I'll sit in the gardens."

"Do you wish for me to join you?" Hannah asked, torn between wanting him to say yes and declining.

"I wouldn't want to inconvenience you."

"You wouldn't be," Hannah said quickly. If Eoin didn't wish to be alone after tonight's revelations, then Hannah wouldn't abandon him.

A shy smile touched Eoin's lips, and Hannah instantly melted. This man had a way of seeping into her heart.

They quickly debarked from the carriage. Instead of heading to the front door, Eoin led Hannah to the garden gate. She could detect the sweet scent of honeysuckle mixed with the more pungent lavender. "It smells like a cottage garden."

"My understanding is that my late grandmother planted it," Eoin said as he stretched out his fingers in her direction, his white glove glowing in the silvery moonlight. "Here, take my hand. There are quite a few plants stuffed into a small space. They're all overgrown, and the paving stones are uneven and crumbling."

As Hannah threaded her bare fingers between his, she could feel his warmth. A magical sensation stole over her as they slipped through the fragrant, late summer blossoms. Stems brushed against her stocking-covered legs and her boy's breeches. It was strange to discover a little of the countryside's wildness behind the immense townhouse of a duke—especially the former Foxglen's residence.

"I am surprised that the previous duke allowed such a tangle of flowers on his property," Hannah said as she brushed her free hand against the foliage. The scent of mint joined the other pleasant odors. "Did he have affections for his late wife?"

Eoin snorted, the sound harsh. "I do not believe that my grandfather suffered from any emotions of the heart. He cared only about his title and the legacy of the Aucourtes. His marriage to my grandmother was strategic. Her family's lands bordered the ducal estate, and her dowry included a nice plot. He mentioned more than once that he blamed her for my father's dramatic tumble from grace even though she'd died years before his downfall."

"Why would he fault your grandmother?" Hannah asked as Eoin stopped in front of an overgrown arched trellis with a crumbling stone bench beneath it.

"This garden is a perfect example of my grandfather's frustrations with his late duchess," Eoin explained as he sat down and gently tugged Hannah after him. Although Hannah knew it wasn't wise, she couldn't help but snuggle against him. Their conversation seemed random, but Hannah sensed some importance in it—a key perhaps to understanding Eoin's lonely childhood. "My grandmother planted common English posies—even wildflowers—because it reminded her of the small village near her parents' country estate that she loved to stroll around as a young lady. The old duke claimed such acts of whimsy and pleasure in common things influenced my father to sympathize with those allegedly beneath him."

"Knowing your grandfather's temperament, I am surprised that he didn't raze the plants and erect a formal garden." Hannah gave in to temptation and leaned her cheek against Eoin's arm. She could not reach his shoulder, but his broad biceps made a perfect—if hard—headrest.

"I don't think he wished to expend the money. He had little use for the outdoors. He preferred a domain that he had complete control over. Nature, even organized landscapes, displeased him. After all, pruned bushes sprout unwanted branches." Eoin's voice rumbled through Hannah, and she swore she could feel his hidden pain. Hannah suspected that Eoin had been nothing but a piece of shrubbery to Foxglen, and any part of Eoin that had not pleased the duke would have been ruthlessly clipped away.

"You seem familiar with this garden." Hannah squeezed his fingers and then began to trace his palm with her thumb.

"It was my secret escape." Eoin laid his cheek on the crown of Hannah's head—surprising her with the intimacy of the gesture. He was clearly a man who never allowed himself to unbend, but here he was, snuggling with her among the honeysuckle and hollyhocks. "My grandfather did not hear well, and I could sneak away at night. I suspect that the servants knew of my midnight forays, and perhaps even my aunts and uncles did as well. Fortunately, no one ever told him. Even on cold winter nights after I'd suffered through a particularly scathing lecture, I would disappear to this very bench and stare at the stars. I would wonder if my mother and sister were gazing at the same ones. A trite gesture—but it made me feel closer to them."

Hannah's heart flopped in her chest. How did anyone ever call this sentimental man callous?

"I don't find it trite but sweet. And having met your mother and sister, I would not be surprised at all if they'd glanced at the night sky while missing you." Hannah moved her head against his chest now, and she could hear the steady thud of his heart.

"They did seem to have missed me." The wonder in Eoin's voice caused tears to prick the backs of Hannah's eyes. This wonderful man had deserved so much more affection than he'd been given.

Eoin bent to whisper his next words in her ear. "Without you, I do not know if I would have ever found them. I am very grateful that you chose to take pity on me that day at the Black Sheep."

Hannah, however, felt no pleasure in his heartfelt words. Instead, renewed guilt blasted her. "I'm glad to have helped, but it was your own diligence that made it happen."

Eoin straightened, and his gaze locked on some indeterminate spot among the shadowy, moonlit plants. When he did speak, his normally measured voice alternated between hesitancy and then rapidity as if his words had been dammed up and then came out in a single rush before a new set became snagged once more. "You...you do not need to return to the Black Sheep immediately...I mean to say that you can if you want, but there is no need to rush on my part. I...well...I...well, I enjoy your company, Hannah...and it is good to have you here tonight...with all that has happened."

In her turmoil over her original reasons for assisting Eoin, Hannah had utterly forgotten that she no longer had a reason to stay in his residence. Since she had discovered nothing about his aunts and uncles beyond their knowledge of Eoin's mother, she should have been scrambling for excuses to stay. The fact that she hadn't thought of strategizing was almost a relief. She evidently was not entirely mercenary. Unfortunately, her lack of foresight awoke a new sense of guilt. Was she abandoning her family's pain to help heal Eoin's?

His wounds were fresh, and although her father and uncle bore scars—both literal and figurative—the rawness had healed over. However, was even this rationale a sign of disloyalty to her family?

Ugh! It was a frightful mess.

"I suppose from your silence you do not wish…" Eoin's nervousness was palpable, and his anxiousness broke Hannah out of her stupor.

"Oh no! That is not it at all. I was only trying to determine how long I can be away from the coffeehouse. I do not want to shift too much of the burden onto my cousins." The excuse flew from Hannah's mouth before she thought about its implications.

"Then you do wish to stay on for a bit more!" Eoin wrapped his large form around hers, enfolding her into his jubilation.

Bloody hell. She should leave for his sake. But she hated destroying his joy. Besides, she wanted to remain with Eoin, and not because of her investigation.

"Although I didn't let on to Mother and Lizzie, I am not completely sanguine about facing the gossip when the ton realizes that I am the son of Championess Quick. Still, with you by my side, I'll weather the rumors better. You're always so practical, and I know you have no care for what the nobles say."

Eoin was chattering—actually chattering—with excitement. Even his body vibrated with enthusiasm. Could Hannah renege now? She needn't stay for long—no more than a week or so. It would be best if she gave Eoin time to adjust to his new circumstances before she revealed the whole truth.

"It won't be much of a strain on Sophia and Charlotte if I remain here a few days. We didn't anticipate that we'd find your mother and sister so quickly." Hannah paused, debating if she should say the next words. But then she made the fatal mistake of shifting in Eoin's arms and meeting his gaze. The expectant hope in his sea-blue eyes undid her. "And I want to spend more time with you, Eoin, just as we are right now."

# Chapter Seventeen

Eoin had never experienced such joy. His mother and his sister had both openly embraced him. They hadn't asked him to change. Instead, they were the ones willing to uproot their lives. And that... that helped heal hurts that Eoin had long since stopped recognizing.

Now Hannah was staying longer at his home, for no other reason than the fact that she wished to spend more time with him. The glory of that news blazed through Eoin, setting every inch of him ablaze with sweet fire.

Caught in the wonder of bliss, Eoin dipped his head to capture Hannah's mouth with his. But just as his lips touched her soft ones, a terrible hissing arose from the ground.

"Ouch! Ouch!" Hannah pulled back and began to rub furiously at her ankles.

"What happened?" Eoin asked in bewildered concern. He glanced around the shadows, trying to locate what had caused Hannah's distress. Then he heard it. The familiar chirping.

The gosling had found them.

Peering down, he saw an angry shadow darting around Hannah's feet. Reaching for it, he captured the enraged fluff. He could feel some of the rougher juvenile feathers poking out from the down as its stubby wings beat against his knuckles.

"How did you get into the garden?" Eoin asked and then felt ridiculous.

At the sound of his voice, the bird settled and began to chirp happily. Eoin supposed he should be grateful that the creature wasn't honking yet.

"Most likely, the gosling was bothering one of your aunts or uncles," Hannah surmised. "I don't think your servants would have tossed your pet into the wild."

Eoin grunted. "The fowl is not my pet, and this garden is hardly wild."

"Regardless of how you view it, the goose

has most definitely adopted you as its mama." Hannah nudged Eoin's shoulder, which the baby bird did not appreciate in the least. The fluff extended its still relatively stubby neck, its useless wings bouncing furiously.

Eoin shot Hannah a withering look, which was probably lost in the darkness. Still, the expression made him feel better. "I am not the fowl's mother."

"I do believe that it is past time to name your baby. You cannot keep calling it *the fowl*," Hannah teased. "Isn't that right, Little Bubbles?"

"I am not naming the bird Bubbles. That would be absurd."

"Ah. But you will be giving it an appropriate appellation, then?"

"You hoodwinked me into that, didn't you?" Eoin accused in exasperation.

Hannah laughed merrily. "Perhaps. But more importantly, what shall you choose?"

"Gosling? Goose?"

Hannah chuckled again, and the sound of her mirth filled Eoin. He wanted more of this. Yearned for it. What would life be like with Hannah constantly by his side?

"Those are rather uninspired choices, especially for a bird with so much personality."

Eoin lifted the fluff to scrutinize it, but he couldn't see much in the dark. No inspiration came. "Mayhap you should name it?"

"Oh no. I wouldn't dare. It's your pet."

Eoin decided it was futile to debate the fowl's status in his life. Instead, he bent to place the small animal on the ground near their feet.

"Aren't you afraid she'll wander off?" Hannah asked.

Eoin glanced down at the little mite even though he couldn't properly see it. "Not with me here. It'll faithfully stick by my side."

"Ah! So you do admit that you've become a mother to it!"

"Will my capitulation make you happy?" Eoin cast a sideways glance in Hannah's direction. In the low light, he could just spy the outline of her profile, but he wished he could fully see her pink lips parted in laughter and the happy flush touching her pale cheeks.

"Exceedingly so."

A rare chuckle escaped Eoin. "Then I

suppose that I have no choice but to claim parentage to it."

"Her," Hannah said definitively.

"Her?" Eoin pointed at the chick, who was most likely munching happily on bugs. "However can you tell? It is just a ball of fluff that is sprouting feathers."

Hannah shrugged but did not appear shaken in her conviction. "I simply have a feeling that the goose is female. She has that air about her."

Giddy joy shot through Eoin. Unable to contain it, he nearly doubled over with laughter.

"What?" Hannah asked. "Can't you sense it as well?"

"Noooooooo." The denial came out as a helpless, uneven howl.

"Well, I can," Hannah replied loftily.

Eoin tried to get his chuckles under control but found that he simply could not. He realized that he wanted to kiss Hannah—to share this glee with her. Acting on instinct, he started to bend his head in her direction, but then he froze.

"Why are you stopping?" Hannah asked as

she threaded her arms about his neck. "I want to— Owwww!"

"That is why," Eoin explained. "I didn't want you to get pecked again."

"Hmmmm." Hannah kept her hands interlocked behind his head as she glanced down speculatively at the still-unnamed menace. "I believe my ankles can endure, especially since the rest of me will be suffused in pleasure."

Heady need shot through Eoin, and his bliss burst into flames of want. "Suffused in pleasure? I make you feel...like that?"

"Most assuredly!"

Hannah gently tugged him toward her, and his heart bumped furiously in his chest. With his blood pounding this hard, he doubted that he would even hear the gosling's hisses. He hoped Hannah's legs wouldn't suffer too—

*Rawrrrrrrr!*

Eoin jerked away from Hannah. For a brief moment, he stared dimwittedly at the fowl despite the absurdity of the sound emanating from it.

*Rawrrrrrrrr!*

Hannah's nails dug into Eoin's shoulder as they both whipped their heads in the direction of the roar.

"That—that sounded like a bear!" Hannah's voice hovered between disbelief and terror.

"I agree," Eoin said grimly as he launched himself to his feet. The growling had originated from near the garden gate. Eoin quickly placed himself between the entrance and Hannah.

"I know that it is easy to weave fantasies when you're in the dark, but I don't believe we're mistaken." Hannah rose to her feet and stood beside him.

"Get behind me!" Eoin ordered as he strained to listen. To his horror, he heard ominous thrashing through the overgrown foliage.

"Why? Are you impervious to claws and teeth?" Hannah asked, but even as she joked, he could detect the tremble in her pattern of speech.

"I'm more bruin-sized," Eoin said.

"Wouldn't that just make you a tastier-looking morsel?" Hannah quipped. "I'm bonier."

"I—I can't lose you." The words tore from Eoin. "I can handle my pain but not yours."

Hannah fell silent but only for a moment. When she spoke again, her tone had turned serious, which only exposed how much her voice was quavering. "And don't you think it is the same for me? Let's stay side by side."

*Rawrrrrrr.*

Bollocks. The growl was closer now.

*Hisssssssss!*

"Is—is the gosling trying to defend us?" Hannah asked.

"It appears so. Foolish fowl." Eoin bent to capture the fluff, but it darted away from him. He lunged a second time, but his fingers only brushed uselessly against the down.

Heavy footsteps—or pawsteps—thudded against the ground, and the thick vegetation rustled. Not for the first time, Eoin was grateful for the mess of flowers and plants that had served so often as his shelter. But his thankfulness was quickly replaced with an even more crystalized fear.

"We should run for the house!" Hannah grabbed his arm. "It sounds like the bear is stalking us!"

"We can't," Eoin said starkly as his mind tried to determine how they could escape. "The beast is between us and the nearest door."

"Are the walls scalable? Or is there a helpful trellis leaning against the bricks?" Hannah asked. "I am very adept at climbing despite being born and bred a Londoner."

"There's a folly in the far corner," Eoin said. "It will be cramped, but there is at least a door we could shut."

"What kind of a folly? Greek? Roman? Medieval hermit?" Hannah asked.

"Does it matter?" Eoin asked.

"Well, some are holier than others. I mean full of holes, not religiously sanctified," Hannah babbled, and Eoin could hear her teeth clacking together. She was clearly terrified but determined to use humor to calm herself.

"Well, a hermit's hut could be holy." Eoin tried to join her humor as he snagged her hand. Tugging gently on their interlocked fingers, he took a step backward, and she followed suit.

Although Eoin had never tried to flee from a bear, he'd read once that one should never turn their back on an enraged dog. The sight only encouraged the canine to chase. Eoin supposed it could work with bruins as well.

"Only real hermitages. I don't think stone beehives erected for the visual pleasure of the aristocracy count," Hannah shot back as they continued to shuffle backward. The gosling darted in and out of their feet, her small body occasionally brushing against Eoin's ankles.

"That would be too Irish for my grandfather," Eoin replied just as he stepped in a divot. His ankle twisted, and his body began to sway. Thankfully, though, he did not collapse. The fowl chirped, and Hannah tugged at his palm, helping to steady him.

"Hopefully it is not an open pavilion with Greek columns—a pretty structure but not very useful for bear blocking." Hannah spoke with increasing rapidity as they picked up their pace.

"It is thankfully a small tower, not sturdy enough to withstand a Norman invasion but sufficient for a bruin attack."

Sweat had started to drip down Eoin's back even though they hadn't broken into a full run. Surely, they should be close to the folly now. The garden was not a particularly large one, but then again, Eoin had never been trapped inside it with a bear hunting him. That changed perspectives enormously.

*Rawrrrrrr!*

"That definitely sounded nearer." Hannah's voice rose slightly at the end, but she didn't shout. It seemed that the more imminent peril became, the calmer she grew.

"Yes," Eoin agreed as he glanced over his shoulder. He could see stone crenellations peaking over two overgrown rosebushes, but the haven was still yards away.

"Eoin." Hannah's voice was deadly calm now, and there was not a single quaver nor hint of humor.

A burst of strong panic caught in his chest. When he cautiously swiveled his head back around, an eerie, ancient fear swamped him. Every hair on his arms stood at attention, and his flesh turned to goose skin.

"I see eyes." Hannah breathed out the

chilling words just as Eoin spotted bright yellow orbs glowing in the shrubbery.

For a moment, Eoin stood transfixed. There was something mesmerizing about the twin moonlike spheres. His breath came out in uneven spurts, and perspiration now drenched his entire body. But Eoin could not succumb to primal terror. He had to protect Hannah.

He tried to release her hand, but she clung tightly. It was clear to Eoin that Hannah had no intention of permitting him to charge the bear. She obviously wanted them to face the danger together. But Eoin wasn't sure if he was strong enough to allow her. For if she perished...

*Hoooooooooooooooooooooooonk!*

Was that a battle cry? From the gosling? Surely not. Eoin didn't even think that the juvenile could emit such sounds yet.

But Eoin couldn't deny that the shadowy ball of fluff was waddling determinedly in the direction of the bruin. Beside him, Hannah gasped. Her grip on his fingers felt like a vise.

"Fowl, no!" Eoin whispered.

The bird, as usual, ignored him. She was intent on defending him, danger be damned.

The glowing eyes drew nearer, and Eoin could now spy the bear's menacing outline among the bushes. Fortunately, it moved in a lumbering fashion as if its very joints hurt. Eoin, however, felt no solace in the observation. Even if the bruin was indeed old—it still had teeth and powerful jaws.

Eoin reached for his pistol, unsure if a single ball would disarm such a creature. He wasn't a hunter, and he had no idea the best spot to shoot the bear. Although he hated the idea of killing, he had to defend Hannah, himself, and even that wretched, foolishly intrepid fowl.

Beside him, Hannah slowly withdrew her own weapon. Other than those slight motions, neither of them moved. Eoin hoped the bruin would simply grow bored and leave... but couldn't those beasts' sense of smell rival that of dogs and wolves? And with its eyes aglow, was it watching them despite the darkness?

The bear shifted in their direction. Eoin and Hannah sidled backward. The creature took two giant steps forward.

*Hoooooooooonnk. Hissssssss! Hoooooooonk! Hisss! Hissss!*

Eoin watched in half horror, half fascination as the small but fierce puff darted between the shadowy legs of the bruin.

*Rawrrrr?*

Did... did the bear sound confused? Surely Eoin's dazed mind was simply ascribing emotions to the growls.

The beast raised and lowered each massive paw in succession, almost as if it was performing a thunderous dance. In the dark, it was difficult to assess the position of the gosling, yet the little fowl's constant stream of honks and hisses were only tinged with anger and not pain. It must be dodging the claws.

*Rawrrrr!*

In contrast, the bear did sound like it was in perplexed distress. Eoin was oddly certain that the gosling was holding the dreadful bruin at bay.

"We should run." Hannah pulled desperately on Eoin's hand. "Now! While the bear is distracted."

Eoin didn't squander any time by

attempting to form a verbal reply. He just pivoted, dragging Hannah with him. He tore toward the faux tower, glancing over his shoulder every few strides. Each time, he could see a large shadow lunging and spinning as it roared in frustration. Although Eoin couldn't detect the gosling, it was obvious that the clever bird was still weaving underneath the big bruin.

"Will the door be open?" Hannah asked as they neared the tower, which was only a foot taller than Eoin himself.

"Yes," he said. "There is no lock—only simple latches on the inside and out. I suspect it was specifically designed for trysts."

"I would rather we were here for a rendezvous," Hannah huffed out when they reached the little tower. She grabbed the handle of the door and gave a push. "It's stuck!"

"Allow me." Eoin shoved his shoulder against the thick wood, careful not to apply too much force. He didn't want to break a hinge. Thankfully, the oak panel must have only been swollen from the summer's heat and humidity. It groaned in protest but opened readily.

Eoin bundled Hannah inside and then dodged in after her, making sure to keep his body between her smaller one and the opening. As he turned to lock them inside, he heard whistling. Glancing in the direction of the bear, he could see its shadowy form swaying back and forth. Was the bruin searching for its lost quarry?

*Squeak! Honk! Squeak! Honk!*

The little gosling was definitely running toward the folly. Since the bear wasn't moving and was still yards again, Eoin kept the oak panel open a crack.

"I want to give the fowl—I mean, the goose—a chance to join us," Eoin explained to Hannah. "Can you secure the latch when I slam the door?"

"Certainly." Hannah walked over to the jamb, positioning herself behind the stone wall.

Within seconds, a small blur squeezed through the narrow slit. Eoin could feel the gosling's body snuggle against his ankles as he shoved the oak panel closed. Hannah quickly slipped the wrought iron hook into its metal loop.

"There's a wooden bar as well!" Hannah pointed at a slab of oak.

Eoin instantly set it in place, pleasantly surprised by its heft. "The architect of this folly certainly designed a tiny fortress."

"Thank goodness for that!"

*Rawrrrr? Rawrrr?*

The bear sounded distressed again. Eoin peered out of one of the narrow, arched windows. The sky had begun to lighten ever so slightly, and the bear was snuffling along the dirt as it swayed its massive body to and fro.

Suddenly, it lurched forward, its glowing yellow eyes fixed on the tower. It lumbered in their direction and then picked up speed.

"It's coming straight toward us," Hannah said.

"Get back from the window," Eoin instructed as he heeded his own advice. Hannah, however, hadn't needed the warning as she headed for the center of the structure. Eoin joined her, which meant that the gosling followed.

Wrapping his arms around Hannah, Eoin tried to enfold her in his massive frame. He doubted that the bruin would breach the walls, but he would take every precaution to keep Hannah safe. In the darkness, the gosling hissed out her dismay as she pecked around their feet. She went still, though, when the bear crashed against the door. The bruin batted the oak panel a few times, and it sounded like a giant was knocking.

"I feel like Scrapefoot, the fox in that fairy tale about the three bears," Hannah said, her voice muffled as she burrowed against Eoin's chest.

He forced out a laugh. "I don't think this bear is as mannerly as the ones in that story."

As if to punctuate Eoin's statement, a scratching sounded at one of the windows. Although the bruin couldn't shove his full paw through the opening, two of his claws scraped against the inner stone. Then came the nose. It snuffled along the casement, the tip twitching up and down.

"If I was not so terrified, I might actually find that adorable." Hannah shook her head, her ear brushing against Eoin's chest.

"At least the bear is no longer attacking the door," he said.

The beast grunted and slowly withdrew its muzzle. A few seconds later, it tried another window and then another. Finally, the beast heaved a huge sigh. They could hear it take a few steps, and then there was silence.

"Do you think it fell asleep?" Hannah asked as they clung together in the middle of the twenty-foot circle.

"Perhaps, but I don't believe we should check just yet." Eoin glanced warily toward one of the openings. There was a faint glow of sunrise, but the light didn't penetrate into the center of the folly.

"I suppose there are worse fates than being stuck with you in a fairy-tale rendition of a castle keep." Hannah stood on her tiptoes and brushed her lips against the base of his neck.

His groan of delight, however, was promptly drowned out by an indignant hiss. Both he and Hannah looked down so quickly at the feathered malcontent that they almost whacked heads.

"I suppose we should really name the gosling now. She's definitely deserving of one." Hannah's voice was laced with a fondness that Eoin had to admit had entered his own heart.

"I agree."

"Aha!" Hannah poked him gently in the chest. "I hear that warmth in your tone. You can't fool me. I bet that you even have the perfect appellation picked out!"

Eoin didn't try to deny it. "Méibh for Queen Maeve. What better namesake for an intrepid little gosling than the legendary warrior queen of Connacht? The goose, after all, is our feathered savior."

## Chapter Eighteen

"I don't think that bear will ever fall asleep," Hannah moaned.

The sky outside the windows had started to turn a pearly gray. Even the gosling had tucked her beak under a chubby wing stubbled with juvenile feathers. Méibh's little chest lifted and fell as she slept soundly—and given the number of times that Hannah had been pecked in the ankle, her slumber was a very good thing. Now, if only the bruin would rest too. Unfortunately, the bear would stay silent for a few minutes and then renew its quest.

"At least it isn't trying to force its way through the door," Eoin pointed out.

"True." Hannah leaned her head against his shoulder. She automatically anticipated a sharp whack to her thigh from Méibh, but the little gosling was thankfully a deep sleeper.

Eoin slung his arm around Hannah, pulling her close. She wanted to tilt her head back for a kiss, but she had too many worries marching grimly through her mind.

"Do you think the bear is Ursus?" Hannah asked.

"Very likely." Eoin toyed with her hair, and Hannah watched as her red locks slipped through his strong fingers. "Of course, we would be predisposed to make that assumption since we saw him recently. Yet it is also logical to assume that someone from the Horse and Hen released him into my garden. How else could a bear find its way here? It is not as if bruins are wandering amok in Mayfair."

"Agreed. Mayfair is much too dignified a section of town. Why, in Covent Garden you see them all the time. Just the other day, one popped by for a cup of chocolate at the Black Sheep, and he became an absolute bear when we said that we only had coffee." Hannah patted Eoin's arm to temper her sarcasm.

Eoin laughed. "You know what I meant."

Hannah sobered. "I did." She really shouldn't tease him under the circumstances, but she'd always turned to humor in the face of both danger and despair.

"I am beginning to think that the Purveyor has formed a grudge against me." Eoin's grip on Hannah's tightened, and she doubted he'd even realized that he'd given her a squeeze. "I am not sure why he is fixated upon me, but the first attempt on my life occurred after our initial visit to the Horse and Hen. The pattern begins there."

"Have you ever suspected your uncles?" Hannah asked cautiously as a sick feeling coated her stomach. She had to warn Eoin against the rumors about his family—even if she wasn't ready to reveal her own personal connection to the Aucourtes.

"Of being the Purveyor?" Eoin asked in disbelief. "They hardly seem like criminal masterminds."

"Their foolish exteriors could be carefully crafted fronts," Hannah pointed out as she reached for Eoin's hand. Gently, she stroked his knuckles as she thought of the best way to explain. "Your Uncle Hugh would inherit the dukedom if you die. And he has even more motive now that you've reunited with your mother and sister. Didn't you say that he and his siblings receive nothing of value from your grandfather if you interact with your maternal line?"

"That is all true, but how would my uncles and aunts even know about my discoveries tonight?" Eoin pointed out.

"If Hugh was the Purveyor and has sent his underlings to spy on you, he would know," Hannah replied.

"It seems far-fetched to believe that he either has connections to this Purveyor or is the man himself," Eoin said.

"There—there has been something that I have been struggling to tell you," Hannah admitted. "Sophia and I have heard rumors for years involving the Aucourte family."

Eoin exhaled. "Ah. I thought you were holding back something directly pertaining to me. Were you afraid I would be insulted?"

"More...hurt?" Hannah half fibbed.

Eoin gave her a quick squeeze and bussed her cheek. "You needn't have worried. I have no real love for my uncles. They have always despised my very existence—my aunts too. I can imagine any of them indulging in casual illegal behavior, but I cannot picture them summoning enough initiative to build a clandestine network like the Purveyor's. What gossip did you hear?"

"Nothing substantial, but when we attempted to investigate, we heard silence similar to what happens if we inquire about the Purveyor. That is why I think they may be one and the same." When Hannah finished speaking, she held her breath. Would Eoin ask why they had been digging into vague whispers about his family? He was so keen.

Eoin kissed her other cheek. "The Black Sheep is truly a remarkable institution. I thought they had only begun to ferret out mysteries when you helped Lady Charlotte unmask Viscount Hawley as a highwayman. But you have been a secret avenging force in London all along, haven't you?"

Guilt stabbed Hannah. Eoin trusted her

implicitly, yet she had betrayed him. Yes, she was currently loyal, but it had all begun as a ploy. Now that he knew about the danger, did she really need to confess the rest? Would it serve anything but to hurt him and to assuage her own guilt? If he was willing to investigate his own family, did it really matter that she'd begun their partnership with the same intent? Every aspect of their romantic relationship had been real without any manipulation on her part.

"Our coffeehouse has always been a haven for the downtrodden who've been misused by people in power," Hannah said cautiously, carefully skirting around her family's personal history.

"Your father and uncle must have been very unusual pirates," Eoin replied, and Hannah's heart started pounding. Did he suspect? Yet why would he?

"My aunt—Sophia's mother—is the true leader of the group, and her mission has always been to free slaves and children forced into indentured servitude," Hannah explained. "The Black Sheep was a location for people to gather while they began their new life in London."

"A place for starting anew." Eoin nuzzled Hannah's neck, and she could feel him smile as he spoke. "I like that. Although my circumstances were very privileged and never as dire, I must say that I have found more and more of my true self after visiting your coffeehouse."

Hannah's remorse nearly choked her. Her lips parted, and she was a mere heartbeat away from full confession. But just as she started to form the first word, Eoin's mouth closed over hers. His tongue plunged deep, teasing hers. Sparks instantly cascaded through Hannah, setting aflame the energy already stirring inside her from the chase through the garden. She shifted in Eoin's strong arms and cupped his dear face with her hands. She could feel the stubble on his chin. As he deepened the kiss even more, his cheek muscles worked beneath her fingertips.

A moan rose up from deep within her. Oh, how this man could make her feel and forget. They were in their own fairy-tale world—a prince and a maiden locked in a tower with a beast pacing outside the door. But they had each other in this dark circle of stone, and everything without the walls simply ceased to matter.

Eoin still wore the rough clothes of a laborer, and Hannah was immensely glad for his shorter jacket. It made it easier to undo the buttons and slip it from his shoulders. He immediately complied, his lips still locked with hers as he contorted himself to escape the folds of the fabric. She disposed of his waistcoat next, tossing it to the side. She tugged at his coarse linen shirt, pulling it loose from his breeches. Eagerly, she skimmed her fingers up his back, feeling his thick, banded muscles.

He groaned, his mouth sliding furiously against hers. Hannah felt him clumsily work the buttons on her own coat, which she'd donned to wear to Championess Quick's. She debated about helping him, but that would mean pausing her very intriguing exploration of his body. When her hands reached his chest, he'd finally undone the fastenings.

Pulling back, she shrugged off her outer garment with one arm while impatiently tugging at the bottom of his linen shirt with the other hand. "I want to see your muscles, not just feel them."

Her voice was ragged to her own ears, but she didn't care if she sounded needy. She *was* needy.

Eoin flushed, but he didn't protest as he immediately shucked off the material, sending it to join the others on the floor. Hannah scooted back to admire the swell of his biceps and pectoral muscles. Even his stomach had firm ridges.

"How are you so exceedingly fit?" Hannah asked as she moved forward to trace the intriguing dips and swells. Although she'd suspected as much from how his clothes tugged and pulled, his body was magnificent and not one of a scholar.

Eoin's mouth opened, and his throat worked, but no sound came out. Instead, he emitted a sound halfway between a growl and a groan.

"Never mind," Hannah said, finding it rather hard to slip a word between her deep, rapid breaths. She had a much better use for her lips and tongue. She dipped her head and kissed Eoin's chest, reveling in the warmth of his hard flesh. He emitted a rough sound and then buried his mouth against the juncture of her shoulder and neck. They sat pressed together, their teeth lightly scraping against the other's skin as they drove themselves wild with yearning and delight.

Eoin's hands slid under her shirt and swept in wide circles up her back. As soon as he reached the binding around her bosom, he immediately began to untuck the strip of material. He was defter this time. Within moments, her breasts were free, and his hands brushed along their sides. Sweet sensation shot through Hannah, and her head arched backward. Eoin pressed soft kisses along the column of her neck as his hands swept forward to cup her. She whimpered from the sharp shards of desire cascading through her as his thumbs toyed with her nipples.

Oh, she wanted this man. Utterly and completely.

She reached up and undid the tie on her own linen shirt. Pulling out the lacing entirely, she tossed it away. Eoin immediately took advantage of the opening to press his lips against her bosom. The stubble on his cheeks rubbed against her sensitive skin, triggering a wonderful cascade of shivers to course through her. Her breath came in wanton pants, and her body began to writhe as her every fiber begged for a release that only Eoin could give. She buried her fingers in his soft hair until they reached his hair tie. Wanting to stroke the silky smoothness of his locks, she quickly undid the ribbon.

Eoin shifted his head so that his mouth was no longer pressed against her. But his fingers gently massaged, and his cheek still rested on her chest. "The...ground...too...hard?"

It took Hannah a few passion-dazed moments to understand the question, and she likely only managed to divine the meaning because of how much she wanted what he offered. This time she was the one who couldn't manage speech—even half coherent. She shook her head. Eoin smiled against her before he slowly began to lower both their bodies to the dirt floor. Hannah stroked her hand down his back, glorifying in how his muscles shifted. He cradled her head in one hand as her back touched the flagstone. The smooth rock felt cool against her heated flesh, even through the linen of her shirt. She shivered. Eoin pressed closer while still supporting most of his weight on his elbows. His mouth closed over hers again as his thighs bracketed her body.

"I...can't...not...enough." Eoin huffed out the words. Even though they were almost nonsensical, Hannah understood that he was trying to convey how badly he needed her. Part of her thrilled that she'd driven such an eloquent man to fragmented thoughts, but she too felt utterly undone.

*Huck-chrrr-phew! Huck-chrrr-phew! Huck-chrr-phew!*

Hannah froze. For a moment, she wondered wildly if she'd somehow cut off Eoin's airway even though her arms and hands were nowhere near his neck. The horrid, grating sound was not one of pleasure. In fact, it sounded exactly like...

"Is that snoring?" Eoin asked as he raised his chin.

Hannah lifted her head as far as she could without whacking against Eoin's temple. "It certainly sounds like it."

Hannah's gaze shot to the gosling nested in the corner. Although its head was still tucked beneath its fuzzy wing, the bird was not making a peep.

A different kind of energy shot through Hannah as she began to wiggle out from under Eoin. He immediately sprang away from her as he rose from the ground. By the time she'd scrambled to her own feet, he'd nearly reached the window.

"The bear is finally asleep," Eoin said as he shielded his eyes. The sun had risen fully during their lovemaking, and light now poured inside, even reaching the spot where they'd taken shelter.

"I thought bruins slept at night." Hannah vaguely recalled Matthew—who loved all animals—chattering about which animals were nocturnal and which weren't.

"It's most likely exhausted from prowling about," Eoin said as he quickly peered out the opening.

"Well, I am actually feeling remarkably refreshed," Hannah teased. Anxiety had begun to trickle through her again, and humor was the best way to ward off its potentially detrimental effects.

"So am I," Eoin admitted as he stole another gaze outside the folly. This time he didn't pull back. "It's slumbering very soundly. You can look safely from the window next to me."

Hannah quickly hurried over to the opening. And there in a sunny patch lay a great black shape. The beast had flattened a bed of overgrown honeysuckle to form a rather inviting-looking nest. It lay curled up with its light brown snout resting on pitch-colored paws. Each claw was trimmed, and Hannah recognized the scars along its muzzle and its patchy, mangy fur.

"That is most definitely Ursus," Hannah said.

"Yes," Eoin said darkly.

"We should talk about this with the others." Hannah watched the bear's black nose twitch as loud snores escaped him. "It is a most unusual method to kill someone."

"But first we must escape this folly." Eoin stepped back from the outer wall and reached down to scoop up their clothes. "I am not sure how long the bear will rest."

"Of course, the beast decided to bed down just when things had become the most interesting between us." Hannah pretended to grumble as she yanked on her coat. She didn't even bother with binding her breasts. Everyone in Eoin's household knew that she was a woman. The disguise wasn't that good that they wouldn't recognize her in broad daylight.

Eoin cast a wary glance in the direction of the snoring as he buttoned up his coat. "I don't know what to do with Ursus. It is not as if I can deliver him back to the Horse and Hen even if the Purveyor wasn't attempting to engineer my death. That bear was suffering. But I cannot keep him in my garden. Perhaps he can join the other animals at the Tower, although I am not sure if King George will want to add a mangy, skinny bear to the collection. Do you think your friend with the menagerie would take him?"

"He would be delighted to do so," Hannah

promised as she finished fastening her clothing. She didn't need to glance out the window to check if the bruin was still sleeping. She swore that his snores were loud enough to shake the stone walls of the folly.

Eoin, who had already fixed his attire, strode over to where the gosling lay still asleep. "I think it is best to leave Méibh here and to latch the door from the outside. It should hold, and she's safer inside these walls. If she starts honking while we pass by Ursus, we could all die."

"Agreed," Hannah said. "And she'll forgive you for leaving her behind. She is exceedingly tender in her affections for you."

Eoin sent Hannah a dry look. "I was not concerned about that."

Hannah didn't believe him. Eoin might not want to admit it, but he'd clearly developed a fondness for the formerly dubbed "fowl." Unfortunately, now was no time to discuss the degrees of affection between a bird and a man.

Hannah squared her shoulders and tried to calm the beating of her heart. "We should leave."

"Wait!" Eoin kept his voice low, but his urgency was palpable.

"Do not even think of commanding me to stay! I am not waiting here with Méibh while you expose yourself to danger." Hannah jammed her fists against her hips. "We go together."

"I know you wouldn't countenance that." Eoin reached over and began fussing with her hair. "You look... mussed."

Hannah started to laugh and then stifled her mirth. It wouldn't do to startle Ursus with her glee. "I am mussed—although not as thoroughly as I would like."

"But the servants may see you or, worse, my aunts and uncles. All four of them are very prone to gossip, especially Aunt Eliza. She seems to always know every tiny detail about an aristocrat whether in the capital or out in the countryside."

"Eoin, it is very kind of you to worry about my reputation, but I'm not a fine lady. I own a notorious coffeehouse and descend from pirates. Most significantly, I am posing as your mistress. People are expecting me to look tumbled, and I am already a walking scandal. I'm just adding authenticity to the story."

Eoin frowned. "I—I suppose you are right, but I feel like...I should protect you or at least champion you. I do not want anyone to think poorly of you because of my actions."

Hannah softened in a way that only Eoin's sweet words could inspire. "You needn't worry. I truly do not care what others say, and I feel no shame about what transpired between us."

A hesitant but beautiful smile touched Eoin's lips. "Neither do I."

"Then let us cease this fruitless discussion and escape while we can." Hannah lifted the metal latch on the door.

Eoin hurried to her side and removed the heavy bar. She slipped outside before he could. This time she wanted to take the most dangerous position. While he latched the door from the outside, Hannah kept a close watch on Ursus. Thankfully, the beast's chest rose and fell at a steady rhythm while its snores floated through the air.

As soon as Eoin secured the folly, the two of them slowly moved in the direction of the ducal townhouse. Grateful that she wasn't hampered by her skirts and petticoats, Hannah walked as soundlessly as she could manage. Twigs and stems slapped against her stockinged legs, but the thick plant growth at least served to dampen the tread of her feet. Despite his height, Eoin moved relatively noiselessly behind her.

As they neared the bear, Hannah swore that her heart stopped beating altogether. The whole world seemed ensnared in a preternatural calm—or perhaps Hannah's senses had become so finely attuned that everything felt slowed down. She could feel each stem brush against her along with the cool touch of the gentle summer breeze. The bees buzzing around the hollyhocks sounded like the roar of a mighty river, while sweet but cloying perfume from the crushed honeysuckle nearly suffocated her. As she crept past Ursus, she swore she could smell his sour breath as he snored out puffs of hot air.

Although her heart beat as loudly as a drum, she could also hear every exhale and inhalation from Eoin. Each bird chirp seemed to rival a gong's ring, and Hannah kept expecting the bear to shake himself awake. But his grunts remained blessedly steady and deep. At least for several yards.

Thankfully, Hannah and Eoin had already passed the bench that they'd shared last night when the snoring abruptly stopped. Eoin grabbed her hand and tugged her along as they broke into a run. By the time the first roar sounded through the quiet morning air, Hannah could spy the brick of the townhouse.

Even though they hadn't raced for long, her lungs burned. She'd never moved so fast in her life. Ignoring the stabbing in her side, she didn't slacken her pace. Over her own huffing breaths, she could hear the crunch of plants being mowed down by Ursus. Another frustrated roar filled the Mayfair street. Hannah didn't think the bear was precisely hunting them. He was just angry and enraged. Hannah didn't blame the beast. After all, she'd witnessed his awful treatment at the Horse and Hen. Still, her compassion for the animal didn't mean that she wanted to be mauled.

In the windows of the townhouse, Hannah

could see the shocked faces of the servants. Eoin's aunts and uncles had crowded around an upstairs window, watching the proceedings with less alarm than the footmen and the maids. Although Hannah couldn't risk slowing down to study their expressions in detail, she tried her best to observe their reactions. Francis was pointing while Hugh chewed on some sort of pastry fisted in his hand. Lady Joan's mouth was flapping wildly as she presumably chattered excitedly to her siblings. Only Lady Eliza showed concern as she pounded on her sternum—but Hannah suspected that she was more worried about the bear storming through the house and eating her than she was about the safety of her nephew.

Hannah and Eoin tore up the veranda steps just as Smythe threw open the French doors. A growl, closer than Hannah would have liked, sounded behind her. Digging deep inside, she tried to find a last burst of energy. She hoped that the glass could keep the bear at bay.

Suddenly, a hunk of meat sailed over her

and Eoin's heads. She glanced up to find footmen standing in the upper-floor windows and tossing smoked ham. Smythe stepped back to allow Eoin and Hannah to hurl themselves into the drawing room. Then he quickly shut the door.

Hannah glanced through the glass, praying that the bear would not charge through the panels in its pursuit of them. Thankfully, Ursus was happily chomping on his feast of pork.

"You are both unharmed?" the butler asked in his booming tone. Even though his face remained implacable, Hannah noticed that he was scanning their bodies for any injuries.

"We are unscathed," Eoin answered.

"Good." The butler inclined his head. When he lifted his chin again, he added in a dour voice, "I am afraid, though, there will be no meat on the menu tonight."

## Chapter Nineteen

Eoin burst into the dining room with Hannah close behind. Although he doubted that his uncles had the capacity to lead a criminal organization, he could not entirely dismiss Hannah's warning. If one of them was behind the attack, their reaction during the aftermath might be telling.

Three of the siblings were gathered around the window while Aunt Eliza rested against a chair like a limp rag doll. Her ever-present gossip sheets were scattered about her with one spread across her lap like a blanket. Even as a small child, Eoin had always found her antics ridiculous. But perhaps Aunt Eliza had more cause for her behavior back then. After all, her husband had recently been killed in a duel with his mistress's husband. His scandalous demise had left her with scads of debts. Her financial woes had only deepened when a ship that her husband had invested in sank. Shortly afterward, her brother died a traitor's death, and her father decided to instill austerity upon his surviving children.

Of course, Aunt Joan had faced similar trying circumstances when her husband fell from his horse and broke his neck after a night of drunken carousing with her own brothers. He'd been in the middle of an awful gambling streak where, over the course of several weeks, he'd managed to bet and lose most of their sizable fortune, including her generous dowery. Aunt Joan had never succumbed to the vapors as frequently as Eliza, but people handle tragedy in different ways. Eliza's solution had been to retreat inward while Joan had chosen to become more boisterous. She was always leaving home for some gathering or long-extended house parties with her few remaining friends. Eoin was only dimly aware of her schedule. He rarely saw her at major social events, yet she still managed to be gone for longer periods of time than her other siblings.

His uncles, too, were people who Eoin barely noticed. His grandfather had paid them no heed either and considered them spoiled gadabouts. Their allowance had been instantly cut off after his death, and they had to justify any money that he gave them for clothing and entertainment. Eoin's uncles had to ask permission before using any vehicle—even to drive to nearby Hyde Park.

Eoin's aunts and uncles surely possessed the need for a stream of income unconnected to the duchy, but Eoin couldn't imagine any of them presiding over London's criminal elements. Swounds, they could barely govern their own behaviors.

Aunt Eliza seemed to notice Eoin and Hannah's entrance first...at least that was what Eoin interpreted from the low moan that she emitted. Her eyes were either half lidded or fully closed—he couldn't ascertain which.

It was Uncle Hugh, though, who initially turned around. He looked spitefully amused—not the expression of someone whose murderous plans had gone awry. At least, in regards to the amused part. Spiteful would still be fitting.

"I didn't know you could run that fast," Uncle Hugh snickered. "I suppose all those exercises that Father forced you to perform ended up having some use rather than just threshing out your wild oats."

"What exercises?" Hannah asked.

Francis turned around to answer instead of his brother. "Oh, Father was worried that Eoin would become a reprobate like Hugh and me, or worse, a radical like our dearly departed brother. He thought a strict regimen would help release any bad humors before they festered into a permanently spoiled character. I was surprised by your athleticism, Hannah. I wonder if all women could run so quickly if they but wore breeches. Perhaps that's why our forefathers thought skirts were best for females—to make sure they can't dash off!"

Francis finished his statement with a jolly laugh as if he'd made a good joke rather than sounding like an unmitigated ass. Eoin debated about rebutting his uncle's statement, but he figured Hannah could handle it better than he ever could.

"Well, if all fellows shared your level of

prowess, then I would say your assessment is likely correct." Hannah smiled so pleasantly that Francis kept chuckling for a few beats. His face crumpled and darkened when he finally realized her mocking meaning.

"That creature is eating the gammon now!" Aunt Joan grabbed Uncle Hugh's arm. "What will happen when it eats all the food that the servants tossed at it?"

"We shall all die!" Aunt Eliza screeched before she collapsed backward again, this time throwing her hand over her forehead. She reacted so quickly and so theatrically, Eoin still couldn't tell if she was merely play-acting or if she truly was distraught enough to think that a bear could storm through the house, ravaging them all.

"One of the stableboys has already been sent to buy more meat for Ursus, and I've dispatched a messenger to alert a man who is well versed in dealing with wild animals," Eoin explained.

"How do you know what the bear is called?" Uncle Hugh asked.

Eoin watched the man very closely as he answered the question. After all, he'd used the bruin's name to see if it elicited a reaction. "Because I've seen him before."

"Where?" Uncle Francis demanded, crossing his arms over his chest in a defensive gesture. Was he attempting to hide that he, too, recognized the beast?

"Where do you think I would have encountered him before?" Eoin pushed the question back onto his relative.

Uncle Francis immediately puffed up his chest in indignation, but he did not unfold his limbs, choosing to keep himself closed off. "I have no bloody idea! That is why I am asking you!"

"Eoin probably encountered the vermin at some bearbaiting." Uncle Hugh rolled his eyes. "How else would you espy a bear in London? I highly doubt this one is a member of the royal menagerie."

"Oh my! I would be much too anxious to attend one of those bloodsports. I simply wouldn't have the courage." Hannah pretended to shudder. Even acting, she was less dramatic than Aunt Eliza, who emitted a faint groan as if the entire conversation was distressing her.

"Of course you wouldn't. You're a female. Although I hesitate to call you delicate, you still are of the weaker sex. Unlike me, you simply do not possess the fortitude," Uncle Francis snapped, clearly eager to redeem himself after Hannah had so handily won the last round.

"Have you really been to a bearbaiting? I've heard that they are becoming more and more uncommon." Hannah was sweetness personified, and Uncle Francis buzzed straight toward her honeyed words like a doomed housefly.

"*Pushaw.* Although there aren't as many as in my youth or especially as in my father's, there are still plenty. The Black Bird in Covent Garden is particularly popular, and then there's the Horse and…*erm*…Toad." Uncle Francis stumbled a bit on the last word, and Eoin was certain that his relative was going to say the Horse and Hen.

"That means that you have seen Ursus fight, then?" Eoin swooped in now that Hannah had so expertly led his uncle to reveal that he had frequented the Horse and Hen. Still, that information didn't make Francis the Purveyor. It was odd that he had clumsily tried to obscure the name of the tavern. If Uncle Francis was the Purveyor would he really be foolish enough to make such an obvious blunder? On the other hand, if Hugh was the mysterious leader, then Francis would likely know. The two shared everything. Of course, that meant that Francis would have managed to keep such a secret for nearly two decades, which seemed highly unlikely.

"No. What? Who? I must say I'm confused." Uncle Francis tried to cover his discomfort with a chuckle. It did not work.

"Why are you asking my brother so many questions?" Uncle Hugh demanded, physically stepping between his sibling and Eoin. Was Uncle Hugh just trying to defend Francis or was his defensive gesture also about protecting the secrets that the loquacious man might divulge?

"I am simply trying to determine how often Uncle Francis has visited the Horse and Hen. Given its connection to my mother, it is within my interest." Eoin stepped toward Uncle Hugh. He wanted both him and Uncle Francis to feel cornered.

"Don't be ridiculous," Aunt Joan snapped,

but Eoin noticed that she nervously rubbed at her neck. "Why would Francis darken the doors of the place that corrupted our brother? Father would have had his head."

"Gin?" Hannah asked, and everyone in the room swiveled in her direction except for Aunt Eliza. She was still flopped like a doll—this time one who had lost every bit of her rag stuffing.

"Gin is the drink of peasants," Aunt Joan snapped. "It is utterly unsuitable for people of our esteemed palates."

"Your first statement may be generally accurate but not the second. I am fully aware that both Uncle Hugh and Uncle Francis have a penchant for the swill." Eoin advanced on the two men, remembering what Hannah had told him about their special morning "tea." "Don't you slip a flask into your breakfast routine?"

"What?" Hugh blustered. "Why would we—"

Eoin pointed over to the teapot situated near Hugh's abandoned seat at the table. "There's no use in denying it, Uncle. All I need to do is to take a sip of that, and I'll easily confirm the truth."

Hugh's hands balled into fists. "What if we do indulge in a tipple of gin every now and again? Why do our drinking preferences matter? We're not harming anyone."

"Is gin the reason why you started to frequent the Horse and Hen?" Eoin pressed again, watching as Hugh's face turned more and more florid. He'd had no idea that human skin could display such a variety of red and purplish hues.

"I never said anything about the Horse and Hen!" Hugh blustered as he stared unblinkingly at Eoin as if commanding him to believe his words by sheer dint of will.

"Oh, my head!" Aunt Eliza suddenly cried out. "With all this excitement, it is aching so. Must you two argue?"

Eoin ignored her outburst. If his interrogation of her brother was bothering her so much, Aunt Eliza could simply depart from the room. Instead, Eoin continued staring down his uncle.

"You're lying," Eoin proclaimed with calm assurance.

Hugh was anything but sanguine, though. His body began to quaver—but whether in outrage or fear or both, Eoin could not tell.

"How dare you impugn my honor with—"

"Your rapid breathing combined with your reddened cheeks and unwavering stare all indicate that you're not telling the truth." Eoin held up a finger as he listed each sign. "Oh yes, and there's also that bead of sweat forming on your brow."

"You're an uncanny nuisance."

"Then you admit that you've been to the Horse and Hen?" Eoin ignored the worn-out insult and stepped forward again. Hugh tried to scuttle backward, but his brother's body blocked his retreat.

"What if I said yes? What is wrong with me drinking a cheap spirit at some ramshackle venue? I had no funds to spend on brandy and sherry, and then I acquired a taste for the floral stuff. And yes, I like a bit of bloodsport from time to time. So does Francis. We're men." Hugh stood as straight as possible, but his head still was no higher than Eoin's upper chest.

"Do you know the Purveyor?" Eoin watched for Hugh's reaction. Unfortunately, before he could witness it, a scratch sounded at the door before it opened to reveal Smythe, Dr. Matthew Talbot, and Lady Charlotte.

"I am sorry for the abrupt intrusion, Your Grace, but you told me to bring Dr. Talbot to you as soon as he arrived," Smythe intoned.

Eoin battled down his frustration. The distraction had given Hugh enough time to school his expression. Yet despite his uncle's omissions that he'd frequented the Horse and Hen, Eoin still remained unshaken in his belief that Hugh wasn't the Purveyor.

"I hear there is a bear in your garden?" Matthew's words were more a disbelieving question than a definitive statement, despite Eoin having been very clear in his missive to the physician.

At the mention of the bruin, Lady Eliza let out a murmur of displeasure. She turned to the side and rubbed her temples.

"Yes." Eoin pointed his finger in the direction of the set of windows overlooking the garden. "The creature is from the Horse and Hen's cellar. I believe it was used in bearbaiting."

"Oh, the poor thing!" Lady Charlotte said.

Aunt Joan snorted. "I would hardly deem that beast 'poor.'"

Lady Charlotte regarded Aunt Joan serenely. "It must have suffered in the ring as men cheered on the dogs forced to attack it." Then she turned back to Eoin and Hannah. "However did you come to rescue him?"

"We didn't," Eoin said shortly. "He was deposited in my garden."

Lady Charlotte and her husband exchanged a glance, but they didn't ask any more questions with Eoin's relatives present. Instead, they both crossed the room quickly,

"Hmm," Matthew said, sounding more like a scholar surprised by a new fact that he'd read than shocked by the presence of a beast in Mayfair.

"What is it?" Hannah asked.

"It is a black bear," Matthew explained. "They're from the Colonies. I was expecting a European brown bear, but it is not too surprising that one could be shipped from the

New World. I've brought animals home from there myself."

"Do you think you can safely remove him from the garden?" Eoin asked the physician.

Aunt Eliza suddenly sprang forward. With surprising speed, she gripped Matthew's sleeve. "Please save us!"

He gave her a kind smile and patted her hand. "There is no reason for fear. You're safe inside this building, my lady, although I would not recommend a garden stroll at the moment. As soon as my friend arrives with proper equipment and one of the wagons that we've specially designed for transporting large predators, we will safely remove the animal."

"Why not just shoot the blasted thing?" Uncle Francis demanded. "If you're all too lily-livered to do so, I'll volunteer."

"I assure you that it takes much more bravery to capture the animal alive." Matthew's polite scholarly demeanor had hardened.

"I still say that we should—" Uncle Francis began anew.

Eoin rubbed the bridge of his nose, wishing that his relatives weren't so difficult to corral.

"As the duke, I have decided that we're not harming the bear unless it poses an immediate danger to someone. Ursus is contentedly eating in a walled space. We can and shall wait until more help arrives."

"We are doomed!" Aunt Eliza cried.

For once, Eoin had to agree with her. Although Ursus hadn't harmed anyone, it was clear that the bear had been released to kill him. The Purveyor—or whoever was behind the murder attempts—wasn't going to stop. And worse, the killer seemed intent on choosing exceedingly dangerous methods that could easily result in others being injured too. It was past time to discover exactly what was happening at the Horse and Hen.

※

"Ursus seems content," Hannah said later that afternoon as Eoin stood next to her outside the bruin's new home. The summer sun burned overhead, drenching the grassy field in light. Matthew and his friend had created ingenious enclosures with sunken walls that made it appear that the animals were contained only by low-lying hedges.

Ursus ignored their presence as he industriously lumbered around the perimeter of his sizable quarters. The black tip of his wiggling nose did not appear to miss a single, solitary scent. Although Eoin knew little about animals, he swore that the bear radiated joy. Perhaps it was because Ursus still managed to eject a little sprightliness into his otherwise stiff amble despite his obvious age. He certainly was no longer growling and roaring.

"I am glad Ursus can finally receive proper care." Eoin gazed at the bear, surprised by how gentle the creature appeared. Ursus exuded an almost cuddly cuteness until one noticed the fearsome claws and teeth.

"I do feel better after seeing him under more cheerful conditions." Hannah leaned against Eoin and gave his midsection a squeeze. "Thank you for stopping by here."

"It was no great detour. We would have practically passed this place on the way to the ducal seat regardless," Eoin said.

"I hope we do find a clue at your estate, and

we're not haring off on a wild-goose chase when there are better leads in London." Hannah sighed as she let go of Eoin to pick a small leaf from the shrubbery hiding the recessed ha-ha.

"If my uncles and aunts are involved in the Purveyor's business, they would have removed or destroyed any evidence in the London townhouse when I first visited the Horse and Hen. They wouldn't have a chance, though, to sort through their belongings at the Kent property," Eoin said, although that was only part of his rationale. He also wanted to protect Hannah. Each time he'd been attacked, she'd been by his side. He had to consider that perhaps the Purveyor wanted her dead too. It seemed best to remove both of them from danger until they had a chance to discover more about the threat that they faced. Eoin, however, doubted that Hannah would be keen on avoiding peril. She was more apt to hurtle toward it.

"Do you believe now that one of your relatives could be the Purveyor?" Hannah asked as she plucked another leaf and flicked it into the air.

"Not particularly, but my uncles may at least have a connection to him," Eoin admitted as a heavy sadness weighed down on him. He had never been close to the foursome, but it still hurt to think one of his father's siblings might be helping to engineer his demise. "After I napped this morning, certain conclusions became clearer to me."

Hannah turned from pruning the boxwood to wrap her arms around him once more. "I cannot imagine they were easy inferences to make."

"Not particularly," Eoin agreed as he fixed his gaze on Ursus. The bear had stopped to paw rather aggressively at a clump of lavender. Chunks of the plant flew into the air, and Eoin wished that he could root out his own problems so easily.

Hannah did not press for more details, and Eoin realized that she was giving him time to prepare himself. He reached his arm around her and squeezed, glad for this moment of privacy.

"I..." he began and then swallowed. "I realized that someone who knows my routine must have helped plan the recent incident." It made him feel a little better, calling what had happened an incident rather than attempted murder. Still, speaking about last night caused a flurry of angst and rage to swirl in Eoin's gullet. "Sending a bear into a garden isn't a very effective way to kill someone."

"Although it would send a gruesome message to those who are under the Purveyor's thrall," Hannah pointed out. "Even though we lived, it is still a terrifying tale that will be repeated throughout London. For some people, such an experience would be enough to persuade them to halt their pursuit of the truth."

"I had not considered those factors," Eoin confessed, a bit ashamed that his normal logic had failed him. "I was primarily focused on the method than the potential results. Most noblemen don't frequent their gardens at night, nor have I revealed this practice to anyone but you. And even you were not aware until last night."

"Which means that either your relatives or your staff informed the Purveyor about your penchant. Given that Ursus was released into the garden after we'd been lingering there for a while, it is likely someone told the Purveyor about our exact whereabouts," Hannah finished, and Eoin was thankful that he didn't have to explain his uncles' potential perfidy further.

"I share your conclusions." Eoin held Hannah tightly.

"I am sorry." Hannah stood on her tiptoes and bussed his cheek.

The simple warmth of her gesture pooled through Eoin, soothing the raw edges of hurt. Gratitude slipped through him that he had this wonderful, bold woman by his side. Neither of them spoke as they silently watched Ursus utterly destroy the stand of lavender. The bear's claws swiped furiously, scattering dirt in all directions. It was oddly cathartic to watch Ursus take out his rage upon the flowers—almost as if Eoin could find some release as well.

## Chapter Twenty

"You didn't tell me that you owned an actual castle!" Hannah didn't care that she was half hanging out the coach window as the horses started down the impressive driveway. As if nature herself wanted to wreath the sprawling building in glory, the sun was setting on the horizon just beyond the west wing. The pale sandstone glowed a faint pink, and the central medieval keep shot into the sky like a monument to another age. Hannah almost expected the portcullis to open and an armored knight to burst forth on his warmblood. A moat, its waters reflecting the pastel-colored sky, still surrounded the sturdy walls although the more romantic drawbridge had been replaced by a permanent structure.

"It may look picturesque from the outside,

but I assure you that the original parts are exceedingly drafty and damp."

Unlike her, Eoin had remained seated with Méibh sleeping curled up against his thigh. When Hannah returned her gaze to him, she found him staring with patent admiration and affection, but not at the place where he'd spent part of his boyhood. His gaze was most definitely focused on her.

"It is massive. I am glad that your mother and sister are arriving tomorrow to help us search, along with my cousins and friends." Hannah—who never felt intimidated by anything—suddenly felt doubt seize her. The man next to her was practically her lover, yet he also had the responsibility for not just this holding but several others nearly as grand. That was many livelihoods, and not only those of the servants but those of the tenant farmers and even the nearby townsfolk. The choices Eoin made could raise the fortunes of the people around him or destroy their futures. Her grandparents had keenly experienced the latter during the enclosures on Eoin's northernmost estate.

Hannah had thought that her guilt and their mutual family history were keeping them apart—which they were. But those factors weren't the only invisible wedges. What future could she have with a man like Eoin? Although she was very intelligent and exceedingly capable of managing a thriving London business, she had no preparation for running households, especially not for castles and mansions. When one pictured a chatelaine or a duchess, Hannah Wick was not the image that sprang to mind. Quite the opposite, in fact. Did she even want to be bloody nobility? Would Eoin even consider marrying her? Perhaps he just viewed her as a mistress, yet he had worried about her reputation as if she were an actual noblewoman.

Oh, it was all a confusing mess!

"It's just a pile of rock," Eoin said, his voice decidedly bitter.

"Pardon?" Hannah asked as she plopped back down on her seat. She was tired of ogling at the building.

"I saw your face fall." Eoin grabbed her hand and wrapped his fingers around it, just as she'd reached for his so many times these past few days. "That castle has been nothing but an ill-fitting yoke around my neck. I've always been told that I wasn't good enough for it, and I won't have you thinking the same about yourself."

Hannah frowned, more upset by his words than her momentary qualms. "You already are a better duke than your grandfather ever was."

Eoin laughed, the sound short and bitter. Then he sobered. "Being with you has made me more confident to assume that role than a lifetime of my grandfather's lessons."

"Well, I am not surprised in the least. He was terrible at duking."

This time it was a touch more genuine when Eoin chuckled. "Is that how we're describing my duties? Duking?"

"Oh, most certainly. Dukely duking."

"And how would you say it for a duchess? Duchly duchessing?" Eoin's voice turned low and exquisitely soft. A fluttering started in Hannah's stomach, growing until it felt as if even her heart would take flight. But what was even more dangerous was that her mind suddenly formed an image of her and Eoin together—as lord and lady of the manor—presiding over a grand ball where the patrons of the Black Sheep danced with the well-heeled members of London Society.

"I..." Hannah's voice trailed off. She had no witty retort—just a surprisingly earnest want.

Luckily, it appeared that Eoin didn't need a verbal reply. His eyes fluttered closed, and he began to dip his mouth toward hers. Just as she reached up to accept his embrace, the coach stopped. That, of course, woke Méibh, who immediately started hissing. Her beady gaze was most definitely directed at their joined hands.

"Why does this always keep happening to us?" Hannah complained in frustration.

"Perhaps because I am always wanting to kiss you?" Eoin suggested, his voice unexpectedly jolly.

He was showing more and more emotions, Hannah realized, instead of keeping them dammed up like some perfectly engineered Dutch dike. But it seemed like the greatest break had come after meeting his mother and his sister.

"I may have similar desires." Hannah shot him a saucy wink as she leaped from the coach before anyone could help her down.

This time, Eoin's guffaws were from pure delight as he followed her lead with Méibh wedged against his side. When he alighted, he jauntily offered her his free arm. It might be scandalous for a woman of her class to boldly link elbows with a duke and march through the main entrance, but she did exactly that. Fortunately, Eoin hadn't ordered his staff to gather to greet them. Only a butler—who was just as delightfully dower as Smythe—opened the door for them with a deep bow.

Eoin was right. Even in summer, the ancient keep exuded a distinct chill. Hannah supposed that the tapestries hanging from the stone walls were meant to provide some semblance of warmth. However, they were rather gruesome depictions of long-ago battles that most likely featured the Aucourtes. Gaping spear wounds and bloodied battle-axes did not precisely engender a welcoming feeling.

"I suppose you're not interested in a speech about the weavings. If I am wrong, I can happily bore you with a long-winded history of each glorious blow that my illustrious ancestors landed on the enemy," Eoin said rather flippantly as they passed by the grisliest one.

"That would be a correct assumption, Your Grace." Although Hannah kept her tone light, she wondered how long Eoin had been forced to stand, with his neck craned upward, as he practiced recounting Aucourte legends.

"Should we head to Uncle Hugh's chambers first? Or Uncle Francis's? Or do you think we should start somewhere else?" Eoin bent to whisper in her ear despite the fact that the butler had already discreetly left, and there was no need for subterfuge.

Hannah allowed a seductively sly smile to touch her lips. She was rather enjoying Eoin's flirtatious side.

"Why don't we visit your rooms first? I want to see where you spent your boyhood," Hannah suggested.

Eoin instantly stiffened, and his expression reverted back to its usual implacableness. He bent to place Méibh on the ground and then straightened again. "I spent my youth in a different room from the one that I now occupy. Grandfather did not move me into the east wing with the rest of the family until after my twenty-first birthday last year."

"You're only twenty-two?" Hannah asked. She hadn't realized that Eoin was younger than her. He had the reserve and maturity of someone much older.

Eoin nodded before he opened an oak panel, revealing an ancient circular staircase. "I do apologize but the ascent to my former quarters is rather steep and narrow. This part of the castle was never remodeled."

Eoin nearly doubled over to squeeze under the arched lintel. When he'd managed to wriggle his massive form through the stone doorway, he waved with his hand for her to follow. Méibh waddled after him first.

Hannah had to stoop as well but not nearly as far as Eoin had. When she made it inside, she found Méibh bouncing and furiously flapping her stubby wings. The intrepid little goose managed to climb up a few of the stones, but Hannah was afraid that she might take a tumble. Hannah reached down and scooped up the bird. Méibh gave her a vicious peck on the knuckles—as if to inform Hannah of who was in charge. After that warning, Méibh nestled her little body against Hannah's arm.

"I do apologize. I should have carried her." Eoin looked over his shoulder, his entire body taking up most of the corridor. Hannah could imagine him as a medieval knight storming a spire, his sword gleaming, his armor clunking as it scraped against the walls.

"I doubt that you and Méibh would have fit," Hannah pointed out. "Did you live in the keep itself?"

"Yes, which is why I know exactly how drafty old fortresses can be. This one was built in the early eleventh century. When the former Dukes of Aucourte erected modern wings, they all elected to keep the original tower along with the south turret, which is almost as old. They are, after all, testaments to the ancientness of our Norman line. Why build a monument when you can live in one—or at least force your heir to take up residence in it?"

"Isn't this part of the castle absolutely frigid in the winter?" Hannah asked as they passed by an arrow slit. Rays of pearly pink light shined through the opening, illuminating the interior sandstone. A few golden motes danced in the glow, looking a bit like tiny fairies. The stairwell was practically a scene from a fairy tale, but once the biting December winds blew, these steps would be a foreboding, chilly place.

"The whole tower feels like it's made of ice starting in November. Even the massive fireplaces in the main rooms do little to ward off the drafts." Eoin opened a small wooden door. This time, he had to lean his top half into the opening first and then wiggle the rest of his body through.

Even Hannah had trouble. Realizing that she and Méibh could not fit together, she placed the gosling on the floor. The fowl shook her feathers as she proudly left the staircase to rejoin her favorite human.

Hannah's exit also required a great deal

of wriggling her back end—although for entirely different reasons from Méibh's tail shake. When Hannah finally popped out, she found herself in stark, unadorned space. It did not look like the boyhood domain of a wealthy heir apparent to a dukedom. There were no wooden toys tucked into a corner. Tin toy soldiers didn't stand at attention on the mantel. There wasn't even a single novel about buccaneers, castaways, or swashbuckling adventurers—in fact, there was nary a fictional tale on the single plain wooden bookshelf. Instead, it contained the Bible, Machiavelli's *The Prince*, Thomas Hobbes's *Leviathan*, and political treatises espousing Royalist views. The only furniture was a scarred writing desk, an uncomfortable wooden chair, and a thin, narrow mattress, which was really more cot than bed. It was shoved against one wall rather than near the central fireplace.

The room could be described in one word: austere.

Eoin had already moved to the center of the circular space. Despite his modern waistcoat and Méibh's presence at his feet, Eoin still looked like a chevalier. The chamber's high ceilings, bare stone walls, and massive fireplace suited Eoin—or at least the Eoin that Hannah had first met. It was cold and unyielding, yet still in possession of a rugged, rough-hewn beauty.

"From here you can see the entire holdings," Eoin explained, his voice dull. "My inheritance and my duty."

Even standing in a corner, Hannah could espy part of the moat from the narrow windows. Beyond the water, a flat plain stretched in all directions. In the distance, a river curved around the estate, and it sparkled a molten silver in the fading light. Yet she doubted that Eoin saw the view's splendor.

"Was your room decorated like this when you lived in it?" Hannah asked, trying to keep her distaste from her voice. It might be an impressive, historic chamber, but it was not a hospitable living space, especially for a child.

"Yes," Eoin said. "My grandfather did not wish for me to grow up coddled like his five children. He felt that a luxurious upbringing had spoiled them, and perhaps he was not entirely wrong."

"No. Your grandfather was most definitely wrong. I hope you understand that truth. You never should have been treated that way." Hannah's heart ached for the boy he'd been and for the man he'd become.

Eoin walked over to the tall mantel and stood next to it, his head level with the massive piece of timber. "In the winter, he used my sources of heat as punishment if I did not learn my lessons quickly enough, if I was too rambunctious, if I forgot a detail about the Aucourte past, if I spoke too softly or if my volume was too loud. The list was endless. At each infraction, I would first lose the heated bricks in my bed and then logs on the fire. I eventually realized that much depended upon his mood, and that was when I started to learn to decipher subtle clues that people display about their emotions."

Hannah moved in his direction and pressed herself against his back. Méibh struck at her ankles, but Hannah ignored the insistent pecks. Wrapping her arms around Eoin, she held him tight, wishing she could go back in time and keep the empty fireplace blazing.

"You asked about my muscles." Eoin's voice was even and precise, but Hannah could feel a slight tremor shift through him. "They are in part due to the duke. He believed that he had raised his sons too softly, and that he should go back to the times when noble lads learned to become knights. I always found it odd that he did not encourage me to fight with a sword, but I suppose now it was because of my mother's skill with the quarterstaff. He didn't want me to be anything like her. Instead, he preferred more regimented exercise. I marched, like a soldier. He commanded me to run circles around the outer moat as he felt it expunged a boy's natural tendencies for wildness. I suppose he wished to physically exhaust me into obedience. Despite being servant's work, I was ordered to muck out stalls or shovel during the planting of the kitchen garden—alone, of course, because I wasn't to mingle with any commonfolk."

Eoin spoke his words in a fast rush, and Hannah didn't try to interject. She just leaned her cheek against him and listened. Although tears gathered in her eyes, she didn't let them fall for fear that Eoin might feel them despite the layers of silk and linen separating them.

"After I outgrew my reedy, gangly adolescence and began to acquire muscles, Foxglen ordered me to stop. He blamed me for looking too much like a laborer," Eoin continued in the same matter-of-fact tone. "By then, I'd come to like exertion. It drove out my frustrations and bitterness. My mood always seemed to lift afterward. When I no longer had permission to haul loads, I was stuck in this room with my books. Although I have never minded reading or even quietude, I found myself growing increasingly restless. It was as if something was ramming against the insides of my stomach, begging for release. Eventually, I decided to try hefting my own weight since I had no access to anything else heavy. I lay flat on the floor and lifted myself upward. Sometimes I would push myself up and down in rapid succession, and other times I would hold up my weight until my arms nearly gave out from under me. Anything to relieve my internal tumult."

Eoin fell silent, and Hannah continued

to hold him. She thought he'd turn around and embrace her, but instead he reached up and viciously scrubbed his face. Embarrassment roiled off him, and Hannah experienced a rush of impotent anger toward his grandfather. How could he have made this wonderful, strong, kind man feel like he was inadequate?

"Do you still exercise in that manner?"

"Yes." The admission came out as a guttural groan.

"Good. I think it was very clever of you to devise such a method. Perhaps you should teach me it." Hannah stretched her entire body so that she could press a soft kiss against the nape of Eoin's neck. Méibh hissed, but Hannah ignored her. Thankfully, the stubborn gosling had at least stopped pecking so furiously.

"You do not find it strange? Or me strange?" Eoin asked.

Hannah shook her head. "Of course not. In fact, I very much like the results."

"You have mentioned liking my physique once or twice, haven't you?" A tiny bit of emotion had reentered Eoin's voice, and Hannah's heart swelled with relief.

"I have." She bussed his neck again. "And now that I know how you earned those muscles, I appreciate them even more. They're badges of ingenuity and perseverance."

Eoin's responding chuckle started out a bit rusty and then turned full and bright. "Are they, now?"

"Most definitely, and I would very much like to explore them." Hannah undid the buttons to his outer garments and ran her hands up the ridges of his stomach to rest upon his chest. Her exploration was well worth Méibh's bruising strike to her ankle.

"The fowl is attacking you, isn't she?" Eoin asked.

"Just ignore Méibh. I certainly am." Hannah ran her fingers back down Eoin's abdomen toward the hem of his shirt. She wanted the garment off.

"I don't want you hur—" Eoin began to say, but before he finished, footsteps pounded on the steps.

Hannah sprang back, nearly tripping over Méibh. The gosling immediately began to circle around, flapping her stubby wings and extending her neck. The pounding of feet grew nearer, and Hannah reached for the pistol that she carried in her pocket. Every attack had occurred either in Eoin's home or on his property, and she didn't trust that even literally fortified walls could keep peril out. They'd been focusing on the Purveyor being a family member, but he could be one of the servants too.

Eoin was frantically rebuttoning his shirt. Every few seconds, he cast a nervous look at the doorway.

"I would reach for a weapon rather than worrying about putting yourself to rights," Hannah pointed out. "The servants already think I'm your mistr—"

"Eoin!"

Was that Elizabeth Quick? She wasn't supposed to arrive until tomorrow.

"Eoin!"

Yes, that definitely was Lizzie. After her warning, Hannah was not likely to forget her voice.

"On second thought, button faster." Hannah shoved her gun back in her pocket.

Although her hair wasn't mussed, she nervously reached up to pat it.

Eoin had just finished securing the last fastening when his mother and his sister burst into the room like two avenging Amazons. Even attired in serviceable dresses instead of their Holland trousers, the two looked formidable. The extra fabric might obscure their toned muscles, but no amount of flounce could ever diminish their innate physicality.

His sister raced across the room and caught him in a fierce embrace. It was probably good that Eoin had exercised as much as he had or Lizzie might have snapped him in two. Méibh pecked furiously at her skirts, but the prizefighter ignored the feathered assault.

Eoin's mother hung back, her hands opening and closing. She clearly wanted to hug her son, but obviously thought she'd lost the right.

"Go ahead," Hannah told her quietly. "He wants to be held by you."

Championess Quick didn't need additional encouragement. She shot across the room with a fleetness that had made her a formidable opponent in the ring. In one giant swoop, she gathered both her children into her arms. Méibh went wild, but no one paid her any regard.

"We heard about the bear!" Lizzie said. "Why didn't you mention it in your missive to meet you here?"

"I didn't want to worry you," Eoin said, which earned him a light bop on his shoulder from his sister—at least Hannah assumed the bop was light. With Lizzie, one couldn't be sure. Eoin showed no reaction to it, though.

"That is a silly reason," Lizzie informed him. "We've fretted over each other for nearly twenty years because we didn't know what the other was enduring. Keeping secrets won't stop the worrying."

"You are unharmed?" Championess Quick asked, pulling back from her children to run her gaze over Eoin.

"Yes," Eoin said. "Méibh, the fowl currently at my feet, distracted the beast long enough for Miss Wick and I to reach shelter."

Both women glanced down at the gosling, who was currently stuck in Lizzie's petticoats.

Lizzie lifted her outer skirt, and Méibh popped free—a ball of frustrated rage.

"She does appear to be a scrappy warrior." Lizzie peered down at Méibh as the little bird tried to charge her again.

"My kind of fighter." Championess Quick chuckled, and Hannah caught a glimpse of the real woman beneath the reserved façade. Each one of her layers was so much like her son's.

"How did you hear about the bear?" Eoin asked. "Do you know Dr. Matthew Talbot?"

"There's talk of it all over London!" Lizzie said. "It's not every day that a duke is nearly eaten by a wild beast in Mayfair."

"I wouldn't say nearly eat—" Eoin started to say.

"They say that you wrestled with it." Lizzie poked her brother in the ribs. "Which, if that is the case, we need to get you into the ring with that kind of talent."

"There was no wrestling," Eoin said quickly. "Only running."

"That does not nearly make for as good a romantic story as the one being told."

Lizzie sighed theatrically before she sobered. "Although I am glad that you weren't actually grappling with a toothsome predator."

"Romantic? Why would you say that?" Eoin asked as he shot a worried look at Hannah.

"People are claiming that you tackled the beast to save your ladylove. All of us commonfolk are atwitter that a duke risked life and limb to save a coffeehouse proprietress," Lizzie babbled on, apparently oblivious to her brother's growing horror. Hannah didn't mind the rumors, but she knew Eoin was worried about her nonexistent reputation.

"Has Miss Wick's name been bandied about?" Eoin asked, his normally even voice tight with concern.

"Yes. Her ownership of the Black Sheep has made the tale even juicier, especially since the establishment was instrumental in bringing down the late Lord Hawley." Lizzie continued to gush. "I cannot imagine how the stories will grow when they discover that you're the son of Championess Quick. There won't be enough seats at the amphitheater to hold the crowd!"

"Darling"—Championess Quick rested her

hand on her daughter's arm—"I believe that your brother is worried about Miss Wick."

"Oh," Lizzie said and turned to Hannah. "I apologize if I sounded insensitive. I've just never cared what anyone said about me as long as it brought in customers."

"I am the same way," Hannah assured her and then turned to Eoin. "And I truly mean that, Eoin. These rumors will only increase the Black Sheep's revenue. I am not a highborn lady. Being perceived as wild and wanton will only help my business."

The color, however, did not return to Eoin's face. "I should never have allowed you to play the role of my mistress to aid in the investigation. I didn't thoroughly consider the cost to you."

Hannah strode forward and grabbed both his hands. Méibh immediately flew into an indignant rage, but fortunately, Hannah had plenty of experience with irate birds. "But that is what I am trying to tell you, Eoin. There is only gain for me. I don't mind the tittle-tattle."

"But what if you are propositioned or worse

because of this?" Eoin squeezed her fingers. "I don't want you harassed at the Black Sheep."

"I know how to handle unruly customers," Hannah promised. "There will always be that sort of man who thinks he can take liberties simply because I work for a living. The gossip doesn't change that. Aye, the annoying attempts may increase for a time, but offensive demands are nothing new."

"Then take the protection of the Aucourte name." Eoin dropped to one knee, his fingers still gripping Hannah's.

Hannah glanced over at his mother and his sister in panic. Lizzie was barely holding in her laughter while his mother's expression had once again gone blank. Even worse, Hannah could hear new footsteps pounding up the stairs. In less than a minute, they would find themselves invaded once more.

Hannah frantically glanced back at Eoin. She understood the reasons behind his sudden action, but no woman wanted to be proposed to in this manner. Hannah could only feel uncomfortable embarrassment...and perhaps an underlying confusion as to her own desires.

She yearned for this man on an elemental level, but did she want the life that he offered?

"Eoin, perhaps we should discuss this in priv—"

"Unhand my daughter, you blackguard!" A familiar voice rang through the ancient tower.

Her hands still gripped by Eoin's, Hannah whirled toward the doorway. Sure enough, her father was wedging himself through the narrow opening.

"Papa!" Hannah cried out, unable to fully grasp what her own eyes were telling her. But even as her mind scrambled to understand, her heart immediately recognized with each frantic thump that the situation was not good. "What are you doing here? You're supposed to be in the Caribbean!"

# Chapter Twenty-One

*Papa?* Eoin glanced frantically from Hannah to her apparent father and then back again. The two shared little resemblance. He was a handsome fellow, but in a more rugged way than Hannah's classic beauty. His hair—threaded liberally with silver—must have been a dark brown in his youth. And while his eyes were lighter like Hannah's, his irises were a striking cornflower blue with nary a hint of green.

Yet both father and daughter carried themselves in the exact same manner—with a boldness that would not yield to anyone or anything. Neither hid their feelings but permitted them to flow unabashedly even in the presence of strangers.

And right now, the emotion rushing from

Mr. Wick was not just exceedingly palpable but also very easy to identify. Rage. Pure, unadulterated rage. The kind that only a parent protecting their young could muster.

Had the man heard the rumors swirling through London? Had he come posthaste to demand that Eoin take responsibility? If so, Eoin was already down on one knee.

"As long as your daughter accepts my troth, I will happily marry her." Eoin forced the words out as quickly as he could, as he debated whether he should rise to greet his potential father-in-law or, if given the circumstances, it was more polite to remain kneeling.

"Unhand my daughter this instant and get to your bloody feet, so I can properly beat some sense into you, you young, insolent whelp."

"I am proposing," Eoin frantically tried to explain. "You do not need to force me—"

"Force you? Are you daft, you great nob? I don't want my daughter wedding a stinking Aucourte."

"Pa—pardon?" Eoin asked, thoroughly confused.

"Papa, please calm yourself," Hannah said. "Eoin is only—"

"Eoin? You call him *Eoin?*" Mr. Wick bellowed at his daughter. Eoin tensed, ready to jump up and place himself between them, but Hannah did not seem at all perturbed by her father's shout. Or at least she didn't look cowed. She seemed exasperated. Exasperation, that was good, right? Perhaps it was common for her father to bluster at Hannah's suitors.

"You should listen to your daughter, Mr. Wick, and regain your composure. Elsewise, you will be the one being taught a lesson by me." Lizzie stepped forward and smacked her right fist against her open left palm. Eoin suppressed a groan. Although he appreciated his older sister's immediate and unquestioning support, her assistance was the exact opposite of helpful.

"This is a family matter. I ask that you stay out of it." Mr. Wick didn't even bother to turn toward Lizzie. His angry glare was apparently reserved just for Eoin.

"As Eoin is my brother, this farce does very much involve me." Lizzie's left hand also formed into an ominous ball.

"As much as I appreciate your support, this is something I must handle myself," Eoin said quietly just as their mother whispered loudly, "Lizzie, do not interfere unless Eoin specifically asks us."

"I don't bloody care how you're related," Mr. Wick thundered as he stomped closer to Eoin. "I just want this nob to stand up and let go of my daughter."

Punctuating his words, Mr. Wick bent over and grabbed Eoin's lapels. He started to yank, but Méibh took violent umbrage to the fact that someone was touching her human. She attacked in a flurry of feathers and rage.

"Owwww!" Mr. Wick leaped backward, and Méibh followed, her beak striking furiously. Mr. Wick tried to sidestep her, but she was intent on wreaking the most amount of damage.

"Owwww!" Mr. Wick grabbed his left ankle and hopped on his other foot. "Ye gads! How can such a tiny bird inflict more damage than Pan? Its beak is flat. Pan's is sharp."

Hannah shrugged, seeming entirely unconcerned about her father's predicament.

"Pan is vicious but lazy. Méibh pecks with more zeal."

"Owwwwww! Can you call off your attack goose?" Mr. Wick gripped his other leg now, and Méibh fluttered her stub-wings as she assaulted whatever her beak could reach.

"She doesn't listen to my commands," Eoin said as he bent down to catch the battle fowl. When he cradled her in his arms, she calmed slightly. Yet her neck still moved furiously, and she landed a few strikes against Eoin's arms.

With the gosling secured, Hannah turned toward her father, her arms akimbo. "Why you here? How are you even here?"

"I am the one who should be asking the questions. I walk in to find you with an Aucourte—"

As Eoin's initial shock began to ebb, it struck him that Hannah's father seemed particularly obsessed with the Aucourte name. But why? Had Eoin's family harmed Hannah's in the past? But if that were true, why hadn't Hannah told Eoin? Maybe she simply did not know.

"You interrupted my proposal, so I think that entitles me to a few inquiries." Hannah marched over to her father, her stride almost identical to his.

"Your mother and I sent a letter ahead, but we must have arrived before it," Mr. Wick snapped. "We thought we were overdue for a visit, and seeing what trouble you've gotten yourself into, I daresay that we were right."

"I am exactly where I wish to be, Papa," Hannah said.

Eoin should have felt comforted by her words, but he didn't. There was something in her intense expression, like she was trying to send her father a wordless message. Eoin could not help but think that he was missing something critical.

"No! I won't have you putting yourself in danger for a revenge that should be mine." Mr. Wick was no longer shouting, and his earnest worry was apparent now that his volume was lower. "You need to end this ruse."

Revenge? Ruse? A sick feeling twisted through Eoin, mixing with the anxiousness that he already felt at meeting Hannah's father. The man clearly despised him or at least his family.

"Papa, this isn't the time to—" Hannah began to say, but Lizzie out-shouted her.

"What is this about retribution and schemes?" Lizzie stormed toward Hannah. "What is your father talking about? Were you using my brother? You promised me that you wouldn't hurt him."

"Oh, do not act as if your family is the victim in this!" Mr. Wick was once again roaring as he rounded on Lizzie. "I return home to hear that my daughter was not only attacked by a bear, but that she was cavorting with the new Duke of Foxglen."

"She's the one who installed herself as my brother's fake mistress!" Lizzie shouted right back. "I was worried that she was after his money, but she assured me she was not. Perhaps she was plotting something else!"

Eoin's head was spinning so furiously that he could not extract one single logical thought. Or perhaps too many facts were hitting him at once, preventing him from putting them in a proper order. He could grasp only one at a time. "Lizzie, what are you talking about? When did you talk to Hannah about me?"

"That is between us women," Lizzie said succinctly.

"Did you threaten my daughter?" Mr. Wick snapped.

"Papa—" Hannah tried to interject, but her father talked right over her.

"Was she not good enough for your precious family? Because she was the daughter of pirates? You Aucourtes are nothing but a family of thieves. Your grandfather stole the land that my family had tilled for generations and hid behind the law. And then when my brother and I snared a few rabbits to help feed our families, the damn duke used his connections to have us sent to the Colonies as indentured servants. My brother was fourteen, and I was but twelve. We were locked up with hardened criminals for over a month before Sophia's grandfather rescued us. And you—you have the audacity to claim that my daughter could hurt your brother!"

All of Eoin's swirling thoughts settled. An empty coldness rushed to take their place. He turned helplessly toward Hannah. "Did you know about our mutual family histories when you agreed to help me?"

All color had fled from Hannah's normally pink cheeks, and her freckles stood out against the pale whiteness. She looked younger and vulnerable, and the sight sliced at Eoin. He didn't want to hurt her. For a moment, her eyes flicked away, but she clearly forced her green gaze back in his direction. She did not verbally answer his question, but she nodded—a short, fast bob, but it was an affirmative.

"Then why—why did you help me?" Eoin's throat ached as if he'd pushed giant boulders up his esophagus instead of words. He dreaded the answer, yet he needed to ask the question. Not just for his sake but for hers. Eoin didn't want Hannah to be forced into playing a charade. She shouldn't have to feign to like him to achieve recompense for what his grandfather had done to her family.

"At first—and I mean at first—I wanted to learn more about your uncles," Hannah explained.

Eoin's rationality returned and, with it, almost blinding pain. "That's why you knew about the rumors that my family was involved in illicit activities. You were hoping to destroy the Aucourte name just as you did with Viscount Hawley."

"I cannot deny that's why I initially agreed to help, but even in the beginning, I—"

"You promised—" Lizzie began to rail, but their mother grabbed her arm.

"Lizzie, you are not helping. Let your brother and Hannah discuss this."

"But—" Lizzie began to protest, but their mother simply marched over to the open door with her daughter in tow. She splayed her hand over Lizzie's head and half guided, half shoved her through the narrow opening. Lizzie's protests were muffled by the thick stone walls, and Eoin's mother quickly exited the room after her eldest. When she pulled the oak panel shut, the chamber fell silent.

"Father, you should follow Championess Quick's suit. She is right. This is a matter between Eoin and me." On the surface, Hannah's voice sounded crisp, but Eoin didn't like the brittleness that he detected. Perhaps he did mean something to her, but now...now he doubted everything. He'd been a fool to think that someone had wanted him simply for himself, not because of the happenstance of his birth. Even in Hannah's eyes, he'd always been his grandfather's heir.

"Hannah, as your father—"

"You have taught me how to defend and think for myself, Papa. This is the part where you let me make mistakes and clean them up myself." Hannah pushed her father toward the exit.

"But—"

Before Mr. Wick could finish his protestations, Sophia popped into the room, followed by an older version of Hannah. Mrs. Wick looked precisely like her daughter and her niece Charlotte except that silver mixed with her red hair and she also moved in a quieter, more contained manner. There was no marching, no bold jerks, and no shoulders thrust forward as if in preparation to charge the enemy.

"I am sorry," Sophia burst out as she gasped for air. "We tried to stop Uncle. We've been chasing him all the way from London. I'd hoped that he would calm down after I revealed your location and plans, but as you see, the information only escalated matters."

Hannah's mother sailed over to her husband like she was crossing a ballroom. She lifted her hand as if executing a move in a country dance. In one quick, elegant action, she snared her husband's ear. Then she swept back toward the staircase.

"Owwww!" Mr. Wick roared, but he did nothing else to stop his wife. For a pirate, he had a very low pain tolerance.

Mrs. Wick paused at the threshold. "I do apologize for any interruption. Please continue your conversation in peace."

She shoved her husband toward the exit with a lot more force than Eoin's mother had used with Lizzie. Mr. Wick's shoulder cracked against the stone, but he did not cry out this time. Instead, he obediently left. His wife followed. Sophia only lingered long enough to mouth "I'm sorry" and "good luck" to her cousin.

Sophia tugged the door behind her, yet neither Eoin nor Hannah spoke. He listened as the footsteps grew fainter and fainter. Dread filled him, and part of him wanted to bolt. But he'd never fled in his entire life. No matter what, he'd endured.

Hannah finally broke the awful quiet. "I am sorry. I truly am. From the beginning, I did intend to help you locate your sister and mother. That wasn't a lie nor are my feelings toward you."

Hannah looked earnest standing there, her hands clenched and tears glistening in her eyes. She'd always showed her emotion readily. Hell, she'd won Eoin over with her boldness on the night that they'd met. The instant she'd run her eyes unabashedly over his body, he'd fallen for her. She hadn't hid her appreciation for him... or, at least, her appreciation for his physical form.

It had felt good, so good to be wanted for exactly who he was. But it had been a lie. Perhaps not then, on that road. But later, when Hannah had discovered his identity. How could she have still desired him? She'd even planned to betray him or, at least, his family. She wouldn't have known then that he held little affection for his aunts and uncles.

Eoin glanced away from Hannah. He

normally read people so clearly but not her, apparently. He'd never sensed her lies, not even when she admitted to knowing rumors about his family that she'd never shared with him prior. Their trust had never been mutual.

"I'll leave if you want." Hannah's voice sounded small, and it ripped at him. He didn't want her feeling diminished. He loved her brashness and confidence. Yet still he could not look at her.

"Don't go. Not yet." He barely recognized his own voice. It sounded as shredded and mangled as his insides. "I need a moment to compose myself."

"I do not blame you for being angry. You do not need to hold back for my sake." The softness of her tone caused another deluge of pain.

"I'm not angry," he said. And he wasn't. His grandfather had destroyed her family and the lives of countless other tenants. He wanted to be a different duke—a better one, who bore his responsibilities to society, not to well-heeled London Society but the one that included everyone, no matter their wealth or circumstance of birth. But even if he understood her motivations, he still felt not just hurt but rejected.

He stared at the bare stone walls, tracing the mortar joints and cracks with his eyes, just as he had when his grandfather and tutors listed all his faults.

"Why didn't you tell me?" he finally asked. "I know why you said nothing in the beginning, but why not when we"—*Kissed. Embraced. Shared secrets*—"grew closer. Did you think I would want to hide my family's crimes?"

"Because I was a coward." Hannah spoke bluntly, her voice harsh in condemnation of herself. "I didn't want to hurt you, but I was also afraid of losing you."

Her words should have mollified him or at least soothed his agony. And they did... but not enough. Hannah had lied before, and Eoin had trouble believing that anyone wanted him for himself.

"I was my grandfather's puppet"—Eoin still couldn't turn in Hannah's direction—"and this was the attic where he stored me. When he died, I was left empty. Then I met you, and

I started to believe I wasn't just a shell. You didn't tell me what to do or how to think, and you chose to be by my side simply because you enjoyed my company. That gave me confidence to trust my own inner thoughts and desires. I even started to act upon them. And now I learn that our entire relationship was predicated on a lie. You didn't break my trust just in you but in myself."

Hannah made a guttural sound that echoed Eoin's own pain. He yearned to take her into his arms, to comfort both of them. But he couldn't reach out. Not yet at least.

Resolutely, he walked over to one of the deeply recessed windows. He leaned against the stone sill, feeling the coolness of the rock even as the summer heat bore through the glass. "I understand why you made the decisions that you did. I realize that my family was ultimately at fault. But even if I comprehend why, I cannot stop my emotional response. I have spent too many years suppressing my feelings, and they will no longer be suffocated under logic, I am afraid."

"I—I don't want you to do that either. I want

you to be free of all the unnatural restraints that your grandfather foisted upon you." Hannah's voice sounded teary, and Eoin scraped his fingers against the sandstone. But he kept his gaze on the lands that were now his burden.

"I may very well work through this, Hannah." Eoin felt something wet strike his cheeks, but he did not reach up to wipe the tears away. It would hurt Hannah more deeply if she realized he was crying. "I know you say that your affections for me are real, but I must relearn how to believe your claims."

"Do you wish for me to leave now that you have said your piece?" Hannah was back to being unusually meek.

"It may be for the best. I need quietude, Hannah, to make sense of all this."

"Do you wish for me to depart altogether or just to leave this chamber? If I promise to stay out of your way, should I continue to help investigate?" Hannah asked. "It is the least I can do."

"You may help look for clues with the others," Eoin allowed. "I am not banishing you from an entire fortress—just one particular tower. There's nothing in here of import anyway. The family never uses this drafty place."

Eoin heard Hannah's footsteps cross the room. The wooden door squeaked open, but it did not shut immediately.

"You are wrong about one thing, Eoin. There is something very valuable in this turret, and that is you."

Then Hannah was gone, and Eoin was alone. Again. Except for one very overprotective gosling.

He buried his head in his hands and stood frozen, his shoulders shaking with silent sobs. He'd cried every night in this room after his grandfather had ripped him from his family. And then one evening the tears hadn't come, and he'd felt... nothing. He'd become as barren as this empty chamber until he'd met an irrepressible redhead on a moonlit country road.

But now... now he was sore afraid he would be hollow again.

## Chapter Twenty-Two

"What is the point of teaching me to think and fight for myself if you're going to literally storm castles and treat me like some bloody damsel in distress?" Hannah asked as she, Sophia, and her parents were scouring Lord Hugh's personal rooms. The rest of her friends from the Black Sheep had arrived in the morning, and they'd split into groups. Eoin—who could barely even look at Hannah, let alone speak to her—was searching with his sister, his mother, and Powys. Charlotte, Matthew, and Calliope formed the third contingent.

"You were with a bloody Aucourte who was proposing marriage to you!" her father grumped as he withdrew yet another bottle that still smelled faintly of gin. Fortunately, this one was empty. They had found several bottles under the bed that Hugh had evidently used instead of a chamber pot. Apparently, he'd been hiding the extent of his drunkenness from even the servants like a small child would sweep evidence of a broken plate under furniture. He must have worried that the staff would report him to his father.

"Marriage! Marriage!" Pan cackled gleefully as he soared around the room. He was very pleased with himself today, especially after he'd flown into the hackney carriage after Sophia and Hannah's mother. Since they were chasing after Hannah's father, they'd just brought the cheeky creature along.

"Yes, he was proposing, Papa! Which, last time I checked, is not dastardly." Hannah slowly lifted the lid of a battered trunk, half afraid of what she would find.

"Well to be fair, a betrothal could be perilous," Sophia said as she pulled open a drawer in a massive writing desk situated near the window. "Consider Viscount Hawley. Any offer of marriage from him would have been very hazardous for the poor lady receiving it."

"Not. Helping," Hannah said between her gritted teeth as she paused from her search to send Sophia a scathing look. "Besides, Eoin is nothing like that murderous fiend."

Frustration filled Hannah, although most of her fury was aimed at herself. Yes, she could blame her father for barging into the room yesterday, but she was the one who hadn't mustered up the courage to tell Eoin the truth. If she had, she likely wouldn't have wounded him so deeply. And it hurt, knowing how much she'd injured him—nay, crushed him. She'd spent the whole night lying awake, just wanting to rush to him and offer comfort. But she'd lost that right. He'd asked for distance, and it was her duty to provide it, no matter what it cost her personally.

"Please cease calling the new Foxglen by his given name. Familiarity with a man that high in the instep will do you no good," her father complained as he continued to pull disgusting glass containers from below Hugh's feather mattress. "And why have I been assigned the filthiest duty?"

"Because you deserve a little purgatory,

dear," Hannah's mother said in her dulcet yet crisp tone. In this, Hannah entirely agreed. She'd earned some penance herself, which was why she'd volunteered to search the cavernous trunk. Although as of yet, she'd discovered nothing but winter blankets.

"You cannot be happy that Hannah is cavorting with a duke!" Her father looked more horrified by the idea of Hannah's mother approving of her relationship than of Hugh's foul mess.

"You forget that I am the daughter of a nobleman," Mama pointed out. "And once upon a time, I was sneaking out of my bedchamber to meet a dashing former pirate who swore he was now a respectable proprietor of a coffeehouse."

"Well, that was different. I possess a proverbial heart of gold." Papa sent his wife a wink, which she pointly ignored.

"So does Eoin," Hannah replied fiercely as she thought of how she'd driven a dagger through his sternum. "He has grand plans for his estates that will benefit the tenants. I even helped him scour the account books to find ways to save money in order to enact more improvements. He isn't his grandfather, and he isn't his title either. He is so much more than that." And she should have made that abundantly clear to Eoin.

"But—"

"Oh, for pity's sake, do not become Lord Capulet." Mama peeked out from the garderobe that she'd been sorting through. She was in charge of checking Hugh's clothing for evidence and comparing his possessions to the late duke's expense records for his eldest son.

"You dare to use *Romeo and Juliet* against me? That is our story!" Papa dramatically clasped his hand over his heart. Her mother had taught him to read using the play, and he took great pride that he could recite passages from it. He'd always seen himself as Romeo to Mama's Juliet.

"Now your daughter is one of the star-crossed lovers, and you're the crochety father. The late Duke of Foxglen was a terrible villain of a man, but that does not make his grandson one," her mother said, and Hannah nearly barreled across the room to hug her.

"Eoin is a victim of his grandfather as well," Hannah pointed out. "What the old duke did to you and Uncle was unconscionable, and I am not trying to diminish what you suffered. But that man is dead, and perhaps so, too, is the revenge that we sought."

"She is right," Sophia said as she sorted through a pile of missives. "Imagine being ripped away from your mother at the age of six."

"His maternal parentage is surprising," Papa admitted, his tone begrudging. "And I've never been one to chase after ghosts. I gave up destroying the Aucourte name decades ago. My family and the Black Sheep were always more important to me. But that doesn't mean that I am happy to see my daughter with the current Foxglen."

Hannah's anger toward her father started to dissipate. He was hot-tempered but so was she. But after his blood cooled, he was a kind and caring man who would do anything for his loved ones and even rid himself of valid, long-held grudges.

"The first step that Eoin took when he

became a peer was to find his mother and sister." Hannah paused to stare pleadingly at Papa. If she and Eoin were to reconcile, she didn't want to badger her father for his approval. "It's exactly the same choice that you would have made under the same circumstances."

"Perhaps he is not utterly a bad sort," Papa grumbled, but Hannah knew that, for him, it was a capitulation. He might not be completely convinced, but he'd come around once he'd witnessed more of Eoin's true nature... that is, if Eoin wished to still be part of Hannah's life.

"Eoin is truly a wonderful person," Hannah said as she pulled out a featherdown comforter. Beneath it lay neatly rolled-up scrolls. "Oh! I may have found something!"

As Hannah unspooled one of the parchments, everyone hurried to her side. Maybe this was proof of Hugh's involvement with the Horse and Hen. Although Hannah's desire to destroy the Aucourte family name had faded, she desperately wanted to protect Eoin. If they could unseat the Purveyor, then Hannah could honor Eoin's wishes to have time away from her. But until he was safe, she didn't want to leave his side.

"Ugh!" Hannah wrinkled her nose as the canvas unfurled to reveal a naughty image of a well-endowed woman pleasuring herself.

Sophia looked over Hannah's left shoulder and clicked her tongue. "I don't believe a real woman would have those proportions."

"She wouldn't," Hannah's mother agreed succinctly as she took up a position at Hannah's right side.

"What are you three talking...oh." Hannah's father took several rapid steps backward as he covered his eyes.

Mama laughed. "You act as if you'd never seen a scandalous drawing before! If I recall, you used to—"

"Mama!" Hannah shouted in horror, just as Papa cried out desperately, "Not with my daughter holding it!"

Sophia laughed unabashedly as she reached for another scroll. "Let's see if this one is any better...Oh, it's three people this time...I don't think that particular position is anatomically possible."

"And now I am leaving the room," Hannah's father announced before he literally scurried out the door with their laughter ringing after him.

◦◦◦

"What we discovered in Hugh's room only proves he has the mind of a lusty, lazy adolescent." Hannah summarized her group's findings as everyone crowded into the great hall.

"I agree with Hannah's initial assessment that he simply cannot be the Purveyor. He can barely take care of himself," Sophia chimed in.

"Francis's room was in a similar state. We did discover that he has an enormous amount of expensive shoe buckles. Given the old duke's accounts, I do not think that Foxglen purchased them." Lizzie spoke instead of her brother. Eoin had positioned himself toward the edge of the group, despite the entire investigation centering around his safety. He was studiously avoiding Hannah's gaze, and she'd forced herself to accept the distance even as it sliced deep.

"Hugh had expensive waistcoats, many embroidered with gold and silver threads, and in the latest styles. They weren't listed under his expenditures either," Hannah's mother added.

"We checked the sisters' rooms and found nothing particularly out of the ordinary," Charlotte reported. "Both women had a few expensive baubles that didn't match the records, but nothing to the extent of the men's. Eliza possesses a well-organized and extremely large collection of gossip rags. We did discover a diary of sorts in Joan's that lists bets that she makes. She seems quite fastidious about it, recording both her successes and losses."

"Would her winnings be enough to explain the extra finery?" Sophia asked.

"If you include her brothers' possessions, then no," Charlotte answered. "On average, she loses more than she wins. But she did earn enough here and there for a trinket or two. She is also not betting enough to gamble away a fortune like her husband did. She only plays with pin money."

Hannah sighed as worry and frustration

burgeoned inside her. "All we have discovered is that the brothers likely have another source of income."

"That is still valuable information." Sophia reached over to pat Hannah's arm. "It could be an indicator that either Hugh or Francis is the Purveyor, or at the very least, they are helping him."

"Why are we only searching their rooms?" Hannah's father asked. "Perhaps the men made them as disgusting as possible as a deterrent? If so, it worked on us."

"The castle is massive." Eoin spoke for the first time, his gaze on everyone but Hannah. "We figured it would be best to start in the easiest place for my aunts and uncles to stash objects."

"But where would you hide things?" Papa pressed. "You were a boy here. What nooks and crannies did you play in?"

"I was not permitted to roam. My grandfather found rambunctious curiosity inappropriate for his heir." Eoin gazed unflinchingly at Hannah's father. "I have read most of the tomes in the library, and I can tell you the tale behind every portrait of my ancestors, but I know little of the actual building. I sometimes escaped to the gardens, but there aren't any structures or follies on the castle's grounds that would be suitable for squirreling away records."

"You know your family history, though," Sophia pressed, leaning forward. "Did you ever hear mention of a secret tunnel in case of a siege? Perhaps one leads to the river. Or a priest hole?"

"No, especially not the latter." Eoin held himself extremely stiffly, and Hannah wanted so desperately to squeeze him. "The Aucourtes have always been staunchly anti-papist since Henry the Eighth broke with the Catholic Church."

"That is not precisely true," Championess Quick said. "Your paternal grandmother was Catholic. She taught your father his catechism before she died. Her teachings, in fact, began his interest in the Church."

"But she was only an Aucourte by marriage," Charlotte pointed out, "and she lived here over a hundred years after the priest hunts under Queen Elizabeth."

"True," Championess Quick agreed, "but she wasn't the only wife with Catholic sympathies. Now that I think about it, your father did mention a priest hole. One of his female ancestors had hidden her crucifix and other items of worship in it."

"Do you remember where it was?" Hannah asked as she bounced one of her legs impatiently. She wanted to fly from her seat and chase down the clue immediately.

"Oh, I was never here before yesterday," Championess Quick said, "and I haven't thought about that conversation in over twenty years."

"The east wing was added less than half a century ago, so it would either be in one of the old towers or the west wing." Eoin rattled off the information until he paused. "There were major renovations to the south tower in the fifteen hundreds. At that time, the Aucourtes were still earls, and I believe the modifications were a wedding gift for a new countess. She insisted on having one of the solars redecorated before marriage. We should start there."

Matthew spoke up. "I know a trick for

finding hidden rooms. Where do you keep your candles?"

---

Ten minutes later, everyone had gathered in the tower across from the original keep. Thankfully, its staircase, although still twisty and narrow, had much larger openings into the rooms than the older, unrenovated structure, so it had been easier to reach the old solar, where they were standing. Square-shaped wooden panels completely covered the room's sandstone walls. Although the extreme use of oak felt overbearing, it was still more welcoming than the bare rock of Eoin's boyhood chamber, and the false work would be a perfect way to hide a chamber.

"This room does feel smaller than mine although it could be just the effect of the paneling." Eoin glanced around the chamber. "And the towers were built almost a hundred years apart, so there is no telling if their outer dimensions are the same."

"We'll soon see." Matthew lit a candle

and then slowly began to pace the perimeter. When he passed any joinder, he ran the flame up and down the seam.

"What precisely are you testing?" Calliope asked.

"If there's an empty chamber behind one of the walls, the draft from the crack might blow out the light," Matthew explained.

"How do you bloody well know that?" Powys asked. "Is that standard knowledge of physicians?"

Before Matthew could answer, the flame winked out. "Here." Matthew began feeling around the area, searching for a trigger to open the obscured door.

"Let me help," Calliope offered. "My ancestral seat is full of hidden passages."

"Of course it has those," Powys muttered.

Calliope shot him a glare. "Must you always comment snidely about my family and me?"

Powys was not chastised. In fact, the rascal even grinned in what appeared to be a genuinely friendly smile. "Yes. You are, after all, a muse, and I am a playwright. I can't help that you inspire such lines."

"That is only because your unrefined mind can't truly comprehend the brilliance that I engender." Calliope flounced over to where Matthew stood.

Lizzie leaned over to her brother and asked in her unintentionally booming voice, "Lovers' quarrel?"

"It is *not* a lovers' quarrel," Powys snapped. "It is simply a quarrel quarrel."

"Ah yes, your mastery of the English language is nearly Shakespearean." Calliope didn't even spare Powys a glance as she tapped on her chin and studied the decorative scrollwork that ran parallel to the floor and was positioned about a third of the way up the wall.

"What are you looking for, Calliope?" Hannah asked, desperately wanting to end the spat—whether it was between lovers, enemies, or an amalgamation of both.

"An uneven part of the carving. Perhaps it sticks out a little more than the other designs or it is further depressed. Anything that could be pushed or jiggled," she explained.

"I am good with details," Eoin said

woodenly as he joined Calliope. His broad shoulders seemed locked in place as he clasped his hands behind his back. When he stiffly bent to study the artwork, Hannah swore that she could hear his body creak.

"Here," Eoin declared after just a few minutes. "The center of this flower is higher than the others."

"Try moving it," Calliope suggested.

Eoin placed his thumb on the oak circle, and a clicking sound filled the air. Several wall panels popped open at the exact spot where Matthew's candle had been extinguished. The physician stepped back and motioned for Eoin to take the lead. "This is both your castle and your search, Your Grace."

Eoin hesitated, and his aquamarine eyes found Hannah's. Bittersweetness blossomed inside her as she realized that he still instinctively turned toward her for advice. Yet she'd tainted their bond. Before his gaze could skirt away, Hannah tilted her chin toward the hidden passage in encouragement.

Eoin audibly sucked in his breath and marched over to the gap. Gripping the oak, he yanked back on the paneling to reveal a narrow space. Matthew relit his candle and handed it to Eoin, who stepped inside the room.

"Is there anything in there?" Sophia called as she stepped closer.

"I think..." Eoin's reply was muffled. "The passage runs the entire length of the wall, and it appears as if something is piled at the end."

Hannah heard Eoin's footsteps as he moved unseen. Then there was a pause followed by banging noises. Eoin grunted but it sounded like it was from exertion, not pain. Still, Hannah wanted to confirm he was uninjured, but his mother was quicker.

"Are you fine, Eoin? Nothing fell on you?"

"I'm...unscathed," Eoin answered between huffing breaths. Loud scraping echoed through the room. Moments later, a dust-covered Eoin appeared hauling a massive trunk that looked very similar to the one that Hannah had sorted through in Hugh's bedchamber.

"Bollocks, not another one of those!" Hannah's father groaned in dismay.

Eoin paused in trying to wedge the chest

into the main room. "Should I not have brought this for everyone to see?"

"Pay him no heed." Hannah's mother shot her husband an exasperated look. "It is just that we found rather naughty pictures in the last one."

"How naughty?" Calliope asked brightly.

"How disheartening is it that I had the very same question?" Powys asked.

"Do not get excited. They are very unrealistic," Sophia reported.

"Well, they are fantasies, are they not?" Powys pointed out.

"Should I…uh…um…just open this in the priest hole?" Eoin asked, his face a deep scarlet.

"Ignore them all." Hannah swooped in to rescue Eoin as she glared at each of the troublemakers. "This is serious. Banter can happen later."

Eoin reached for the latch and paused. "It's padlocked."

"I can take care of that." Matthew, whose face had also pinkened at the mention of scandalous drawings, walked over to Eoin.

Kneeling down, he produced a set of picks from his boot.

"Who are you?" Powys asked rhetorically, but then he glanced over at Hannah in mock sheepishness. "Pardon. That question was not central to the mystery at hand."

Within seconds, Matthew opened the chest. This one contained neither blankets nor rolled-up scrolls. Instead, books lay in neat stacks.

"Those look like the diaries that Joan uses to keep track of her gambling losses and wins!" Charlotte called as she hurried over. Eoin reached for one of the journals and handed it to her.

"Is the penmanship the same?" he asked when she flipped to the first page.

Charlotte's eyebrows rose as she started furiously scanning the record. "I—I am not sure. It is written in a very odd style, and I cannot decipher anything."

Eoin grabbed another book and scanned it. "It appears to be some sort of code."

"Code?" Sophia stepped forward to snare a volume. "Who would write in code?"

"The Purveyor would!" Hannah's heart thumped wildly. Unable to contain herself, she darted over and plucked up a journal. Thumbing through it, she found an odd combination of letters, squiggles, and numbers. Yet everything was precisely organized into what appeared to be paragraphs.

"I wonder if there is a word key to the cypher?" Sophia asked.

"I was thinking the same thing myself," Matthew said.

"I'll pull out the rest of the chests," Eoin said before he once again disappeared into the priest hole. The men went to help him while the women continued to riffle through the current trunk. Although Charlotte had unearthed a physical set of keys, they found nothing else other than more coded record books.

Hannah kept staring at the odd text. Although she had no prayer of reading it—at least quickly—there was a noticeable pattern. It was clear by the spacing that the jumble of letters, numbers, and symbols represented words. Each paragraph started with three to five words, and the first ones often consisted of just a few letters. Those that didn't start with a short collection of symbols seemed to almost always contain a long word, then one with two characters, and finishing with another lengthier amalgamation. And the two-character words were always and invariably the same. The first short words also repeated frequently.

"They're names!" Hannah hollered to no one in particular.

"Pardon?" Sophia asked as she lifted her head from the trunk she was searching.

"Here!" Hannah stabbed at what was an obvious record, but of what she did not know. "This right here, before the dash, it's most certainly someone's title. See that two-character word? That must be 'of.' The other shorter ones might be Mr., Mrs., Miss, Hon., and so forth!"

Sophia opened a book and ran her finger down the page. "I do think you're right!"

"Which means we can figure out what some of the symbols mean," Charlotte cried out in excitement.

"But even with knowing a few, it will take

ages to figure out," Hannah sighed. And during that time, the Purveyor would still be trying to kill Eoin.

"What's happening?" Powys asked as he helped Eoin drag out another trunk.

As Sophia told the men about the discovery, Hannah glanced back at the writing. When she spoke, she mostly muttered the words to herself. "I don't think this is a simple account book. There are too many words, nor do they appear in list form."

Sophia scanned the journal that she held. "I see what you mean."

"Do you think they could be descriptions of bets?" Hannah asked.

Charlotte looked over Hannah's shoulder and then shook her head. "The entries are much longer than those in Joan's diary."

"It is as if they are telling a story or recording an event in the person's life," Hannah mused as she rubbed along the ink, almost as if she could conjure the author's thoughts.

"Also why bother writing a bet in code?" Powys asked. "The entire point of recording a wager is to create evidence if the other person tries to wriggle out of the agreement. You wouldn't wish to keep it a secret."

Secret. The word rushed around Hannah's mind and tugged at a half-forgotten memory.

"We know that the Purveyor began by selling gin," Hannah said slowly.

"From the little that I know, that is correct," Eoin's mother confirmed.

"But gin no longer makes a profit." Hannah tapped her foot as she thought. "Thus, the Purveyor must be selling something else now."

"There's the bearbaiting and boxing, not to mention the tavern itself. Entertainment can be very profitable as both Championess Quick and I can attest," Powys pointed out.

"But none are illegal." Eoin's voice was measured and distant, and Hannah knew that he was working through the facts just like she was. "There must be something illicit that the Purveyor wishes to hide. If not, why would he try to kill me for poking around his enterprise?"

*Don't go chasing after spirits and secrets.*

The half-remembered words ushered in an epiphany. Hannah slammed the book closed.

"I've got it! I know what's recorded in here!"

Before Hannah could say more, Lord Percy burst into the room, followed by a vaguely familiar and very raggedy boy. As the youth nervously worried his fingers, recognition slammed into Hannah. He was the adolescent who frequented the Horse and Hen—the young man who Eoin had twice saved.

"The Black Sheep is going to be attacked in two days hence by the Purveyor," Lord Percy gasped out.

## Chapter Twenty-Three

Ever since Eoin had learned Hannah's true motivations for assisting him in his search for his mother and his sister, he'd felt numb. It was as if he'd once again become an automaton—only he wasn't governed by clockwork but by unrelating logic. He'd sorted through Francis's belongings and felt…nothing. Even when the group had discovered the priest hole, he hadn't experienced a single spark of adventurous energy. He'd just wanted the whole affair to be over. If they unearthed damning evidence indicting his uncles, then the Wicks could have their revenge, and Eoin could have his peace.

But then Lord Percy had burst into the solar and announced that the Black Sheep—Hannah's home and livelihood—was under threat. And although it was the Purveyor who was planning the attack, the fault was entirely with Eoin. He'd dragged Hannah into this dangerous debacle.

He would not allow any harm to come to her or to the establishment that she and her family had labored to build. Eoin's need to protect sliced through the hazy cocoon surrounding his emotions. He would bring down the Purveyor—no matter who was behind the appellation.

"What?" Sophia cried. "How would you know? Why?"

"This brave young man, Peter, told me when I was having coffee at the Black Sheep. Fortunately, I knew you would all be here today," Lord Percy said theatrically as he swept his arm toward the waif from the Horse and Hen. The boy was clearly frightened. He clawed at his own hands as he stood with his face directed straight at the ground.

Hannah hurried over to the lad, her countenance soft and welcoming. "Are you hurt at all, Peter? Did you escape from the Horse and Hen?"

Peter's chin jutted out defiantly even as it wobbled. "I can come and go of my own accord. Nobody noticed me."

Eoin noticed that the youth didn't answer Hannah's first question. Given the life he led, Peter was probably always suffering from some bruise or wound.

"You didn't come to us for aid?" Hannah asked.

Peter shook his head and then jerked his chin in Eoin's direction. "I owe that big man a favor, and I've come to repay it. Mr. Jenks was calling for men and lads to burn down the Black Sheep. We're supposed to make it seem like a right old riot. I remembered you telling me to head to that coffeehouse if I ever wanted to work for someone other than a kidsman. So I knew it had something to do with the two of you."

"Thank you," Eoin said as he walked over to the youth, trying not to step too close and crowd him. "I'll reward you handsomely, and I can offer you a place to stay too. I won't make you pick pockets or fight other boys."

The youth puffed out his chest. "How am I going to learn to defend myself if I stay out of the ring?"

"I'll teach you," Eoin's mother said. "In fact, I'll make you my student."

Peter seemed vastly unimpressed. "Who are you?"

"I'm the Duke of Foxglen's mother and Championess Quick," she answered.

The boy's eyes grew huge. "I thought he was a toff! But, cor, he's your son! Everyone knows about you. You're famous at the Horse and Hen!"

"Then you know that I can protect you," Championess Quick said.

"We can," Lizzie chimed in. "You'll be safe with us, and we'll teach you how to fight anyone, even adults."

Peter glanced at them skeptically. "You want me to tell you about the Purveyor, don't you?"

"You still have a place with us even if you say nothing more," Championess Quick promised. "You've already put yourself in danger to warn us about the Black Sheep, and we will protect you."

Eoin's worry increased. "Your amphitheater! If they are attacking the coffeehouse, your establishment could be next. Even if the Purveyor has no connection to my uncles, he still knows that I was asking about you or at least about the woman who used to work at the Horse and Hen."

"Although we do not know for certain that the Purveyor knows of our connection, I will increase our guards, and I can send some to the Black Sheep as well." His mother reached forward—likely to pat his hand—but she stopped midair. Pain washed through Eoin as he wished the strain between them could disappear. But his mother's misplaced guilt would take time to ebb.

"The Purveyor does realize that you're Eoin's mother," Hannah said definitively. "In fact, the Purveyor knows the secrets of a lot of people, especially high-ranked ones. I suspect that he may even know secrets of the Crown itself."

"What do you mean?" Lizzie demanded, her hands on her hips as she towered over Hannah. It was clear that she hadn't forgiven Hannah for misleading Eoin. "Did you really discover something about those notebooks or is this another one of your games?"

Eoin rubbed his thumb against his other fingers and wished that his sister weren't so dedicated to her role of an avenging Fury.

"Hannah would not lie about this. It will do us no good if we attack each other."

"The Purveyor collects and sells secrets," Hannah explained. "Those books are his records. It makes sense why they would be in code and why each entry is relatively long."

"However did you arrive at that conclusion?" Sophia asked.

"When Eoin and I first went to the Horse and Hen, an elderly man stopped us in the street and told us not to chase 'spirits and secrets.' I never paid him much heed, especially when we found Championess Quick and Lizzie. But then it struck me. What if the man wasn't talking about ghosts but about gin? And if that part was true, maybe the first was accurate too."

Despite everything, a swell of pride burst through Eoin at Hannah's brilliant deductions. She was a clever one, indeed. And unlike him, she didn't rely on her logic alone, but her feelings as well.

"But secrets could mean so much," Sophia pressed, obviously not as completely won over by her cousin's theory as Eoin was.

"True, but spirits turned out to be what the Horse and Hen initially sold, so what if they were selling secrets too? The right type of information could be used to extort great funds."

"If the rumors about the Aucourtes engaging in illicit activity are true," Eoin added slowly as his own mind began to process the implications of Hannah's conjectures, "then perhaps some of that knowledge is treasonous. If the Purveyor knows secrets about the people in power, it makes sense how he could suppress almost all gossip about him."

"But how could the Purveyor acquire such critical intelligence?" Calliope asked. "It is not precisely an establishment that caters to nobles."

Mr. Powys snorted. "You do realize that you nobs employ plenty of us commonfolk who are more than willing to sell your precious confidences."

Hannah nodded. "Not to mention that the Horse and Hen may own the brothels lining the street. Plenty of nobs visit those, and they might stop by and gamble on a bloody fight too."

"It makes sense that the Purveyor could

parlay his original business into the new one. If you can't pay for gin or if you suffer significant losses during a bet, just pay in secrets," Eoin added as everything became clearer. "And ones that could be sold for political reasons would be the most valuable. Imagine what France would pay for intelligence about the Crown."

"You're right—even about the treason. There's always French blokes pretending to be English at the Horse and Hen." Peter's voice was quiet and extremely hesitant, but he spoke audibly enough. His eyes remained trained downward as he scuffed at the floors with his bare toes, which stuck out from his tattered, too-small shoes.

"Well, the solution is simple," Lord Percy said. "We alert—well, I suppose I don't know who we alert—the Royal Guards, perhaps, or maybe the dragoons—and then we have them storm the Horse and Hen tonight."

"With what proof?" Eoin asked. "All we have are piles of journals that no one can read and vague rumors."

"Peter can collaborate!" Lord Percy went to touch the boy's shoulder but immediately stopped when the youth flinched, his blue eyes wide in his pale, pinched face.

"I don't believe that Peter would feel comfortable talking to soldiers," Hannah gently pointed out. "And they wouldn't listen to him either."

"But we know the Purveyor must be one of Eoin's uncles." Lord Percy frowned.

"Unless they just help maintain the books." Eoin still couldn't believe that either Hugh or Francis could be the mastermind.

"Peter, would you feel comfortable describing the Purveyor to us?" Hannah asked. "You don't have to tell us if you don't wish to. We won't get mad or punish you in any way."

Peter glanced up at her, then away, and then up again. Gone was the defiant boy who'd tried to pick Eoin's pocket. But Hannah and Eoin had been in Peter's sphere then, and he'd been following the code that he'd been raised under. Now he was standing in a literal castle surrounded by ancient wealth and being asked to reveal the identity of a most likely violent man with untold criminal connections.

"Nobody sees him—at least not more than

a glimpse or two." Peter spoke haltingly, yet clearly. "Mr. Jenks is who speaks for him. I saw the Purveyor once or twice, though. He has curly blond hair and blue eyes, and he's always surrounded by doxies."

Shock flowed through Eoin. "That description does match either of my uncles."

"Is that enough proof?" Lord Percy asked as he lifted his heels and then plunked them back down in an eager bounce.

"What would we even report?" Eoin asked. "It sounds too fanciful. My uncles might not be well liked in Society, but I, myself, can hardly believe what we've uncovered. I highly doubt I could convince others to take such drastic actions as summoning a small army."

"Well, then, we just create our own." Lizzie slammed her fist into her palm. "We have plenty of fighters. If they want to start a riot at the Black Sheep, then we do it at the Horse and Hen first."

"No," Hannah and Sophia said immediately.

"Too many people could get hurt," Sophia said.

"We need a better plan." Hannah began

to pace rapidly around the room. "What we require is proof, and we'll likely find it in the Horse and Hen."

"How?" Powys asked. "It is not as if you can simply stroll inside the tavern. It is clear you'll be recognized. In fact, any of us will likely be noticed. This Purveyor must have been gathering a great deal of information about the Black Sheep. I agree with Miss Quick's plan. Some of my workers at the Grand would be willing to help storm the building."

"I do not want anyone unnecessarily injured either, but a preemptive attack may be the only option. Trying to locate the Purveyor's den would be nearly impossible in that rabbit warren of connected buildings," Championess Quick pointed out. "I couldn't be your guide. I barely recall the old twisting passages, and I am sure they have been modified during the past twenty years. Not to mention that any room of interest would likely be locked. The Purveyor could not have survived this long if he was not a cautious man."

"But we have the set of keys that Charlotte found in the trunk. Perhaps they are for the

Horse and Hen!" Hannah tore over to the table, where a big cast iron ring lay. When she lifted it triumphantly into the air, a pleasant jangle filled the room. Although everyone else seemed skeptical, Eoin couldn't help but feel a swell of charged energy about Hannah's plan. He'd watched as this woman barreled her way through every social strata in order for him to discover his mother and his sister. She didn't care about the odds; she just turned them in her favor.

"That only solves one of the issues that my mother listed," Lizzie said, her feet spread apart as if she were participating in physical rather than verbal sparring. "Almost everyone agrees with my plan."

"Bollocks! Bollocks! Bollocks!" Pan cried out after being unusually quiet during the entire conversation. Perhaps castles intimidated the feathered fiend.

"Well, almost everyone but the parrot," Lizzie corrected, "which shows how bird-witted your scheme is."

"Pan is extremely intelligent, not to mention very discerning," Hannah replied haughtily, seeming more perturbed by the criticisms against her pet than herself.

"Although I might not agree with Hannah's assessment of Pan," Eoin said slowly, "I don't believe we've heard all the details of what Hannah is plotting."

At his words, Hannah glanced in his direction, and her green eyes searched his countenance. She'd been so bold in these last few minutes and exactly like the woman he'd originally met. But now he saw her hesitancy and her remorse. His support had surprised her, perhaps even touched her. But what shocked him was how much she had apparently wanted it and maybe even needed it. He wasn't sure where they stood, but he knew one thing. In this, he believed in her.

So he nodded—one short dip of his chin. That was all it took. A confident grin spread over her face, and the doubt in her eyes vanished.

"Is there another part of your plan, Miss Wick?" Eoin's mother asked.

Hannah's smile grew even wider. "Most certainly. It all begins with a distraction, and that's where I will need your help."

# Chapter Twenty-Four

"Halt! You're not allowed to enter!" The guard positioned his burly body in front of the Horse and Hen's cellar steps.

Lizzie marched over to him, matching his stance. "I'll give you one opportunity to step aside."

The man snorted as he ran his gaze up and down her body, the gesture both lewd and dismissive. Hannah's own blood steamed, and she could only imagine Lizzie's ire. The foolish sentry had no idea the fury that he'd just triggered.

"How is a doxy like you going to stop me?" the fool chortled.

"That was your chance." Lizzie smiled. It was not kind. The hapless watchman was still laughing when Lizzie's fist caught him in the temple. He blinked. Once. And then he crumpled to the ground.

Lizzie glanced over her shoulder at the group of mostly female boxers behind her. "The way is clear."

Championess Quick was the first to step around the unconscious sentinel. Lizzie followed with Hannah close behind. This time, she wore women's clothing rather than a lad's. Many of the women wore masks, which Calliope had provided. The Quick women, however, had chosen to enter barefaced.

Eoin's mother marched straight past Ursus's empty cage. When she burst into the main room, she spread her feet wide and planted her fists against her hips. She'd donned her famous Dutch trousers and plaited her hair into a braided crown about her head.

"I heard this establishment has been maligning my name!" Championess Quick didn't even need to shout. Her deep sonorous voice boomed easily around the cavernous chamber. The men gathered for the fight jostled each other and pointed to the entranceway. Although there were a few whispered voices declaring her identity, the room grew unnaturally still as the crowd sensed an upcoming spectacle.

"Folks here have been saying that I've forgotten my beginnings. Worse, they are disparaging my prizefighters! They have called my people weaklings who do not have the stamina for a real fight. We cannot let such aspersions stand!" Eoin's mother cried.

She was magnificent as she pumped her fists into the air, her biceps bulging under her white shirt. Beside her, Lizzie emitted a battle cry that rivaled those of the famed Valkyries.

"This... is highly unorthodox and unacceptable," Jenks cried from the ring, sounding more like an aristocratic matron upset that a luncheon was ruined by bad behavior than a master of ceremonies for brutal fights.

Immediately, the crowd began to boo at Jenks. Raised voices sounded around the room as the gathered throng clamored to watch the unplanned bouts.

"Let 'em tussle!"

"I'll bet on the Horse and Hen boxers!"

"Have you gone daft? That's the infamous Championess Quick."

"Let's see how much fight the old girl has left in her!"

"You're nothing but a coward, Jenks!"

"Lily-livered ninny!"

"Fight! Fight! Fight!"

"What is this I hear?" a new voice bellowed through the crowd. Like Championess Quick, the dark-haired man didn't need to scream to project his words through the room. He strolled through the throng like a prince or perhaps a god, Dionysus in particular. In fact, during the last and only time that Hannah had encountered the Duke of Blackglen, he'd been wearing a Bacchus outfit at one of his famous masquerade balls. Yet the notorious rogue didn't need to don robes and reveal swaths of his chiseled chest to evoke the sense of debauchery. Even in his more formal attire, Lady Calliope's half brother radiated sensual wickedness. Perhaps it was the way his sculptured lips quirked just slightly at the ends, drawing attention to his sharp cheekbones. Or it could be the ever-present naughty gleam in his sapphire-like blue eyes. Then again, he had a way of seeming to stand straight yet slouch at the same time as he glided with an elegance that was both lazy and commanding.

Like at his parties, the Duke of Blackglen wore no mask. However, the revelers that he'd brought with him did. Eoin was among the legendary peer's entourage, and so were the rest of their friends from the Black Sheep. But there were still other nobles eager to participate in what Blackglen had promised to be a grand lark.

Hannah hadn't been positive that Calliope would be able to convince her sibling to join her scheme. Fortunately, the man had leaped at the opportunity when they'd offered him the bait: a rematch against the famed Lizzie Quick.

"I'd heard rumors that the Horse and Hen offered the most thrilling fights in London—better than any of the shiny but boring amphitheaters that are popular right now." Blackglen spoke with a laconic drawl that, despite its slowness, or perhaps because of it, was utterly compelling. "Yet what do I witness when I step inside for the first time? A cumberground sniveling about something being unorthodox! What is unconventional about a challenge? I say that trying to scurry away from a match is actually what would be heretical in prizefighting!"

"Hear! Hear!" Cheers rose up as men clung one-handed from the hodgepodge of wooden support structures while they waved their other fists in the air. Among the chorus of affirmations were the whispers of people proclaiming the presence of the Duke of Debauchery.

Jenks looked around wildly, appearing as cornered as Hannah had felt when the spineless man had tried to force Eoin into the ring. Clearly, the man realized that the Horse and Hen had been invaded, but he was utterly powerless to stop it. He kept glancing up, and Hannah tried to follow his gaze. Could there be a secret space where the Purveyor could view the action similar to the room at Championess Quick's?

"If you are not willing to have your men

spar with Championess Quick's fighters, then I will volunteer myself. I have been waiting for a rematch with Lizzie for years!" Blackglen slowly circled, his arms raised as he addressed every inch of the crowded, underground structure.

"Prepare to lose once more!" Lizzie shouted back.

Hannah nodded to one of the women who'd entered with them and had been tasked with carrying the equipment. The prizefighter tossed two quarterstaffs, and Lizzie easily caught one in each hand. She turned and gently threw a rod to Blackglen. Although he plucked it from the air, his movements weren't as seamless as Lizzie's. The left corner of his mouth flattened ever so slightly, and it was clear that he'd noticed the difference and didn't like it.

The bout between them was going to be interesting. It was too bad that Hannah would miss it.

The crowd parted to allow Lizzie and Blackglen to head into the ring. Lizzie marched with a fierce purpose while Blackglen seemed like he was simply taking in the sights at the Tower of London. Jenks quivered like a hare as he once again swung his gaze wildly around the room. He was clearly looking for assistance or maybe a sign on how to proceed. Whatever he wanted, he wasn't finding it.

Lizzie reached the pit first, and the noise in the room rose to painful levels. Just when it seemed like the shouts could not grow in volume, Blackglen entered the arena. More screams erupted. Tension swirled between the two contestants as they faced each other. Lizzie was not a small woman, but Blackglen had a few inches on her vertically and clearly outweighed her by several stone. Hannah knew, though, that what Lizzie lacked in size, she could make up for by being quick and light on her feet. Moreover, she'd already defeated Blackglen once before. The outcome of this bout was no foregone conclusion.

"Well?" Blackglen asked Jenks in that perennially cavalier way of his. "Are you going to start the fight or must I find someone to even do that?"

Blackglen's statement inspired more

invectives from the crowd aimed at the master of ceremonies.

"Lily-livered bastard!"

"Coward."

"Chicken-hearted knave!"

At each insult, the light in Jenks's eyes grew wilder and wilder. The man was clearly only accustomed to stirring up a frenzy rather than being on the receiving end of fury. With palpable reluctance, Jenks shouted for the bout to begin.

Yet neither Blackglen nor Lizzie flew at the other. Instead, they slowly circled, each on the balls of their feet, each gripping their quarterstaff tightly, each entirely focused on the match.

Although Hannah had staged this fight, it wasn't a fake one. The goal was for the two opponents to draw out the match as long as possible, but Hannah knew that both wanted to win.

"We need to go," Sophia hissed in Hannah's ear as she tugged on her arm.

Hannah nodded. After all, that was why she had engineered this whole performance.

With everyone distracted, she and Sophia gathered the rest of their family and friends along with Eoin. Championess Quick had told them where to find the initial passageway from the cellar, and Peter, who'd remained safely behind at Championess Quick's, had confirmed that the hidden hallway was still in use.

They'd agreed to split into two groups. To Hannah's surprise and relief, Eoin had volunteered to join hers. Although she knew that it didn't mean he'd forgiven her—or was anywhere close to fully trusting her again—she was glad that he felt comfortable enough to search with her.

Matthew—with his lock-picking abilities—headed up one of the teams while Eoin carried the set of keys that Charlotte had found. It wouldn't be easy finding the codebook, especially when they didn't even know how many rooms they would encounter. But they could always stumble across some other damning evidence.

"You lead," Eoin told Hannah softly as they ducked behind the barrels and crates that obscured the entrance to the rest of the building.

"Are you certain?" Hannah asked nervously.

"Until I met you, I'd never embarked on a real adventure," Eoin replied. "You have more experience."

Hannah's heart squeezed so tightly that she almost reached up to rub it. She had wanted to fill Eoin's solitary existence with so much joy. But she'd lost that opportunity.

"Understood." Hannah's voice sounded strained even to her own ears, and she busied herself with pulling out the dark lantern that she'd hidden under her skirts. Lighting it, she slipped into the opening, which was only slightly roomier than doorways leading to the circular staircase in Eoin's boyhood tower.

Along with a ground-floor tunnel that branched off in both directions, there was one set of rickety stairs leading straight up. If Hannah was correct that Jenks had been glancing toward a secret room, then this passage was almost directly opposite it. By Hannah's calculations, they were currently standing directly under the Horse and Hen's tavern room. Thus, the steps likely led to the public house. If Hannah wished to reach the Purveyor's lair, she'd need to remain subterranean. Hannah led her group to the right while Matthew's team went left.

The air smelled damp and rotten. It wasn't just mildew but the stench of decay. Hannah had difficulties imagining the spoiled Hugh or Francis scurrying along the smelly corridors in their finest silks and shiny shoe buckles. But someone intelligent enough to run a massive criminal organization would be clever enough to obscure their true nature.

At the thought, an odd sensation whispered through Hannah. "I think we've missed something."

"Pardon?" Eoin asked as he followed close behind her, his pistol in his hand. Her father, mother, and Sophia had also drawn their weapons.

"I feel as if we've overlooked something important—or didn't put the pieces together properly." Hannah paused to rub at her temples as if that could somehow massage her nascent thoughts into being.

"We've got no time, lass," her father warned. "We'll discover all the facts soon enough if we find this bastard's lair."

It didn't surprise Hannah how quickly Papa's anger had transferred from the Aucourte family in general to the Purveyor in particular. The shadowy figure had declared war upon the Black Sheep, and her father was practical enough to believe that any enemy of his enemy was now a friend. But it was more than just necessity. In the carriage ride over with her mother, father, and cousin, Hannah had explained her growing esteem for Eoin. Hannah knew that Papa wouldn't allow the past to interfere with his daughter's current happiness.

"Yes, you're right," Hannah said, shaking herself from her momentary reverie. She'd had enough time to think. Now was the occasion for action.

She stormed ahead, twisting through the passage as it narrowed and then suddenly turned into a sizable storage room before constricting again. The tunnel-like structure was mostly dark. In a few places, the plaster had crumbled away, and the lathe had broken.

Light from the main underground room oozed in through those sections, along with the shouts from the crowd. By the sound of it, Lizzie had landed at least two strikes against Blackglen while managing to dance just out of reach of his quarterstaff.

"There's a staircase," Eoin whispered near Hannah's ear, and for a moment, she needed to close her eyes against the onslaught of unexpected emotions. It reminded her too keenly of their embraces—embraces that would likely never occur again.

Hannah focused instead on the rickety jumble of wood, which was more akin to a ladder than steps that led to a hatch in the ceiling. The group hadn't transversed enough ground to reach what Hannah suspected was a secret viewing area. But she also didn't know if such a place even existed.

"I'll go first," Eoin said.

Before Hannah could stop him, he'd scrambled up the haphazard arrangement of planks. Luckily, it held his weight. Eoin pushed on the trapdoor, but it only opened a scant inch.

"Is it latched from above?" Hannah asked as she started to climb too.

"Yes, but I can easily break it." Eoin shoved on the wood. The sound of metal scraping against metal was quickly followed by the cracking of oak. The covering popped free.

"Not subtle but effective," Hannah's father said quietly.

Both Hannah and her mother shushed him, but fortunately, Eoin didn't appear to hear. He was already pushing his head and shoulders through the opening.

Two women screamed—the sound high and piercing. The rumble of a man's voice followed. Eoin quickly ducked back down, slamming the broken hatch behind him. Even in the low light of the lantern, Hannah could easily detect his blush.

"That was one of the brothels." Eoin sounded choked even as he managed to speak succinctly.

Hannah's father started to laugh heartily, but her mother shoved her elbow in his gullet. He instantly doubled over before he straightened.

"Ow!" Papa rubbed his belly and shot his wife a baleful look. "What? It was amusing."

Hannah's mother did not deign to answer. Her expression, though, was withering.

"Let's keep exploring!" Hannah attempted to assuage the awkwardness. Unfortunately, her overly bright tone only drew more attention to the situation. Quickly, she jumped down from the ladder, allowing Eoin to follow.

Their group moved quietly forward. A few minutes later, Hannah spotted another trapdoor in the ceiling. This time, though, there were no stairs or ladder.

"If you get on my shoulders, you could push it open as long as it's not latched," Eoin suggested—his usually steady gaze flicking back and forth from Hannah's face. It was clear that he still felt uncomfortable around her, and her parents' presence wasn't helping.

"That should work." Hannah almost winced at how stiff she also sounded.

Hannah handed her lantern and pistol to Sophia while Eoin bent for Hannah to climb onto his back. Fortunately for her sanity, her petticoats provided enough layers that she didn't feel his muscles against her thighs.

*This is simply the most practical solution*, she reminded herself sternly. *This is not an excuse to be physically close. It is the only option.*

After Eoin stood up, Hannah quickly clambered to his shoulders. They needed to move efficiently, and her heart couldn't handle much more.

This trapdoor had a lock installed on it, but thankfully, the second key that Hannah tried worked. Once unlatched, the wood panel was light enough for Hannah to easily push it upward. Peeking through the small crack that she'd created, she spied nothing but darkness.

"I need a light," she whispered.

Sophia held up the lantern, and Hannah snagged it. Using one hand to raise the door, she lifted the lamp and allowed a small glowing circle to escape into the blackness. Copper winked, and cobwebs hung like the Spanish moss that grew on the island home of Hannah's aunt. Emboldened, Hannah laid the lamp on the floorboards above her and hoisted herself into the room.

"Hannah?" Eoin whispered from below, his voice threaded with worry.

"It's just an empty space." Hannah spoke in her regular tone as she retrieved the lantern and held it high above her head. Sure enough, disused stills shined in the warm glow. "This chamber must have been used for gin production."

When Hannah walked, she sent puffs of dust into the air. There were no windows here, and she could spy no other entrances. It would have been a very secure place to make illegal spirits, and by the sheer quantity of equipment, it must have been an extremely successful operation.

She rapidly walked the perimeter of the warehouse-like facility. She hoped to find some abandoned records that might prove the identity of the Purveyor. However, she came across nothing but a few angry rats.

"Are you safe up there?" Eoin wasn't even trying to hide his worry, but Hannah still didn't know how to interpret his concern. It was clear that, despite her lies of omission, he still cared for her. But was it enough? And was it fair for her to push for a relationship despite all that had transpired?

"Yes," Hannah said, careful to speak at a normal volume instead of raising her voice. Even though it was clear that the place was abandoned, she had no idea how thin the walls were or what establishments were on the other side. "They must have made gin here before the increase in grain prices."

Scanning the space one last time, Hannah headed over to the trapdoor. When she peered through the opening, she found Eoin looking up expectantly. As she considered the drop, she realized that it might have been easier climbing up than down.

"If you sit and dangle your legs, I should be able to lift you down," Eoin suggested. Of course, he'd registered her dilemma almost immediately.

Hannah hesitated. This would be even more like an embrace. But she really had no choice.

Eoin encircled her legs with his arms. As he held her high and straight in the air, she rested her hands against his shoulders. Pushing off, she avoided sliding down his chest. Yet even as she kept their bodies separated, the pose was still one of a celebrating couple. It was akin to how a groom would lift his bride above his head as they spun around in utter glee. But this was a mission, not a passion.

Hannah landed lightly on her feet, but her heart fell with a dull thud. She glanced at Eoin, and an unfamiliar wave of awkwardness nearly drowned her. Forcing her eyes not to dart away, she nodded sharply. "Thank you."

Then she spun with military precision toward the unexplored part of the passage. Her body was so stiff that she practically marched. She could hear Eoin and her family following. The tunnel veered to the right, and Hannah wondered if they were crossing under the alley above them. After a short while, the passage turned right again. They were definitely parallel to where they'd been previously.

Hannah's heart kicked up in her chest, and nervous excitement pumped through her. They were headed in the direction of the suspected secret room. But before they reached where she assumed it would be, they discovered another set of stairs.

"Based on how far we've traveled, I believe we're under the other brothel." Eoin's face was a bright red once again, and the tips of his ears had even begun to turn mauve.

"I shall check, then," Sophia said as she boldly marched up the steps with her gun in hand. She carefully lifted the unlocked trapdoor a few inches and then let it silently fall back into place.

Without any other reaction, she climbed down and gave Eoin a curt nod of acknowledgment. "Your assumption is correct. Let's proceed."

Hannah once again led the way. Just as she thought they were nearing the potential hidden lair of the Purveyor, the passageway had a strange jog. Although the fieldstone walls appeared to be solid in the glow of their lanterns, Hannah wasn't so certain.

"We should investigate here." Hannah lifted her light high as she studied the mishmash of rocks.

"Any reason?" her father asked as he nudged at one of the larger pieces of sandstone with the toe of his boot.

"Eoin's mother and sister have a hidden room in their amphitheater from whence they can view the bouts. I thought I noticed something similar in the main room under the Horse and Hen. If I am correct, the hidden solar should be located above us."

"Perhaps the Purveyor was inspired by the priest hole to create a hidden chamber," Sophia said. "Or rather a hidden staircase within an already secret tunnel."

"Does that mean we should try the candle trick?" Hannah's father asked.

Hannah's mother shook her head. "We already know that it is behind that bulge."

"But it is stone!" Papa protested.

"It's likely just a façade of hewn rocks adhered to a base of wood." Eoin headed over to the wall and studied it carefully. "Which would still make it dreadfully heavy to move. There must be a mechanism involving pulleys."

"It would also be exceedingly expensive to create," Hannah said as she looked for anything unusual on the already uneven walls. "Which demonstrates how much wealth the Purveyor must have accumulated."

"And it shows an almost obsessive suspiciousness and fear," Eoin said. "We are so deep within the bowels of this convoluted maze, yet the Purveyor still felt the need to obscure the entrance to their inner sanctuary?"

"Well, we are here poking at rocks." Hannah's father dragged his hands over the bumps and divots.

Hannah noticed one particularly large pebble that stuck out from the others and was smoother and more evenly shaped. Experimentally, she traced her finger over it. Sure enough, it didn't feel like a rock but a paper-and-paste creation. Curious, she fiddled with it and found it was hinged at one side. Opening it carefully, she discovered an iron lever sticking out. Curious, she pulled it. The scrape and clang of chains filled the air, and the fake wall slowly groaned open.

"Fascinating!" Hannah's father kept his voice soft, but his excitement made his whisper sound like a shout.

"I should go first." Eoin immediately started to wedge his body into the hidden space. He paused, and for a moment, Hannah was afraid that he'd become stuck. However, after a few moments, he managed to wriggle through. Hannah followed suit, and she marveled at his ability to squeeze inside. She, herself, had trouble fitting. Perhaps the Purveyor had a way of opening it farther. She could not fathom either of Eoin's uncles voluntarily squishing themselves on a daily basis just to enter their secret office.

The clandestine staircase was not a hodgepodge of boards and questionable timber. This one was stone and circular. In fact, it reminded Hannah keenly of those at the ducal seat. Had the Purveyor purposely re-created parts of the castle here—perhaps as a way of declaring his own power and dominion when he had little chance of becoming the heir as a second or third son?

Yet as Hannah climbed each step behind Eoin, she felt less and less certain that they had arrived at the proper conclusion. It was as if all the facts were lining up perfectly but were somehow still askew when it came to pointing out the culprit.

"Have your pistol ready," Hannah

whispered to Eoin's broad back. She wished that she'd pushed ahead of him and had taken the more dangerous position.

"My weapon is already drawn," Eoin promised her, and she thought she detected a bit of warmth to his voice. Perhaps her worry had touched him.

"I still feel that we've miscalculated," she admitted as she held her own firearm tightly.

"Doubt is plaguing me too," Eoin confessed, his voice so low that Hannah strained to hear it. "Well, perhaps not doubt, but I can't help feeling as if we're lacking a crucial deduction."

"If you wish to turn around, my family and I can proceed instead. We began this fight. I promise we will not take action against any of your relatives without consulting you." Hannah leaned as close to Eoin as possible as she kept her voice barely audible. Fortunately, her father was still trying to navigate through the small opening and was blocking Sophia and Hannah's mother. Although both her parents and her cousin had agreed in the carriage that Eoin would ultimately decide his uncles' fate, this was a private conversation.

Eoin's steps faltered, but he didn't stop his ascent. "This is my responsibility, too, especially if it involves Uncle Hugh or Francis. But do you mean..."

Eoin suddenly trailed off, and Hannah tried to peer around his broad shoulders for a glimpse of his face. That, however, proved impossible as his back occupied the entire passage.

"We've reached the trapdoor," Eoin whispered. "There's a lock on it, and I suspect it may be latched from the inside as well."

Hannah pushed the keys into his hands. "Here. Try these. But don't enter until my parents and Sophia join us."

Fortunately, her father appeared just as Hannah heard the key turn in the lock. To Hannah's relief, her father whispered to her that Matthew's party had met up with theirs. When he tapped her shoulder twice, she knew everyone was assembled on the staircase or at least as many of them as would fit.

"We're all accounted for and ready now," Hannah told Eoin as her heart rammed against her chest.

Eoin nodded once and then gave a mighty push on the trapdoor. Metal screeched as the wood panel tore from the hinges. Eoin surged forward, and his shoulders cleared the hatch before Hannah even heard the oak covering thump against the floorboards.

She scrambled to follow, wishing that her palms weren't so sweaty. She might be the daughter of a pirate, but she was accustomed to more clandestine activities. She'd never stormed anything before.

When she popped into the firelit room, she immediately leveled her pistol toward the group of figures clambering to their feet. Their backs had been toward the exit, and they'd been seated in chairs in front of a latticework that had obscured them from the crowd below. From their forms, it seemed as if there was one man surrounded by a bevy of smaller, slender women. All of them wore cloaks.

Yet there was something amiss about the tableau before Hannah—something that felt... off or at least unexpected. For a moment, Hannah couldn't determine what.

And then it struck her. The man had not been sitting in the central position.

"Turn around!" Eoin commanded.

The women shrieked and clutched the hoods around their necks as they spun. The man moved stiffly, his hands down at his sides. Hannah expected his features to be obscured, but his head covering wasn't that deep.

But he wasn't Hugh, and he wasn't Francis either. But he certainly looked like them. Close enough to be a cousin or perhaps even a half brother.

"Who are you?" Eoin demanded, his voice as cool and distant as ever. His hand gripping the pistol was just as steady.

But Hannah's focus was no longer on the gentleman. Instead, she swept her gaze over the women. They'd started to drift around, seemingly overwrought by the unexpected invasion. Hannah had witnessed similar behavior before, and suddenly the elusive fact slammed into place and all the rest aligned.

She watched the fluttering women. On the surface, their movements seemed driven by chaotic panic. But their frantic darting was not random—at least not for one of the ladies. Although she wrung her hands and her steps seemed erratic, she consistently moved toward the right wall. Hannah studied it, wondering if it contained another secret passage or priest hole.

The small room was certainly richly appointed with oak panels akin to those in the ducal estate. Yet it was decidedly an intimidating décor with a series of grotesques. Hannah cocked her head as she realized the carvings created a ladder. Glancing up, she noticed that the ceiling was comprised of recessed wooden squares—a perfect way to obscure another trapdoor.

Sure enough, the woman who'd been moving with intent reached the series of miniature monsters. The cloaked figure grabbed two of the lower creatures and placed her daintily slippered foot on the other. She began to scale the wall with surprising alacrity.

Hannah rushed over and grabbed her leg before she could ascend any farther. A familiar high-pitched scream filled the room as the fleeing figure tried to shake Hannah loose.

However, Hannah had plenty of muscles from hefting heavy trays of coffee.

"Unhand me this instant!" the woman yelled. Although Hannah still couldn't see the lady's face, she was certain of her identity—all of her identities.

"I have no intention of doing so, Eliza Aucourte, or should I say, Lady Purveyor?"

## Chapter Twenty-Five

At the sound of his aunt's name, Eoin turned from the man who looked like a combination of Hugh and Francis. He saw Hannah clinging to the legs of a cloaked woman who was scaling a set of grotesques.

Had he heard correctly? How could his timid aunt be here? She could hardly muster enough energy to lift her head from the settee, let alone find the vigor to literally start climbing the wall.

"I said unhand me, you uncouth coffee maid."

The shrieking woman certainly sounded like a louder version of Eliza. But still? Eliza? And who was the fellow with the face of Eoin's uncles?

"I am a proprietress!" Hannah tugged hard against her captive's legs, causing Aunt Eliza to tumble backward. Hannah kept her hold, guiding the struggling female to the floor while keeping her in a tight grasp. No sooner had the culprit's feet touched the ground than Hannah yanked down her hood.

Sure enough, a red-faced Aunt Eliza was revealed. She screeched out a string of extremely rude words as she wriggled and thrashed. Although Aunt Eliza might not have been as weak as she pretended, she couldn't break Hannah's grip.

"So that is the Purveyor," Hannah's father said, his tone practically nonchalant. But then again, he'd served under a female pirate captain, and more importantly, he'd never met Eoin's aunt.

Aunt Eliza. The idea of her as the Purveyor still boggled. Yet as the initial shock began to dissipate, Eoin methodically reexamined the facts. Her exaggerated histrionics would have obscured the normal visual clues that he gathered about people, and her theatrics had typically made him glance quickly away. He'd foolishly dismissed her, believing that there was nothing to observe.

Aunt Eliza was the one who was always reading the paper. Gossip. She adored it. And evidently, she'd parlayed it into a profession—a treasonous but lucrative vocation, nonetheless.

"I do not know what you are talking about!" Aunt Eliza cried. "What is this about a purveyor? I was abducted by that man over there! He claims he is my half brother, and he wants revenge on my family! Please unhand me! My nerves can no longer tolerate this! Oh dear, I am feeling so very faint!"

Upon her last exclamation, Aunt Eliza simply collapsed against Hannah. However, Hannah was not so easily fooled, and she kept her arms tightly banded about the older woman.

"Oh, stop feigning to be a silly goose!" Hannah harrumphed. "We know you aren't the flibbertigibbet that you pretend to be."

Aunt Eliza only moaned weakly, her head lolling against Hannah's shoulder. This time, Eoin did not immediately look away, but he studied her closely. She was an impeccable actress. Even her skin had turned as white as early morning mist. But considering that her entire illegal business was about to be exposed, it was no wonder that her already pale cheeks had lost even more color.

"I didn't take her captive!" The Hugh look-alike crossed his arms over his barrel-like chest. "She is..."

Eoin's potential half uncle suddenly went silent. Eoin glanced back at his aunt and found her glaring at her underling. She'd cleverly angled her head, so that Hannah's elbow was shielding her face from everyone except her accomplice. But Eoin was just at the proper angle to catch a glimpse of her glower.

Eoin stepped between his aunt and the fellow. Pointing his chin toward the desk and then the chests in the room, he addressed his friends. "I believe we'll find more proof of the Purveyor's schemes in there."

"I smell smoke!" Aunt Eliza cried out as she now flopped her head against Hannah's arm. "It is a fire! We're all doomed."

"You may be," Hannah informed Eliza blithely, "but the rest of us will be just fine."

Everyone from the Black Sheep swarmed

to the desk and the chests. The other hooded females shrank against the wall. It was clear that they were not going to defend Eliza. Eoin's long-lost uncle nervously watched the proceedings.

"The authorities will likely believe you were in charge." Eoin advanced on the man.

"We're all going to die, Paul!" Eliza shrieked again as she lifted her head to gaze straight at her minion.

"It is clear that my aunt has artfully arranged matters to make you the scapegoat for her crimes. If she has indeed been engaged in treason, the sovereign will easily believe her manipulations. But if you are honest, we may be able to persuade King George otherwise." Eoin made certain not to appear either too threatening or too cajoling.

Paul rubbed his hands against his breeches as he glanced warily between Eoin and Eliza. The flickering firelight reflected in the sweat beading upon the man's forehead, casting him in an almost shimmering glow. Paul's tongue flicked out as he licked his lips.

Yes, the man was about to crack—and

Eoin wanted him to break in his direction. "Why do think Aunt Eliza chose you? It is clear that she wanted you to be mistaken for Uncle Hugh or Uncle Francis, but if you believe they will be found guilty over you, you are sorely mistaken. They will fight the accusations and will win simply due to their noble status."

Paul's whole body jerked. "But they know everything!"

"The gin!" Hannah cried out. "Eliza must have been bribing them with gin and money!"

"It now makes sense how they could afford clothing that my grandfather hadn't financed," Eoin said before he turned his attention back to Paul. "But even if it can be proved that they accepted bribes, that does not make them the masterminds. And the king will punish the leader the most."

"The king! Why would King George bother himself about a handful of nobs paying a few pence for their indiscretions?" Paul worked at his neckerchief, his blue eyes flicking anxiously to Eliza as if he expected some explanation or perhaps a savior. He received neither.

"Do not try to fool us," Eoin said. "We know the Purveyor has been selling secrets to the French."

"How? How do you know that?" Paul swung so fast in Eliza's direction that his perspiration flung into the air, winking in the firelight.

"Here is one of the log entries." Sophia walked over to them, jabbing her finger at the account book. It was still in code, but Sophia must have been gambling on the fact that Paul wouldn't know the difference.

"I—I cannot read."

"An excuse that will not save you, I am afraid." Eoin kept his tone steady as his calm delivery seemed only to make Paul unravel more. "But I am literate, and I can assure you that there are plenty of records that will damn the Purveyor. Now, I ask again. Is this your study or is it the clandestine office of another?"

"It's La—"

"No." The single word from Eliza was not a shriek or even remotely a scream. Despite the loudness of her exclamation, it was almost tranquil, especially in contrast to her normal hectic shouts.

Eliza straightened in Hannah's arms, and her face suddenly transformed. Her soft edges hardened into sharp corners, and her lips thinned. Her eyebrows, which always seemed to be permanently raised, fell to normal levels. Her vapid blue eyes even seemed to shrink in size, but Eoin supposed it was only the effect of the intensity of her stare.

She looked indescribably fierce despite her small stature, and her frailty all but vanished. With a regal air, she regarded each person gathered in the small room.

"No," she repeated. "I will not have my story be told by a man. Not again. I wouldn't be in this fix if my father and late husband hadn't been in control of my destiny. If my deeds are to be proclaimed, it shall be by my own lips."

"You admit to being the Purveyor?" Hannah asked.

"I am one of the most feared figures in the stews—especially for the nobles who haunt the dark corners." Pride buzzed through Eliza's voice. "And I—I built this empire myself with no assistance from my brothers. That dolt before you is merely a figurehead, and Hugh and Francis are annoying leeches."

"And you began in the gin trade," Hannah said.

Eliza laughed. It was not a melodic sound. "You are surprisingly clever. My nephew is too. That is why I knew that I must stop you both when you began sniffing around the Horse and Hen. If only my idiot brothers hadn't mentioned the place. If Eoin discovered my operations, it was obvious that he'd feel honor-bound to report me. Insufferable prig."

"You must have started peddling spirits after the deaths of your husband and my father," Eoin mused aloud as he began to put the fragmented pieces in order.

Before she spoke, Eliza clenched her jaw hard enough that her cheek muscles bulged. "Father arranged my marriage yet blamed me for a poor choice in husband when Algernon lost our fortune and left me penniless. But I'd been secretly saving my pin money for years as I never trusted Algernon's business acuity. When I moved back home and your father died, mine imposed draconian rules. I refused to be punished for mistakes not of my own making. I decided I needed my own source of income. I didn't have the funds to purchase a building, but I knew that the Horse and Hen had been abandoned. That is where I set up my first stills."

"You must have had another source of income," Hannah speculated. "I know how much capital is needed for a business, and I cannot imagine that you saved enough money by not buying fripperies."

A wry smile twisted Eliza's already thinned lips. "I did say you were intelligent. And you are right. I knew secrets about my friends, and I sent them anonymous letters demanding payment, or I would air their affairs. I suppose it was my first foray into what would eventually become my most profitable venture."

"Why boxing matches?" Eoin asked.

Eliza shrugged. "I learned from my husband not to invest in one thing. The gin business made money, but what if something figuratively sank it like Algernon's literal ship? The Horse and Hen was already known for fights, and creating a place to gamble would earn me more funds. When gentlemen wagered more than they could afford, I decided to demand something else of value from them: secrets. When grain prices increased to the point that I would lose money on gin sales, I simply transitioned entirely over to gathering valuable information. Some I found on my own through reading gossip rags and making deductions, and others I paid for. I still had the boxing matches, and I opened the brothels where the workers would gather confidences too. And yes, I didn't stop with trifling scandals. I know everything about this sodded country from the military to Parliament."

"And you tried to have me killed," Eoin said flatly, "and Hannah too."

Eliza shrugged nonchalantly. "I didn't personally try to cause you injury. I don't soil my hands that way. But one cannot conduct businesses like mine without employing those who are comfortable with violence. There have been occasions where I needed to permanently stop people who'd learned too much. I am not so weak as to let my enemies live."

Eoin suppressed an urge to shiver at his

aunt's bloodless delivery. Did his coolness affect others in the same way?

Even though his aunt's callousness chilled him, he could not help feeling a degree of respect. Yes, she had acted viciously without demonstrating any remorse. But she'd also created a business empire.

"What was Paul's role?" Hannah asked.

Eliza made a dismissive sound. "Do you expect people to listen to a woman? I needed a man to be my public face. I knew Father had scores of by-blows, and it wasn't difficult to find one desperate enough for coin to fill the role. My only regret is that my useless brothers followed me one night and demanded that I pay them. Luckily, the louts never understood the full extent of my fiefdom. And toward the end, they'd begun to fear me."

Eoin was most definitely intimidated by his previously bothersome, silly aunt. She'd certainly played her role perfectly. She was evil and hard-hearted but still brilliant. If Aunt Eliza had been given better opportunities to use her intelligence, Eoin wondered what she would have accomplished in the light.

"What shall you do with me?" Eliza asked defiantly. "If you report me to the Crown, you may lose all favor. It would be dangerous having two traitors in the family, and the secrets that I've sold to the French have not been middling. I don't do things in half measures. Do you really believe Father would wish for you to further sully our family's name by revealing what I've done?"

Eoin glanced at Hannah and her papa. "I am not the one who was hunting you."

As much as it hurt that Hannah had not trusted him with her family's story, he understood her need for revenge. Although Eliza had nothing to do with what had befallen Hannah's father and uncle, she'd destroyed people's lives just as readily. She dealt in blood whether she committed the crimes directly or indirectly.

"Mr. Wick, as my grandfather was the ultimate judge in your case, you and the Misses Wick can decide my aunt's fate." There. He'd given Hannah what she'd set out to accomplish. Perhaps now they could begin anew without their families' pasts hanging over their heads.

"Eoin, let's talk in private." Hannah glanced over at her cousin. "Sophia, could you restrain Lady Eliza?"

"Most definitely," Sophia said.

Dread lined Eoin's stomach as he started down the circular staircase with Hannah following him. He was only now starting to accept the revelations that she had shared yesterday. He did not know if he could handle more.

Hannah tapped his shoulder when they were halfway down. "We've gone far enough. I don't think anyone will overhear."

Eoin carefully pivoted in the tight space and found that his face was nearly level with Hannah's. It would be so easy to kiss her here... physically at least.

"What is it that you wanted to say?" Was that his voice? He didn't realize that he was capable of sounding so sharp and anxious.

Hannah gnawed her bottom lip, and Eoin instantly felt a stab of guilt. He hated seeing her without her confidence. But he was struggling so hard to regain his own.

"I—" Hannah swallowed audibly and then began anew. "I wanted to tell you that I spoke with my parents and my cousin in the carriage ride here. We want you to decide how to handle this situation as long as you stop your aunt from causing further harm. We will not seek for her sins to be publicly aired."

Eoin had girded himself for more disappointment. He hadn't expected this. "But your family has sought justice for years. I've always understood that, Hannah."

"The perpetuator is dead," Hannah pointed out. "I should have recognized that long ago."

"Your family suffered because your father and uncle were simply trying to survive. My grandfather insisted that they receive extreme punishment for poaching a few hares. In contrast, my aunt has confessed to killing people to obtain wealth and power." Confusion doused Eoin. "Why would you not demand that she receive the strongest sentence possible?"

"Eoin, do you know why my father never pursued the rumors about the Aucourtes?" Hannah asked.

Eoin paused, thinking about what Hannah had told him. "He didn't want to jeopardize the Black Sheep, since it was still a relatively new establishment. I imagine your safety and your mother's also played a role in his decision."

Hannah nodded. "He cared more about the people in his life than he did about old wounds, even extremely painful ones."

"But revealing my aunt's perfidy will only ensure the Black Sheep and your safety," Eoin pointed out, still immensely befuddled.

"But you, Eoin—you are one of those people who I care about. Quite ardently. I do not wish to harm you. I never did. My father, my mother, and Sophia, they all recognize your importance to me. We mutually agreed that you would decide the fate of the Purveyor if they turned out to be your family member. As I said, our only stipulation is that Eliza can no longer wreak harm. But you may keep her villainy quiet."

He was important. To Hannah. Enough that she would entirely give up her pursuit of the Aucourtes simply to preserve his feelings.

Eoin felt shaky—as if a single touch would cause him to crumble. Such fragmentation would not be destructive but transformative. Did he have the bravery to emerge anew?

"You were not swayed by Aunt Eliza's tale?" Eoin asked as he struggled to fully comprehend the fact that Hannah and her family would sacrifice so much just for him.

"I can understand, to an extent, the desperation that she experienced at the hands of her father and husband. I witnessed what my cousin Charlotte endured when she was almost forced to wed Hawley, but Charlotte never hurt others in her bid for freedom. I cannot condone the suffering that your aunt knowingly wrought. She deserves punishment, Eoin." Hannah began to reach for him, but she snapped back her fingers before they could touch him.

She'd always been like that, offering him comfort even before he, himself, realized that he needed solace. No wonder he'd come to love her so readily. She was spirited yet immensely kind and compassionate—the perfect companion to his reserved and overly analytical nature.

"I agree that my aunt needs to face the

consequences of her behavior." For the moment, Eoin chose to focus on the external problem rather than the emotions bubbling inside him.

"I could send Aunt Eliza to one of my remote properties and hire guards to watch her," Eoin said. "But she is exceedingly clever, and I would not be surprised if she could revive her operations while under observation. And we are at war. If she has sold important information that would put our soldiers and sailors at risk, we must adequately warn the military. I see no choice."

"Your aunt may very well be right. The king may not reward you for your honesty," Hannah pointed out.

"Unlike my grandfather, I don't view my reputation by how others perceive me," Eoin said. "If I am to value myself, I must make choices that I think are right. I cannot in good conscious try to hide my aunt's crimes when they can continue to injure people."

To Eoin's surprise, he noticed a sheen in Hannah's eyes that didn't come from her lantern's glow. "That is why I could not help but fall in love with you. I could never abide peers, but you are a true noble, in the original sense of the word."

"You... you fell in love with me?" Eoin's heart swelled in his chest to the point that it almost physically hurt. He yearned to gather Hannah into his arms, but the curve of the stairs made that nigh impossible.

Hannah clapped a hand over her mouth. "Oh, I shouldn't have burdened you with that."

"It's not a burden," Eoin said quickly. He could manage to lean a few inches and kiss her. But an audience lurked upstairs, and his emotions were a frightful mess. "I... I... love you too."

It was surprising how hard it was to say those words.

"Is that why you asked me to marry you?" Hannah asked. "Not because of my reputation?"

"I am not sure if I can properly separate the two," Eoin admitted as his stomach simultaneously fluttered with joy and twisted into knots, leaving it a wretched mess. "I know that I wished to keep you by my side regardless, but I also do not want to be the cause of your name being sullied. I would have eventually proposed marriage, but the gossip spurred me to act more quickly."

"And here I am, rushing things again with my questions." Hannah grinned, her smile not as bright as usual but still a true one.

"I must admit that I am a muddle right now," Eoin confessed.

Hannah reached out, and this time did pat his arm. The simple gesture sent a rush of warm comfort rushing through him.

"You have endured more than your fair share of emotional revelations these past few days." Hannah gave him an additional squeeze. "We'll have plenty of time to discuss our relationship when things are more settled. I am impulsive, but I know you need time to employ your logic. And I will always find the patience to wait for you, darling."

Darling?

Hannah's fingers dropped away. "Now I've done it again, haven't I? You can ignore the last word."

"I liked it... my love," Eoin told her as he clumsily tacked on the endearment. Acknowledging they were sweethearts, now that, he could handle. No matter what, they meant something to each other.

Hannah's entire face shined with so much joy that Eoin almost did kiss her. But this still wasn't the place, and she was right that he needed time to fully think through all that had happened.

"Five days," he promised. "In five days, I shall come to the Black Sheep, and we can discuss everything. By then, I should have dealt with my aunt and will have had the opportunity to unravel my emotions."

"Five days," Hannah said, her green eyes shining as brightly as cut gems. "I'll be waiting."

## Chapter Twenty-Six

Hannah was not generally one for pacing, but then again, she rarely had time when she wasn't occupied with some task or another. But she and her cousins had decided to close the doors of the Black Sheep on the day that Eoin was scheduled to arrive. Hannah's meeting with him was too vulnerable, too personal for a large audience. She would have even sent her cousins away if she hadn't needed their support while she waited.

Hannah should have insisted on setting a time. But she hadn't realized that she'd be so bloody nervous.

She hoped, oh, she *hoped*, that they would reconcile. If she could bring herself to trust their parting words, she wouldn't worry at all. Yet doubt had crept in. She'd sorely wounded

Eoin, and his sense of betrayal could have caused him to change his mind.

But what if he hadn't wavered? That, too, was a frightening prospect. He clearly would not make Hannah his mistress. If they were to renew their relationship, Eoin would insist upon marriage.

But could Hannah become a duchess?

"You are orbiting again," Sophia pointed out.

Hannah wrung her hands. She did not normally twist her fingers any more than she typically strutted aimlessly about the room. "I can't help it. I cannot stop."

"What is worrying you?" Charlotte asked.

Hannah barked out a short laugh. "Everything. Will he arrive? What will I do if he doesn't? What happens if he does? What if everything between us goes right?"

"Worrywart! Worrywart! Worrywart!" Pan cried gleefully from the rafters.

"Oh, do be quiet, Pan!" Hannah shouted in irritation. "I *will* make a fine duchess!"

"So that is what is bothering you," Charlotte said quietly.

"Yes!" Hannah huffed out. "I am the

daughter of a pirate and the proprietress of a coffeehouse. I'd make a bloody terrible peeress."

"I personally think you'll make a fine one," Sophia said. "You've successfully run this coffeehouse since you were seventeen, and you've always had a head for figures."

"Peeress! Peeress! Peeress!" Pan croaked as he tapped his gray foot in time with each word.

"I agree with Sophia," Charlotte said, entirely ignoring the parrot. "You would have no trouble managing a household, and it is not as if the butler and the housekeeper won't be able to guide you."

"Handling the accounts and organizing the staff are the least of my concerns. I'd have to entertain nobs!"

"You're a fine hostess here," Sophia pointed out. "I mix up the brew, and you make the customers feel at home."

"It is hardly the same set of etiquette and rules!" Hannah protested. She'd increased her speed to a pace where she almost felt dizzy. But still, she could not slow down.

"I must second Sophia again." Lady Charlotte stood up from the chair where she'd been sitting.

Intercepting Hannah, she placed her hands on her shoulders, forcing her to stop. "You will never follow the proper protocol. It's simply not in your nature. But you will be a duchess and, thus, allowed to be eccentric. That means that you can continue to draw people to you with your own unique appeal, just as you do now."

Hannah huffed out a sigh, which was half frustration and half relief. Charlotte was a kind but honest sort. She wouldn't say those words if she didn't believe them. And Charlotte was in the unique position of understanding both the aristocracy and the world that Hannah inhabited. And Hannah's mother had been born a noble. The damn ton couldn't entirely dismiss her lineage... but...

"I don't even like nobs!" Hannah practically wailed as she tossed her head back. Then realizing what she said, she quickly amended, "Except for you, your brother, your husband, Eoin, my mother, Calliope, and I suppose some of our new members aren't terrible sorts."

A half smile curled Charlotte's lips as she dropped Hannah's palms from her soft grasp. "You do realize that you've listed almost every noble who you've had the chance to spend time with. There are absolutely horrid ones like Eoin's grandfather and his aunts and uncles, along with Lord Hawley and my parents. But there are good and bad people of all ranks and positions."

"I feel as if I will sacrifice my ideals if I become a duchess," Hannah ground out as she started to rub her fingers together again. "Oh, why did Eoin have to be a bloody duke?"

"But think of the good you could do as a duchess!" Sophia grabbed Hannah's twisting hands. "Eoin is clearly inclined to champion reforms. You've already told your parents and me how he plans to help his tenants. What if you were his North Star, helping to guide him on that path? Imagine what such a duchess would have meant to our grandparents and fathers? Their lives would have taken an entirely different trajectory. And Eoin will sit in the House of Lords with your cousin. He and Alexander have the opportunity to accomplish more if they work together, especially if you are there helping Eoin to devise laws that will benefit folks like our customers!"

"I...I never thought of it that way,"

Hannah said as a kind of peace started to flow through her.

"Do you love Eoin?" Sophia asked her.

"Yes," Hannah said without a moment's hesitation. "We...we just fit together. I am not sure if I can explain it more than that. When we argued, I felt a loss, even though I could still feel that connection."

"That is how it is with Matthew and me," Charlotte told her.

"Do you picture yourself married to him? In a partnership with him?" Sophia continued to press.

"If he wasn't a duke, then I most certainly can. I can see him coming to the Black Sheep and us finding a small place of our own nearby. We would sup together and tell each other about our days," Hannah said, finally admitting to the daydreams that she'd worked so hard not to envision.

"Try envisioning living on one of his estates," Charlotte prompted.

"I suppose I imagine us going over his ledgers. I really enjoyed when we reviewed accounts together, and he was exceedingly happy with my assistance," Hannah said. "I know nothing of agriculture, but I wouldn't mind learning if he would let me implement my ideas."

"I will not lie to you." Sophia held her gaze, her golden brown eyes somber. "Your life will change. Even if you work at the Black Sheep when you are in London, there are many times when you will need to travel to Eoin's holdings. But that does not mean that you will not embrace your new circumstances. You, my cousin, will shine wherever you go."

Guilt stabbed Hannah. "But that means leaving you alone to run the coffeehouse."

Sophia grinned. "I'm perfectly capable of operating it myself. But do not forget that I have Charlotte's help now."

"I'm happy to take over the accounts and your hostess duties," Charlotte said. "It is time that we officially announce my part ownership."

"You would both do that for me?" Hannah asked as a happy warmth filled her. She was blessed with her family.

"And for the Black Sheep." Sophia gave Hannah a gentle nudge.

"And for myself," Charlotte added. "I don't

want to remain in the shadows. I am a noble who chooses to operate a business."

And Hannah could be too. After all, so had her mother. It would not be easy entering the rarefied world of the aristocracy, but Eoin was worth it.

Just then a knock sounded on the door. Excitement and joy fluttered through Hannah.

"I think it is time for Charlotte and me to retire to our quarters upstairs." Sophia immediately started to leave the room, but she did pause long enough to address the parrot. "Come along now, Pan. Hannah doesn't need a feathered chaperone."

"Beast with two backs! Beast with two backs!" The bird screeched out the words, but remarkably, he complied. As soon as Pan landed on Sophia's shoulder, Hannah swore that the little imp sent her a wink.

But she had no time to consider the antics of a parrot. She needed to prepare herself for when she opened the door.

As she strode across the familiar, creaky floorboards, anticipation crackled through her, prickling her flesh. She wished she could steady her heart or, at the very least, her breathing. But both were terribly erratic.

What if Eoin had come to say good-bye? Had it been presumptuous of her to think that he'd make her—a proprietress of a coffeehouse—his duchess? Yet he had already proposed to her. But then she'd gone and nearly smashed his heart apart. And he'd had time to reconsider his unorthodox decision.

Oh, she was an utter mess.

Before her trepidation could overtake her, she flipped the latch and yanked back the door. Eoin stood before her—his face alive with emotion. His stoicism had utterly vanished, and Hannah had no trouble reading his anxiousness. After all, it mirrored her own.

But Eoin's nervousness wasn't what held Hannah in thrall. It was the softness in his blue-green eyes. It was not the visage of a fellow about to cast a sweetheart aside. It was exactly how Eoin looked before a kiss.

Relief flooded Hannah, along with utter joy. Eoin wasn't here for an ending, but for a new beginning—a beginning that Hannah absolutely wanted to embark upon.

## Chapter Twenty-Seven

It hadn't taken Eoin very long to conclude that he needed Hannah Wick in his life—preferably on a permanent basis. All it had taken was walking into his London townhome and realizing that she wasn't coming back. She'd brought so much light into the grim, overbearing mansion.

*And I will always find the patience to wait for you, darling.*

For the past five days, Hannah's words had reverberated through Eoin's very being. But it turned out that he was the impatient one. Still, as much as he wanted to dash to her side, he hadn't.

Hannah had been right that they both required time to sort through their emotions, and he'd needed to deal with his aunt's treasonous operations. Even as he rode in the carriage to speak with the king, he'd thought of Hannah. He hadn't just wished for her to be by his side, but he'd marveled at how she'd sacrificed her revenge for him.

He'd come to accept that she'd truly grown to care for him, even if their relationship had begun with lies—or at least with omissions. Slowly, a confidence had built inside Eoin, a belief that he could be loved and cherished, that he wasn't just an empty puppet filled only with his grandfather's goals.

"It's been five days." The inane announcement slipped from Eoin's mouth before he could stop it. It was neither the most romantic nor cleverest of statements, yet his simple words caused a massive grin to spread across Hannah's face.

Before he could react, he found himself enfolded in an exuberant embrace. Hannah smelled of coffee, nutmeg, and home. Eoin buried his face in her red tresses, which were escaping from the bun at the nape of her neck.

He accidentally knocked her mobcap askew, but Hannah didn't seem to care as she drew him inside the coffeehouse.

"I missed you so much." He squeezed his eyes shut as he tried to absorb every detail about her body pressed against his. Nothing in his life had ever felt this welcoming.

"As did I." Her voice was muffled by his chest, but he could hear her clearly enough. Which was good because he wasn't ready to let go.

"Thank you," he breathed out. It was important, and he wanted the business with his aunt to be completely resolved between them.

"For what?" Hannah asked as she laid her cheek against him, her arms still tight around him.

"For allowing me to address Aunt Eliza's crimes."

Hannah shifted so she was looking up at him. Her chin poked into his waistcoat, but he didn't care.

"What did you decide?"

"I confessed her crimes to King George.

He does not want rumors circulating, and I believe he is embarrassed that the Crown's secrets were being disseminated by a seemingly penniless widow. If Eliza had been a man, she likely would have been executed. Instead, King George is sending her to the Colonies."

"What about your Aunt Joan and your uncles?" Hannah asked. "Will they be punished too?"

"I do not believe that they were aware of her more treasonous endeavors, but King George wishes for them all to be deported. I suspect that he's worried that my uncles will spread rumors. And to be honest, I am astonished that they kept Eliza's secret identity for so long. I suppose it was the stream of coin for their silence, which has dried up now." Eoin really did not wish to speak about his relatives, but it needed to be said. Hannah and her family deserved the resolution.

"So they are facing the same fate as my father and uncle?" Hannah asked.

"They will be set up with a house and land, so it is not akin to what your family faced,"

Eoin admitted. "It is not, perhaps, the revenge that you wanted. They will, however, be living rather close to the frontier, as the king fears that Eliza will try to reestablish her business, especially if they settled in Boston, Philadelphia, or the Tidewater."

Hannah's embrace did not change—not even by a fraction. She just kept holding him, her eyes soft with affection. The last tension that Eoin had been holding inside finally loosened.

"It will still be difficult for them, especially if they are far from any city," Hannah said. "And there is some poetic justice in the fact that they have been sentenced with the same banishment. But I meant it when I said that my father, Sophia, and I are willing to forgo the old injuries. I'm ready to start anew, Eoin. With you."

For a moment, Eoin could not speak. So many emotions erupted inside him that he could not tell where one started and the other ended. As much as he wanted to bask in them, he couldn't dismiss his logical side. At least not yet.

"I will still be the Duke of Foxglen." Eoin watched Hannah closely as he spoke. He did not want to force her into a marriage that would ultimately chain her down. "The king has no intention of stripping my title. I am not sure that I have earned his trust, but that is of little consequence to me. I will likely never be a favorite, but I will always be a noble, and so will my wife and children."

Eoin took a steadying breath. Hannah's lips twitched, and he could tell that she itched to speak. Yet she maintained her silence as she watched him with a promising warmth. Her unusual restraint was for him, and that gave Eoin the confidence to continue.

"My offer of marriage still stands, Hannah." Eoin's heart pounded so fiercely that his vision seemed to fade at the edges. He'd never experienced such a case of nerves. "I wish to remain by your side. Not just for a few weeks. Not just for a few years. But for the remainder of my future."

Hannah's mouth opened, and Eoin hurried to say the next. "I know you are worried about life as a duchess, and I have thought about your concerns. Perhaps a longer engagement might help ease your fears. It will give you time to consider your new life. Where I am able, I can adjust my lifestyle to accommodate yours as much as I possibly can. Obviously, the needs of the estate are great, and I know neither of us wishes for me to neglect those dependent on my lands. To be clear, I am not demanding that you give up your interest in the Black Sheep. When we are in London, you may still work here as you wish. It is unconventional, yet I will also be the duke whose mother and sister operate a boxing establishment. When we exchange vows, I want us both to be assured that we have an understanding of how we will jointly grow together."

"You are the most remarkable man." Hannah's eyes glistened as she tugged on Eoin's neck.

Mesmerized by the love shimmering on her upturned face, Eoin leaned down for a brief but brilliant kiss.

"A long engagement is perfect. After all, we are not the most typical of couples." Hannah continued to stare up at him, her expression as open as ever. "But know that I do wish to marry you."

"Even if it means being the Duchess of Foxglen?" Eoin asked, trying hard not to allow euphoria to overtake his rationality. Hannah had listened carefully to him, and now it was her turn to speak. He couldn't smother her words with kisses, no matter how much he wanted to celebrate their love.

Hannah nodded solemnly. "You weren't the only one who spent the last five days in contemplation, although I must admit that my revelations were rather last minute. Yet their newness has no bearing upon my conviction that they are right."

"What are your revelations?" Eoin asked as he reached up to run his hands through her flyaway strands. Tenderness and ferocious need warred inside him.

"That I can accomplish much good as a duchess—your duchess." Hannah cupped his face with her right hand, and her thumb gently stroked across his cheekbone. "I believe in the vision that you have for your estates, and

I can take pride in helping you bring it to fruition. My cousins have assured me that they can run the Black Sheep in my absence."

Eoin trembled, undone by both her touch and her words. "You will make me a better duke, Hannah. You already have."

"And I will be sure to remind you of that." Hannah shot him an impish look, which quickly melted into something much sultrier but no less mischievous. "I think we've had enough of practicality… at least for the moment."

Before Eoin had a chance to respond, Hannah pressed her lips against his. Any lingering shred of rationality burst into iridescent flame. His mouth eagerly worked against hers.

This wasn't just a kiss. It was a homecoming.

Despite how interlocked they'd been before, they still managed to press closer together. He swore he could hear her very heartbeat, and that it was as gloriously rapid as his own. His hands trailed down her shoulders, while her fingers explored his.

He could never get sated. He needed to feel her, to assure himself that this was real. He wasn't alone anymore. He had a helpmate, a partner, a sweetheart.

Hannah leaned back, and he almost moaned in protest. But then he heard her words. Those three short yet all-encompassing words.

"I love you."

He thought he was already consumed by fire for her, and there was no kindling left. He was wrong. Somehow, more heat flared through him until he felt utterly incandescent.

"I love you, too, Miss Hannah Wick... my soon-to-be duchess." He pressed a kiss against her nose—a lighthearted gesture that he could never have imagined making before he met Hannah. She had utterly and completely transformed him.

"And you are my thoughtful, kindhearted duke—the only one who could ever convince me to become a bloody nob."

# Epilogue

*Approximately a year later*

"I wonder if we should start offering the Black Sheep as a venue for wedding breakfasts?" Hannah mused aloud as, despite her voluminous wedding gown, she wedged herself between Sophia and Charlotte on a settee that should truly fit just two.

"This is your *own* wedding day," Sophia chided her. "You shouldn't be thinking about the coffeehouse!"

"It is always the time to consider business." Hannah reached forward and popped a sugar-coated almond into her mouth. "Do you think Alexander will agree to plan them for us? He did such a brilliant job on yours, Charlotte, and now mine."

"I believe the anxiety would destroy his

sanity." Charlotte waved her hand in the direction of her brother, who was nervously guarding the cake. Although Pan had been plied with fruits, his amber eyes kept focusing on the delicacy. Not to mention the presence of a monkey, a terrier, an extremely fluffy rooster, and a full-grown goose.

"Alexander is also consumed by his duties as a duke," Sophia pointed out. "How many new reforms are he and your new husband championing in Parliament, three? No, four, isn't it?"

"It may soon be five. Alexander wants to push for a cruelty-against-animals prevention act," Hannah said. "He and Eoin were discussing it two evenings ago."

"Matthew mentioned it as well," Charlotte said. "If they have success with stopping bear-baiting and cock and dog fights, he's hoping that they could propose measures to help the Scottish wildcat."

"The three of them are always trying to find supporters when they stop by for coffee." Sophia shook her head. "I never thought the Black Sheep would be at the center of parliamentary work."

"It has changed since when my parents first opened the doors." A rare surge of sentimentality tore through Hannah, although she supposed she was extra emotional today. Still, she hadn't expected to feel tears prick the backs of her eyes. She glanced around the comfortable back room and imagined how it had looked three days ago when she was last serving coffee. "Papa, at least, never would have imagined that fine ladies would be clamoring to gain entrance, or that they'd be so willing to sit and chat with actresses and seamstresses."

"Not to mention female boxers," Charlotte added, using her chin to nod at Championess Wick and Lizzie, who were chatting with a few of their fighters. Peter stood close to the women, eagerly listening to the conversation. Their amphitheater had only exploded in popularity once their identities had been revealed to the public. Everyone wanted to watch the sister of a duke take to the ring.

The populace was even more scandalized to learn that the Duke of Foxglen's fiancée was the proprietress of a coffeehouse. The fact that she intended to retain ownership had caused even more heart palpitations among the nobs. They'd been even more aflutter when she and Eoin had welcomed Peter, an orphan from the stews, into their home and educated him.

But Hannah found that she cared naught for the rumors. In fact, she rather liked inspiring a rush of whispers whenever she entered a ballroom. After all, it resulted in more customers the next day at the Black Sheep.

"There is my bride!" Eoin strolled over, his face no longer indifferent but beaming. The man hadn't stopped smiling since she'd walked down the aisle, but then again, neither had Hannah.

Oh, how she loved her husband. The past year had only assured her of that. True to his word, Eoin had made every effort to arrange his schedule so that they could spend the maximum amount of time in London. And he'd included Hannah in his plans for improving the lives of his tenants.

"You two are the most radiant couple!" Calliope observed as she wandered over. Méibh—who was waddling at Eoin's side—hissed at her. Although Méibh had eventually learned to accept Hannah's presence near Eoin, she relentlessly guarded him against all others.

"This is one of those rare times where I must agree with Lady Calliope." Powys drifted over too.

"If you actually listened to what I said, you would find that I am exceedingly reasonable." Calliope sent a decidedly smug smirk in Powy's direction.

"Ha! If you think—"

Hannah arched her eyebrow. "Didn't you two declare a truce today as your wedding present to me?"

"We did," Calliope and Powys sighed in unison. Of course, that caused them to turn and glare at each other.

Fortunately, Alexander chose that moment to join their group. "What mystery do you think the Black Sheep will encounter next?"

"That is a good question," Charlotte said. "Judging by the other wedding breakfasts held at the Black Sheep, there should have been a knock at the—"

Just then the sound of a fist pounding

against wood broke through the babble of conversations.

"Door," Charlotte finished as they all turned in the direction of the sound.

"Well?" Hannah asked as she stood up excitedly. "Who's going to let our visitor in?"

# About the Author

**Violet Marsh** is a lawyer who decided it was more fun to write witty banter than contractual terms. A romance enthusiast, she relishes the transformative power of love, especially when a seeming mismatch becomes the perfect pairing.

Marsh also enjoys visiting the past—whether strolling through a castle's ruins, wandering around a stately manor, or researching her family genealogy online (where she discovered at least one alleged pirate, a female tavern owner, and several blacksmiths). She indulges in her love of history by writing period pieces filled with independent-minded women and men smart enough to fall for them.

Marsh lives at home with Prince Handy (a guy who can fix things is definitely sexier than a mere charmer), a whirlwind (her daughter), and a suburban nesting dog (whose cuteness Marsh shamelessly uses to promote her books).

Marsh loves to interact with her readers on social media:
www.facebook.com/violetmarshauthor
www.instagram.com/violetmarshauthor
www.X.com/vi_marsh_author